A PRINCE IN CAMELOT

Third book in
the story of
DRAGON'S HEIRS

COURTWAY JONES

POCKET BOOKS

New York   London   Toronto   Sydney   Tokyo   Singapore

An *Original* Publication of POCKET BOOKS

POCKET BOOKS, a division of Simon & Schuster Inc.
1230 Avenue of the Americas, New York, NY 10020

ISBN: 0-671-73408-3

First Pocket Books printing July 1995

10 9 8 7 6 5 4 3 2 1

POCKET and colophon are registered trademarks of
Simon & Schuster Inc.

Cover art by Teresa Fasolino

Printed in the U.S.A.

ACKNOWLEDGMENT
AND DEDICATION

As my two favorite authors, Shakespeare and Tolkien, have said, "Once more unto the breach, dear friends, once more" . . . "Third time pays for all." Who would have thought it would take four years to write a trilogy? Who among you would have enlisted with me in this venture, had you known? I am not less grateful to my readers who remained faithful than to those who, knowing me, might have guessed how it would go. Of these, my own champion, Lilian Fuller Jones, must take first place. My advisors, Carroll L. Riley and Brent Locke Riley; my computer guru, Nancy Lieppe; my artist, Harry Lieppe; my agent, Knox Burger, and his partner, Kitty Sprague; and my editor at Pocket Books, Claire Zion, with her assistants, Amy Einhorn and Dudley Frasier; stalwarts all, know I could not have done this by myself. I thank you and dedicate this final book to you in acknowledgment of my debt.

DRAMATIS PERSONAE

BRITONS OF THE ISLES

Arthur	High King of Britain, son of Uther Pendragon and Igraine the Gold
Ayres	Farmer in Caerleon
Brastius Redbeard	Warden of the North
Cador	Duke of Lyoness
Colin	Ship Captain in Lyoness, father of Eliza
Constantine	Son of Duke Cador
Ector	Arthur's protector as a child, Kay's father
Gorlais	Duke of Cornwall, husband of Igraine the Gold, father of Morgan
Kay	Arthur's seneschal, son of Ector

DRAMATIS PERSONAE

Lot	King of Lothian and the Orkneys, husband of Morgause
Myrddin	Arthur's tutor, guardian of Nithe
Ninian	Bishop, father of Nithe
Samana	Arthur's first wife, daughter of Cador
Torre	Son of Pellinore and Ayres's wife
Uther Pendragon	Arthur's father, High King of Britain
Vortigern	(deceased) King of Britain, father of Guenevere

BRITONS FROM OVERSEAS

Ban	King of Armorica, brother-in-law of Uther Pendragon, father of Lancelot
Bors, Senior	Brother of Ban, brother-in-law of Uther Pendragon, father of Bors, Jr. and Ector De Marys
Bors, Junior	Cousin of Lancelot
Ector de Marys	Cousin of Lancelot
Lancelot	Son of Ban, cousin of Arthur, Bors, Jr. and Ector De Marys

JUTES AND SAXONS

Hilda	Lady of the Lake, mother of Nithe, sister of Guenevere

DRAMATIS PERSONAE

Horsa	Jute Chief, father of Rowena
Guenevere	Queen to Arthur, daughter of Rowena
Kesse	Chief of the Saxon raiders
Rowena	Queen to Vortigern, mother of Guenevere

GAELS

Aggravain	Son of Lot and Morgause, enemy to Guenevere
Gaheris	Son of Lot and Morgause, killer of Morgause
Gareth	Son of Pelleas and Morgause
Gawaine	Son of Lot and Morgause, cousin and close friend to Arthur
Igraine the Gold	Wife to Gorlais and Uther, mother of Arthur and Morgan, sister to Morgause
Mordred	Son of Arthur and Morgause
Morgan	Daughter of Gorlais and Igraine the Gold
Morgause	Wife to Lot, mother of Gawaine, Gaheris, Aggravain, Gareth, and Mordred

PICTS

Brusen	Mother of Pelleas, sister to Pellinore, wife to Pelles

DRAMATIS PERSONAE

Elaine	Mother of Galahad, lover of Lancelot, daughter of Brusen and Pelles
Galahad	Son of Lancelot and Elaine
Lamerok	Son of Pellinore, lover of Morgause
Pelleas	Son of Uther Pendragon and Brusen, High King of the Picts, lover of Nithe
Pelles	Old king of the Strathclyde, husband to Brusen, father of Elaine
Pellinore	High King of the Picts, brother of Brusen
Viki	Adopted daughter of Pelleas

THE ROYAL BLOODLINES OF BRITAIN

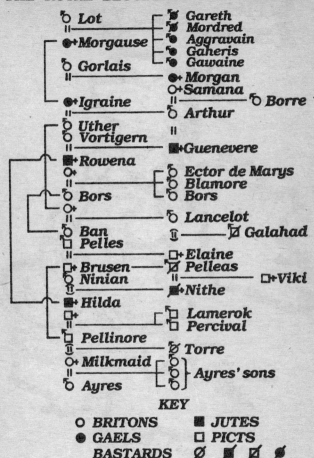

KEY

○ BRITONS	■ JUTES
● GAELS	□ PICTS
BASTARDS	Ø ◪ ◪ ◉

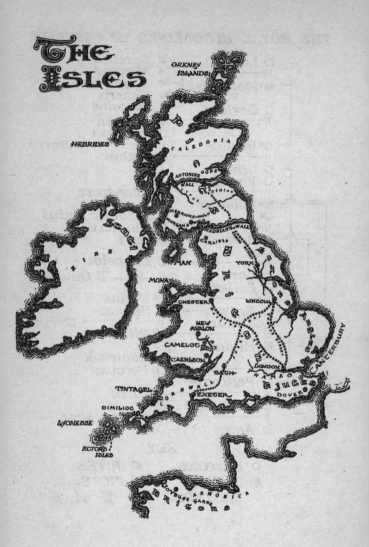

PART I
The
HURLEY PLAYER
479 - 484

Odoacer the Ostrogoth rules in Rome while, in Britain, King Arthur's bastard son dreams of being acknowledged by his father.

CHAPTER
I

hen I was small, I dug turnips with Hal, the head gardener. Hal had cut down a shovel to my size; I carried it everywhere with me. I remember we had been joined by a puppy that attacked the clods of earth we turned over as if they were rats, growling ferociously the while. Even Hal smiled.

The day Borre joined us to watch, Lady Miriam found us so. "That dirty beast! That mongrel's been dragging the wash off the lines. I want it drowned!"

I stood and backed away while Borre gaped up at her. Lady Miriam was squinting in the sun, with her white face showing the two spots of color she got when she was angry. She plucked her eyebrows clean in the Roman manner so that her eyelashes appeared to be eyebrows arched over two red eyes. It was scary!

"No need for that, Mistress," Hal said and, scooping up the puppy, cracked its neck with his hard, cruel hands. The puppy yelped once as it died. Hal licked his upper lip when I turned my shocked gaze on him, perhaps embarrassed at his betrayal of our acceptance of the puppy's comradeship. Borre fled to find his mother, Samana, but I couldn't move.

"Throw that on the compost pile: bury it so I don't have to smell it every time I walk past," Lady Miriam ordered. Hal tugged at his forelock in acknowledgment.

That released me and I dropped my shovel and ran off after Borre, ignoring Lady Miriam's screamed command for me to get back to work. When I reached the kitchen where Samana was to be found early and late, I saw Borre sitting in Samana's lap, so choked with tears he could hardly get his story out.

Samana raised a warding hand, totally absorbed in her child, and I stopped. There wasn't room for both of us in her lap. When she looked up, I was backing out the door, ignoring her look of sudden distress and welcoming words. I ran to the tool shed where I'd long ago found an empty chest to store my treasures safe from discovery. From it I took out the seven-colored plaid that had been wrapped around me when they found me as a baby lying in a broken boat washed up on the beach. I covered my head with the plaid and stuffed a fold of it into my mouth so no one could hear me crying. Crying's for babies, but it was my dog, not Borre's! I swore to myself I'd never dig turnips again.

From then on I spent most of my time with other boys, growing up without talking to adults other than Samana. Some mornings when the tide was out we played king of the castle on the beach, Borre and I, our backs against the sea, defending our sand fort against a double handful of the fisherfolk children. They'd help build it until it was a true king's hill, and then Borre and I would mount it and try to hold our position against the others. Oh, they pushed us backwards into the water eventually: there were only two of us and many of them, small, dark, naked, and sneaky. Picts they were. Borre is a Briton, blond and sturdy, and Samana says I must be a Gael because of my red hair. Not Picts, either of us.

Of course we were naked, too, but we had clothes, neatly folded and placed on a flat rock out of the way of the sea spray. They didn't have any, not for summer wear, anyway. Borre and I were said to be kings' sons and were supposed to wear clothes sometimes.

This early spring morning we had struggled against the others for hours when they murmured to one another in Pictish and backed away, staring past us at the sea. We knew this trick. If we turned our heads to look, they would rush us, take us by surprise, and push us into the water. They had done it before. This time, however, the surprise came from behind us.

"Does it always smell this bad down here?" a low, clear voice complained.

Borre and I whirled, surprised to see a fine, big curragh floating just behind us, a seagoing, two-man boat no less than six paces long and with a small, low cabin aft. The speaker was not a man, but a woman who, I guessed, would be tall standing. She was dressed in something green and shadowy and seemed to be as old and almost as beautiful as Samana. She was smiling at us. I noticed her eyes were the gray you sometimes see in the sky at first dawn, as luminous as that. Her hair was black and cut square at the shoulder like a helmet. It bounced when she moved her head, with flyaway strands escaping and coming back to fall neatly into place like the tide.

Borre had moved close to me, and I put my arm around his shoulders. He expected me to look after him, for at almost twelve, I'm half a year older than he and sturdier by half again. "I don't smell anything but fish," he said defensively.

"Yes, that's it," she agreed, nodding and still smiling. "Fish. Fish guts in the sun. Fish that have been dead for hundreds of years, but perhaps a tang of something else?"

Borre sniffed again. "When the breeze comes from the land you can sometimes smell the manure piles," he offered. "We keep cows. Pigs, too," he added, to be honest about it. Pig manure stinks.

"That would be it! How could I forget?" She turned to a man sitting amidships keeping oars sculling gently to hold the boat off the shingle. "Look at them, Myrddin. Do you remember Arthur when he was that old? The bigger one has the same scowl he wore half the time!" She spoke to the man in Latin, thinking, perhaps, we did not understand. She was wrong. Samana made us learn Latin.

The man smiled and nodded. He was also sitting, but gave the impression of immense size, and his tunic was brown and trimmed with fur. His hands and forearms were gnarled and scarred across the knuckles like Borre's grandfather, Duke Cador, but much larger than the duke's. This man was a warrior, or had been. His hair and beard were dark brown streaked with gray.

"You would be Mordred, wouldn't you?" the lady asked in British, looking at me.

"I'm not either," I said in a low voice, speaking Latin to show her she wasn't so smart.

"His name is Dylan the Orphan," Borre offered in Latin, following my lead. "Dylan means 'son of the wave' in British. He's a king's son like me. Samana said so!"

The boat lady nodded. "Is he now?" she asked. "Well, I should have known Samana would teach you Latin, as befits kings' sons."

"Do you know my father?" Borre asked in a surprised voice. He was always asking strangers that. I wished he wouldn't, for then they'd ask me about my father. I haven't got one.

"Oh, yes," she said, "very well, indeed, if you're Mordred."

"I'm Borre! My father is Arthur the King! My mother is Samana!"

"That would be right, too. I'd forgotten," she admitted. "But Dylan the Orphan also has the look of Arthur's kin. It's his eyes. Arthur's cousins have eyes of that same vivid blue; all of Morgause's children have them. In truth, no one else has eyes quite like those of Morgause and her sons."

I looked at Borre and he looked at me.

"They're blue all right," he said seriously.

"So are yours," I muttered again. What did that prove? I looked

6

back at the boat lady, who was watching me expectantly. Then I glanced at the man at the oars, but couldn't see the color of his eyes. They were deep-set under heavy brows and shaded from the light.

"Who is Morgause?" I asked.

"Why, I would have thought she was your mother," the lady exclaimed. "Don't you know?"

I shook my head. "Samana takes care of me."

"Ah! Well, she would then, wouldn't she?" the lady said pleasantly, as if that explained everything. It didn't.

"We've come to see Samana and ask her to take on another boy. He can help you defend your sand castle, for he's another brother. Come out, Gareth. We've arrived!" she shouted, looking back at the cabin.

Lud, she thought she knew a lot. She was wrong about this Morgause, though. I guess I'd know if my mother was someone named Morgause! What kind of a name was that? She was right about seeing that Borre and I needed help defending the sand castles, but another brother? How could that be? Borre and I weren't even brothers.

She must have been watching us for quite a while. I wondered why I hadn't noticed her. The waves slapping against the shore make a lot of noise and must have covered the arrival of her boat.

A sturdy boy as big as me stumbled into the sunlight from the boat's tiny cabin, rubbing his eyes. He was followed by three large gray puppies, jumping up on him for attention. I wondered how they had all fitted under the cabin's roof.

"He's wearing shoes," Borre whispered.

He was, too, along with a woolen tunic, blue and embroidered at the neck and sleeves. Even my dress-up tunic was not as fine. "He must think he's grown up," I whispered back. Shoes!

"Stop it," the boy commanded, pushing the puppies away. They

7

all sat and gazed up at him, panting anxiously, wondering what they had done wrong.

I wasn't allowed a dog of my own. This boy had three! Lady Miriam didn't like dogs, especially in the house. Even the duke had to keep his dogs in the kennel.

"I told you about these lads," the lady said to him as he stared at us. "The bigger one is your brother, Mordred, who wants to be called Dylan the Orphan, and the other is Borre, who is your cousin."

Listen to that! I thought. Even after Borre told her my name, she's still calling me Mordred. She probably doesn't listen any better than Lady Miriam. I wouldn't be a grown-up for anything.

The boy looked at me intently out of eyes as blue as mine are said to be. He was only nearly as big as I, I thought.

"How old are you?" I asked, wanting to settle the question of seniority right away.

"Nine, going on ten," he said confidently and a little scornfully. "I'll be ten at Beltane." He knew how old he was!

Only nine? I thought in relief, but shook my head. Beltane, the Great Mother's spring feast . . . I celebrated my birthday at Pentecost, fifty days after Easter, because that's when they found me in the broken boat. Since Easter comes on a different day every year, so does Pentecost. It sometimes came as late as June first, the date of Beltane, so I was about two years older than he. I looked at him carefully again. He might even be bigger than I. "You can't be only nine," I said, "I'm almost twelve. Besides, I'm a high king's son like Borre. I've got a seven-colored cloak! I'll bet your father isn't even a high king." I wasn't sure about that, but I thought, if he had been Arthur's son like Borre, the lady would have said so. And it wasn't really a cloak, but a plaid, a blanket.

"My father is too a high king, isn't he, Nithe?" the boy protested, turning to the lady for confirmation.

"Indeed so. Gareth's father is Pelleas, High King of the Picts," she affirmed.

"Picts don't count," I said, dismissingly. "Besides, I don't believe it." The fisherfolk were Picts. How could they have a high king? Anyway, though the Picts were broad and strong enough, they were also short. This boy was too tall to be a Pict, though I still thought he was probably older than nine. Ten, maybe. Not eleven, though.

"Truly, being the son of a Pictish king does count," the lady said. "Furthermore, Pelleas is brother to Arthur, your own father."

"That's Borre's father," I said, but half aloud. The lady couldn't tell us apart now. Lud, she was dumb! Besides, I didn't know who my father was. He was a king, though, a high king. Only high kings wore seven-colored cloaks like mine.

"Can you fight?" Borre asked the boy.

"Yes," he said. "I'm very strong. My father is a Geen."

"What's that?" Borre asked.

"A Geen is a giant," the tall lady explained.

Lud, now the lady couldn't keep her stories straight. One minute the boy's father was a Pict, the next, brother to the High King, and now, a giant. I decided I couldn't believe anything she said.

"Pelleas is the biggest man in the islands, stronger even than Myrddin." She smiled back at the man at the oars.

He returned her smile, his eyes glinting as he looked up at her, and spoke for the first time. "Do you think we could go ashore?" he asked in a deep voice. "I'm getting butt-scald."

I decided the big man didn't believe her either.

"Do I have to stay here?" the boy interrupted, plucking at the lady's sleeve. She had risen and was picking up a rope attached to the boat's bow.

"A boy needs kinsmen to stand beside him," the lady said to him. "Except for you, these two boys are the bravest in Britain. Tell them about the puppies," she encouraged.

"Nithe says one of these is for each of you, but this is the best of them. He's mine," the boy said, clutching a shaggy ruff. I don't know how he could tell them apart. "They're all half wolf, and very fierce," he added.

"They aren't really," the lady said gently. "Your father would never give you anything so dangerous, even if he keeps them himself. I've told you that before. They're called wolfhounds, but they're just dogs."

Maybe she told the truth about this for they didn't look very fierce. They were young and fat with big clumsy paws. I would have done anything to have a dog of my own.

"I had a dog once," I announced. I did, too. I always thought of the dog that Hal the gardener killed as mine.

Borre gave a pull on my tunic, and I put my head close so he could whisper to me. "Let's do take him. We can make him get food for us."

I nodded. Borre had to wheedle food from Samana at the kitchen door now because he was the younger. He hated begging. "You can stay," I decided, "but you have to do what we say. Come along, we're going to ask for something to eat, and then you can watch me play hurley." I kept looking at the puppies, trying to decide which of the other two I would take, and wondering how I could hide it from Lady Miriam.

"I'm very good at hurley," he announced, and scrambled out of the boat along with the three animals. He was just talking. He didn't even have a hurley stick!

I picked up mine and looked meaningfully at Borre. He grinned back; he knew what I was thinking. If you play hurley, you carry your stick everywhere! We dressed and I draped my folded seven-colored cloak carefully over my shoulder before we set off together to the kitchen. I always wore my cloak now. I liked having it near me, feeling the touch of it on my skin.

The fisherfolk boys tagged after us, knowing we would share

whatever food we were given. As Samana said: a king's son must be generous with his followers, even if they're just Pictish fisherboys.

"And why would a king's son have to beg food?" the boat lady asked me. She was following us. She was much taller than Samana and dressed in a tunic and boots, almost like a man. The boatman with her was a giant in truth, a head taller than anyone on the island. I wondered if he was a Geen like Pelleas. I decided not to let him get too close to me.

"We get regular meals," I protested.

"Oats and barley porridge for breakfast," Borre said proudly, for that's what the men ate, too. "And fish stew for supper, usually," he added with less enthusiasm. We never ate at the table in the main hall where meat and root pies were served. I don't like fish much.

"You don't take a meal at noon?"

Didn't she know anything? "Who would cook at noon? The flies are too bad," I said. Anyway, Samana always gave us something at the kitchen door when we got hungry at midday, apples or bread and cheese. No one else ate then.

One of the puppies jumped up, caught the edge of my tunic in his teeth, and tugged. I stopped and looked at him, wondering what he wanted.

"He wants to play," the boat lady told me.

I loosened my belt of linen rope and offered one end of it to the puppy. He immediately released my tunic to fasten on the rope, making ludicrous growly sounds as he tried to pull me forward. This was a game I knew, and I could win while he was this small. He was tireless and willing to pull all day, but Borre was hungry.

"Come on!" he said. "Play later!" I picked up the puppy, and he squirmed so in frantic kissing that I almost dropped him. I didn't, though. I pretended I didn't like it and scolded him, but he knew I didn't mean it. I wanted this one. Gareth had made a mistake, picking as he had. This one was best.

"Why are we going to the back door?" the boat lady asked.

"You want to see Samana, don't you?" I replied. She was walking beside me, while the giant followed us both.

"Yes."

"She runs the kitchen and spends most of her time working with food." I said. "Lady Miriam doesn't go back there much, except to give orders. You·won't have to see Lady Miriam if you come this way."

"I thought Samana was the house chatelaine, as Duke Cador's daughter. She's mother of the duke's heir," the lady said.

"Not any more. Not since the duke married Lady Miriam," I said, and spat carefully to one side to show what I thought of that.

"Samana has to stay in the kitchen." Borre said, glaring. "Lady Miriam is over everybody now."

Both Borre and I knew the story of how Lady Miriam had taken Samana's place. Borre hated it, for he loved his mother fiercely.

"That must be hard on Samana," the lady said thoughtfully.

"She doesn't seem to care," I assured her. "She's happy, no matter what Lady Miriam says."

It was true. Everyone loved Samana. When anyone needed anything from the castle, they went to the kitchen door to find Samana, just like we did. Nobody asked Lady Miriam for anything. Samana always listened, not caring whether the person was important or not, and almost always would find some way to help. Lady Miriam might be the chatelaine, but Samana was the heart of the place and everyone knew it, including Lady Miriam.

Lady Miriam did not like being ignored. Consequently, she didn't like Samana or Borre. And she didn't like me any more than she liked dogs. I wondered how I could keep this one. I knew I'd never let Hal the gardener come near it.

Borre reached the door in front of us, and by his squall of rage I thought Constantine was probably sitting on Samana's lap, eating a cookie. Constantine, like everyone else, loved Samana. He was the son of the duke's second wife, Lady Miriam, while Samana was the daughter of his first, so Samana and Constantine were brother and sister. In truth, though, she was more like a mother to Constantine than Lady Miriam ever could be. Lady Miriam had no love for anything except her church. However, Constantine is supposed to stay away from Samana entirely, for Borre has warned him. Borre is very jealous.

I put the puppy down and ran to stop the fight that was sure to be in progress if Borre caught up with Constantine this side of the great hall door. I didn't care about Constantine, but Samana got upset when Borre and Constantine fought, and I didn't like to see Samana distressed.

I arrived in time to see Borre punch Constantine on the back of the head as Constantine tried to flee, sending the smaller boy sprawling. Constantine would have been smarter to stay on Samana's lap. Borre wouldn't hit him there. Samana had her fist clutched in Borre's tunic, attempting to hold him back, delaying him long enough to allow Constantine to escape, while Constantine bawled at the top of his lungs for his mother. I grabbed Borre just as he twisted free of Samana's grasp and slammed him against the wall, knocking the breath out of him.

"Look, manure head," I yelled. "See what you've done? He'll have Lady Miriam back here to yell at Samana now!" I hated it when that happened.

"I don't care!" Borre cried wildly, which was untrue. "Let me go!" He struggled in my grasp, turning his head to yell, "Crybaby Constantine!" at the open door after the fleeing child.

I held him with one hand clutching his hair and raised up my hurley stick to threaten him. We were both surprised when one of the puppies leapt to snap at my wrist and the other defended me, snarling viciously. I let Borre go and snatched up my protector while Borre picked up his. They kept growling at one another. The wonder of it, having the dogs fighting for us, set both Borre and me laughing. I wouldn't hurt Borre. We both knew that, but the dogs didn't.

Samana was looking sternly at us while the boat lady stood to one side, leaning against the worktable with her arms folded and her long legs crossed. She was watching us with her head cocked on one side and seemed amused until Lady Miriam burst in, carrying a whip. Constantine was with her, peering out from behind her skirts.

"What's going on here? Where's that wild brat of yours?" she screeched at Samana. "And dogs in my kitchen? Out! Out!" She waved the whip wildly.

"It's my fault," Samana said, making gentling motions with her hands. She had flour on the front of her blue tunic from the bread-making, and a dusting of it on the tip of her nose. It would have been funny at any other time. "Borre found Constantine sitting on my lap," she explained. "You know how jealous Borre gets, but I really can't help it, for Constantine is my brother. I do love him!"

Lady Miriam advanced toward her, the whip half raised, and said, "Aye, it's your fault!"

"No, it's mine!" Borre yelled, coming to stand bravely in front of his mother. Samana reached over to put her arms around him and dragged him backwards, bending over him and shielding him from Lady Miriam's whip.

As I gazed in horror it cracked across Samana's back, and I heard her cry out in pain. Anger flashed over me suddenly like the tide rushing up one of our narrow bays. It engulfed me, taking away my sight and hearing as I ran at Lady Miriam and crashed into her, knocking her off balance. I grasped the hand that wielded the whip and bit it.

14

Dimly I heard her cry out as someone grabbed and shook me. I let her go, kicking out with my feet and hitting something solid at least once as I was raised high in the air. My sight cleared, and I saw Lady Miriam before me, wiping blood from her mouth where my foot had struck her. Before I could kick her again, a huge hand imprisoned my legs. What was this? I panicked, helpless.

The dogs were going crazy, yipping and jumping up on everyone, but quieted immediately when a deep voice above me ordered it. Ah, Lud! I was in the arms of the giant boat man!

Hampered by her voluminous skirt, Lady Miriam struggled to pick up her whip from where she had dropped it on the floor. She tugged frantically to free the whip from where the giant boat man had it trapped beneath his foot.

"Ah, Myrddin! I know you, false druid. Release my whip!" she raged. It was almost the only tone of voice she ever used.

"False druid?" the boat man asked. "I gather you mean false because I am a druid," the boatman replied in a mild voice that belied the sternness of his face. "I am no druid, though I may have been mistaken for one once or twice. As I recall, it's possible I may even have encouraged the misunderstanding." As he continued to speak softly, he placed me on my feet by his side in an absentminded kind of way, keeping a heavy, restraining hand on my shoulder.

A druid! I leaned back and looked up at the tall, bearded man. So that's what they looked like. I knew about them: the priests of the old gods, outlawed by the Romans hundreds of years ago. They were said to live hidden in the oak woods and to hold dread ceremonies by moonlight. Lady Miriam stopped trying to free the whip and stepped back from him as though she saw something menacing in his eyes.

I twisted my head to look up at him again, but found myself patted gently as if I needed reassurance. Suddenly, I wasn't afraid of him any longer, no matter how Lady Miriam felt.

When I turned back I found Lady Miriam looking at me with a loathing so intense it was like a physical blow. Well, I didn't like her either, but I had reason. She had my dog killed!

The boat lady had come up beside Samana and, after looking her over intently to determine whether the lash had cut her, hugged her warmly. Without releasing Samana, she turned to speak to Lady Miriam. "Likely you remember me as well, Lady Miriam," she said.

"Nithe?" Lady Miriam asked doubtfully, but in a tone that implied she did not care who the woman was.

"Aye, Nithe, though I am now known as Nineve, Lady of the Lake. You would do well to remember I am also foster sister to Arthur, the High King."

"The royal bastard," Lady Miriam sneered.

"The High King," the boat lady corrected in a level voice. "He is your husband's liege lord. At King Arthur's request I am here to ask Cador, Duke of Lyoness, to receive Gareth, son of Pelleas, high king of the Picts and Morgause, queen of the Scoti, as a page in his house." This was delivered formally so no doubt could exist about the request.

Lady Miriam was still too angry to accord the boat lady the respect due her station. "Another royal bastard?" Lady Miriam spat. "This one out of the witch Mōrgause? What do you people think this place is? First Borre, and now another? No, by heaven, I will not!"

"Borre is no bastard," Samana said in a dangerously quiet voice. I had never seen her angry before. "When raiders killed my mother and brothers, my father married you to get an heir. When you proved to be barren, he contracted me in marriage with Arthur for one son. Borre is my father's heir by contract with King Arthur!"

"Oh, I know you were married to Arthur by druidic contract to provide my husband an heir when I had not. Our good priest said that didn't mean a thing. He said my husband, Duke Cador, required a Christian heir, one born to a marriage sanctified by the church. Well, I wasn't barren! He has an heir now in my son, and if you weren't Duke Cador's daughter, he'd have sent you packing long ago, both you and your brat."

"You'd like that, wouldn't you?" Samana asked. "But there it is: I am Cador's daughter. You'll find my father will honor the marriage contract he signed with Arthur when the time comes. Borre will be his heir! And Gareth is welcome here, despite what you say; you know my father will insist on it!"

"This one must leave, at least," she rasped, glaring at me. "Even Cador's indulgence won't extend to this nameless animal when he finds I've been kicked in the face and bitten!"

"This boy is not nameless," the boat lady said. "I do not know why you are not aware of it, but his name is Mordred, and he is the son of Arthur, the High King, and Queen Morgause."

"That one?" Lady Miriam asked in horror, putting her hands to her cheeks. "Everyone has heard of him! Had I known who he was, he would never have spent a night under this roof! He's an abomination, a child of incest!" She backed away from me, making a cross with the index fingers of her outstretched hands, looking at my face only from under lowered brows.

"How could you not know?" the boat lady stormed, putting her hands on her hips and leaning forward to glare at Lady Miriam. "I heard Gawaine promise to place the baby Mordred in your hands. What did he tell you?"

"Gawaine did not bring this child to me," Samana said in a troubled voice. "Are you sure? Arthur's son? I truly didn't know."

"There is some riddle here," Nithe straightened up and muttered in reply.

"Riddle? I'll give you a riddle," Lady Miriam said in a voice barely under control. "How could there be three kings' sons who are brothers, though two of them are not related?"

The boat lady stared at her, stony of face.

17

"Too deep for you, is it? The solution is easy when you know that kings and queens breed like pigs! I'll give you a hint. The father of the first is also father of the second, and the mother of the second is also mother of the third."

"I didn't need the hint," the boat lady responded coldly. "The answer is when they are royal bastards, but it is a false riddle, as Samana has already told you."

I like riddles. I'd been thinking about this one, trying to understand it, not listening to the grown-ups much, when I heard Lady Miriam hiss sharply and spit out the words, "However he came, he can't stay in Lyoness any longer. Even the king can't ask that of me!"

She was pointing at me! Did she mean to send me away from Borre and Samana?

"Samana may win the folk over by giving stores from the kitchen to beggars behind my back," she continued, "but this place is in my care. I'm the duke's wife!"

"Lyoness may be in your care, but it's in Arthur's gift. These islands are royal property," the boat lady retorted. "When I tell him how his son has been driven from your roof, perchance he will find a new caretaker."

"How dare you speak so to me?"

"I think I begin to see why it is that the duke spends so much time in Camelot," the boat lady said in a deceptively sweet voice.

Lady Miriam turned livid and gasped, "Go! Leave my house! And take this living affront to God with you," she shrilled, pointing at me. Her hand was bleeding where I had bitten it. "It makes me shudder to be in the same room with such a monster, as it would any honest Christian." Then she turned and fled from the room. My last view of her was as she slapped Constantine out of her way. I almost felt sorry for him. He was a crybaby, though.

I turned to look at Samana and found her looking back at me in deep concentration. "I don't see it," she announced. "I know every line in Arthur's face and can trace his likeness in Borre, but not in Dylan."

"You have never seen him glare in that special way, angry and arrogant?" the boat lady asked.

"He never showed such a face to me." Samana replied simply, reaching out to touch my cheek. "Dylan has the look of a king's son, I grant you, but more like Arthur's cousin Gawaine than Arthur himself, don't you think?"

"The boy spoke of a seven-colored cloak," the giant boat man said. "Do you still have it?"

"This is it," I said, and picked it up from where it had fallen when I attacked Lady Miriam. I unfolded it and held it out. It was not big, having been made for a baby, and a little faded from wear, but it was still handsome.

"Ah," the man announced, "it is the plaid of clan Merrick, the royal house of the Scoti. No wonder the boy looks like Gawaine. He is Gawaine's brother, if I am not mistaken."

Gawaine was one of King Arthur's chief knights! Was he truly my brother, I wondered?

"Then it is so," Samana said sadly. "He is Mordred."

"Yes, that settles the matter," the boat lady said briskly. "We must leave here. Myrddin and I have houses on Ector's Isle. We will all go there." She was still holding Samana protectively, and Samana reached out an arm to me, pulling me in and hugging me.

"I will not leave," Samana said stoutly, freeing herself from the boat lady's embrace. "My son is Cador's heir. The duke, my father, parted Arthur and me as soon as he knew the child was on the way. Do you think I can forget that? After paying such a price, I will not have my son cheated of his legacy."

"Then I will take Mordred back to Camelot," the boat lady declared. "It is time Arthur had a look at his son, anyway. It may be the only one, except for yours, that he will ever have."

19

"His wife is barren?" Samana asked.

"It has been ten years and no child. She may be cursed, as folk say." She turned to me. "Get your clothes. We're leaving."

"Me, too," Gareth declared stoutly. "I won't stay here!"

"Ah," Nithe sighed, "I can't say I blame you."

I looked up at Samana, speaking for the first time, "Borre needs me, Samana!"

Borre tugged at her arm, imploring her with his eyes not to send me away.

She hugged us both, but said, "You'd have to be separated anyway. It is time for Borre to go away for fostering. Sir Ector fostered Arthur and will take Arthur's son. Borre's a big boy now."

"Mama!" Borre cried in protest.

"You will come back," she told him. "I will hold your place here; you are my father's heir. Hush now. You know it must be so!"

"I could go with him," I offered desperately. All kings' sons are sent away from home to be trained for knighthood in other royal houses. I knew Borre had been fearing it.

"No, love, it's late for Borre; it's over late for you. Come to that, you were fostered here. No, it is time for you to seek a knight among your father's men who will accept you as a squire. Nithe will help," and she looked to the boat lady for confirmation.

The boat lady smiled and said, "Besides, you will have Gareth to look after, too, won't you?"

"Gareth takes care of himself," the boy announced stoutly.

I stepped away from Samana and glared at Gareth, taking my unhappiness out on him.

He glared back.

I wondered what he could do to make me like him, but I looked back at Samana and nodded. Maybe it was time to seek my father. Was it truly King Arthur? Could that be? I knew my father had to be a high king, for only kings are allowed to wear seven-colored cloaks like mine, but King Arthur! Why, that made Borre and me true brothers after all.

This did not seem the time to ask the questions that were in my mind like why did the Lady Miriam call me an abomination? Was that some kind of an animal? I had bitten her! Why had she called me a monster? When she struck Samana was the overwhelming wave of anger that had washed over me monstrous? Why did the boat lady say my mother's name was Morgause? But, most of all, was I truly the son of Arthur, the High King, like Borre? I wanted to hear that again.

CHAPTER

II

The giant boatman sailed off alone, on business he did not explain, and the boat lady bespoke a craft that did not smell of fish to take us to Britain. One of the fishermen, Colin, had a new curragh that merely smelled powerfully of fresh-tanned hides and the sheep fat used to waterproof them, a stink almost worse than the smell of fish, to my mind. The boat lady engaged it, grumbling. She was hard to please.

If I'd known how sick I would become sailing on the open sea, with the wind whipping up waves as tall as my head, I would not have gone, even if it meant I would never have a dog of my own. I missed Samana and Borre. That new boy, Gareth, liked boats! Why didn't he stay behind instead of Borre? I could hear him laughing. Vomiting again, I thought I'd teach him different if he were laughing at me . . . if I lived.

It pitched for hours up and down, up and down, all the way from Cador's Island to Exeter, the port in Cornwall. No one else seemed affected, and only the puppy at my feet, whimpering over my distress, made the trip bearable. He kept up a continual whining growl, forcing his nose under my arm as I sat disconsolately on the deck, my head over the rail, vomiting repeatedly. He snapped once at the boat lady when she came to comfort me, so she kept her distance thereafter, standing by Colin as he guided the boat with an arm draped over the tiller.

"Why did you name the boat *Hammerhand?*" I heard her ask him.

"It's what we call the boy," he told her, and I knew he meant me. "He can hit a hurley ball the better part of a mile."

Lud, I can't do that!

"Mordred?" she responded with surprise in her voice.

"Dylan the Orphan," he corrected her. "That's his name, Dylan the Orphan. The boy is the only three-goal hurley player in the islands. I won this boat betting on him against off-island teams."

"But he's not yet twelve!" she retorted in disbelief.

I'm almost twelve, I thought.

"Maybe," the captain replied. "The Irish think he's Lugh of the Long Hand. Seems their god likes hurley and takes the guise of a boy in games. The Irish won't play against Dylan the Orphan, but they'll bet on him every time. Only mainlanders can be lured into matches any more. Stupid clods!"

I remembered that game, the first time I'd ever made four goals by myself. I'd had to. The Irish were better than we were. They'd called it hurling, but lots of their words were funny. After the game they tried to get Duke Cador to give me to them, saying I was probably one of them anyway, with my red hair.

"What is it he does?" the boat lady asked, evidently fascinated by what she'd heard from Colin.

"He's too small to be in the scrimmage, so he plays goalie; and when the other side makes a breakaway and streaks toward our goal, Dylan the Orphan steals the ball from them and runs through the field of players without a hand being laid on him. When he outruns them all, he tosses the ball up and hits it through their goal, farther than anyone else can drive the ball. Wouldn't think there was that much power in him, but the boy says it's all in seeing the shot in his mind. I don't know . . ." he finished, as if that weren't reason enough. It was, though.

Another wave of nausea gripped me and I threw up again, losing interest in the conversation. I am good at hurley, but it made little difference in how I felt right now. Samana told me when I was small that I get sick at sea because of the storm I endured as a baby, the only survivor of a boat swamped by high waves. She said that Lir, the sea god, was angry that I escaped. I don't remember it, but I can get queasy just climbing on the deck of a boat in harbor. Other boys my age work with their fathers as fishermen. They have less time to practice hurley than I do, but at least they have fathers to work with. When I'm playing hurley, though, I don't think about that much.

I hoped that as soon as I had solid land beneath my feet again I would recover but, in truth, my stomach continued to churn after I stepped onto the shore. I nodded to the captain as he bade me good-bye, hearing his pledge of support for the part I had in earning his boat, should I ever need help. Colin, his name was, he said. I knew that. I'd have been happy enough if he could help me get over puking my insides out. Nothing else was as important as that.

I followed the boat lady up the beach fronting the town. Gareth walked by her side, holding her hand and chattering. How could he be so cheerful?

The town was crowded and dirty. Never had I seen so many houses so close together or smelled anything so foul. Either it was much worse than the beach at home or my seasickness was going to last even longer.

The boat lady took us to an inn and bespoke a room with beds for the three of us. I was asleep almost immediately, though my bed was far from clean. The puppy curled up beside me and kept me company until morning came, waking me by licking my face.

While in the throes of sickness, I'd sworn I would never eat again, but I was hungry after all!

"So, you decided to live," the boat lady said as I sat up, fending off the puppy.

"Is there anything to eat?" I asked. I didn't want to play games with her, or the puppy either.

"I've been to the kitchen and brought you bread, cheese, and fresh apples," she answered, indicating a small table near the wall with a nod of her head. She was standing relaxed, with her arms crossed. I had a feeling she'd been watching me as I slept.

I nodded, and sat before it, drinking first great gulps of water from the two-handed drinking bowl beside the bread trencher. I must have vomited away half my body. I fed the puppy before eating myself, dividing the food into equal portions.

"When you're finished, we'll buy some horses for our trip. Have you ever ridden?" she asked me. She sat in the other chair and played with an extra spoon lying on the table.

I shook my head, my mouth too full to speak. After swallowing, I asked her the question that had been on my mind. "If my mother is a queen, why did Lady Miriam call me a monster?"

She hesitated and I figured she was thinking up another lie.

"Your mother, Morgause, was full sister to Igraine," she said, "the mother of Arthur, the High King. Among Christians like Miriam it is unlawful to beget a child with one's mother's sister. For them, what Arthur did was almost as bad as if it had been his own mother!"

I understood that! It would be like me with Samana, which didn't bear thinking of. "No wonder she called me a monster," I muttered. "Is that what Lady Miriam's riddle meant?"

"Yes. You and Borre have the same father, King Arthur, and you and Gareth have the same mother, Queen Morgause, so they're both your half-brothers."

"They're not related to each other at all?"

"They're cousins, for Gareth's father, Pelleas, and Borre's father, Arthur, are both the sons of Uther Pendragon."

Nithe looked away from me as Gareth rushed in, out of breath and laughing, being chased by his puppy. The dog caught him and jumped on him as the boy rolled on the floor. My puppy growled when they came too close to the table, and Gareth picked up his pet and sat on the bed with him, quieting down.

"But monster?" the boat lady said, looking back at me. "That's nothing. I've been called worse in my time."

My disbelief must have shown on my face, for she added, "There is a strain of wildness that runs in royal lines like ours. In my case I know what other people are feeling without their saying anything. I can also project my own feelings without words, a witch trick, indeed!"

And such a rush of love swept over me that I was almost overwhelmed. Had it come from her? "I get wild sometimes," I confessed. "I was so mad when I kicked Lady Miriam I couldn't see. And all I could hear was this sound like waves breaking against a cliff. It was scary!"

"I never get mad," Gareth boasted.

"I see. Well, your father, Pelleas, has a temper like Dylan's," she told him. "It worries Pelleas, for he is always afraid he may hurt someone he loves, unknowing."

She understood! "Hurley is rough," I confided. "Sometimes I don't care if I hurt people when I play." I wasn't proud of that. I chewed for a while, thinking, then said, "I can tell what other players are going to do before they do it. Is that something you can do, too?"

"No, but Pelleas can. Remember, I told you that your own father, Arthur, is half-brother to Pelleas. Uther Pendragon sired them both, though on different women. It's in your blood, right enough," she stated.

"I thought Pelleas was a Pict. You said he was their high king."

She laughed. "It's hard to tell who is what among the royal families, with all the intermarriage. Your own mother, Morgause, is Queen of the Scoti, a Gaelic tribe originally from Ireland. Of course her sister, Igraine, was one, too, so King Arthur is half Gael. Arthur's father was Uther Pendragon, a Briton. Britons reckon descent through the father, so Arthur was his heir. Among the Gael, though, descent is reckoned through the mother, so Arthur is just another clansman, by their reckoning. Morgause needs a daughter to succeed her."

"How about the Picts?" Gareth asked.

"Picts have kings, but the royal line is female. Pellinore is one of the Pictish kings, and Pelleas was born after Pellinore's sister, Brusen, had an affair with Uther Pendragon. There is no such thing as illegitimacy among the Picts. A child is his mother's. Since Brusen is from the royal line, Pelleas was eligible to become a king. He has done so by being a great leader of men."

"Are you really King Arthur's sister?" I asked.

"We're not related, but I was raised with him and took care of him much of the time when he was growing up," she told me.

"Are you a Pict, like my father?" Gareth asked.

"No. My mother, Hilda, and Queen Guenevere's mother, Rowena, are sisters, daughters of Horsa the Jute, who ruled in Kent. The queen's father was Vortigern, a Briton and the last ruler of Britain recognized by Rome. Arthur married her to give his own reign legitimacy. My father was Bishop Ninian, and his father was a Roman legionnaire who married a Briton after his discharge from the army. Roman soldiers were not allowed to marry but often had families that they recognized after their army service was completed."

"A bishop?" Gareth asked in horrified surprise. "Bishops can't marry."

"I know," she said wryly. Changing the subject she told us, "When I grew up with Pelleas and Arthur, they called me by my baby name, Nithe. They still do. You may call me that, if you wish."

It was better than 'boat lady.' I decided. "Lady Miriam said that woman, Morgause, was a witch," I remarked in an offhand way, but I watched her carefully as she framed a response. It would be no light thing to have a witch for a mother. That might explain the monster thing.

"It is said that she ensorcells men," Nithe admitted. "She is old enough to be my own mother, but she is still beautiful and complains that men will not let her be. It was never a problem for me, so in that sense maybe she is a witch."

I almost understood that. Men bothered me all the time, too, after the hurley games.

"I have a surprise for both of you," Nithe told us when I'd finished eating, and she undid a parcel that she'd laid on one end of the table. It was trousers! I'd never had trousers; only men wore them. They were gray with red checks, very handsome.

"Before you put them on, though, you have to bathe," she announced. "The two of you smell even worse than most boys do."

"Bathe? I never bathe!" I told her.

"I bathe every day," Gareth said proudly.

That was just the kind of thing he would say, but I didn't believe him. "Show me!" I demanded. I could do anything he could.

We left the inn and walked to a nearby building that had steam coming out of the windows. "This is a bathhouse," Nithe told us. "Men and women bathe separately, so I'll see you out here when you're through. Gareth can show you what to do," she added, handing me my new trousers.

"Sure," I muttered, following the boy as he confidently led the way into the interior of the building. It wasn't too bad. He took off his tunic and rolled it with his new trousers and placed them on a shelf before jumping into a small pool filled with water, ducking under to get wet all over.

I did as he did, hoping the others in the room would not notice how clumsy I was at it. There were no other boys, just men, but they ignored the two of us.

Gareth left the pool and walked to a wooden tub of soft soap, taking a handful and lathering it over his body and even his hair. As I watched, one of the men scooped a bucket full of water from the pool and splashed it over Gareth, rinsing the soap off. He served me the same way when I was ready.

I'd gotten soap in my eyes, and it stung so I could barely see to follow Gareth into another bigger room with a larger pool half-filled with men talking and shouting to each other. Gareth jumped in and I did the same, frantic for water to cool my eyes, but this water was hot! I scrambled out, furious, attracting attention and laughter. I didn't care; I'd had enough.

Gareth caught up with me before I could leave the big room and said, "The way out is over here," and dragged me off to the side through another door. He was strong!

There was a small pool in this one, too, and when I hesitated at the edge, he pushed me in. The water was cold, shocking even after the hot pool, but I welcomed it, splashing it into my eyes until the stinging ceased.

Gareth got out before I did and took a white linen towel from a pile by the door. He watched me as I joined him, drying myself. "You've never done this before, have you?" he asked scornfully.

"No, and I'll never do it again, either," I retorted.

He smirked, so I punched him on the nose, hard enough to draw blood and knock him down. He might be as big as I, but he was going to learn to show respect, one way or another. I was happy that when he got up he only nodded to show he understood, though there were tears in his eyes. He left the room and fetched our clothes, handing me mine before beginning to dress himself. Maybe this was going to be all right.

Nithe was waiting for us and smiled approvingly. "You look like high kings' sons, both of you."

"If I have to bathe every time I get a new pair of trousers," I said, "I'm not sure it's worth it."

She laughed. "Tomorrow we'll find a river. Would you like that better?"

I shook my head in disgust, but Gareth said, "I like bathing in rivers." He was still too smart, but he hadn't told Nithe I'd hit him. Maybe he'd started learning how to behave.

Nithe led us to the edge of town where the locals were holding a horse fair. The beasts looked huge to me, but Nithe told us they were only Welsh mountain ponies, sturdy, but certainly no match for King Arthur's chargers.

"Actually, real horses are easier to ride than these creatures. I expect they can jar marble when they trot. They're all the better to learn on, though. If you can endure being on the back of one of these, you can ride anything!"

She selected a gray and brought it away from the others, anxiously watched by the trader. She pulled the lips back to inspect the teeth, dragging the lower jaw down with a grip on its underside to peer into the mouth. "Never stick your hand in a horse's mouth," she instructed me. "Horses bite hard enough to take off your finger. Their upper jaws are wider than their lowers, and they chew up and down, wearing razor-sharp edges on their back teeth."

"Why do you fool with them, then?" I asked, appalled at such a risk. Gareth craned his neck to get a better look, coming closer to the pony than I wanted to. That boy wasn't afraid of anything!

"It's easy to tell how old a horse is by looking at its teeth," she said. "Horses have baby teeth, just like people, and the nippers in front fall out after they're two. All the foal teeth are gone by the time a horse is five; a five-year-old horse is fully grown and as strong as it'll get. Its teeth are cupped until it reaches nine, when they wear flat. What you're looking for is a horse between five and nine."

"What about this one?" I asked, coming to look.

"It's the right age," she said. "See the black spots on the surface of the front teeth? Those are the cups; they disappear in the tenth year."

As I came closer, I could feel she was sending out waves of comfort to the horse, who stood very quietly during the examination. I glanced at the trader. He seemed amazed to find the animal so docile.

"Is this a mean horse?" I asked him bluntly.

"Not mean. High-spirited, like," he demurred.

Sure, I thought.

"I'll take him," Nithe said, grinning, "but I want something steadier for the boys. They've never ridden before."

"I have just the mare for this one," he said, nodding at me, "and not a day over ten," the trader averred, "though Mistress will see that the cups are gone," he said in a confiding voice. He led out a plump beast of a dark chestnut color, placid enough to look at.

Nithe inspected the teeth and pointed out her findings to me. "As the man said, the cups are gone, but look at the nippers. They're triangular! And the corner teeth in the upper jaw are round, not sharp like a horse of, say, sixteen. This horse is probably eighteen, an old lady in truth."

"But see how fat she is," the man pleaded.

Nithe ignored him and led out another beast. "This one is a little over ten, maybe twelve," she said. "Its nippers are rounding." She pointed them out to me. "You like her?" she asked.

I walked around her, as if evaluating her points, but truly seeing only a pony of my own. The puppy followed closely after me, watching anxiously, trying to fathom what my concern might be.

"She has a nice short, straight back, and her rib cage is well sprung," Nithe said helpfully. "She'll be easy to sit."

"Hmmm," I responded.

"She walks well," Nithe added.

I glanced at Nithe suspiciously. Was she laughing at me?

"Well, look yourself," she invited. "There's a good slant from the stifle to the hock, and the hocks are straight to the ankle, as they should be. The pasterns connect to the feet at a good, workmanlike angle."

I didn't know any of those words; she was laughing at me! "I like her," I said simply, reached over to pat the pony's side. She eyed me in a way that suggested she had no more confidence in me than I had in her.

"Good," Nithe said. "I mentioned that horses sometimes bite. They kick, too. If you stand close to them, though, it's harder for them to get you."

"Buy me one, Nithe," Gareth commanded. "Get me a big one."

I paid no attention as Nithe selected a mount for Gareth and another beast for a pack animal, dickering with the trader all the while. I concentrated on my pony. Maybe this wasn't going to be easy. I took an apple from my belt pouch and stepped up to the mare, offering it on my flat hand so she could take it without biting me. She accepted it greedily, rubbing her nose against my shirt when she finished, asking for more. I gave her my other one, patting as she ate. She whuffled her breath on my neck, smelling me, and nudged me again. She liked me!

I patted her side and, as she turned her head to watch me, vaulted onto her back and clutched her mane for a handhold. She saw me settled and stood quietly, looking ahead, waiting for the signal to move forward.

"You're ready?" Nithe asked, coming back to me.

"Yes," I said. The puppy still watched, sitting some distance away looking worried.

"Well, first let's get a blanket for you to sit on. Your trousers are for dress-up, not for every day. Horses sweat and their hair will stick to your bare legs like glue. It's quite unpleasant."

I slid off the horse and petted her some more while Nithe took her tether and fashioned what she called a hackamore to fit around the pony's head. "I want you to be able to guide the horse with pressure from your knees, but at first you'll have to be able to move her head one way or another by pulling it around with the rope. Gently, though! You can lead her that way, too," she added. "Just hold the rope ends and walk; don't look back at her. She'll follow."

I led the mare to the trader's hut, where he kept a few blanket pads for sale. Gareth had already picked out the one he wanted, and the trader had helped him up on the pony's back. It could be a sister of my own, a fat, brown mare. Nithe selected blankets for us and a long horsehair rope to tie our supplies to the pack animal. After she paid the trader we rode back to the inn to stable our beasts. Nithe looked over the feed pails and selected a gallon bucket, saying to the stable boy, "I want each horse to have one of these filled with oats, today and tomorrow, along with as much hay as they want to eat afterward. Be sure they have water available."

The boy nodded and scurried away.

"I have to buy some supplies for the trip," Nithe told me. "Do you want to come along, or would you rather stay here?"

"I'll come," Gareth announced, and headed for the door.

"I'll stay with the horses," I said. "I want to make friends with them."

"All right; just don't give them any more apples today. I don't want them to get colic."

"How can you tell how much to feed them?" I asked.

"When they're working, horses should be given a pound of oats

33

for every hundred pounds of weight. I judge these ponies at about eight hundred pounds, so I ordered a gallon of oats."

"A pint's a pound the world around," Gareth recited, smirking in the doorway, "with eight pints to the gallon." Show-off! I might have to punch him again.

Nithe smiled, hearing the old nursery rhyme, and left me to watch the stable boy, who bustled about without speaking to me, conscious of his responsibility. He was no older than I, but considered himself vastly superior, by his manner. The puppy settled down next to me, content to rest while I talked quietly to the mare. She paid little attention to me, but she knew I was there. I'd have to think up a name for her and for the puppy, as well.

I was happy next morning to leave the inn at Exeter, and happier when we rode beyond its gates and eventually beyond its smells. "How do folk stand living there?" I asked.

"The crowding or the smell?" Nithe asked, watching me as I let the horse go at its own speed.

"Both," I replied promptly.

"It's something you get used to, like the smell of your harbor back home, I expect. I don't like town living myself," she added.

It was not the same, I thought. Anyway, I didn't mean to get used to it.

"Are you comfortable on that mare?" Nithe asked after a time.

"Yes, riding's easy," I boasted. It was, too, even when Nithe urged her horse into a trot. I understood what she meant about it being a rough ride, but I soon let myself melt into the pony's stride, moving with her instead of bouncing on her back and it was easy, like I'd said. Gareth had no more trouble than I did.

I decided to name my pony Sam, after Samana; it made me less lonesome, somehow. I called the puppy Fat Nick, for he was as stocky and greedy a creature as Samana's kitchen scullion of that name. I had liked him. I had never seen anyone so eager to please and be of use as he. and the puppy resembled him in that, too.

We were days riding north, taking our time, with Nithe giving us lessons in horse-handling on the way. "Your father, Arthur, was mad for horses when he was a boy." she told me, watching with approval as I vaulted onto Sam's back. Sam was very patient, standing quite still. Nithe made me vault up from either side and from behind the horse, explaining that I should catch my weight with my knees and thighs so I didn't pound on Sam's back with my backside.

"It would be easier on the horse if I just jumped up," I told her.

"I can do that," Gareth said, clutching at his pony's mane and scrambling up. He'd tried to vault but was too young and clumsy still.

"Very good, but there isn't always time for that," Nithe said. "Anyway, it's part of a knight's training, and it would be good for Dylan to have it behind him. It's best learned young. Your turn will come."

"A knight's training?" I said, surprised.

"You're a king's son. Kings' sons are expected to be knights." Nithe said, eyeing me in the way she had, as if she expected me to do something funny. "What did you expect?"

"But I'm only eleven!" I protested.

"Almost twelve, you said. Anyway, for most boys, knightly training starts even younger. First you're a page at eight, then a squire at puberty, and with luck and skill, a knight at fifteen."

"I don't want to be a page." I objected. I didn't even want to be a knight, but I didn't say that. "Duke Cador had pages. They had no time for hurley or anything!"

"Oh? And what do pages do then that keeps them so busy?"

"Pages have to know how to wait on table and run errands and carry messages," I exclaimed in an exasperated voice. I thought maybe she was laughing at me again.

"Hmmm! That's part of it, of course. And that's what happens when you're sent out for fostering," Nithe said gently. "Borre is going to have to do all that at Sir Ector's house."

"But why? Why does a knight have to know all that?"

"He doesn't," she said. "Chances are, however, a boy's been spoiled rotten by his mother, for she'd know she was going to lose him as soon as her husband decided it was time for the boy to go. What a page really learns is unselfishness, conforming his actions to the needs and wishes of others. Knights are supposed to serve. Christian humility is one of the most prized and honored of knightly attributes."

"I don't need to know any of those dumb things," I said sullenly.

"I do," Gareth said brightly. "I'm going to be a knight of the Round Table."

I glared at him thinking everyone knew about King Arthur's Round Table, that assemblage of the finest knights in the world. They wouldn't want a baby like Gareth.

Nithe clucked in what might have been disapproval if I hadn't seen the smile tugging at her lips. She might think it was something to laugh at, but I was serious. Hurley is important! And who cared what Gareth wanted, anyway?

"Well," she decided, "that's enough talk for now. We can make a few more miles before camping. There's a small stream that runs into the river ahead where we can bathe."

She meant it, too. She made us bathe every night before we ate, though she didn't make us soap ourselves. We could use sand to scrub the dirt off. At home I'd gotten wet most days playing by the sea, but that was not intentional. Fat Nick loved bathing, and having him in the water with me helped make it bearable. Gareth and his puppy joined us, for Gareth never waited for an invitation before thrusting himself forward. Still, while the four of us were splashing water at one another. I could forget what a pest he was most of the time.

Sam the mare and Fat Nick the puppy became friends on the road. Even when we were traveling, the puppy could frolic around Sam's feet without being kicked. He was somewhat more cautious around the other two horses, as was I, but I had no fear of them. Nithe showed me how to groom them, and it became my chore as cooking was hers. I liked it. Gareth mostly played with his dog. He said he didn't have to do chores, and Nithe just shrugged. I guess he'd find out different when he became a page.

Fat Nick was into everything. He had grown even in the short time we'd been together and thrived on the diet of oatmeal and rabbit meat. Nithe set snares in the grass before we slept each night, and we had rabbit for breakfast. On the evening of the fourth day out Fat Nick, who had been scouting ahead, came running back to us, barking. I hushed him and he led us toward a grove of trees, looking back often to make sure we followed. Eventually, we heard cries for help coming from the woods.

"Let me go! Oh, no, how could you!"

Fat Nick took us to the edge of a clearing, and we pulled up to determine what was going on. Out in the open a woman broke free from a circle of men and ran toward an old apple tree, climbing it as easily as a boy might. Lud, she was naked!

Some of the men had loosened their belts, so that their trousers hung around their knees, and stumbled after her awkwardly. She kicked at the hands that reached for her, plucking small green apples from the tree and throwing them with considerable force and accuracy, judging by the yells we heard.

"Ow! Oh, you'll pay for that, pig girl!" one shouted.

She drove her attackers a short distance away from the tree, where they huddled together and pointed at her from time to time with one hand while holding up their trousers with the other.

Nithe said, "I'll distract them while you free the girl," and spurred

37

her pony, yelling at the top of her voice. She smashed into the knot of men at a half gallop, though they tried to scramble out of her way at the last minute. The horse kicked and bucked at the impact, tossing her to the ground, but in an instant she was up with a knife in each hand, slashing and stabbing at the temporarily hobbled men. What kind of fool would run around with his pants down?

I rode under the tree yelling "Jump!" and the woman dropped onto Sam's back as lightly as any trained knight. She clutched at my tunic to steady herself, screaming curses over her shoulder as Sam took us out of the camp. The pack pony ran at Sam's left flank, frightened by the shouts. Gareth had its lead rope and pulled her to a halt when I stopped Sam. I cut the thong that tied my hurley stick to the bundle lashed to the pack pony.

"Run and hide," I told the woman. "I have to go back and help Nithe!" and jumped to the ground.

Before I'd taken more than half a step, the naked woman brought me to a stop by yanking on my hair. "Give me that knife!" she ordered.

I passed it up and she released me. With Fat Nick running beside me, barking hysterically, I went to Nithe's aid. As I'd told Nithe, hurley is a rough game. If you strike a man on the outside of his knee at just the right place, you can pop it and cripple him for a time. Two of the attackers were still on their feet, and I hit one from behind with my hurley stick. The man collapsed and rolled on the ground in agony, clutching his knee with both hands.

The woman I'd rescued raced back into the fray, launching herself from Sam's back at the last man fleeing from Nithe's attack. The naked woman buried my belt knife in the man's back, knocking him to the ground. Flinging herself on top of him, she stabbed him again and again, screeching in rage, "Whoreson dog! My father will have your guts for rope!"

"That's about all they'll be good for," Nithe remarked, wiping her knife blades on the grass and sheathing them.

I stepped up beside her and together we watched the survivors stagger to their feet and limp, groaning, into the woods. The woman rose and whirled to face us, crouching defensively.

"Hey, we're your friends, remember?" Nithe said, eyeing her intently.

Fat Nick quickly scooted several paces away, cocked his head, and studied her while Sam, Nithe's pony, and the packhorse clustered together nervously at the edge of the woods with Gareth, bowing their heads to snatch mouthfuls of grass from time to time.

I could feel the wave of calmness that emanated from Nithe and the woman relaxed slowly, finally standing erect. She was really naked: no clothes at all. I'd never seen a woman before without anything on! Looking at her carefully, I thought she couldn't be much more than fifteen, if that, but way older than I.

"I'm ruined!" she sobbed, dropping my knife and hugging herself. Nithe reached out her arms offering comfort, and the girl almost collapsed against her.

"Get something to wrap her up in," Nithe told me. "She's shaking with cold."

I found an embroidered cloak cast upon the ground not far from the wagon and brought it back to them. Gareth rode cautiously back into the clearing and slid off his pony, coming up to Nithe for reassurance. I tethered all the horses to a sapling not far from where I built a fire. Cutting dried meat and roots from our stores into small cubes, I placed them in the pot I had put to boil over the flame, along with a handful of barley. I'd seen Samana do it often enough. She'd said barley stew would cure anything. It couldn't hurt.

When I brought a bowl of it to the woman, blowing on it to cool it, Nithe looked up in surprise. Nevertheless, she took it from me and spooned it into the woman's mouth, coaxing her to eat as she might a child.

Gareth helped himself to a bowl and found bread and cheese to go with it. He ate more than Nithe and me put together, and more often.

Later Nithe joined us at the fire. "She's asleep," Nithe said. "The soup did the trick. What made you think of it?"

"It's what Samana always did for us," I said. "Is she going to be all right?"

"Maybe, in time," Nithe said. "She blames herself in part, and that is hard to forgive. Her father is rich and was sending her off to marriage with an old baron, who had gone through three wives already. Her father wanted the lofty connection as much as the baron lusted after the young body."

"Are we going to take her to him?" I asked, frowning.

"Is it likely?" Nithe asked. "The only part the girl had in all of this was seducing her father's under steward to cheat the baron of a virgin. She'd likely have gone along willingly enough after that one act of protest, for she had nowhere else to go."

"What went wrong?"

"The steward knew the girl would be inspected at the baron's castle and found not to be intact. Likely the baron would send the girl back and keep the bridal presents. The under steward would be flogged, at the very least. He wasn't going to risk it."

"But why were they attacking her?"

"The under steward invited his comrades in to share the feast after he had finished with the girl to involve them in the betrayal. He didn't want anyone bearing tales back to the girl's family." Nithe leaned over and threw another stick on the fire. "Poor child," she said. "The girl believed the under steward was in love with her. She killed him for his faithlessness."

Served him right, I thought. "What will we do with her?"

"Take her along with us. She says she can use the bridal presents to set up an inn at Caerleon, just across the river from Camelot. She'll have a better life of it there than with either her father or the baron."

Nithe and I dragged the body of the under steward into the woods where the crows and foxes could find him, not deeming him worth the effort of burial, as Gareth curled up in his cloak by the fire to sleep. He liked sleeping almost as much as eating.

I cut the under steward's belt free with his own belt knife, a blade better than mine. The belt pouch was filled with coins.

Nithe peered within, hefting the pouch as she did so. "You've found the bridal present," she said. "Must be twenty pieces of gold here, a veritable fortune. The baron will miss this more than the girl."

"Will he look for her?" I asked, shaking my head when Nithe offered to give the pouch back to me. It wasn't mine!

"Probably not. He'll think the girl's father changed his mind, like as not. Anyway, once she's under the protection of Arthur's laws, she'll be safe. He doesn't allow marriage to be forced on women, and she doesn't want to marry anyone now. Maybe never, after what happened to her."

I couldn't blame her. "It wasn't her fault," I muttered.

"Of course it wasn't her fault," Nithe snapped. "It's how she feels about it that matters." And she rolled herself up in her cloak to sleep, snorting indignantly from time to time.

When I awoke next morning I saw the woman already up and dressed in a sober brown dress, rummaging through bundles that had been part of her equipage. Gareth was squatting off to the side, one arm around his puppy's neck, watching her. With her light brown hair in a single braid hanging down her back, the woman looked not much older than I. She used the belt knife I'd given her to open the parcels and cut off gems sewn on some clothes, scattering the mutilated garments carelessly while placing other everyday items of wear in a neat pile. She put the gems in the money pouch I'd taken from the under steward. Good, I thought.

"Lady Malguin is getting rid of her finery, bidding good-bye to that sort of life," Nithe said as I leaned on an elbow to watch her. "She means it to look like bandits attacked the party. The dead under steward in the woods wears her father's livery, and word will get back when he's found."

"Lady Malguin? She's just a girl!" I objected.

"She tells me her marriage contract was signed. In law she's a baron's lady, and deserves the title. Lud knows it's cost her dearly enough!"

"Won't her family grieve for her if they think she's dead?" I asked.

"Not much, from what she says. They'll feel worse about missing the chance to be related to the baron, foul as he is."

"I guess she'll want to keep her horse, though," I said, hoping the answer was 'no.' A number of horses were grazing near ours . . . six, seven, eight in all, ponies except for the palfrey that probably had been the girl's steed, a mare fine enough for a baron's lady.

Nithe followed my gaze and said, "Nice, isn't she? Lady Malguin says the mare is her only friend."

I got up and spooned out a bowl of oatmeal mush from the pot over the fire. It was gummy, having cooked too long.

"If you'd get up with other folks, you could eat better," Nithe remarked.

"Can you read my mind?" I asked. I remembered how she'd looked fighting with a knife in each hand, and marveled how quiet and pleasant she seemed this morning. I wondered how old she was and why she traveled around alone. She could take care of herself, of course; but if I'd been a little older, I might ask her to marry me. I'd never seen anyone like her.

"I can read your face," she replied, grinning.

I didn't like that. I put the bowl down and walked over to the woman. "Malguin," I muttered to myself. Strange name. Who would name a baby something dumb like that? "Do you need any help?" I asked.

She looked up scowling on hearing my voice, then made a gesture of denial. "I'm sorry," she said. "You startled me. Do you want your knife back?" She seemed reluctant about it.

"Keep it if you want," I said. "Your servant had a better one I can use."

"Thank you. It makes me feel safer to have it at hand." She looked at me for a moment before adding, "You're just a boy. There's no harm in you . . . I didn't thank you for helping me get away. Never had I wanted anything so much!"

"You could have kept on running," I said. "Why didn't you?"

"I was angry" she said, "more angry than I've ever been in my whole life. I didn't stop to think about what I was doing. I just had to make him pay for what he tried to do to me."

"Tell me something," I said as she stooped back to her work. "How did you learn to throw as straight and hard as you do? Some of those green apples raised lumps on the heads of the men who'd treed you."

"Ah, you remember they called me pig girl?" she asked, straightening up once more. "On my father's farm it was my task when I was younger to take the pigs out into the woods to find acorns. I'd climb the trees and shake down nuts to feed the pigs, or throw rocks at the branches in the trees too big to climb to knock them loose. It's not so long ago that I've forgotten how to climb and throw!"

"That sounds like hard work for a girl," I said.

"Females were not highly valued in my father's house. I was glad enough to be outside, away from the more onerous chores. Indeed, I never minded being called pig girl. It was something I liked to do." She gave me an apologetic smile and started sorting clothes again.

I nodded, letting her continue without further interruption. If I'd been as frightened as she was, I would have kept on running, I thought. She had courage to return to kill the under steward, no matter why she said she did it.

We left before midday, with small packs of Lady Malguin's goods on the extra horses. She talked very little, so Nithe chatted with Gareth and me, saying quietly out of earshot once, "It will take some time for Lady Malguin to recover from what happened to her. The best thing we can do for her is to give her a chance to work things out in her head."

I didn't know exactly what Nithe was talking about, but followed her lead, speaking to the woman only when she asked a question.

Gareth, who usually chattered so incessantly that I rarely listened to him, asked me one morning as I helped load the packhorse, "Would you tell me about hurley? I know I said I played, but I don't really know much about it."

I glanced over at Nithe to see if she'd put him up to asking the question to make friends with me, but Nithe was absorbed in lashing some of Malguin's goods on one of the horses.

"Well," I said slowly, tugging at a strap to tighten it, "hurley is a game in which two sides vie against one another to hit a ball between their opponent's goalposts set at either end of the field. The field is a hundred and eighty Roman paces long and a third as wide. You spend most of your time running and dodging"

"Why it's nothing more than field hockey," he said scornfully.

"Field hockey?" I shouted in outrage, drawing Nithe's startled attention. Even Malguin looked up. "Girls play field hockey!"

"I like field hockey," Gareth said defensively. "What's the difference?"

"The field is only half as long in field hockey," I informed him coldly, "and you can only advance the ball by hitting it. In hurley

44

you can carry it on your stick if you're skilled enough. You use body blocks in hurley to stop an opposing player, and no contact is allowed in field hockey. There are other differences, but you don't know enough about it to talk to." I finished explaining and brushed by him, determined to ignore him from now on. I knew he was just telling a story when he said he was an expert hurley player. He didn't even have a stick! Field hockey!

We journeyed for a week before coming to an arm of the sea, skirting it to the east. A few more days brought us to the Usk River and we rode along its east bank until we came to a crossing place above the tide. On the top of a low hill we could see Camelot, Arthur's castle. It was immense, dull gray in the light rain. As we watched, the rain lifted and the sun's light turned the wet gray walls to silver. Fairy folk might well live in such a castle, I thought. "It's stone!" I said. "Even the walls are stone!"

For once even Gareth had nothing to say.

"They were wooden posts once, like most forts," Nithe told us, "but Arthur wanted something that looked Roman and would resist fire. Roman forts were all made of stone, even the buildings inside."

A red dragon floated over the highest turret.

"It's Arthur's banner," Nithe said, watching my face. "It's hollow and when the wind fills it, the archers know how to adjust their aim. Arthur does nothing for mere show."

I decided to ask the question I'd avoided before, dreading the answer. "If Arthur the High King really is my father, why has he never sought me out?"

"Maybe he didn't know you were lost," she answered, glancing at me out of the corner of her eye.

That was no answer, but about what I'd come to expect from her. I knew that if I pressed her, I might hear something I didn't want to hear. I felt resentment: What was so wrong with me that my father would be ashamed to acknowledge me as his son? Whatever he had done in the past was not my fault! I decided I would not speak of it again but wait to see what happened. I'd made my way without a father all my life. I had a seven-color cloak; let that be my father!

"My mother gave me away when I was younger than you," Nithe said, surprising me. "I was raised by Myrddin, the one you call the giant boat man."

"Truly? Why would she do that?"

"I was considered a disruptive influence in the quiet religious community in which she lived. She had a choice: to give up her position as Lady of the Lake or to give up her daughter. She made the right one, I think. I needed a stronger hand than hers."

Mostly when grown-ups said they understand how you feel, it sounded false to me. But Nithe knew! And I thought she still felt anger for being sent from home; she didn't have to say that. I wondered how anyone could be as beautiful as Nithe, fight as fiercely as she could at need, and still remember what it was to be a child. If only she didn't have this notion about bathing!

After crossing the river over the stone causeway laid in its bed, we turned away from the town toward a prosperous-looking farmhouse.

"Ayres, the cowherd, lives here," Nithe said. "He owns this small pasture on the edge of Caerleon, and he might part with it, the very spot for an inn," and she indicated the plot on our left. It was perhaps twenty acres, protected from the north wind by trees clustered on a small hill behind it, and fronted on the road from the ford to the town. I could see it was cut off from the rest of the farm by a spur of the hill and would not be convenient for the farmer to use.

Lady Malguin looked at the spot with more animation than she'd shown in days. "That would do very well," she said. "What would it cost, do you think?"

"I know little about such things," Nithe said. "Ayres is an easy man to deal with, though. I think he might like an inn handy where he and his sons could relax and drink among friends after a day's work, away from the swarms of children at home."

"Sons?" she asked frowning.

"They're harmless, all very shy, with the exception of the oldest, Sir Torre. He's been knighted by Arthur and stays at Camelot most of the time. The others, twelve in number, if you'd believe it, all work for their father."

"Their poor mother," Lady Malguin muttered.

"She's as happy a person as I know. Some of her boys are married and their wives cluster around her, vying to see who can best serve her."

The farmhouse was surrounded by a low fence with a gate to keep the geese from escaping the yard. They splashed out of their small pond, coming to challenge our entry like so many guard dogs. Fat Nick didn't know what to make of them and nearly got stepped on by Sam, crowding under her as she stood, shifting her weight from foot to foot.

A stout woman in a long wool gown came to the door of the house, a low, rambling, plastered building with a red tile roof. She hailed us. "What service can I give you?"

"Shame on you, Cousin, not to recognize one of your own!" Nithe said, dismounting and waving the geese back. They quieted for her.

"Ah, my lady! Shame, indeed! But it's been years since I've had the pleasure of greeting you!" She hugged Nithe and kissed her soundly, giggling, to add, "Cousin, she says!"

"I'd like you to meet my friends," Nithe said. "This is Lady Malguin, who would like to speak to your husband about setting up an inn."

"Lady Malguin?" the woman we'd rescued asked, as if startled to hear her name. "I don't think so. I've never liked the name Malguin, and with the title it sounds worse than ever. My friends used to call me Mal."

"Lady Mal, then," Ayres's wife said comfortably, bobbing a bow to her.

"Standing beside Lady Mal, the red-haired boy is Dylan the Orphan, the pride of Lyoness," Nithe said, continuing the introductions.

"I'm Gareth, son of Pelleas," Gareth offered, not waiting on others to make himself known. Pushy.

"Welcome, I'm sure, all of you," Ayres's wife said. "Ayres is taking a nap, but the girls will wake him now that we have company. But tell me why is Lyoness proud of this young man?" she asked, folding her hands across her ample belly and looking at me with a smile.

"I'm told he's the only three-goal hurley player in the islands," Nithe replied.

"Hurley, is it? Wait 'til the boys hear that! They're mad for hurley. But such a lad, yet!"

"Makes you wonder what he'll do when he's had his growth, doesn't it?" Nithe said gravely enough, but winking at me.

"I'll be bigger than him," Gareth exclaimed. "My father is a Geen!"

I gave him a sour glance. I was sure I hadn't stopped growing.

Young men came to stand behind their mother, stepping aside for an older man to walk up to us. "Lady Nineve!" he exclaimed. "Goodwife, why haven't you invited them in? Come in, come in! The boys will take your horses." And he ushered us all into the house.

I looked around with wonder. I'd never seen such a place. It was handsomer than Duke Cador's, even. There were tiled arches everywhere, framing corridors that ran off in all directions. The floor was a mosaic, small pieces of colored stone forming a picture of a man in a chariot drawn by two white horses.

Seeing my face, Ayres said proudly, "It was a Roman manor

house once. We've rebuilt it along the original lines, including the baths and hot air ducts underneath the floors."

"Did you do the work yourselves?" Lady Mal asked.

"Me and my sons. There's nothing in building one or another of us can't do."

"Ayres is the son of a Roman soldier, discharged in Britain at the end of his service," Nithe told us, as we were urged to take seats on fine carved chairs.

"A centurion, my father was," Ayres said proudly. "He taught me Latin, and I've tried to teach the boys, but none of them took to it. It's a shame. I like to hear my father's tongue. It's why I'm always so happy to see Lady Nineve," he finished, beaming at her.

"I speak Latin," Lady Mal said, with a proper Roman accent. It was as good as Samana's.

"What?" Ayres exclaimed. "Why, that's wonderful."

Using Latin, Lady Mal proceeded to tell Ayres of her interest in establishing an inn; and they talked together through the afternoon, supper, and until past time for bed, making plans and discussing terms.

"My sons and I will build the inn and take payment in the gems from the store you've shown me. It will be a brave thing to see our women decked out in jewels for mass on Sunday. I can get them evaluated fairly at the castle. Kay, the king's seneschal, will buy any you choose to sell, paying in barrels of wine and beer, like as not," Ayres summed up.

I yawned, bored with the long discussion, and one of Ayres's sons led Gareth and me down a corridor to a small room with two clean, comfortable beds. Fat Nick and I settled down in one, and Gareth and his puppy in the other, leaving the rest of them still talking.

CHAPTER

III

woke with Fat Nick jumping up and down on my back, stiff-legged, barking his head off. I rolled over, tumbling him to one side, and found my room full of people staring at me and talking. They were Ayres's sons. Gareth was not among them.

"He's not big enough to be a three-goal player or even play against men," a tall person said slightingly.

"Lady Nithe said so," one of Ayres's sons insisted.

Several others agreed with the speaker. "That's Dylan the Orphan! You've heard of him!"

"Ah, the boy wonder! Of course I've heard of him. But what makes you think this is the lad?"

"Because I say so!" I answered. I didn't like to be talked about as if I weren't there.

"Would you come play with us?" one of Ayres's sons asked. "We have a game against the squires from the castle this morning. It's Pentecost and we always play them on that day. They always beat us," he added. Perhaps he thought it would be different this time.

I stared at him . . . Pentecost. I had been found in the broken

50

boat the day after the feast of Pentecost and brought to Samana, where all small things in need of mothering were brought in Lyoness. Since then it was reckoned as my birthday. I was twelve now, truly.

"The king will be there to watch," he added as inducement.

"King Arthur?" I asked, excitement rising within me.

"There's only one king," the tall man answered. "Of course, King Arthur."

"Let me eat first. I play better when I'm not hungry," I said, and pushed through the crowd, following my nose to the kitchen. I found Gareth there, stuffing himself, with Ayres's wife hovering over him, watching him with admiration.

"Come, sit," she ordered, and placed a steaming bowl of oatmeal before me, swimming with fresh butter.

"It's good, Dylan," Gareth said after a huge swallow. "I'm not going on to Camelot. Torre says the food is better here."

"See, Torre, he called him Dylan! I told you!" one of Ayres's sons said with conviction. "I told you it was Dylan the Orphan!"

"You're a knight? Do you know King Arthur?" Gareth asked while I ate. It was good.

"He made me," Sir Torre said simply. "When he married Guenevere, he set up the Round Table with knights given him by Guenevere's father. The Round Table is the finest group of knights in the world, all sworn to live by the Pentecostal oath. Twenty-eight more knights joined the Table, but the first he made with his own hands was Gawaine. I was the second. My father had brought me to the king saying I was no good on the farm, spending all my time in knightly drill. I serve the king now."

"What's the Pentecostal oath?" Gareth asked, always ready with a question of some kind.

"Arthur proclaimed it when he established the Round Table. On admission each knight must swear to fight only in just causes, to be merciful, and always to put the service of ladies foremost."

"That's all?"

"It's quite enough. It's not easy to determine which side of a quarrel is the just one or to remember to be merciful in the heat of battle. It's even harder to put oneself at the service of ladies, for sometime ladies want things that are neither just nor merciful. You see?"

I did, though Gareth looked doubtful. I had a sudden recollection of Nithe and Malguin fighting the under steward and his men. I'd helped, but they could have done it by themselves, like as not.

I held out my bowl for more oatmeal and asked, "Who is a lady?"

Sir Torre looked surprised. "It's a matter of birth," he said. "Ladies are born into noble households. Females born into families among the lower orders are not ladies, though they may be most respectable," he added, glancing at his mother.

She ignored him, placing another bowl of hot oatmeal before me and beaming. She approved of my appetite and my appreciation of her cooking.

I knew what he meant. Samana had told me there are only two classes in Britain: those that owned and those who were owned. The lowest of orders, the serfs, were bound to the land and could not leave without their master's permission. Even a free man, like Colin the ship owner, could not use his own property without the Duke Cador's permission. It wasn't fair.

"Why are you playing against Camelot if you're a knight of the Round Table?" I asked.

"It isn't me. It's my brothers. Knights don't play hurley. Maybe they would if you could play it from horseback, but that's impossible."

I thought a moment: it might be possible to play from horseback, striking the ball as it rolled along the ground. Probably you couldn't carry it on the flat blade on horseback, though. That was hard enough to do just running.

"Do you bet?" I asked.

"Yes, out of loyalty to my brothers. It's fortunate my father has a deep purse," he replied ruefully.

"You'll win this time," I said. I'd show him I was not too small to play hurley!

The game took place in a large meadow before the castle where shades had been set up over a wooden stand at midfield to shelter Arthur and his party. There were fifteen of us on each side, as usual in match play, though any number might take part in a pickup game.

We assembled before the royal box, and I saw a man there looking at me curiously, though no more interested in me than I was in him: King Arthur! Oh, let it be now . . . he must know who I am, I thought.

The king was a strongly made man of middle height, not yet thirty, with blond hair and mustaches and a golden dragon torque around his neck. The lady he escorted was as tall as he, looking more Saxon than British. She must be his queen, Guenevere, I decided. Nithe walked with the two of them, dressed much more richly than I had seen her before, in a long gown of forest green. She winked at me and spoke to Arthur, who nodded, looking at me. Even then he didn't speak! Maybe he wants to see me play first. Good. I'd show him!

"Don't stare, boy," Sir Torre admonished me, walking to the center of the field to begin the game.

I took my accustomed place as goalie, stripping off my tunic and placing it carefully behind one of the goalposts. Not all the others took their clothes off. I wondered why? Their tunics would get all sweaty if they ran as hard as they should to play good hurley.

Sir Torre dropped the ball for the scrimmage and, following my instructions. Sir Torre's brothers allowed the squires to capture it and run toward our goal. I made a feint of running toward the youth who carried the ball on the flat of his blade and veered sharply off to intercept the soft pass he flipped to a teammate. When I had run completely through the other players, dodging with ease blows meant to stop me, I dropped the ball and hit it far over the goalie's head, through the posts set up at the other end of the field. Perhaps I was showing off, but King Arthur was watching!

Folks from Caerleon had come to see the match, taking a half holiday. I saw Lady Mal and Gareth standing beside Ayres's wife along with several of her daughters-in-law. They were all cheering, but they weren't alone. Most of the townspeople joined them. I wondered if they usually cheered for the castle.

"Did you bet?" I asked Sir Torre during the rest period after the first goal, when he came on the field to drop the ball for scrimmage to restart the contest.

He laughed. "I'll be rich if you can do that again!"

I scored four goals, one in each quarter of the game, and no one else scored on either side. In truth, I am a four-goal player when I want to be, but no one has ever been ranked that high.

Sir Torre led me up to meet Arthur after the game at the king's request. Sir Torre made me dress first. "Show a little respect, boy!"

"That was splendid, Dylan," Arthur said as I trailed Sir Torre, a bit resentfully, to meet the king. How had I not shown respect? "Do you always play so well?"

"Always," I said, looking directly at his face. He seemed amused at my bluntness. Fat Nick had bitten through the rope that restrained him and ran to join me, jumping up to lick my face.

"My dog used to enter tourneys with me," Arthur said. "Yours may become as large as she was."

"He's a wolfhound," I told him.

The king laughed. "Hardly that I think. Perhaps he'll grow up to hunt bears, but he'll never catch a wolf."

I must have appeared to resent his criticism, for he said hastily, "I can see his mother must have been a wolfhound, from his coat, but I would think his father was a mastiff, by his heavy bone. The dog I spoke of was wolf and mastiff. I never saw a finer beast."

That was better. I nodded with as much dignity as I could muster, dirty and sweating the way I was.

"You'll have to become a page and join our court," he continued pleasantly, and he smiled a blinding, welcoming smile that made me look at the ground in sudden embarrassment. I knew the king meant by that I would be his page, not just another page, but it wasn't enough!

"No, there'd be no time for hurley," I blurted, shaking my head for emphasis. Oh, dumb! What did I want?

Nithe rolled her eyes up in dismay.

"I'm a high king's son," I added desperately. Didn't he understand? "I'm not going to be anyone's page!"

"Ah, I see," he said, his smile changing to one of amusement. "Who is your father, then?"

"I don't know," I muttered and looked away. Why didn't he know?

"I had that problem once," the king told me kindly. "But you're wrong about not having time for hurley. Ask Sir Torre."

I glanced up at Sir Torre, who nodded gravely, so I changed my mind. "I will, then," I said.

Arthur smiled again, and rose to leave. For a moment I poised myself to chase after him—I'd have followed him anywhere—but a huge man loomed up behind Arthur and said, "A king's bastard, is he? The countryside is fairly littered with kings' get, eh, Torre? Bring him to me and let me get his neck under my arm. I'll show him a new use for that stick of his; give him a hiding. Teach him some manners."

Sir Torre's hand tightened on my shoulder but he didn't push me forward, just the same.

Nithe stepped from the queen's side and faced the giant. "I brought the boy to Camelot, Pellinore," she told him with her hand hovering near her dainty belt knife. "He is under my protection, and for your information he is no king's get, as you call it. He is a true high king's son, as he claims—not yours, though," and she turned to stare at Arthur.

The smile left my father's face as he looked intently first at her and then back at me. "He's the image of Gawaine as a boy," he said finally, paling.

"Is he not?" Nithe agreed, challenging him somehow.

Arthur turned abruptly away and left the stand, followed by his retinue. The queen gave me a look of loathing in passing. I thought she'd guessed who I was, if Arthur had not! My disappointment was so strong I felt tears sting my eyes.

"Wait here for me," Sir Torre said. "I'm going to collect my bets before my friends forget what they owe," leaving me with his brothers, who were all filled with the joy of our victory. Some of the squires we had played against came to talk with Ayres's sons. "This must be Dylan the Orphan," one of them said, nodding at me. "How did you get him to play for you?"

"He's been staying with our father," one of the brothers replied.

"He's my brother," Gareth announced, pushing through the crush until he stood before me. There was pride in his voice. This was the first time Gareth had claimed me for a brother. I'd missed Borre. It would be good to have someone to take care of again.

Gareth had refused to leave Ayres's house and Ayres's wife's table. Nithe had offered to present him to King Arthur, since neither Pelleas, his father, nor Morgause, his mother, were in residence at Camelot. Gareth had decided if I could refuse to enter pages' training, so could he. He spent all the time he was not at table or asleep, working and caring for Ayres's draft animals, oxen

56

with huge brown eyes and patient ways. He'd found a chore that was more play than work to him.

I glanced up at Lady Mal, who had followed him, but I spoke to Gareth. "Did I do well, brother?" I asked. I would not have him rejected as Arthur had rejected me.

Gareth nodded, suddenly shy.

Lady Mal put her hand on his shoulder, and he stepped back to press against her. She was beaming at me; I realized she'd hoped I would do that. Probably she'd put Gareth up to it in the first place, but I didn't care. I felt good about that, anyway.

Sir Torre joined us. I feared he might be angry with me for taking the king's offer, but instead he was delighted. "I'll make you my squire, though," he said. "You can skip the page part, if you want to. If you can outplay the other squires, I don't see why you should be held back."

"I won't have to hang around waiting to be ordered here or there?"

"Not a bit of it. You will have to live in Camelot, like the king said, but that's where I am most of the time. There's a bed in the stable's tack room you can use. I am the king's Master of the Horse, and it is my duty to oversee the care of all beasts in the royal stables. As a matter of course, mine are there as well. You will take personal care of those I own, feeding and grooming them yourself, and seeing to their needs. You will particularly see they are properly shod, and learn how it is done, for a horse may throw a shoe where there is no farrier to correct the matter."

"I'll be a horse groom?"

"Not just a horse groom; you'll be my horse groom," Sir Torre said. "You might say I'm the king's horse groom if you like. It is not dishonorable work."

"No," I agreed. The idea pleased me very much.

"You'll also have to keep my gear in shape. Not just the horse gear but my armor and weapons. Fortunately, I don't have all that much. My brothers have been taking turns polishing and sharpening such items as I own, and they'll see you right. It won't be like working with the other stable lads."

I agreed. I liked Ayres's sons.

"Do you hunt?" Lady Mal asked Sir Torre.

"No," he said shortly. "I have too clear a recollection of knights trampling my father's field chasing some stag, heedless of the damage they do to standing crops to take any pleasure in it. If I did," he said, turning to me, "you'd come along and carry my bows, arrows, and boar spear. I'd carry my own hawk."

"It sounds like fun," I said.

"You can go with the other lads to beat the woods, driving game toward the hunters, if you have a mind to," he offered kindly.

I nodded. I'd think about it. It didn't sound as much fun as running after stags on horseback, but only knights did that.

"One more thing. If we go to war, you'd have to ride with me. You'd carry my shield and extra weapons, handing them to me at need. If I took prisoners or captured horses, you'd mind them for me."

"Would I fight?"

"Only if you were attacked. It happens sometimes. War is usually just a series of single duels, with enemy knights engaging each other all over the battlefield. Foot soldiers with spears usually fight the spear men of enemy knights their master is engaging, coming to his rescue if he falls. They don't bother anyone else."

That part sounded dumb to me, but I told him truthfully, "I'd like helping you. Would your brothers come, too?"

"Some of them. Those with wives would stay with my father and work the farm."

"I like the farm," Gareth announced, riding beside Lady Mal.

"So do I, but I have no rights there," Sir Torre said. "When I was made a knight, I lost my position as Ayres's eldest son. That's the lot of most knights, however. Knights are usually younger sons of kings or barons. They have no property of their own or any hope of getting any. Only the eldest son inherits. That means a knight must attach himself to some propertied noble and fight his liege lord's battles in return for support."

"It sounds dull," I said.

"Sometimes it is. Until recently King Arthur was rarely in Camelot, though. He's pretty well tamed all the bad barons and reduced the number of robbers on the king's highways."

I wondered what would become of me if my father did not acknowledge me. I'd probably end up as a knight retained by some bad baron someplace near Camelot. Maybe I could go and join Pelleas, the high king of the Picts. If I brought Gareth along, he'd have to welcome me. I'd think about it.

I ate with Ayres's family after the match and waited with them to see the knights' tourney that afternoon. At first I was thrilled as the knights thumped each other, and cheered when one or another landed on the ground with a clang. My own brother Gawaine was one of the best, surpassed only by Sir Lancelot. I wished I could run up to Gawaine as Gareth had run up to me, but until King Arthur had spoken, how could I?

I soon became uncomfortable at the tourney when I saw how the horses were suffering. The first time one of the long ash spears broke and long splinters were driven into a horse, I was shocked. The second time I was outraged, and on the third time, I turned and left, riding Sam all the way back to Ayres's farm by myself. Some of those horse were used again and again, with splinters still sticking out of them!

When the family joined me later, they asked whether I'd taken some hurt in the hurley game.

"No, it was the horses. Do the horses always get hurt like that?" I asked.

"Those weren't their good horses," Ayres explained. "War horses are clad in tough leather armor like their riders and usually come to little harm. These tourney horses get patched up after every meeting. If one dies, there's little lost."

I shook my head slightly, but didn't respond. He didn't understand. A horse was a horse. Lady Mal told me later that she agreed with me. She wouldn't even eat meat because she hated to have animals suffer. I wasn't that tenderhearted; I just hated to see people hurt animals for fun. After that, I didn't even want to seek out my brother Gawaine quietly, as I had planned. I decided I didn't like knights much, except for Sir Torre.

Torre moved me to Camelot as he promised, and I took up my duties as his squire. Gareth continued to stay with Ayres's huge family as another son, being watched over by Lady Mal. We saw each other from time to time, for Sir Torre was very devoted to his family, and I always accompanied him on his visits home. Gareth soon took a place beside Borre in my affections, and Lady Mal ranked only second to Samana.

The work in Camelot filled my days, with the exception of the rare holidays we spent in Caerleon. The stables were in the outer bailey, the outer courtyard, protected by a stone defensive wall. Though removed as far as possible from the castle, because of the flies attracted by the horses, we saw as much of Arthur the King when he was in residence as the castle folk did. He inspected the stables, kennels, and mews daily.

I followed him around, out of sight, just to look at him. I saw him give the smile of welcome to his favorites and began to understand him better. It was as if he were saying, "My horse!" "My hound!" "My hawk!" But it was more than that, for it held a commitment, too, as if he'd die for one he loved. If he offered me the opportunity to serve him again, I'd make him feel that way for me, I swore to myself. I would!

Sir Torre knew about my spying, for I was forever lurking around, trying to stay out of sight when he was talking to the king. "The king's three loves are horses, hounds, and hawks," Sir Torre said, nodding when I told him about the king's talking to his animals on his morning rounds. I felt much the same, though I placed hurley over hawks.

I played with Ayres's sons against Caerleon and Caerwent in the great meadow before Camelot over the next two months, and we won both times. I had chances to score half a dozen goals in each game, but I limited myself to three in each to keep my average up but not look greedy. Instead, I passed off to one or another of the brothers and let them take the score. It pleased them immensely.

One grabbed my hand and squeezed it overhard, beaming. "Never have I scored a goal before," he said, "and with the father and mother and the wife and the little ones watching and shouting and cheering my name! Never!"

I thought it was pathetic.

Another one of them told me, "Torre asked the lady Nineve whether we could adopt you into the family, but she said no."

Sir Torre came up, counting his winnings, and overheard the statement. "She wouldn't say why," he observed, looking down at me. "She said I could ask you."

"I'm waiting for my true father to claim me," I said.

"Who is that?"

"Arthur the King," I said, half-defiantly. I didn't expect him to believe me.

He stopped fingering the small coins and dumped them unceremoniously into his belt pouch. "I see. You probably don't know, but my own true father is King Pellinore. He forced himself on my mother while she was still a maid. She said he'd found her milking cows in a barn where there was no one to protect her. He even took her dog with him as he left, saying he wanted something to remember her by."

I didn't usually pay much attention to adults, but I could see that though Sir Torre's gaze was calm enough, his tone was bitter. Fat Nick nudged my hand with his nose, and I thought if someone wronged me and then stole my dog, I'd be mad, too. "Does King Pellinore claim you?" I asked.

"Oh, yes. That's why I'm not considered Ayres's eldest son any longer. After the king knighted me, Myrddin told everyone about how I was conceived. Do you know Myrddin?"

I nodded. Myrddin was Nithe's giant boat man.

"Well," he continued. "I said Pellinore had dishonored my mother, but Myrddin held that since Pellinore was royal it was an honor, really, particularly since my mother wasn't married yet. Pellinore agreed and embraced me. Myrddin apologized to me later, privately, saying that he had only wanted to spare me from being snubbed by the others, seeing my mother was a commoner." His words were still light enough, but there was no smile on his face. The hurt he'd felt for his mother still showed after all those years, and I warmed to the man.

It was some saint's day. I didn't know whose, but Sir Torre said we could skip the feast that followed the game. Lady Mal and Gareth had come to watch me play and rode back with us to the farm, nearly an hour's distance from Camelot. We left the general rejoicing and high spirits behind us, though Lady Mal and Gareth a few paces ahead of us were blithe enough. I was tired and Sir Torre looked pensive.

I broke in on his thoughts. "You believe me, then?"

"About King Arthur being your father? Oh, yes," he said absently. Rousing himself he looked at me and asked, "Who was your mother?"

"Nithe says it was Queen Morgause."

"That one! You're Mordred, then?"

"You know about me?"

He nodded in a companionable way. "I heard stories about the king's dalliance with Queen Morgause when he was little more than a boy. You know I've been with Arthur almost since the beginning. I remember I'd also heard he sent you to Samana under Gawaine's care. I was supposed to go along on the trip to Lyoness, but Ayres needed me on the farm for harvest. I still owe him respect for having raised me."

"You don't think me a monster like Duke Cador's wife says? The queen looked at me as if I were dog's dinner!"

He looked embarrassed. "My family, Ayres and my mother, I mean, are not Christian, so neither am I. A man sleeping with his aunt is considered something of a joke among those who do not follow the cross; in large families it happens, seeing the two may not be much different in age and handy and all. Only Christians, like Arthur's queen, would be much bothered by a thing like that."

"My father turned away from me!" I said, tears welling up into my eyes, remembering the distress on Arthur's face.

"He was surprised, is all. The king moves quickly enough in battle, but new ideas are hard for him. Don't worry. With the king's sister as your champion, you'll win through!"

"Nithe?" I asked.

"The lady Nineve! They were raised together, and if anyone can bring him around it's she," he said comfortingly.

I hoped so, but she hadn't had much luck so far, I thought.

The talk turned to the duties I'd have as squire to Sir Torre at the feast he said would be held to honor the queen's birthday. Lady Mal dropped back to ride with us and listened closely, for she knew much about the preparation and serving of food. "When we dine with the king," Sir Torre said, "you'll stand behind my seat and select for my plate food from the tureens and platters the pages carry . . . such morsels as catch your eye, tasting everything first, of course."

"Tasting?"

"You might take several bites to determine in some cases," he said smiling.

"Several bites. Yes, I can do that," I said. The thought of Gareth as a squire came to me unbidden. There would be scarce anything left after he'd tasted dishes!

Lady Mal added, "The purpose in having a taster is to keep oneself from being poisoned."

"What?" I cried, not as pleased as before.

"Only Pictish kings poison their enemies," Sir Torre assured me. "The occasion will not arise," and he reproved Lady Mal with a slight frown.

He might as well scold the sun. "You must help your master ready himself for the feast," she continued, unabashed, "attending him on his rising, dressing him, fetching water for him to wash, emptying his slops jar, and scouring it to keep it fresh . . ."

"I won't then!" I shouted, breaking in on her list of servile tasks. "Not even pages do all that!"

"Squires serve their masters in whatever way their master wishes," Sir Torre said calmly. "I will not use you so, though it is true some squires perform such functions. All knighthood is service. Pages serve, squires serve, and knights serve. Only barons and kings live without serving someone else."

"I'm going to be a baron then," I said.

"You sound like Gareth," Lady Mal said teasingly.

"Sometimes food goes bad in the kitchen," I said, ignoring her teasing. "It even smells bad. Do I have to taste that, too?"

"If you have any doubts, you can always slip a suspect morsel to one of the hounds that roam around behind and under the tables at mealtime," Lady Mal answered.

"That's no help," Sir Torre grunted. "The king would rather lose a page or a squire than a hound anytime."

When the queen's birthday feast arrived, Ayres's wife gave me new clothes to wear, a green jerkin and red and gray trousers so

I would not shame her son. We were all in our places when the queen entered on the king's arm, smiling and speaking to favorites along the way. The king placed her between his seat and Sir Lancelot's, much to her advantage. Sir Lancelot was bigger than the king and as dark as the queen was fair. King Arthur's golden hair and mustaches made him handsomer than either to my mind, however.

On the other side of the king sat Gawaine, my brother. He had the same copper red hair as me. Gawaine was taller and leaner than King Arthur. I found Gawaine looking at me curiously several times, as if he wondered who I was. The king never glanced in my direction.

While waiting for the food to be served, I looked around the great hall. I judged it was twenty paces across and sixty long, with great oak beams running up the sides of the walls, supporting the vaulted ceiling. The walls were of dressed wood, smoothed and oiled so that they shone in the glow of the wax-dipped candles gracing the two long tables. Shields painted with individual knights' identifying blazons were hung from the walls behind the seats. The king's household sat at one table and some of his men-at-arms at the other, so that the diners faced each other. Sir Torre's place was directly across from Nithe, and she smiled or winked at me from time to time as I stood behind him, nervous about making mistakes. I knew she was teasing about my refusal to be a page.

I wasn't a page, though. I snapped my fingers and pages came running, most of them older than me. After inspecting the platters they carried, I would select a sample and eat it while they waited and then nod for them to serve my master.

Sir Torre beckoned me forward and muttered behind his cupped hand. "No more. I can't possibly eat all this!"

There was a lot of it. At Duke Cador's table on ordinary days there was one hot dish, soup or fish mostly . . . not much meat. Here there were joints and fowl and baked fish, course after course.

I tasted everything, even after Torre was through eating, as if trying to find something that might tempt his appetite. In truth I was hungry and was not allowed to sit and eat with the queen's guests, so I made out the best I could with tastes.

As for the wine, I sipped it only, not sure if I liked it. One of the pages smirked at the doubt on my face, and I poured the glass of wine on his foot saying, "This is sour. Bring something sweeter," and stared at him.

He turned color but lacked the nerve to make a scene in the king's presence. There was little of that. Most of the squires liked me. I'd promised to play hurley for them when they were not contending with Ayres's sons, and won their support that way. Even a few of the pages came to me asking me to keep certain of the other squires from bullying them. A few words in the right ear was all it took to bring a change in behavior. Many people called me friend.

Most of the horses were turned out to pasture after the last haying, and there was little to do around the stables at Camelot. Sir Torre turned me loose to help with the work on Lady Mal's new inn. Ayres's sons had been trained by master craftsmen when Arthur built Camelot, and had become proficient enough that the inn was constructed before winter set in. I helped where I could, followed by Fat Nick, who was under foot most of the time. I grew used to hearing him yelp as he got stepped on or kicked, though never hard, for everyone knew him for my own.

Lady Mal had an open house when the work was complete in the fall, and folk from town and castle came to drink her wine and ale and eat her food. Ayres's wife and daughters-in-law helped in the huge kitchen and waited table. "They'll eat you out of house and home, Lady," the goodwife grumbled as smoking joint followed smoking joint into the eating hall.

"Only tonight. If they like what they see, they'll be back with pennies in their hands," she promised.

I sat on a high stool and talked to folks who were eager to meet Dylan the Orphan, the three-goal hurley player. Sir Torre insisted, saying that I was a celebrity, and folks who would not have come otherwise would be there just to shake my hand. It seemed fanciful, but Lady Mal looked anxiously at me, hoping I would agree to the plan. I felt responsible for her after rescuing her from the apple tree and played the role assigned me.

After the food had been cleared away and folks settled down to serious drinking, Lady Mal surprised us all by taking a lute from an embroidered case and strumming on it to quiet the crowd. She began to sing, in a voice of remarkable sweetness and power, a ballad I'd heard in Duke Cador's hall in Lyoness. Shouts of approval followed, and on impulse I tossed the few coins I owned toward her, sitting on my high stool in the corner. My gesture inspired others until I thought the cost of the feast might well be covered. Lady Mal obliged us by singing for another hour, song after song, some in response to requests from the topers. Who would have thought this quiet woman could do such a thing!

I was sleepy when the last guest left, and Lady Mal told Sir Torre she wanted me to stay over and sleep by the fire in case some latecomer wanted service. Fat Nick could wake me up. Sir Torre nodded and left with his brothers for home.

As they shut the door, Lady Mal barred it and said, "That was only a pretext. There will be no more guests welcomed tonight. I wanted to say privately to you that this is your home anytime you wish to stay. I haven't forgotten what you and Lady Nineve did for me. She is so far above my station I probably will never even see her again, but you are like a little brother."

She took me to a small room near the kitchen where it was warm and showed me a bed. "This room will be kept for you," she said. "Come and go at will," and she kissed me on the cheek, closing the door on Fat Nick and me. Pig girl . . . I wouldn't call her that, for other folks might misunderstand, but that's the way

I'd think of her. I threw myself gratefully on the bed and went to sleep. I had one friend, at least. She was as nice as Nithe.

Someone scratched at the door of my room before I was fully awake and one of Ayres's sons poked in his head. "Sir Torre wants you. Queen Guenevere has decided to move the entire court to London for the winter season. You have to help him get ready."

"London?"

"Aye. She does it every year. Didn't you know?"

I didn't. Why would she want to leave Camelot, I wondered. I found bread and cheese in the kitchen and joined Ayres's family down the road without seeing Lady Mal. She'd slept late today. Torre had a jumble of clothes and armor on the floor of the main hall, trying to decide what to take with him. His mother stood by with folded hands as usual and commented on each item as he picked it up.

"No, gosoon! That's a summer shirt. You'll not need it in London. Take the brown one there and the two green ones. That will give you a choice and a spare." He obediently dropped the light tunic and picked up the three his mother had indicated were appropriate, handing them to one of his sisters-in-law, who folded them and tucked them into an open leather sack.

"Good! You're here!" Sir Torre said on seeing me. "Get your clothes together and then help me sort this gear. You'll have to take care of it on the road. I'll need helmet, mail, a long sword and a short one, a shield, and two spears. Everything has to be shined or I'll catch hell. Use sand and a little water on them, will you?"

"Will we be fighting robbers on the way?"

"No, we won't even see robbers. They may come at night to steal a cow or two, but they won't attack a party as large as ours."

"Why do you need armor then?"

"For the tourneys, of course. They have them at Christmas, Easter, and Pentecost, if we're still in town."

"That's not real fighting, is it?"

"No. King Arthur's mercenaries, the real fighters he got as part of Guenevere's dowry, don't even come to London. It's just the court that's moving. That includes all the sons of client kings, kings he's conquered and who have sent their heirs to Arthur to hold hostage for good behavior. Arthur's father, Uther Pendragon, kept his hostages naked in a pit, feeding them on scraps like dogs. King Arthur's way is better. He's made them all knights of the Round Table."

"Does that include Gawaine and Lancelot and King Pellinore?" I asked, for the idea sounded fantastic to me.

"Of course not. Gawaine and Lancelot are relatives. King Pellinore is an ally. There are scarce twenty hostage-guests."

"Will they fight in the king's wars?"

"No, but they'll take part in the tourneys, if they can find someone to lend them horses and armor. Likely, they'll come to me, for I have charge of the horses. They'll probably want my armor as well," he grumbled. I now understood why Sir Torre kept his best equipment at Ayres's house.

Sir Torre's brothers did most of the work in readying his gear for London, teaching me what I didn't know, oiling the leather straps and burnishing the iron. It was interesting for its own sake. I liked his great sword but was surprised that it had a rounded point.

"Swords are used for slashing," one of Ayres's sons told me. "If Torre wants to stab someone, he'll use a dagger," and held out a wicked spike of a knife for my inspection. "It'll slip between the links of the chain mail," he explained, though explanation was hardly necessary.

In truth, there was little to do, for Torre's armor and weapons were a source of pride for the whole family and were kept shining at all times. I suspected we went through the formal process of cleaning and sharpening for my benefit, so I would know how.

"When do we leave?" I asked when the last piece had been inspected and set aside for packing.

"In three days," Sir Torre said. "Some of the baggage has gone on ahead, though the queen keeps winter clothes in the London palace." Sir Torre sounded as if he were looking forward to it.

"You like London?" I asked.

"Oh yes. It's good to get away from home from time to time. Here I'm always surrounded by friends and family. There I can be completely by myself in a crowd of strangers if I want to. No one pays any attention to anyone else there."

The afternoon before we left Nithe came searching for me. She found me in the stable, grooming Sam.

"I've come to say good-bye," she told me.

"You're not coming with us to London?" I felt a sinking feeling. I loved this splendid woman. How could I let her go?

"No. I'm out of favor with the king just now, not to mention his wife," Nithe said. "If it were just Arthur, I could bring him around to accepting you publicly as his son, as he has acknowledged to me in private, but with the queen always listening, I can't budge him. He's besotted with Guenevere and fears to offend her. Having done just that, perhaps I can understand why."

"You got into trouble over me?" I asked, glad to have had a friend speak for me. It didn't help, though, if I was the cause of her leaving Camelot.

Sam whinnied and turned to glare at me for leaning too hard on the currycomb.

"It wasn't your fault," Nithe said. "I did it as much for Arthur's sake as yours. He needs an heir and Guenevere can't give him one. Usually I can talk to her, for our mothers were sisters, and I'm closer to her than any of her ladies. It isn't even Guenevere's fault." Nithe sputtered, hitting the stall side with her fist and blowing on her knuckles ruefully afterward.

"Whose then?" I asked, wondering if I had an unknown enemy.

"My father, Bishop Ninian, is in residence," she explained. "He told the queen you should be confined to a monastery where you could spend your days on your knees, praying for forgiveness."

"What did I do?"

"Nothing!" she sputtered wrathfully. "Nothing at all! He wanted you to pray for Arthur! He wanted the same thing for me when I was a child, holding me a product of his own sin. He considers you and me beyond redemption ourselves."

"I'll run away!"

"No need. Arthur could see the unfairness in that and refused to permit it, but he admitted if you were brought forward it would reflect on Guenevere's barrenness. Hard choices serve no one well." She picked up another currycomb and worked on Sam's other side. She'd never been groomed so thoroughly.

"Will you stay at Camelot?" I asked, hopefully, but I knew she wouldn't.

"No, it is time for me to seek out Pelleas. I should have done it long ago, but I so valued my freedom I put it off. I just hope I haven't waited too long."

"Are you married to Pelleas?" I asked.

"Not yet, though he's asked me," she replied with a wry smile. "I hope he's not forgotten. If things go too badly for you here, come to us at Mona. They play hurley there," and she smiled at me. "Of course, you may not be able to leave Camelot. Arthur is not reconciled to the idea of losing you."

"He has not come again to watch me play."

"He wants to know each detail of every game, however," she replied.

"If the queen has given my father no heir," I said, returning to the earlier discussion, "why doesn't he set her aside?"

"Her kinsmen, the Jutes of Kent, would rise against him were he to do that. It would bring more trouble than any possible gain that could come from it. Guenevere's father gave Horsa, the Jutish leader, all of Kent in exchange for his daughter Rowena. Horsa, in turn, promised to close off Kent to any but close kinsmen, forcing their distant cousins, the Saxons, to seize what lands they could north of Kent. Besides, the only woman Arthur has ever really loved is Samana. If he could take her to wife again, he would."

"He was the king. Why did he let her go?"

"Samana insisted in abiding by the terms of the marriage contract. She was to provide her father, Duke Cador, an heir. And I expect Kay worked on Arthur, telling him he needed to marry into royalty to secure his throne against challenge. Guenevere's father was King Vortigern, the last king of the Britons to be recognized by Rome. A child by Guenevere would have no rival claimants. Arthur's bastard would have to fight as Arthur has done. You may have heard that there are those who believe Arthur's real father was Igraine's husband, Duke Gorlais, not Uther Pendragon. Even those who say different realize that Igraine was still married to Gorlais when she conceived Arthur. The marriage was consummated a bit prematurely, you might say."

"Samana didn't remarry," I said.

"Arthur knows. If things ever developed for him that made it possible to take her back, he would. Until then, even if no heir comes, Guenevere is safe and can be as arrogant as she pleases."

Nithe hugged me and left, tears running down her cheeks. She cried silently, as I did. She seemed more like my mother than even Samana then, for Borre had always stood between Samana and me. With Nithe gone, I realized my only protection against the queen's displeasure was Sir Torre's standing in the court. I hoped it was enough. Worse, no one was constant in my life. I'd never felt more alone.

The road from Camelot to London was Roman-built to service the fort at Caerleon. Its stone surface was heavily rutted by iron-rimmed wheels over the years, but it was still better than the dirt roads that turned to mud with every summer shower. The oxen hauling the queen's wagons could travel no faster than four leagues a day, and on horseback we overtook them the third day out. Even the queen rode.

I was on Sam, positioned in the train just behind Sir Torre, and led a packhorse with his battle gear strapped on. As Sir Torre had said, no one expected any trouble from raiding parties of Saxons, Picts, or Scoti with so large a party, but Arthur left nothing to chance. Sir Torre rode with the advance guard, so we were out of the noise and dirt that the main group suffered. His position as a senior knight made my own situation pleasant, as I shared some of his respect. Even my own endeavors on the hurley field would probably not have served me so well had he been a junior knight. I was fortunate.

Each morning and evening we dropped to the rear of the column to inspect the cattle herd that Ayres's sons drove behind the main body. We always found his brothers complaining of the dust they were obliged to breathe at the rear of the procession. They also grumbled about beasts stolen each night by robbers, who drove them off quietly, a few at a time. The knights wouldn't bother themselves about problems of that order. Ayres was merely a peasant farmer, after all.

Sir Torre was philosophical about it. "If the cattle weren't traveling to the London market under the protection of Arthur's party, we'd have lost them all."

I thought they could have been better safeguarded, but kept my peace. It wasn't my responsibility.

After Exeter and Caerleon, I didn't expect to be surprised by London, but this city was bigger, smellier then either, and had not only more people but more of many kinds and colors. There were black men! Magnificent they were, both broader and taller than any but the giants like King Pellinore and Nithe's boatman, Myrddin.

The king's horses were kept in the Roman fort set into the northwest corner of the walled city. The knights and squires were housed there as well: only the pages had beds in the London palace. Sir Torre was invited to eat with the king the third day we were in London and took me along to attend him.

"The king's London quarters were once a Roman public bath-house," Sir Torre told me. "He's had it refurbished and added to, but his main court is the old hall that once served the Romans as a gathering place to gossip before and after bathing."

At least, I thought, he didn't open it as a bathhouse again. I couldn't see any point in bathing all the time. I'd found no matter how clean you get, it didn't last more than a day, and you'd have it to do all over again if you wanted to stay that way.

Sir Torre's seat was next to that of my brother, Sir Gawaine, the one the king thought I resembled. I noticed the king looked from the knight to me several times during the evening, comparing us. Sir Gawaine's squire was a man but a few years younger than himself, an unusual thing. I'd heard that his brother, Gaheris, acted in that capacity, though knighted himself. He'd be my brother, too! He didn't look to be a comfortable man to know, though, with a harsh face and raspy voice. He seemed impatient. Never-theless, as Sir Torre told me, a brother can be trusted. Sir Torre had paid me a great compliment in preferring me to any of his own.

Two court pages greeted Sir Gawaine with hugs and kisses; they were his sons, Lovel and Florence, red-haired like their father, and about my age. The three of us could have passed for brothers. They didn't know who I was either, or they'd have to call me uncle! I'd made Sir Torre promise not to reveal my identity to anyone until my father spoke of it openly, so I passed as Dylan everywhere.

Pages were a little in awe of me usually, knowing about my hurley prowess. I was always friendly with these two; it would be easier to be called kinsman later if I were approachable now. Still, it was difficult to keep a straight face when I sampled food from dishes they held. Florence whispered to me that the food was better in the kitchen. It often reached the king's table somewhat cooled by the long trip through drafty halls. He offered to take me back later, and I promised to go with him.

After the meal, which lasted the better part of two hours, at least some of the knights were full drunk and clutching at the pages as if they were serving girls in a public inn. "Find some place to wait away from this," Sir Torre told me.

"I'll be in the kitchen," I told him, and beckoned to Florence to lead the way. Lovel followed as younger brothers do.

"Nobody would bother us," Lovel objected. "They're all afraid of Gawaine. He has a frightful temper, particularly when he's drunk."

"Sir Torre doesn't want to have to fight someone on my account, though it would surprise me if anyone were able to lay a hand on me. Dodging drunken knights can't be harder than dodging hurley players."

"How do you do it, anyway?" Florence asked me as we walked down a corridor at whose end I could see steam coming through an arched doorway.

I thought about it. "I can't tell you," I said. "I just know what's about to happen when I concentrate. I've always been able to do it, though I had to get big enough to run fast before it did me any good."

In the kitchen Florence led me up to a man seated in a raised chair, observing all that went on. "Sir Kay, this is Sir Torre's squire, Dylan the Orphan," he said.

"I've won money on you," he told me in an unctuous voice.

"Could I wait here for Sir Torre?" I asked him. "It'll be some time before he can leave."

"You're welcome. Florence can show you how we do things here. Come anytime, with your friends or by yourself."

I noticed the welcome didn't reach his eyes: they were cold and calculating. I thanked him anyway and allowed myself to be dragged off to a small buttery where Lovel was already sitting at a table with other pages drinking small ale. I don't like to drink, but there were platters of bread and meat so I made myself a meal, not being full in spite of the tastes I took of Sir Torre's food.

"Sir Kay is milk brother to the king. His own mother handed him over to a wet nurse so she could nurse the king herself," Florence told me. He had his nose deep into a pot of small ale.

"He can't have liked that," I said, thinking of how jealous Borre was of Samana's paying attention to anyone else, even me. No, I didn't even believe it. Samana had not done that for me.

"Why not?" Florence asked, surprised, but I only shrugged and wondered if all adults had something in their childhood experiences like that. Nithe had been given away by her mother and viewed with disgust by her father as a living symbol of his own weakness. Sir Torre had been gotten on his mother by rape and was seen as different by his whole family all the while he was growing up. Even Arthur had been stolen away as a newborn baby to be raised in secrecy, if the stories about him were true. My pig girl was ignored by her family and put out to herd swine until she grew enough to catch the eye of an old lecher. And now Sir Kay had been replaced in his mother's arms by Arthur, except it probably never happened. Why would Sir Kay say that, I wondered? He looked older than Arthur; probably he'd been old enough to wean. He'd have hated the one who stole his mother's love, though. I wondered if he still did and if that was the real reason for his coldness to everyone.

There was no hurley to be played in London. It's a rural sport, and summer is the time for it. Anyway, London's too cold for going naked in the winter. The other pages, including Sir Torre's brothers, ran the streets of London like packs of dogs. They fought with shop apprentices and consorted with prostitutes and serving girls in disreputable inns at night. In the daytime they stole food and goods from the stalls by swarming on the poor shopkeepers in such numbers they couldn't all be watched. Every weekly audience before the king, when he heard complaints from citizens, was thronged with merchants seeking redress.

"King Arthur hates London court life," Sir Torre confided in me, "and wouldn't come at all if the queen didn't insist. The one thing that he enjoys here is seeing old friends from his early days, friends made before he was crowned. They formed the core of the troops that Arthur named the London Irregulars, stalwart pike men. They're commoners, of course, and are never found at the palace. Arthur has to go out in disguise, with one or two followers, to see them. Do you know, when he was a boy, he used to wrestle sailors down by the docks?"

"Did you ever see him?"

"No, I didn't meet him until after he became king. Pelleas knew him as a boy, though, and says he was virtually unbeatable."

He was like me at hurley, I thought.

Sir Torre was right. Court life in the city was different from Camelot. Even though it was colder, the women seemed to wear less clothes, drinking to stay warm. They were warm in more than one way, and Sir Torre admitted that the morals of the ladies-in-waiting were not much different from street women's. "There are houses of assignation all over London. This place hasn't changed much since the Romans were here."

Sir Torre had a room attached to the office of Ayres's city farm agent. His name was Hugh, and I liked him. He was a short grizzled man with bowed legs and bad teeth, but he listened to me when I said something. Most adults just pretend to listen.

He explained, when Sir Torre left me behind on some private errand, that he handled Ayres's surplus cattle. Surpluses were supposed to be offered first to the king, but this was gotten around by arranging to trade steers for heifers so the count of animals stayed the same. The heifers were sent to pasture in Kent among the Jutes with rents paid in the milk and cheese they produced. The calves born on Jute land, sired by Jute bulls, became Jute cattle, but presents in wine and goods from the continent were given Ayres in token of friendship. There was no direct exchange of goods, so no gains were taxable.

I guessed that Ayres was richer than anyone knew, but I would not have divulged that information under torture.

Hugh showed me a pallet in the tack shop where I could sleep if Sir Torre's business proved to last through the night, and made it free to my use anytime I wished. He treated me with the respect he might give a man of his own station, the first time an adult had ever done so. From then on, I always stopped a moment to speak to Hugh when I sought out Sir Torre at his room in Ayres's lodgings. I truly liked Hugh.

Sir Torre's friends were another matter. First, they all seemed to be female. More than once I even surprised one or another of the court's ladies in his room.

"You naughty boy! I'll be quite undone!" one gushed at me.

"Dylan will never say anything," Sir Torre assured her.

"There have been other occasions then, with other ladies?"

"I've never seen ladies here before," I told her truthfully, for they were all strumpets, to my mind.

"Ah, the truth is not in you!" she retorted coyly, but seemed satisfied enough. It occurred to me she didn't much care if her conduct was remarked on or not.

Formal meals in the palace were more discreet, with the flirting confined to winking and nodding. Arthur would not permit more license than that, and his cold queen barely smiled at anyone save him and his friend Lancelot, seated customarily on either side of her. Lancelot was the queen's protector, so named by Arthur, who could not risk his own life in meaningless duels. Lancelot's prowess with weapons was so great that no one offended the queen purposely and was quick to beg forgiveness if they did it inadvertently.

I hated the London tourneys. They were as bloody as the practice ones, though more men were hurt and fewer horses because of the higher level of play. As Sir Torre's squire, I carried extra spears when he fought and helped bear him from the field when he fell, which was not often. He was big, strong, skilled, and well-liked except by the occasional jealous knight who grieved over the loss of some lady's interest which Sir Torre might have won. He told me that most of the serious fights were over women, and even with blunted weapons, duels sometimes had dire consequences.

Once, when he had had rather more to drink the night before than usual, Sir Torre was unseated in joust and dazed from the fall. His opponent was a bad-tempered man with a grudge and determined to do him injury as he sat on the ground. The man dismounted and walked up to Sir Torre, drawing his sword as he advanced.

"Come on, Sam!" I urged, and she spurted to the half gallop that was her top speed. I pulled her to a halt and jumped off, picking up a piece of Sir Torre's broken lance as I ran to his side. It was about the same length as a hurley stick. I took a stance in front of my fallen master.

"Move aside, boy! This is between Torre and me!" the knight ordered.

He'd removed the jousting helm and was carrying it in his free hand, for you can't really see, wearing one. The rest of his armor consisted only of helm, epaulets, gorget, and chain mail shirt, for the rules of joust allow only the head and the body to serve as targets. If you're going to fight, it's best to strike the first blow, so I aimed a vicious cut at the knight's unprotected knee. He dropped the helm and toppled sideways, crying out in surprise and pain.

I reversed the shaft and pointed the splintered end at his face. "Drop the sword," I told him. "Drop it or lose an eye!"

"You can't do this!" he sputtered.

"Who's to stop me?"

Heralds came running up with drawn weapons, and I stepped back to straddle Sir Torre, who had passed out again. They assisted the protesting knight to his feet and dragged him off. Sir Torre's brothers arrived just after, out of breath from running, and I walked behind them as they carried Sir Torre, looking over my shoulder for possible interference.

I feared Sir Torre was dead, for he didn't stir. My anxiety didn't lift until we reached his tent at the end of the jousting field, and he sputtered into consciousness when they poured cold water on his face. Such a relief! I didn't think of him as a father but more as a favorite uncle, for he almost never scolded me and didn't seem serious enough to be anyone's father. I loved him, though.

"You're the talk of London," Sir Torre told me later, his face mirroring the gloom in his soul. "So am I, for that matter," he added dismally.

"Would you rather I had let him behead you?" I asked. "That was his intention."

"Oh, surely not! The man's a belted knight!"

"He's a jilted lover," I retorted. "You didn't look into his eyes. I did."

The other squires thought it was hilarious, not being as respectful of the traditions of knighthood as they might have been. At least I now had a reputation for something other than playing hurley.

We stayed four months in London, from the beginning of November through February. The queen would have waited until the onset of spring, but King Arthur would delay no longer. Sir Torre told me the king was fed up with London and wanted to breathe the clean air of Camelot to clear his head.

That spring I was twelve going on thirteen and still growing, though mostly sideways. I couldn't help noticing that while few of the pages were taller than me, all of the squires were; it irked me. Returning to Camelot suited me. I could hardly wait to play hurley again. I stood head and shoulders above them all in that.

CHAPTER IV

ur first hurley match at Camelot was all I could have wished. Camelot played Caerwent and I was with Camelot, leading the squires and bigger pages in victory. Next day I was currying horses in the stables when Sir Torre came up to me.

"You're wanted up at the castle," he said. "Get a quick bath and put on a clean tunic." He was smiling, so I decided I wasn't in any trouble. He walked along and waited for me, but declined to answer any of my questions. I carefully draped my small plaid over my shoulder, just in case I should see the king, and silently accompanied Sir Torre into the great hall. Fat Nick followed us, as was his custom. I didn't think to stop him. There I found the king and some twenty pages: the boys in a state of suppressed excitement and King Arthur smiling.

"Greetings, Dylan," the king said amiably.

"Greetings, Your Majesty," I responded, bowing low. My manners had improved marginally since we first met. After all, I was nearly thirteen now.

The king clicked his fingers and, after looking to me for permission, Fat Nick walked over to be petted. "Brian, the page master, has been knighted." the king said as he fondled the dog. "The position must be filled by a squire, and the boys are allowed to choose whom they will to govern them. They have asked that you be Brian's replacement."

I was aghast. "But, I've never been a page! I don't know anything about it," I exclaimed.

"Then you'll find it an interesting learning experience," the king said dryly.

He was amused, I could tell. The glint in his eye and his carefully blank look informed me I was not going to be allowed to beat the system. Just because Sir Torre had allowed me to skip that part of a knight's training didn't mean I was going to avoid learning what a page must know. I glanced at the boys and saw their anticipation had turned to apprehension. I had never been able to school my face to cloak my emotions. I must have appeared angry, indeed, but it was merely frustration at the king's obstinacy in refusing me recognition. It wasn't their fault, so I smiled at them.

"I hope you won't have cause to regret your choice," I told them. "I expect your tutelage under me will be somewhat different from what it was under Brian." I knew Brian as a somewhat prissy fellow, overfond of fine clothes.

"Will you play hurley with us?" one asked, evidently speaking for them all, judging by the concentration with which they awaited my answer.

I smiled again. Now I knew why I had been chosen, and that it was no conspiracy by the king and Sir Torre to trap me into being something I wished not to be.

"We'll have the finest team in Britain," I promised them.

The boys cheered while Arthur took a gold chain from his neck and gave it to me. "Here is your chain of office," he said gravely. "You are still responsible to Sir Torre, but you will be held accountable for the boys' progress."

I put on the chain and bowed, understanding the king's words as a dismissal but thinking, he likes me! The boys followed me out into the inner bailey, Camelot's walled inner courtyard, while Sir Torre and the king watched us depart. I did not turn to see if they were chuckling, but I suspected as much.

When I stopped and faced the boys, they clustered together before me, looking at me expectantly. "What is it you know and what do you have to learn?" I asked bluntly.

"Some of us know all we are supposed to know as pages," one of the older boys said, "and some of us know very little. We'll help the younger boys with stuff like serving at table on bended knee and helping a knight dress and undress. The Bishop Ninian teaches us to read and speak Latin, Brastius Red-beard instructs us in weaponry, and we learn horsemanship from Sir Torre. No one teaches us hurley, though; we just pick it up as best we can."

"I see. Well, I've already promised to teach you hurley, but it seems to me that there are other things you should know as well. Sir Torre has told me there are kings' sons among you. Many others of you are heirs to rich lands. If you depend on stewards to manage your affairs, you'll likely be cheated. I'll see that you know enough about estate management to govern wisely." A few of the older boys nodded. I had in mind bringing them to Caerleon and working with Lady Mal and Ayres's sons. It might not be customary training, but I saw it as a sight more useful than learning to serve on bended knee.

I realized from then on I was to either watch, supervise, or lead in all the activities with the pages. I decided I would set few rules, past requiring that the older boys help the younger ones. I would abolish all hazing of the younger boys, explaining that in the years ahead, as grown men, the little ones could be valuable friends. I could do this. Maybe I could show the king I was worthy of his recognition.

Sir Torre joined us then and insisted on going with me to meet

Sir Kay formally while the boys went to Latin class. We found him in his office, a small room lined with parchment scrolls on shelves, almost too dark to see in. It was located off the buttery, where giant hogsheads of ale and barrels of wine were stored in a vast room under the kitchen. There, the same temperature could be found summer and winter, a requirement Lady Mal had told us when we built her inn. A few tables had been set up and, even at this hour, some of the seats were occupied by off-duty squires, drinking ale and talking.

Sir Torre ignored them, though a few spoke to me, and I greeted them in return. "Kay," Sir Torre said, "the king has appointed Dylan as page master. I'd appreciate it if you'd give him a tour of the castle."

Sir Kay nodded and rolled up the scroll he'd been reading. He gazed sharply at my plaid and noted, "Royal clan Merrick."

I nodded in turn. I saw no purpose in explaining it, nor did he have questions.

The castle seemed even bigger inside than out. Kay took me everywhere a page might go, mentioning my new responsibility to several functionaries. I noticed people greeted him with respect but not affection, and he, in turn, treated everyone with the amount of consideration their own responsibilities might entitle them, but no more.

The kitchen, up a flight of broad stairs from the buttery, was attached to the main structure of the castle by a covered, windowless hall. On the first floor of the castle proper, in addition to the great hall, was a smaller one he named the queen's hall. It might seat fifty persons. There was also a library, various small chambers that could serve as private audience rooms, several guest rooms for visiting dignitaries, and a guardroom near the main door, where a dozen knights lounged.

On the other side of the door was a staircase leading to the second floor. We mounted and Kay took me into the king's suite, set within the round tower. The room was littered with discarded weapons and bits of armor. Books were piled on chairs and benches. and scrolls of parchment stacked on a long deal table. A few scrolls had been unrolled and pinned to the table's surface. On the side nearest the tall narrow windows were a clothes press stuffed with clothing and. next to it. a big. rumpled bed. There was no mark of a feminine presence anywhere.

He showed me the hallway that led down the side. saying that the household knights had rooms there. including both himself and Sir Torre. To my mind it was more like a barracks or a monastery than gentlemen's quarters. Ayres's house was more gracious.

At the far end was a big open room with rows of beds. "The pages sleep here." Sir Kay told me and. indicating a small cubicle. added. "This will be where you stay."

I looked in. The room held a small bed. a chest at the end of the bed. and nothing else. Indeed. there would have been little room for anything else. Fat Nick was doubtful about it. too. sniffing and shaking his head. He liked the tack room in the stables better. So did I.

We retraced our steps and passed the other tower keep. which Sir Kay said held the armory and treasury and was kept locked. Along that side was a double row of rooms separated by another long narrow hall. much like the one we had just passed through. "The queen's ladies live here." he said.

The room at the end of the hall was the queen's own dressing room. and the hall turned sharply and ran along it to a closed door. As I reached to knock for admittance Kay shook his head.

"Servants do not knock." he said simply. and pushed the door open to a huge sunlit room where the queen and her ladies were chatting and weaving. Narrow windows stretched from floor to ceiling along one side. and the door we entered by was the only one in the room. The room could not be approached directly from the men's side. Just as well, I thought.

"Your Majesty," Sir Kay said, bowing to the queen, "the king has appointed Dylan the Orphan as page master."

The chatter ceased while the ladies looked at me, some tittering and nudging one another. They'd seen me naked, playing hurley. Perhaps I looked strange to them, wearing a tunic.

"When did this happen?" the queen demanded.

"An hour ago," Sir Kay responded without expression.

I was surprised at the sharpness of her tone.

"He should consult with me on such matters before he acts," she said in an exasperated voice.

Her ladies quieted. I gathered a queen in a temper did not like to hear tittering. I was embarrassed, but the queen ignored me and turned back to her weaving, two spots of color on her cheeks marking her displeasure.

Kay bowed and we withdrew. "The queen wished for one of her favorites to hold the post," he explained.

"I'll never be that," I muttered.

I found the boys in the chapel annex and Sir Kay went back to his ledgers. As I sat listening to the bishop's clerk intone Latin, I wondered if the queen's displeasure was based on something more than what Kay had said. Did she see me as a rival to any heir she might produce? I was sure she knew who I was, thinking back to what Nithe had told me of her efforts to get me recognized. Well, there was nothing I could do about it.

Gareth joined the pages for training, at Sir Torre's insistence. "Pelleas expected him to be fostered by Duke Cador in Lyoness, and will be most unhappy if he grows up like a peasant," Sir Torre said. "Having Pelleas unhappy with me is not one of the aims of my life."

Personally, I thought Gareth better cared for in Ayres's household than he would have been in Cador's, having seen both, but I said nothing, particularly since Gareth was so eager to become a knight of the Round Table. He had to start training for that sooner or later.

I didn't know quite what to make of Gareth, though I had long ago learned to love him. He resembled Fat Nick in his insistence on ignoring possible consequences of his actions. It was a wonder either of them had lived to grow up. I worried over both of them, trying to protect them from the more serious results of their actions. Focusing on some concern outside of myself eased my more personal self-doubts.

I measured myself against Gareth continually, and he seemed to grow even as I watched. At nearly eleven, he was as tall as I and broader, not stronger, though. I hadn't grown much in the last year, outside of adding a few pounds of muscle, but I had grown powerful to the point where I no longer avoided the scrimmages in hurley. It added a new dimension to my game, being able to run over instead of around opponents. The added strength hadn't slowed me down, though. In fact, I seemed to be faster as well, both running and dodging.

Lady Mal insisted on testing the boys' skill in waiting table, saying no one ever really served from bended knee even in the king's hall, though it was supposed to be a part of a page's formal training. "No one does that any more," she said testily when I asked about it. "Maybe it was different in Roman times; old ideas die slowly, though practices may change."

The food at her inn was better than Kay's kitchen turned out, and most of the boys were happy to wait table in exchange for free range of the kitchen. A few objected, saying they were of noble blood and couldn't be expected to wait on peasants. Lady Mal noted dryly that if they kept that information to themselves no one would notice, since no one ever looked at the faces of serving folk.

They were all less pleased with the farm work, but I insisted on it. "You'll all own farms some day," I said, "and it will be useful for you to know what can reasonably be expected of a man doing a day's work."

Both Ayres and Lady Mal kept accounts of their transactions and opened them to the boys. The boys barely had enough grasp of numbers to follow the explanations, but saw the need to learn, as perhaps they had not before.

On the feast of Pentecost, my second at Camelot, I realized I was thirteen now. Gareth would be eleven at Beltane. We were growing up. The feast was my first test as page master. I stood beside Sir Kay while he inspected the dishes that came up from the kitchen. It was my responsibility to oversee the pages as they served the food at table. Thankfully, the pages knew what to do but made a point of asking me for instructions from time to time with questions that needed only a nod for reply. It made it seem as if I knew more than I did, and I think the charade amused the king. It must have pleased him too, for he smiled at me at the end of the feast, when he rose to leave the others to their drinking.

All spring and summer I worked with the pages, learning what they knew in the process. By fall I was confident I could discharge my duties without error and looked forward to the formal winter season in London. After harvest when the leaves turned, the queen took the court back to the city as usual. With her customers leaving, Lady Mal closed the inn and came with us, acting as Ayres's agent in place of Sir Torre. Lady Mal had earned Ayres's complete trust and respect, and Sir Torre was happy to be relieved of the duty.

Arthur's mercenaries stayed at Camelot, but the Round Table knights rode in his train. They were properly members of his court while the others were professional soldiers. I was instructed to bring the pages, so I formed them into a guard for Ayres's cattle, knowing the boys would get experience in defending them against robbers.

"Sir Torre told me that raiders don't fight in the daytime unless they come in overwhelming numbers," I said. "Mostly they sneak up, as these robbers do." I mounted the boys, armed them with spears and short swords, and had them ride around the bunched cattle as soon as the sun went down. Nothing happened until the third day out, when the robbers struck. The boys raised the alarm, and I led a picked handful of the bigger boys after them while Ayres's sons roused the rest of the pages to guard against a second attack if this one turned out to be a device to draw off the herd's defenders.

We had better horses than the robbers, who had expected no pursuit, and in the first skirmish all the robbers were downed, speared from behind as we overtook them. When we reassembled to drive the dozen frightened cattle back to the herd, I found I was riding beside Lady Mal on her palfrey.

"You surprised me," I told her, grinning.

"I shouldn't have, if you reflect back," she responded. "Ayres put these beasts in my trust."

She was right in both instances. She had become as self-reliant and independent as Nithe. Indeed, she confided in me that was her goal in life. I'd never had a blood sister, but I felt as close to Lady Mal as if she were one.

We were not bothered again, and I thought maybe in the past the same small gang had driven off cattle night after night. With no effective opposition, there was no reason for them to be content with one raid only. We took their horses back with us, sorry nags that they were, more accustomed to pulling plows than carrying riders, probably. We could sell them in London and divide the money, giving the pages a few coins each to spend in the city.

It was good to see Hugh, Ayres's London agent, again. He took charge of the cattle and the horses we'd captured, paying for the horses on the spot. I gave all the money to the pages, and from then on keeping track of the pages in London was impossible. They were much used by members of the court as go-betweens to set up assignations. There seemed to be a certain license allowed in the city not tolerated in Camelot.

The pages were not kept to lessons; I thought not even to practice hurley with them because of the cold, but they thought otherwise. At least we didn't strip for it. Our activities attracted some attention and Hugh spoke to me about it. "Would you be willing to play an exhibition match? The merchants would put up a prize for the winning team."

"Who would we play?" I asked.

"There are sailors from Lyoness in town who say they know of you. They're willing to form a team."

We played the next day in a field across the Thames, outside the city walls. I was astonished at the crowd. There were thousands of people ringing the field, and the noise of their cheers mixed with the cries of vendors selling food and drink was beyond anything I'd ever known.

I knew most of the sailors. I'd played with some of them and against others when I lived in Lyoness. They greeted me with pride as one of their own, and I realized they wanted me to do well. I still thought it was too cold to strip, but when they did, I followed suit. Lud's balls! With my example to follow, the pages and Ayres's sons did the same, though several of the latter rolled their eyes in mock dismay. Running back and forth soon warmed us up, and I forgot about the chill air.

The game was pure sport and at its conclusion, we decided to divide the prize, though we had won handily. The crowd pushed forward and surrounded us, making way for Hugh as he drove up in a wagon. He gave each player a new plaid, a handsome prize and welcome in the cold after all the sweating. Then he called me up to stand where everyone could see me.

Taking a laurel wreath wrought of gold he held it up and cried, "This once was worn by some noble Roman. We award it to Dylan the Orphan, hereafter King of Hurley!" As he placed it on my head the crowd roared its approval, and the players, pages, and sailors carried me on their shoulders across the bridge and back into the city to drink at inn after inn. There was little work done in London that day.

Next morning Sir Torre roused me from a late sleep in the tack room. He examined my gold wreath as I dressed and splashed water on my face. I drank a copious draught of water to still the dryness that comes the morning after too much ale. No headache, though. I felt wonderful.

I noticed Sir Torre looked glum, however. "You should have been with us," I said.

"My brothers told me all about it," he responded. "This is a pretty bauble," he added, turning the gold wreath over in his hands. "The king's own crown is no finer. It's a pity, though."

"Why?" I asked, surprised.

"Lancelot sponsored a tourney yesterday, and nobody came except the castle folk. Everyone else in London went to the hurley match."

"I didn't know," I said, aghast.

"No, but Hugh and the other merchants did. The king is most unhappy with him."

"But Sir Lancelot blames me, doesn't he?"

"Perhaps. He hasn't said so."

"Very well. In London, I'm king of hurley. You think I should not wear this? Well, I will when I'm in town. When I'm in Camelot, where I'm the page marshal, I'll put it aside. What I won't do is apologize to Sir Lancelot. If people would rather watch me play hurley than watch him punish horses, so be it."

Sir Torre nodded, sadly, but said nothing. I knew he grieved to see a knight of the Round Table held in such low esteem, even if it was by common people. Perhaps Sir Lancelot deserved better, but not from me. He'd never even spoken to me. The pages told me Sir Lancelot ignored all those in the lower orders as a matter of course. It just didn't occur to him to do otherwise, so I should not take it personally. I did, though.

The queen abruptly decided to move back to Camelot. She was displeased, it was said, by the actions of the people of London, and determined to make it known by removing her presence. It was no light matter. The royal court attracted many visitors to London; the merchants would miss the lost sales.

I stayed away from the royals, keeping to the rear of the column with the squires on the trip back to Camelot. If the queen was angry over Sir Lancelot's unsuccessful tourney, I didn't want to be available for her to vent her spleen on.

I stopped off at Caerleon to see Gareth rather than going all the way to the castle. Gareth had remained behind with Ayres's family, at their invitation. I'd missed him. When I first saw the boy, I realized he had shot up again over the winter. It made even more apparent the fact that I had not. Of more import, Gareth had also discovered girls, according to one of Ayres's sons, and with the same enthusiasm he gave each new interest. It should not have surprised me. I had so long thought of him as my little brother, however, that I wondered if we would ever be as close again. I did not want to lose him as I had lost Borre.

At Sir Torre's insistence, Gareth rejoined the pages' classes as soon as they started again, and within a week I found him missing from the Latin lessons. He had grumbled about them, saying he spoke enough Latin already.

I went looking for him in the kitchen, thinking it the one place above all that might attract him. I asked Sir Kay if he'd seen him.

"The tall, dark boy? He may be up in the solar. It seems I've seen him there several times. The queen's ladies seem to have made a pet of him."

I knew the queen's ladies were in the habit of doing that with some of the pages, but Gareth was not the best kind of person to fill that role. He was by no means safe for them to be around now. What worried me was that the fool didn't realize how serious the consequences might be if the queen caught him with one of her maidens.

I looked into the second floor rooms, one by one, and found them all empty. The queen's dressing room was bigger and required that I enter rather than just peek in the doorway, if I were to search properly. The room was awash with light from windows stretching across the south wall, a continuation of the solar where the weaving was done. A blaze of purple fire on her dressing table caught my eye, and without thinking about where I was, I walked over to it and picked up a necklace of purple gems to hold up to the sun's rays.

"What are you doing here?" an outraged voice asked.

I whirled to face the queen, white of face and standing in the doorway. A sly, dark girl watched over her shoulder. I'd seen her with Sir Kay. Hastily replacing the gems, I stammered, "Forgive my intrusion, Your Majesty. I was looking for a truant page."

"And you thought to find him here?"

"This one might be anywhere," I said, coming up to her in an attempt to edge through the door. I had never felt so awkward.

"Who is the wretch who would be bold enough to invade the queen's quarters?"

I thought that Gareth wasn't properly a page at all. I didn't want to get the boy in trouble. "It matters not, since he is not here," I said.

"I see. Warn him, then, that we have had a rash of petty thefts, and it would go hard on him to be found in this room, my room! And I do not expect to see you again in the women's quarters, either!"

"Whatever he might be, he is not a petty thief," I said, lamely.

The queen gave a significant glance at the pile of purple gems and said, "Perhaps he is not."

Her meaning was as plain as a direct accusation might have

been. I bowed and brushed past her, vowing to myself not to return if the place were on fire.

I found Gareth in the stables, asleep in the hay, with a beatific smile on his face. Judging from the hollow next to him, he had not been alone long.

I dipped a leather bucket full of water from the horse trough and dashed it over him. As he sat up sputtering, I leaned over and said coldly, "You like it here? If you play truant again, I'll see that you spend the rest of your life dunging out this stable. Now, get out to the practice field and run around it until the rest of the pages join you. You're getting fat!"

Gareth scrambled to obey, judging correctly that I was more angry than I appeared. Given an excuse I would have dealt with him severely, and we both would have regretted it. Of course, it wasn't his fault that I was found in the queen's dressing room, but I would not have been there had he not skipped Latin class.

The next evening I stood with Sir Kay to watch the pages at supper while he inspected the food brought to the serving table, and one of the pages assigned to the king came running up to me. "Dylan, the king wants to see you up in his room." His eyes were wide with apprehension, so it was something serious. He couldn't or wouldn't tell me what.

I followed the boy out, hurrying since he insisted on it, and found the king with the queen and Sir Lancelot. The king was pacing back and forth, his hands clenched together behind his back, while Sir Lancelot bent over Guenevere as she sat weeping.

She looked up as I entered and stretched out an accusing finger, shrilling, "There's the thief!"

I stopped just inside the doorway while the page fled down the hall.

King Arthur came to stand before me. "The queen says you stole her amethyst necklace," he said. The king was usually so pleasant a man that his anger was all the more startling. His face was flushed and his eyes were as cold and blue as mountain ice.

How could he say this to me? I was so shaken I could barely blurt out, "The queen is mistaken. I have never stolen anything in my life!" That was true. How could he doubt it?

"Did she not find you in her room holding that same necklace?"

"The purple one? Yes. I picked it up to admire it. Perhaps I should not have touched it, but I wasn't thinking."

"And what were you doing there in the first place?" Sir Lancelot asked, coming over to stand beside the king.

"I was looking for my brother, Gareth. Sir Kay told me the queen's ladies have adopted him as a pet. I didn't want him to be there."

"He never has been!" the queen said, flushing. "What are you suggesting?"

I shrugged. Was she calling me a liar as well as a thief? "Then Sir Kay was mistaken," I replied in an insolent voice.

Sir Lancelot raised his hand to strike me, but King Arthur caught his wrist and stopped the blow. "If the necklace is returned, nothing more will be done about it," the king said. "See that the pages learn of this. If more rigorous measures must be tried, they will be."

I bowed and left, so furious I could not speak. The king let Sir Lancelot and the queen lodge false charges against me without hindrance. He must hate me! He must believe what they said!

When neither the king nor the queen came to supper, I left one of the pages in charge and rode over to Caerleon to see Lady Mal. We sat together at her regular corner table in the inn as I told her what had happened. She sipped a white wine as I drank ale. "They were handsome beads, but nothing particularly valuable," I concluded my account. "You have as fine a set. Why the fuss?"

"My amethyst beads are just that, true colored quartz," she said, shaking her head. "The queen's were Arthur's betrothal gift and are said to have once belonged to Alexander the Great. They are corundum gems, like the ruby and the sapphire from far India, and immensely costly."

"Who would know that?" I asked.

"My father traded in gems, and it was no secret among such people," Lady Mal said. "I doubt if many in Camelot knew, however—the king and queen, surely, or the gift would have been pointless. And Sir Kay, of course. He knows everything there is to know about the king's treasure."

"It was Sir Kay who sent me to the queen's quarters in search of Gareth," I said, frowning.

"You think he might have stolen the necklace to get you into trouble? Why would he do that?"

I considered it. "I don't know," I admitted, "but I sense something false and cold in the man. Even so, why would anyone believe it of me? What would I do with purple beads? I couldn't wear them myself, and I have no sweetheart to give them to."

"I agree. You would be a fool to take them after being found with them in your hand," Lady Mal said. "Maybe they think you put one of the pages up to it."

"The suspicion would still fall on me," I said, shaking my head. I wondered what the rigorous methods King Arthur spoke of might be. He had never allowed torture.

The next morning the story of the loss of the queen's necklace was talked of all over the castle, along with its recovery. It had been found, broken, lying before the queen's door. Sir Kay claimed one of the beads was missing, that the inventory showed the necklace consisted of forty-three beads, and now there were but forty-two.

The queen wore it at supper that evening, pausing to look coldly at me as she passed by my station. The king ignored me. I had lost whatever goodwill Arthur had for me. I felt I could never win his regard now.

That first occasion the queen wore the necklace after its recovery marked the beginning of a pattern. Though I had never seen it on her before, now she wore it every night, and every night she spoke to Sir Kay standing beside me but not to me. Sir Lancelot did the same, but the king had no word for either one of us. Sir Torre told me that all of the older knights believed I was guilty of the original theft and that I still held the single bead that was missing.

One could not tell that the necklace had even been broken, to look at it, much less that it was shorter than before. When I had held it up to the light I'd noticed that the beads were graduated in size, with the biggest near the bottom, and that still appeared to be the case. I even wondered, as the weeks wore on, if the necklace had ever been stolen in the first place. Perhaps the queen merely wished me ill. It preyed on my mind to the point where I found excuses to be elsewhere when the queen passed. I missed the feast of Pentecost, spending the day at The Pig Girl, the name Lady Mal had chosen for her inn. I thought maybe I was the only one who knew why she called it that. I heard guesses from her patrons, but never spoke of it myself. If Lady Mal wanted others to know, it was for her to say.

As for the feast, I thought the pages could do very well without me. It was my third Pentecost since coming to Camelot to seek out my father. I was fourteen.

It was Lady Mal who told me that the woman who was said to be my mother had came to court on that day, having been driven from her home in the north by Picts.

Gareth went to see her and came back from the visit saying she wanted to see me. "I'd forgotten how much she looks like you, with the same bright blue eyes and dark red hair," he said.

It was true then! I had a mother, and she wanted me! If it hadn't been too late in the day, I'd have set out immediately on hearing that. As it was, Sir Gawaine sought me out that night in

The Pig Girl. He was sharing a table with his brother. Gaheris, when I entered, followed by Fat Nick.

"Over here, boy," he called. He'd never spoken to me before, and as I came up to his table he said, "Sit down. Sit down! What will you drink?"

"Ale," I responded. I was used to having people buy me drinks to be seen with the famous hurley player, but I was surprised that Gawaine would do so.

"Why didn't you come to me, boy, your own brother?" he asked reproachfully.

He knew! "How could I come to you before my father had claimed me?" I asked, but beamed with joy to have him speak so.

Gaheris reached over to pat Fat Nick, ignoring me. One of Lady Mal's serving wenches brought me ale, and when I looked up, Lady Mal waved to me from her high stool behind the bar.

"But we're kinsmen! It has naught to do with the king! I'm offended, boy! Seriously!" Gawaine insisted. I could see he'd been drinking for some time and, knowing his temper, I might have left had he not clamped his bony hand on my arm. I wanted no quarrel with him, so I leaned back in the chair to show I would stay. He released me.

"Kinsmen. Aye, there's that," Gaheris sneered.

Fat Nick nudged at his hand, and the man turned his attention back to the dog. King Arthur had been right. Fat Nick was no wolfhound. He had grown as tall as one, certainly, and as shaggy, but twice as heavy and could run no faster than I.

"You've seen me wear the clan Merrick plaid, and never questioned it," I retorted, rattled by his attitude.

"Ah," Gaheris said contemptuously, and spat on the floor. "Our father traveled much and never slept alone. He has bastards in every village in the north of Britain. They all think they're clan Merrick, not knowing that the Scoti reckon clanship through the mother," he explained, looking over at me briefly, but keeping his

99

hands on the dog. I had never seen Fat Nick take to anyone so.

"The boy's right, Gaheris!" Gawaine growled back at his brother. "We should have asked. Go see her," he told me. "She wants to talk to you."

"Gareth told me that, too," I said. "I'll go tomorrow." Gawaine was gazing at me in vast approval, an emotion perhaps enhanced by the ale. Nevertheless I felt gratified by his acceptance, no matter what Gaheris said.

"Gareth! Morgause said Gareth was another one!" Gawaine exclaimed. "He's that tall, dark lad that plays hurley with you?"

"You didn't know about him, either?"

"No, we'd left home before he was born. The birth was hushed up, for Morgause was over forty, and our father was dead. She didn't want the scandal."

"Is that why she sent me away, too?"

"That was the king's doing," Gaheris said unexpectedly, scowling. "Having a bastard out of his own mother's sister embarrassed him. He pays too much attention to those Romified exquisites from Brittany, Lancelot and his cousins."

"Enough of that!" Gawaine said sharply. "You forget I'm a Christian, too!"

Gaheris merely shook his head obstinately, refusing to look at either of us.

Gawaine sighed and said, "The king had me bring you and your wet nurse to Exeter when you were but a babe. I'd had enough of the simpering wench, so I paid passage for the two of you on a fisher boat bound for Lyoness."

"It was lost at sea," I told him. "I was found in a broken ship's boat, washed up on the beach. No one knew who I was until Nithe came for me."

"Ah, I hadn't known! Be sure you tell this to our mother. She's wondered why she'd heard naught of you all these years."

"I will then." I was so happy to hear that my mother had been concerned over my fate. I did not think how she might have suffered in the process. At least I could make it up to her, if she'd let me.

"Will she claim me despite the king?" I asked.

"She does what she damn pleases, our mother," Gawaine said with quiet pride. "She was head of Clan Merrick, royal house of the Scoti, for long years, and is used to having her way.

Clan Merrick! Myrddin, Nithe's giant boatman had said my seven-colored cloak was the royal plaid of the Scoti! "And Gareth?" I asked.

"We'll help the boy," Gawaine said. "He's old enough to be a squire from the looks of him."

"Yes, but he has some notion of winning the king's regard on his own merit," I said. "He doesn't want to be given special consideration just because he's Gawaine's brother."

"Daft," Gaheris murmured.

I agreed but held my tongue. I didn't approve of Gaheris.

Next day I put on my best tunic; I even bathed. Fat Nick waited for me in the garden when I entered the castle. He'd often hunted rabbits there, which was fun for him and no harm to them. He'd never caught one.

Morgause had been assigned living quarters upstairs in the queen's wing as far from the queen's own room as possible. As King Arthur's aunt, she was entitled to quarters in the castle, but the queen did not have to make her an intimate.

I was not a servant here so I knocked before I entered. She opened the door to me with her own hand, and I saw she was livelier and more beautiful than Guenevere, being all warm gold in color in contrast to the queen's cool ivory.

"My baby!" she cried, and rushed to embrace me, weeping and kissing me at the same time. It was damp; I was embarrassed.

"Sir Gawaine said you wanted to see me," I said, unnecessarily, but I could think of nothing else, stiff in her embrace.

"In truth, I didn't know you were here or I'd have come to

Camelot sooner!" she said, dragging me to a couch to sit beside her. She had taken as much trouble with her dress as I had, for she was arrayed in a gown of fine green linen, as if she were going to dine with the king. A shawl of the seven-colored Merrick royal plaid was thrown over her shoulders.

"It was not for me to say," I muttered.

"Truly," she said, holding my face between her two hands and gazing into my eyes, "I'd heard one of Lot's bastards was a famous hurley player. Everyone teased me about it! I had no idea you were my own Mordred."

"I'm called Dylan," I responded, perhaps sounding more ungracious than I intended. I freed myself from her grasp, but gently. These kin did more touching than I liked.

" 'Son of the wave,' " she agreed. "Gareth told me you were found alone in a ship's boat, swaddled in a blanket like this," and she stroked the shawl lightly.

So, it was Gareth who'd told her about me. I might have known. "I have it yet," I said, and took it from my shoulder to place in her hands.

"I made this for you, wove it with my own hands," she said, her eyes luminous with tears. She stood, took the one she was wearing, and, putting it over my shoulder, fastened it with a massive gold fibula. "You must let me exchange it for this one. You should wear it on all formal occasions," she added. "I will own you my son before all the world!"

This was unlooked for! "But King Arthur . . ." I said in protest.

"Pooh for King Arthur!" she retorted with spirit. "Among our people it doesn't matter who a man's father is."

"Why was I sent away, then?" I asked with a bitterness that surprised me. I thought I had my emotions under better control than that.

She put her hand on my chest and gazed earnestly into my eyes, "To protect you from my husband, Lot. We were estranged, but he would not have accepted a bastard with any grace. He's been dead for years, and what he might think or do no longer matters."

"And why was I not sought for after he died?" I asked, still not satisfied.

"I was the head of clan Merrick and not always able to do as I might wish, any more than Arthur is," she said, moving away from me to look at me better. "I have since passed over my clan responsibilities to my sister's daughter, Morgan, and need no longer answer to anyone but myself. My dear, I've often wondered about you, wondered which would be best for you: to bring you to Camelot against the king's wishes, or to let you stay safe in Lyoness."

"How would you know whether I was safe or not?" I argued.

"Gawaine told us he had put you in the care of a ship's captain and paid for your passage to Lyoness, along with your nurse. We assumed you were in Samana's care all these years. Don't you see? We felt it was up to you to make a choice, whether to claim your kinship with us or not. We had no idea the ship had foundered in a storm and that only you, a tiny baby, had survived, with no one alive to know who you were! Poor baby, was it very hard?"

"No, not hard," I said honestly. "The fisherfolk brought me to Samana, and I fared well at her hands."

"I've wondered, why did you come to Camelot, then?"

"Lady Miriam sent me away when Nithe told her who I was. She called me a monster," I added, unwillingly.

Morgause looked astonished. "Why would she say such a vicious thing?"

"She said I was a child of incest," I muttered.

"Incest? But Arthur was my nephew, child of my sister Igraine, not my son!"

"Nithe said Christians think it's almost as bad," I said.

"Christians!" She made it sound like a curse, staring into the

103

distance for a moment, obviously struggling with her temper. "Ah, they have their place, particularly in these times," she muttered as much to herself as to me. "It is not well to scorn Christians when the king is one!"

Then she turned and laid her hand on my arm, looking earnestly into my face. "I'm a priestess of the Great Mother and a member of the royal house of the Scoti. Women rule among the Scoti. What I have done has been in duty. As clan head I had a responsibility to provide an heir, to bring a daughter to the clan to take my place when I could no longer serve. My choice of consort was limited to males within royal lines, princes of the blood. Lot gave me three sons and no daughters. Arthur gave me you, and Pelleas gave me Gareth. I am past childbearing years now, which is why I was deposed by the clan in favor of my sister's daughter, Morgan."

I tried to keep my face impassive as I heard this extraordinary discourse. I had to say something, so I said, "Then the Scoti do not consider Gareth and me illegitimate?"

She shook her head. "That's not the point," she replied, seemingly exasperated with my lack of comprehension. "Bastardy is not considered an honor among the Scoti, but neither is it a curse. It's just not important!" Perhaps she thought me stupid, for she asked earnestly, "Do you understand? Among the Gael, in royal lines the only forbidden matings are father-daughter and mother-son." A rueful look crossed her face and she added, "I did nothing wrong under clan law except to bear sons instead of daughters."

"But Britons think differently," I stated baldly.

"Oh, they once reckoned descent through their mothers, like the Scoti," she said. "The Britons had more contact with the Romans than we did and adopted Roman rules of descent. That doesn't make them right."

That sounded as if it might be true enough. "Gawaine is as

old as King Arthur," I said, for the difference in age between her and the king still seemed strange to me.

"Older, years older," she said, "but any woman can take a youth half her age to bed, if she wishes. Arthur had little to say about it."

I must have looked as appalled as I felt, for she laughed, "Don't worry, I draw the line at sons, though you are a very pretty fellow. You have much of the appearance of Arthur and even your grandfather, Uther Pendragon. Uther's mother was a Roman, short and stout, and both Uther and Arthur inherited Roman strength and short stature from her."

I had a Roman grandmother? Truly, I didn't know anything.

"Come sit by me while I weave," Morgause said comfortably then, as if satisfied that all questions between us had been answered. "This is my favorite occupation. You must come and see me often and talk to me; it helps to have a conversation going while I'm working. I find, left to myself, that I think too much and keep losing the pattern. Now tell me about yourself. What have you been doing?"

"Well, I was squire to Sir Torre," I said, "and now I'm page master here at Camelot."

"Torre is a nice man," she said absently as she untangled strands of thread.

"I play hurley," I said, not thinking of anything else to say that might interest her. "Would you like to come and watch me sometime?"

"Oh no, dear, I don't care much for games. There doesn't seem to be much point in them, does there?" She looked up with a condescending smile and added, "It isn't as if they were real!"

"I suppose not," I said lamely. I left her presence soon afterward, somewhat confused, and wandered out into the garden to collect my dog. I wanted to trust her, but the hurt was too old and deep. Maybe in time . . .

Over near the castle wall I saw my brother Gaheris in a hot dispute with Sir Lancelot, watched by the queen who was kneeling with her hands covering her mouth.

"You killed the dog over a rabbit?" Gaheris shouted in outrage.

"It was the queen's pet," Sir Lancelot retorted angrily.

"But a rabbit?" He waved his hands, leaning toward Sir Lancelot, who fended him off with the point of his sword.

Suddenly I saw to one side, lying in the long grass, a tawny form that could only be Fat Nick. I ran over to find him cut nearly in two, with a rabbit pinned underneath his paw. He'd finally caught one, and it turned out to be the queen's pet! Sir Lancelot waved the bloody sword to the endangerment of the queen, all unknowing in seeming grief.

"Oh, Nick!" I cried, and the two men stopped quarreling as I sank down beside my friend. He was still warm, but quite dead. Over a rabbit?

"You, Sir Lancelot? You killed my dog?" I asked, knowing the answer. It wasn't a question so much as an accusation.

"He had no business here in the queen's private garden," Sir Lancelot said stiffly, red of face.

"He had the king's leave," I said, my throat so filled with tears I could barely make a sound. It was true. Sir Torre had told me so.

"You should have had him on a leash," Sir Lancelot responded coldly. He stooped to wipe his sword clean on Fat Nick's ruff, and I whirled and pushed him away, overbalancing him so that he fell against the queen.

"Don't you dare!" I yelled.

Sir Lancelot leapt to his feet, dropping his sword and, instead of coming to the queen's assistance, reached for me to punish my insolence. He wouldn't have caught me, but before he could even try, Gawaine stepped up beside Gaheris saying, "Have a care, Lancelot. The lad is our brother!" I hadn't even seen Gawaine, so intent on going to Nick had I been.

"I might have known!" The queen cried, rising and pulling her clothing into order. "It's clear where he learned courtesy! Come, Lancelot. Lead me away from here!"

Taking the queen's arm and ignoring Gawaine, Sir Lancelot said menacingly to me, "I'm not through with you yet, boy!"

"Nor I with you, Outlander," I retorted. The damned Breton!

"Hush, lad!" Gawaine said, in a scandalized voice. "He's the king's favorite!"

"The queen's, too," Gaheris added loudly enough for them to have heard. Sir Lancelot hesitated in his stride, but the queen yanked him violently after her. Gaheris laughed.

"Would you have the man call you out?" Gawaine hissed between his teeth.

"I wouldn't mind," Gaheris answered. "On foot, with long swords, I'm the better fighter. He knows it, too. He'd never challenge me and give me choice of weapons in a duel."

"Ech!" Gawaine retorted in disgust. Nevertheless, Gaheris might be right. Sir Lancelot was a superb, if horse-punishing, rider, unmatched with a lance, but Gaheris had a six-inch advantage on him in reach and a reputation for ferocity the equal to any among King Arthur's knights. I felt him more my brother than ever before.

Disregarding the blood, Gaheris picked up Fat Nick and carried him for me out behind the stables. We buried him there, in a place the dog had chosen in years past to sun himself while waiting for me. I had not looked for kindness from Gaheris, but then his feeling seemed to be for the dog, not for me.

"A lovely beast," he said to himself sadly before he walked away. He said nothing to me.

I cried for Fat Nick, crouched over his grave, alone and miserable, as I'd cried over the puppy Hal the gardener had killed. I hadn't cried since until now. I also vowed revenge. Sir Lancelot would pay for this!

CHAPTER
V

Expressions of regret over Fat Nick's death came from many of the castle folk, squires, pages, and retainers alike. The dog with his gentle manner had made many friends for the two of us. I had offers of puppies to take Nick's place, but turned them all down, well-meant though they were.

Of the knights, only Sir Torre spoke to me in condolence. Sir Torre wanted to complain to King Arthur, himself.

"The king loves dogs and has often remarked how much yours looked like his old pet, Cavell. He'll make Lancelot apologize."

"Please don't do that," I said. "This is between me and Sir Lancelot. I'll find payback on my own."

"I feared you might think that," Sir Torre said with a sigh. "I've talked to Gawaine about it. He and I will sponsor you into the Round Table if you promise not to seek a quarrel with Sir Lancelot. Gawaine and I have agreed it's better so."

"Knighthood? You want me to be a knight?" I shook my head vigorously. The idea was ridiculous! "But I'd have to stop playing hurley," I explained, when I realized Sir Torre was upset. "I'm not ready for that."

I was not ready to forgive Sir Lancelot, either. He owed me a grievance: I'd been too young to do anything to Hal the gardener when he killed the puppy, but Sir Lancelot's killing Fat Nick was another matter.

The year passed and I fulfilled my duties as page master without incident, but without joy. The king seemed indifferent to me, never speaking or seeming to see me when he chanced to look my way. Fall came and the remove to London occurred on schedule, as did the move back to Camelot in the spring. My mother did not send for me again, and even Sir Gawaine seemed not to be interested in me, though he was amiable enough when we met by chance. Gaheris occasionally nodded gruffly in acknowledgment of our kinship, but offered no friendship. Not even Florence and Lovel, Gawaine's sons, paid any more attention to me than did the other pages. Everyone seemed to be waiting, as I was myself, for King Arthur to make some move toward me. We waited in vain.

The opportunity to even the score with Sir Lancelot came at Pentecost, my fourth at Camelot. I was fifteen. In the morning we had a hurley contest, as last year, with the castle against the best players from several of the small towns, Caerleon and Caerwent particularly; outlying farms like Ayres contributed players as well. It was understood by everyone but me that I would play for the castle. When we stripped and walked onto the field, I could hear tittering among the court ladies and felt many eyes on me. Ladies were not accustomed to seeing grown men naked, except at hurley. A hush fell when I lined up with the commoners.

"You surprise me," Sir Torre said as he walked out to drop the ball between the two lines of players to begin the contest.

"I stand with your brothers," I told him. There were two of them beside me, nudging one another and grinning. Sir Torre kept a straight face, but he was not displeased.

As I played, I decided it would be my last game. I was now one of the oldest players, and the others could no longer match my strength. Usually I tried to keep from scoring too many points to avoid looking like a show-off, but this time I wanted to do more. I wouldn't score myself, but pass off and block for others. It was a brilliant strategy in that all of the Camelot players keyed on me, and our other men were open for passes. We won ten to nothing, the most lopsided final score anyone had ever heard of. The common folk loved it if the gentlefolk did not.

When the game was over, so many people surrounded me I was borne away before I could free myself. Most alarming were the young women, who insisted on hugging and kissing me and surreptitiously caressing my naked body to the point that I was in a fair way of making a rare show of myself. Ayres himself took pity and brought me my plaid, saying I would catch cold if I cooled down too quickly. I ate with him and his family, all seated around a huge picnic lunch, with my pig girl as a guest rather than a hostess this time.

"Greetings, hero!" she called out as I came up.

She was laughing at me, which was well, for it brought me back into countenance.

"It was fun," I admitted, sitting down in the grass at her side, but glancing nervously at the knots of young women who clustered and giggled when I chanced to look up.

"You look very festive," I said.

"And you look ready for bed," she said.

I clutched the plaid more closely around me and glanced at the women again, who were standing almost close enough to hear us talk.

"You took a worse mauling from them than from the squires," Lady Mal teased, following my gaze.

I smiled, but it was true. If I hadn't already decided to stop playing hurley, that would have done it. It was becoming too dangerous.

That afternoon, Sir Kay, who was in charge of the festival, had arranged for a chicken pull. He said it was an old Roman contest, to see which horseman was skillful enough to snatch loose a chicken buried up to its neck in the earth. The knights vied for the opportunity to compete.

Sir Lancelot took his turn after waiting until most of the others had failed, so as to appear to better advantage when he won. He insisted that his black stallion be brought to him.

"You rode him yesterday pretty hard," Sir Torre demurred. "Why don't you use another horse?"

"Nonsense! Bring him," he ordered one of the grooms.

Sir Torre bit his lip but said nothing. It was Sir Lancelot's horse, not his.

I knew why the horse was not fit. Sir Lancelot customarily used a heavy iron bit, jerking at it to effect the rearing posturing that looked like horse mastery but was in reality an attempt by his mount to avoid the pain of the bit. He claimed the maneuver was useful in battle to strike down infantry, for the stallion's hooves were iron-shod. Yesterday, however, he'd merely been showing off for the queen. The black's mouth had been cut in the process and was still tender.

When the horse was trotted up, Sir Lancelot leapt into the saddle and leaned forward, urging the stallion into a full gallop. He leaned over the side, pulling at the rein to turn the horse's head so he would just miss stepping on the chicken, and the horse stumbled. Sir Lancelot missed the chicken. He completed the turn, coming upright as he did so, and brought the horse to a rearing stop by pulling savagely back on the bit as he slid off its rump. The horse whinnied in pain.

"He must have a loose shoe," the angry knight said accusingly to Sir Torre.

"It wasn't the horse's fault," I muttered. Unfortunately no one else was saying anything just then, either out of astonishment at

Sir Lancelot's failure or at his blaming it on another, and my voice filled the silence.

Sir Lancelot whirled to face me. "You have no standing here, bastard! Do not presume to speak before your betters."

It was too raw an insult for Sir Torre, and he calmly unsheathed his sword, saying, "Kneel, Dylan."

No sooner had my knees touched the ground than he hit me on either shoulder with the flat of the blade, saying, "Rise, Sir Dylan."

The crowd that had watched the hurley match had followed me over to see the chicken pull. They cheered as I rose slowly, my eyes challenging Sir Lancelot, too angry myself to find voice. King Arthur seated in the royal box eyed us both silently, his face impassive, but the queen's own face was white with rage.

"Very well, Sir Dylan," Sir Lancelot said to me tauntingly. "I say the horse is ill-shod, probably your handiwork of a few days ago before you reached your present exalted state. If you pull the chicken from the earth riding this horse, I'll give him to you. If not, acknowledge yourself a liar and braggart!"

This was patently unfair, as I am sure he knew. No one else had been successful yet. Chicken-pulling was hardly a practiced skill for knights. I nodded, however, and approached the horse; the beast was nearly unstrung by the bad handling. I cursed to myself, for he was a favorite of mine. I'd brought him apples in the stables and petted him when the grooms avoided him because of his bad temper. No one had ever ridden him but Sir Lancelot, who had broken him himself, using the heavy cruel iron bit.

The horse sniffed me suspiciously, but let me slip the bit from his mouth and rubbed my chest with his face when I unfastened it and threw the tormenting thing away, fashioning a hackamore of the reins. I led him apart from the crowd and vaulted onto his back, talking to him all the time in the low voice I always used with him. He quivered for an instant at the unaccustomed burden, but stood quietly enough, responding to pressure from my knees when I urged him into a walk, and then a run. I allowed the reins to lie loose on his neck, turning him with my knees. Oh, he was a sweet horse!

Then I tried running with him, vaulting on and off his back, holding on to the saddle, and finally leaning over in the maneuver I would have to use to reach the chicken. I detached my belt and tossed it to the ground, retrieving it by leaning so again and again without his stumbling once.

The contest had stopped while everyone watched me put the great horse through its paces. When I rode back toward the crowd, they separated to let me through, and I ran straight at the buried fowl, plucking it neatly from its earthy nest and waving it as it squawked and flapped its wings, bleeding from a torn comb. The crowd that usually cheered Sir Lancelot, the foremost knight in the realm, cheered me. King Arthur looked astonished. Never had he seen his favorite in such a light. The queen was close to tears.

I brought the poor bird up to Sir Lancelot and tossed it to him, feathers flying, as he stood pale and aloof. "Here is my part of the trade," I told him, "and I must thank you. It isn't every new-made knight that receives such a gift."

He fended the bloody chicken off with his hand, muttering a curse, but replied, "The horse is yours. I trust he doesn't stumble with you in some more dire time as he did with me," and he turned and walked away.

I waved to the still-cheering crowd and took the horse back to the stables to tend his torn mouth. I swore I'd never use a bit on him of any kind. His mouth was ruined, with old scar tissue showing how hard his life had been. He was about eight, judging from his teeth, and in the prime of his strength, otherwise.

"I'm sure Sir Lancelot called you by some outlandish battle name," I told him. "The grooms all call you the Black Devil, but I'm going to call you Black Nick, after a friend of mine." Horses don't respond so much to names as to tones of voice, and doubtless he didn't understand me, but he nuzzled at me. I found a piece of barley sugar for him; it would ease the raw places in his mouth.

Sir Torre found me there hours later, grooming the horse and talking to him. "There's nothing wrong with this horse but bad treatment," he fumed, indignant over the slur Sir Lancelot had put on Sir Torre's management of the stables.

"True," I agreed, "and now everyone knows it."

"I ought to call him out!"

"In his present mood he's capable of killing you," I told him. "You have nothing to defend from him!"

He snorted, and to distract him I said, "I must thank you for knighting me as you did." It was completely unexpected. I thought it was necessary to keep vigil, fasting and dedicating oneself to God and swearing knightly oaths and the like before one could become a knight.

"Let me swear myself your liege man," I said, kneeling before him and offering him my belt knife. I had no sword.

"This is a fine blade," he said gravely as he inspected it. "How did you come by it?"

"I took it from a man I helped kill when I was but a boy," I said. "He had hurt a friend of mine."

"A boy? You're hardly more than that now, are you? I should have asked before. How old are you, anyway?"

"I've never known when my birthday was for sure, but I think I was just twelve when I came to Camelot. That was three years ago. I'm fifteen."

"Good," he said. "That's old enough for knighthood. Arthur was crowned at fifteen. Now, I regret that I cannot accept your service. It is no fault of yours, but the rules of chivalry hold one must have rank to bind other knights so. I have none. But I will swear allegiance with you, friend to friend, and you will ride at my left side as I go to battle, if you would."

It was a position of trust, and I was touched by it. He pricked his palm with my knife, and I extended my hand to him. He made a shallow cut on mine and clasped it with his own bloody hand. "This is a bond older than knighthood," he told me.

As he gave me back my knife I seized his hand and kissed it. He had been good to me. I may have made some dangerous enemies, but I had also made some stalwart friends.

Sir Torre was determined that I should learn jousting, little as I cared to do so. "Knights fight with spears, often as not. You could get challenged and not be able to defend yourself," he insisted. In this he was backed by Gawaine and, surprisingly, Gaheris.

"Why should I have to defend myself?" I said in a mulish fashion. "I could just walk away."

"That you could not. If you wouldn't fight, you could be slain like a dog," Gaheris said. On seeing me frown, he amended it by saying, "Well, what chance did Fat Nick have?"

He was right, but I tried one last plea. "I won't have time for that as page master."

"That's over, I'm afraid," Sir Torre said. "When I knighted you, it moved you beyond that duty; only a squire may hold the post."

I said good-bye to the boys that evening, giving them my gold chain of office to bestow on another page master. "You must choose another leader," I told them. "I did not plan to leave you so soon, but we do not control all the chances in our lives."

"No," one of the boys said flatly. "You've taught us how to look after each other. That's what we'll do. You keep the chain; we will not seek another to take your place."

Since I was no longer page master, Gareth stopped page training, saying he had all he wanted or needed, since he was going to be a knight of the Round Table anyway. I didn't argue with him. I thought much of it was pointless, myself. He took to following me around, saying he was my squire, until I took pity on him and confirmed it. He was happiest watching the jousting, though I was in constant fear that Black Nick would get hurt by some awkward spear thrust.

The stallion was so used to running at other horses and crashing into them that he needed no guidance from me, and I could concentrate on handling my weapons. I learned quickly in scrimmages against other new-made knights and soon was able to deflect my opponent's lance point from making full contact with me after suffering several jarring falls.

My brother Gawaine took responsibility for training me in the tactics of tourney fighting. Among other things he told me, "As a rule, the bigger the man, the longer the spear; and the longer spear strikes first. If you are seen to flinch from it, you'll be considered a coward."

"And if I let the longer spear hit me full on, I'll fall every time."

"True. The trick is to make it look like the other man missed. Got it? You dodge the blow but as unobtrusively as possible. That way, you don't get hurt, but you don't appear cowardly."

I gathered that knights were more concerned with appearances than with reality. Some knights, at least. Those who lacked Gawaine's counsel seemed to get knocked off their horses with some regularity.

I heeded Gawaine and became sufficiently proficient so that my tutors grudgingly admitted I could learn no more from instruction. All I needed now was practice, which I did on my own. A swinging swivel target had been set up near the tourney grounds or lists, as Gawaine called them. I ran a dozen passes at it, occasionally accepting a challenge from one of the fledgling knights or even an ambitious squire for a practice half-speed joust.

I found I could still tell what was about to happen just before it occurred, as I could in hurley. As my skill increased, the knowledge made me unbeatable at that level of challenge. By the time Guenevere decided to move the court to London for winter, I was as ready for novice runs as anyone could be. Sir Torre promised that if I showed myself a punishing opponent I would be left alone, but I would have to find my place in the pecking order first. Maybe, but I'd seen barnyard fowls with more sense than to seek confrontation. I decided I had no need to fight in London unless challenged, and if I avoided the lists, that wouldn't happen. I took care not to announce my decision, for I wanted no argument, but my mind was made up.

Lady Mal rode with us, as she had last year, to manage the sale of Ayres's cattle. The pages volunteered to ride guard with me and Ayres's sons and grumbled because we suffered no raids. They had been looking forward to another skirmish like last year's. I was just as happy to have an uneventful trip, marred with nothing except continual rain. Mostly I ignore the weather, but to be out in it when it's unpleasant makes that hard to do.

Hugh, Ayres's London agent, was happy to see us, installing Lady Mal back into the room she'd taken over from Sir Torre. Sir Torre had found another one nearer the London palace for his dalliances. I went back to my sleeping pallet in the tack room. There was little to do once the cattle had been delivered, and Lady Mal donned a youth's clothing to roam London with me, unremarked. Ladies didn't go where she wanted to go, though we saw common women everywhere. Together we poked into market stalls to buy iron tools for Ayres's farm and drank ale in the more reputable inns to compare them with her own.

I was often recognized and given free drinks. "I saw you in a match against the Irish when I'd gone to Lyoness to deliver iron goods," one might say. "You scored four goals, one in each quarter."

"Hmmm," I'd retort.

"They say you've decided never to play again," one said.

"I'd play in a minute if I could get away with it," I admitted. "I've been enjoined not to fall into scandal, and Sir Torre assured me that playing hurley as a belted knight would do just that."

"You could go in disguise," one young knight from Cornwall said once, "as knights always do when they seek adventure." He said his name was Sir Tristram. Sounded like he made it up.

"I don't know how I could disguise myself playing hurley," I replied, "unless I wore a loincloth, perhaps." I was aware more people looked at my private parts than my face when I played. I couldn't disguise that. I was no longer a hairless boy.

Lady Mal laughed and turned the talk to court scandal, of which she knew an inordinate amount. Some of it was even true, possibly. "They say the queen and Sir Lancelot are lovers," she said, watching the man for his reaction.

"The queen is his chosen lady, and the king has appointed Sir Lancelot her champion," Sir Tristram retorted somewhat primly.

I didn't give a damn one way or another, but I quickly tired of gossip and found an excuse to leave. Still it bothered me.

"Did you just make that up?" I asked Lady Mal.

"You've never heard that? It's common talk in London. They say it's the reason why she likes to come here and loathes to leave each spring. There's no opportunity for secret assignations in Camelot as there is in London."

We encountered Sir Tristram again a few days later talking to fellow knights from Cornwall.

"They're saying raiders came to Lyoness," he told us grimly. "They abducted the daughter of Duke Cador, a woman named Samana. I knew her as a girl."

I felt the blood drain from my face. Samana! I nodded, fighting to control my emotions. I loved Samana!

"She was my foster mother," I exclaimed. "How long ago was she taken?"

"It's been months," one of the knights said. "They came in the fall just after harvest, as they always do."

The man upended his belt pouch on the table. "Saxon jewelry

from raiders we killed," he explained. "Do you know where we can sell it here?"

Lady Mal suggested Hugh, and we brought the men to his shop and waited until he'd concluded trading with them. "Each of you select a piece for yourselves," he said to us afterward. "I am grateful for your bringing them to me."

I took an amber necklace whose color put me in mind of my dog, Fat Nick. The stones had the same golden glow as his eyes. I went out by myself that evening, leaving Lady Mal talking with Hugh. I had much to think about.

The London docks are quiet at night, and I strolled toward the waterfront. If I'd been paying more attention, I could have avoided the skinny arm that snagged my own and dragged me toward a darkened doorway. I recovered my balance and stopped, still out in the fading sunlight of late winter, looking at the person who had caught me unawares.

"For a Roman penny I'll let you see what I have," a girlish voice said coaxingly in good Latin. It was a young whore from the docks, I thought, though the Latin surprised me, coming from such a person. I loosened her grip on my arm.

"Why would I care?" I asked. I'd had my fill of young girls offering themselves to me for free. I didn't have to pay if I wanted that kind of thing.

"For two pennies I'll let you touch," she said in a desperate voice.

"And for three pennies?" I asked cynically.

"No, there is no three," she said. I looked at her more closely. Her clothing was plain but good, if dirty, and maybe she was younger than she had looked at first.

"What kind of whore are you?" I asked coldly.

"No kind," the girl said angrily. "I'm just hungry."

"And if no one buys a look and you are hungrier tomorrow, what will you sell then?" I asked, as angry as she. I hated the need some people had to take such measures just to feed themselves.

"I don't know," she said. "I don't think I can get hungrier."

She had been about to cry, but the roughness in my voice brought her chin up.

"Where is your family?" I asked.

"I don't know that, either. I don't even know where I am, and I've not been able to find anyone who understood either Latin or Pictish until you came along."

"This is London," I informed her bluntly. "Not many people speak Latin near the London docks, but there are always Pictish sailors about. Go back down there. You have only to ask around to find one."

"I'm afraid of the docks," she said. "When my parents were away, Saxon sailors came raiding to our island and stole me from my home. They were going to sell me someplace, but I escaped at night and jumped into the water. They thought I drowned, but I can swim, and I came safely to land. Now it seems as though I may starve to death before I can find help! I haven't eaten in days! If I go back to the docks, the Saxons will surely catch me again."

"You're positive they were Saxons?"

"Yes, tall, blond men, they were, though not as tall as my father. He would not have let them take me!" She was on the verge of tears again.

"Sometimes bad things happen that cannot be prevented," I agreed, thinking of Samana. "Did you see a woman of middle years with them, a captive like yourself, but blond and blue-eyed?"

She shook her head glumly, "Not on my boat. There were other boats, though."

I sighed. "What is your name, then?"

"Viki," she said forlornly.

"Well, Viki, I will help you. I understand something of what it is to be alone. Come with me." She followed me back to Hugh's quarters.

Lady Mal didn't seem to believe her story. She studied the girl and looked over at me as the three of us sat together in her room. Hugh had left food there for me, a generous portion that was to be my supper. The girl fell on it frantically, at my invitation.

"Did she tell you she was a princess?" Lady Mal asked in a sarcastic voice.

The girl looked up at her flushing at the sneer in her voice. "I am a princess!" she exclaimed. "My father is Pelleas, the Pictish king. He will reward you well for any help you give me." Her tone was haughty enough for any princess, and her Latin was rather better than Lady Mal's, though she prided herself on her speech.

"Indeed," Lady Mal said. "King Pelleas, you say. Well, it isn't always easy to tell about kings' get." Her glance rested on the girl's dirty clothes and smudged face. "For instance, you'd never believe that Dylan here is a king's son, would you?"

"No," she replied coldly, looking me over in the same way. Lady Mal's eyes widened to hear her, and I felt myself redden slightly at her frank appraisal.

Lady Mal, on the other hand, was delighted with her high spirit. "In that case," she said laughing, "you can stay here until we find some way to return you to your people."

A bath and clean clothes turned Viki into a beauty, with chestnut curls clinging to her head like a boy's cap. They were soft to the touch, as I discovered by accident. My discovery didn't pass unnoticed, though, for I saw a startled look come over her face when my fingers lingered for just an instant longer than necessary. What it did to me was to make me realize I could never rest properly again out of her presence.

It was good I had no other duties, for they would have been slighted over the next month. The weather alarmed Londoners for its wind, cold, and rain. Ordinarily it would have kept me under Hugh's roof like a cat, refusing to move from the fire. As it was, I never left Viki's side, except to sleep, for she and Lady Mal thrust me out of their room when they tired of my company at night. I would then take to the street and watch their lighted window until they retired.

I slept but little myself, but never had I felt so alive. I wanted to touch her hair again, to take her in my arms and tell her how I felt, but hesitated to try. What I would do if she rebuffed me I did not know, but feared the test. This was no wench who'd seen me in the excitement of a hurley game, straining to throw herself at me.

At her insistence, we escorted her to the docks every few days to find Pictish sailors and question them. When she claimed to be the daughter of Pelleas, she was given a most polite reception. A week before King Arthur declared the London visit at an end, we encountered searchers sent out by Viki's father. "Princess! Your father is about to invade Saxony looking for you!"

"Poor Geen! I didn't mean to worry him so," she told the gray-haired man who accosted us.

"Ah, well met! What do you here? Never mind, there will be time for tales on shipboard. We must sail on the tide. Pelleas will have my head on a pike if we delay longer than the time it takes to load food and water for the trip."

Viki turned and stuck her tongue out at Lady Mal, who merely grinned in return. They had long since become firm friends. I couldn't smile. I hadn't thought of the possibility of losing her. But I had barely come to realize the strength of my feeling for her, reluctant, perhaps, to risk the pain of loss again.

"It's four hours until the tide turns," she said. "I must bid good-bye to those who have sheltered me here. I'll be back in time," and we returned to Hugh's house.

Hugh and his wife kissed her and gave her good-bye gifts, which brought tears when adversity hadn't. They gave her an impromptu farewell feast, but I couldn't touch the food, though Hugh's good-wife was a better cook than Ayres's daughters-in-law even.

"I'll take her to the boat," I told them all when it was time to leave. "I found her and wish to finish the adventure as it began."

I could have said more, but no one hindered me, and Viki and I walked off together. She turned and waved once more at the corner, then tucked her hand under my arm.

"You appear to have something to say to me, I think," she stated.

After a few steps during which I tried to frame a reply, I muttered, "What I had in mind would be easier for me to say to a girl from the docks than to a princess."

"That would be something improper, then, maybe to do with a Roman penny?"

I laughed but shook my head. "I am the illegitimate son of King Arthur and his mother's sister," I told her baldly. There wasn't time to lead up to such an admission in a gentler way. "I'll probably never be acknowledged by my father for the connection is considered scandalous. Perhaps it wouldn't have mattered to a girl from the docks with no family of her own."

"Pictish women choose their own mates," she told me. "My family would never think of hindering my choice, whoever it was."

"Even so, your father is half-brother to my own father, if my friend Nithe was correct. Nithe was very good to me when I was a boy," I added, knowing not what else I might say. Viki squeezed my arm but let me talk on. "Even such allowance as Picts give their women would not extend so far!" I blurted.

"No, not if Pelleas were my true father. I was an orphan and chose him as I'm choosing you, Dylan. Together we chose Nithe to be his wife and my mother." And she kissed me.

I hadn't said no to all the girls who pursued me, but I had never been kissed like that before. "I had a betrothal present I'd planned to give you," I mumbled, and drawing the amber necklace from my belt pouch put it into her hands.

She studied it carefully, nodded and said, "Put it on me, Dylan."

My hands trembled as I obeyed her. Her chestnut hair curled around my fingers as I had remembered. "I touched your hair once before," I said inanely.

"I know," she replied serenely. "And you must know this, Dylan, my love, that I would not leave you now except for the pain my absence has caused my family. Will you not come back with me?"

"I will seek you out when I am no longer a nameless bastard," I told her. "I will not wait forever for my father's blessing, though."

"Fine. The sooner the better. I will not wait quietly forever, either, Dylan," and she bade me leave her to find her way to the ship by herself.

I watched her go, following to see she met with no misadventure before she reached the ship and was hustled aboard. Only then did she look back and, seeing me, wave. It seemed I had only to learn to care for someone to lose them: Borre, Samana, Nithe, Fat Nick, and now Viki.

I wondered why I had not gone with her? Had she truly wanted me to? Would she wait for me to come for her? If so, how long? King Arthur had much to answer for.

Walking back to Hugh's stables, I noticed the cold. I hadn't been aware of the chill when I was with Viki. It might be long before I was as warm again.

CHAPTER VI

he day after Viki sailed away, Lady Mal insisted we find Sir Torre and prevail upon him to come with us to settle accounts with Hugh before we all set off for Camelot. I brooded on Viki's leaving, ignoring Lady Mal's bright chatter until we encountered Sir Torre riding slowly down the street near the palace. "Oh, very well," he sighed, giving in to her repeated request, nodding his head, then wincing as he pulled up short to avoid a pushcart. He'd drunk too much wine the night before to be easy with sudden motions.

We had to thread our way between wheeled pushcarts all the way from a few feet before Arthur's palace to Hugh's warehouse near the docks. "In Roman times no wheeled vehicles were allowed in the city until after sunset," he muttered.

"It must have been hard on the merchants," I said.

He shrugged slightly. He didn't care about merchants. I knew at heart he had no more interest in trade than Sir Lancelot did.

Hugh was waiting for us. "I have the tallies here," he said, looking first at Lady Mal and then at Sir Torre.

Lady Mal said, "I have Sir Kay's requisition slips that you asked me to bring," and gave them over. "We furnished the royal household one steer each day for the ten days of the trip," she added.

"Good." Hugh said. "I'll debit them against the king's account and credit Ayres's."

"Does the king ever pay?" I asked.

"Oh, no, but he does allow his debts to count against taxes. Each of these slips of paper is worth the cost of a cow at tax time. Now, that brings the tally to one hundred and nineteen beasts delivered."

"So many?" Sir Torre asked in surprise. "It's never been over a hundred before."

"It was that good last year, too. In the past you lost a couple of animals to robbers every night on the road." Hugh told him. "During these two trips under Dylan, a better guard was posted than you had in other years."

It was true, but I wondered how he knew.

He saw the question on my face and answered it. "I've talked to the pages who helped you. They are proud of what they accomplished."

"The pages?" Sir Torre said. "You got those lazy brats to take cattle guard seriously? They've always complained that it was not proper page duty, caring for the animals of a cowherd like my father."

"If we are supposed to get the protection of a large party because we furnish them fresh beef, it seems to me the protection should be real." I protested.

"Oh, no doubt." Sir Torre agreed. "Before, though, we were happy to bring in three out of four animals we started with. Traveling alone, we would have lost them all."

"The pages say they all want to become squires for you, Dylan." Lady Mal said, looking at me closely.

"They can't do that, can they?" I asked in horror.

"I don't know why not." Sir Torre mused. "There's always a

crowd of youngsters around Sir Lancelot, hoping he'll sponsor one or another into the Round Table."

"But I'm not in the Round Table. What could they want from me?"

"Do you want in? Between us, Gawaine and I could get you accepted, despite any opposition Lancelot or the queen might raise. We've talked about it often, you know."

Gawaine? Often? I didn't believe that! "It can wait," I said. "But do the pages expect it? Is that why they want to squire for me?"

"No," Lady Mal told me. "You're their hero. They don't care if you belong to the Round Table or not."

I shook my head. This could be a problem! "I couldn't even mount them," I said.

"I have a consignment of light horses destined for Armorica," Hugh said. "They eat them there but pay next to nothing for them. You might take those. The boys could ride them back."

"And I have the twenty fenced acres attached to the inn," Lady Mal said thoughtfully. "Besides, the inn's stables never hold more than a few animals. You could keep them there."

"They'd need more to eat than what they can graze in your meadow," I objected.

"Well," Sir Torre observed, "my father always puts up more hay than he can use, and if your squires help with the haying, he'd give you enough fodder to winter your horses over."

That was so. "It would be years before I could pay you," I told Hugh.

"That's not really true," he said diffidently. "Your commission is based on the number of cattle you deliver. I think Ayres will be as pleased as I at the way you fulfilled that responsibility the last two times. Accounts do not have to be settled evenly; they just go on as long as each party is satisfied. I am satisfied."

With that I decided to take as many of the pages who wished it into my service as squires, always allowing for the king's permission. I'd start a band of mercenary soldiers. In a few years, when the boys got a little more size, we could hire out. In the meantime, I could train them. Teaching them to play hurley was as good a way as any to form them into a team.

The next day the pages came to see me in a body, over a score in number. I knew them all. They had all been my charges when I was page master. They'd asked Lady Mal to be their spokesman.

"Sir Dylan," she said, "most of these boys are the king's pages who are coming into manhood and must choose a knight to follow. Some of these who aren't ready yet will be in the next few years. All of them would choose you if you would have them."

"I would be proud to have you," I told them, and it was settled.

The pages loved the horses Hugh showed them, and each of the larger boys had chosen a favorite by the next day. None of the horses had ever been broken to ride, but the boys had them following on halters before the day was out. By the time the king was ready to leave for Camelot a week later, everyone was mounted.

On the trip back, all my thoughts were of Viki, and I paid little attention to much of anything else. Had I made a mistake, letting her go without me? Should I follow after her even now? I wanted to stand in my stirrups and scream with frustration. As it was, I let the pages herd the few cattle we drove to feed Arthur's party on the trip home to Camelot. Sir Kay's kitchen staff butchered and cooked the meat, and the pages brought back food for us. We ate separately from the rest. This all happened around me, and if any problems arose, I was not aware of them.

The oldest pages stayed with me when we reached Caerleon. "We don't declare until Easter," one of them told me, "but the priests always try to get some of the pages to choose the priesthood. They'll complain that you are not a Christian. The choice is ours, however, for it's King Arthur's rule that no one be coerced. The priests don't respect that in practice, of course, so we'd rather stay away from them."

They moved with the horses into Lady Mal's stables, at her invitation, waited tables in exchange for food at the inn, and lived better under her care than they had at Camelot.

Gareth moved from Ayres's farm to the room Lady Mal had set aside for me, somewhat crowding it. He and Lady Mal came to an agreement. Gareth would keep order in the common room at night when some of the drinkers tended to get rowdy, and she would feed him. I thought it might turn out to be an expensive arrangement for her, but she said Gareth would earn his keep, for he was as amiable as he was big. At nearly fourteen he was larger than any man in Caerleon, or in Camelot, for that matter, but being thrown out by Gareth was almost a friendly act.

The inn was full every night, and not just with commoners. Sir Lancelot's cousin Bors, a red-faced lout who more resembled a butcher than a knight, often brought some of his friends to drink and hear Lady Mal sing. They said even King Arthur came more than once with Sir Lancelot, though I didn't see them.

Sir Torre told us that Brastius Red-beard, Arthur's Warden of the North, had returned to Camelot, much worried. Arthur was calling a special meeting of the Round Table after hearing his report, and I was requested to attend. This was the first notice the king had taken of me since the theft of the necklace. I hid my excitement, but I was as jumpy as before a hurley match.

Sir Torre was as mystified as I. "Maybe he plans to acknowledge you!" he said.

I dared not hope it.

As Sir Torre described it, the Round Table always met in a circular room open to the sky, modeled after a Roman atrium. Fellows of the Table were protected from the elements by a roofed colonnade that followed the wall line. The great wheellike table, after which the fellowship was named, dominated the space, and a hooded fire in its open center kept the room warm enough for comfort. It was not used in winter, as the court was always in London during that season.

I had never attended a meeting before. Sir Torre told me that only knights were permitted, with fellows seated and other knights standing behind them to serve as pages. It was an honor for an outsider to be present, he insisted. I didn't feel it quite as I should have, perhaps.

The first thing I noticed when I entered the room was that the table was painted. A red dragon ran the length of its surface, with its head depicted just in front of the king's seat. The dragon's face was turned toward me, and I could see its blackened nostrils. It looked real enough, as if it once had magically breathed fire. I wondered if it had.

Sir Lancelot raised an eyebrow when he saw me take my place behind Sir Torre. We were stationed directly across from King Arthur with Sir Lancelot on one side of him and King Pellinore, as Senior Knight, on the other. Beside Pellinore was an empty seat with the words *Siege Parilous* written in gold lettering. Gawaine sat on the other side of it with his brother Gaheris beside him.

I recognized a few other knights: Bors, of course, Sir Lancelot's cousin from Brittany. I thought knights in peacetime didn't seem to have anything to do but hunt and drink. Bors seemed to prefer the latter, though maybe he was hunting more delicate game. Still, Lady Mal kept him at arm's distance, though she didn't prevent him from spending his money.

Sir Kay, looking odd without his apron, saw my eye on him and nodded. I had never been able to make up my mind about Sir Kay, but he treated me civilly enough. He seemed an odd choice to be a Round Table knight, but maybe the fact that King Arthur had been fostered in the house of Sir Kay's father had something to do with it.

"Brastius Red-beard, Warden of the North, has brought us a

disturbing challenge from the Picts," Arthur said to open the meeting. "Tell them about it, Brastius."

A gray-haired man with a rusty beard rose and said, "Sire, distinguished colleagues, guests, the king of the Picts of Strathclyde, speaking for all the Picts and for the Scoti of Eire, has challenged Arthur's court to a game of hurley."

The unexpectedness of it brought a sudden shout of laughter, which was punctuated with derisive remarks like, "Why not a Maypole dance?"

Brastius reddened and raised his hand peremptorily. "Am I to be mocked, Sire?" he demanded angrily. I gathered he was neither thick-skinned nor patient.

"Quiet!" Arthur barked. He was not amused, either. A sullen silence fell upon the group; these men were not used to being checked, even by the king.

"It is no matter for laughter," Brastius grated. "To you hurley is a game for boys. Among the Picts and the Scoti it is a training ground for war. Are you not alarmed to hear they have come to a common purpose, even if it is only hurley? I tell you, they see this as a serious test of courage and skill. If they can defeat us in hurley, the Picts will come over Hadrian's Wall in a buzzing swarm, and the Scoti ships will raid our coasts from Dimilioc to Mona."

"Let them come," Bors growled. "We'll beat their backs like the dogs they are."

"Will you? Dogs? Perhaps, but such a pack of dogs as you have never seen before. There are thousands of them. Among these two peoples every man sees himself as a warrior. What are our thousands? Peasant farmers, guarded by a few hundred knights. Can you be everywhere at once? Who will keep the eastern Saxons in check if Arthur's men are fighting in the west and in the north?"

No wonder Arthur looked grave, I thought. Perhaps he could defeat any one of these foes in a pitched battle, but his forces were too limited to fight on more than one front at a time, particularly against night raiders who stabbed and fled.

"I played hurley when I was a boy," Gawaine said. "I could strip down again, if necessary."

"Even among the Picts and Scoti hurley is a young man's game," Gaheris observed sourly. "When was the last time you ran farther than from the table to the bar for another pitcher of beer?"

"We could combine the Camelot team with recruits from Caerwent and Caerleon," Sir Torre said. "They beat the Irish the last time we were challenged."

"Our hurley players are boys," Brastius said grimly. "These are men. The Scoti are big and the Picts are fast." He was silent for a moment before announcing, "They will be led by a Geen."

There was a sudden intaking of breath, for Geens were indeed perilous.

"Who?" Arthur asked.

"Lamerok," Brastius answered.

"My son?" King Pellinore asked in a surprised voice. "Why, he's little more than a boy himself, all arms and legs!"

"He's twenty now," Brastius said dryly. "Perhaps you haven't seen him lately. He's as big as you are."

"Well!" King Pellinore said, seeming immensely pleased, but attempting to hide it. "Well! I am sorry, Sire," he continued, turning to face King Arthur. "I trust Brastius is wrong about what this portends, but you have no chance against these men. I've seen Picts play when led by a Geen. Used to do it myself, you know."

So, I thought, King Pellinore was a Geen. Why, he was no bigger than Gareth! On consideration, however, that gave me no feeling of ease when I considered playing against such a man. I had seen Gareth handle a drunk a head taller than me in The Pig Girl not three nights ago. It had taken him little effort, and would have taken less had he not been considerate of the man's feelings.

"We have to win," King Arthur said flatly.

"Would you like to wager on it, Sire?" Pellinore asked blandly.

"We won't play with boys, either, Pellinore. I admit Gawaine may be past his prime for hurley, but Dylan is not. I'd be inclined to back him against anyone, even a Geen!"

I felt an enormous rush of pride. My father believed in me!

"You like your chances enough to bet, then?" Pellinore persisted. "There is land in contention between our two castles . . . the west side of the Usk over to the east side of the stream that waters my valley. Would you like to have that under your control?"

"I control it now," Arthur said testily. "They pay my taxes."

"They pay mine, too," King Pellinore said laughing mirthlessly.

"We could set it up as an independent barony, I suppose, with the winner to name the holder. I'd give it to Dylan."

"Dylan!" Bors snorted. "A bastard without family?"

"His blood is as good as yours, Bors," Gawaine snarled. "Dylan is my brother!"

I saw King Arthur flinch as if he'd been struck when he heard Bors's words and bite his lip at Gawaine's retort. He did not speak, however.

"Well, Arthur, since Gawaine is your kinsman," Pellinore said, "and Dylan is Gawaine's brother, it seems you plan to name a kinsman as baron. Well, I'll do the same. If Lamerok leads his team to victory, I'll name him Baron of Caerleon. Is it a wager?"

"It is," Arthur said grimly. "Sir Dylan, you have my authority to choose anyone in the kingdom to play with you," he said, looking straight at me for the first time since the theft of the necklace. The impact of his gaze on me caused an answering surge of emotion in my chest.

"Get them ready," he ordered me. "We will hold the match the day following the feast of Pentecost." He then rose and turned to Brastius, who was still standing. "Tell them, Brastius. Tell them to bring their best men, for we would scorn beating any other

Tell them!" He stamped out, in a fine temper, as far as I could see.

I was not the happiest of men myself. If I was to be only Sir Dylan to my father, it wasn't enough. But another thought stayed me from declaring I would not play; if we won, I would be made a baron and have a name to offer Viki! I would play . . .

Before Sir Torre and I left Camelot for Caerleon, young knights who had been squires with me and had played hurley with me and against me from time to time, came up to offer their services. I told them all the same thing: "Come to the great field in front of the castle tomorrow two hours after sunup." I'd rise at dawn, but it would take half that time just to ride back to Camelot. I could stay over in the barracks; I didn't want to.

Sir Torre rode back to Caerleon with me, and together we thought of some twenty men that we'd have to consider as possible team members. Torre was as knowledgeable as I; he'd been a fine player himself when he was younger and still coached the castle team. He agreed to work in that role with me. I'd be playing and would lead from the field.

"My father will be excited to hear of the wager," he said. "He's complained for years of the necessity of paying taxes to both kings."

"I wasn't even aware of it," I said. "How heavy are they?"

"Why, a tenth each way. Of course, the church gets another tenth."

"A tenth for the church? Not from me," I said.

"That may change if you become Baron of Caerleon."

"There will be no tithing for anyone," I declared. "I've never seen why one man must give the fruit of his labor to another without his leave," I said. "Can you imagine me collecting a tenth part of Ayres's wealth each year? Why, I haven't spoken to him about the oats and hay I need for the squires' horses this winter for fear he'll yell at me. I've been using the inn's supplies."

Sir Torre laughed. "You're not afraid of what the king might say, but you fear my father?"

"Well, I value your father's good opinion," I said.

"Ah! Hmmm . . . both Hugh and I know how highly my father thinks of you, but despite what we've told you, you won't believe he's given his approval to the commissions you've earned."

"Yes, you say that and Hugh says that, but Ayres hasn't mentioned it. I won't believe it until I hear it from him."

Our conversation put Sir Torre in high good humor, and he insisted on my accompanying him to Ayres's house, where he related the whole story to everyone.

Ayres grinned throughout the recitation, seeming particularly amused at my discomfort.

"Stop teasing the boy," his wife said finally. "You must know, Dylan, that Ayres claims you as a kinsman, a fourteenth son, no less, though you'd think I'd remember a thing like that if it were true!"

"It's true enough for me," Ayres said. "I can't tell you how relieved I'd be to hold my land under you rather than being claimed by rival kings. Of the two of them, I'd choose King Arthur for master, but no one's asked my opinion about that!"

No one had asked my opinion about whether or not I wished to play for Britain, either. It had been taken for granted that the king's word was law and my obedience would be unquestioned. If I became Baron of Caerleon, that would change, I vowed to myself. I might be a landless knight now, but no lord had claim on me as liege-man. I would offer my services as friend to friend where I met with friendship, the same as now, but not as vassal to liege lord, were I Baron of Caerleon.

Some of Ayres's sons and grandsons wished to be considered for the team, and other hurley players I knew from Caerleon and Caerwent sought me out that night and early the next morning before Sir Torre and I set off for the practice field. We brought the pages over in a wagon to keep them from wading the ford over the Usk. Fog rose from the surface of the water, damping the voices of the boys behind us as Sir Torre and I led the company to the great field. An even greater company met us there. I recognized old teammates among them, but there were others, too, knights like Gawaine and Gaheris and even King Pellinore. Not one of the knights from Brittany was present. Neither was my father.

Sir Torre made a speech. "Thank you all for coming out this cold morning, gentles and peasants all. I want to assure you, however, there will be no distinctions among us on the playing field, bound as we are in defense of king and country. All who participate will be honored, each according to his merit and station. You may not be chosen to confront the enemy in person, but your contribution will still be valued. If you need anything to help bring a victory to Britain, ask it of me. In all else, Sir Dylan will be your captain."

There was a cheer following his words, and I kept my face as blank of emotion as I could, only glancing out of the corner of my eye at Sir Torre's brothers, who stood near. I found them grinning openly, watching me. I'd have to be careful or everyone would know how I felt about such nonsense! It was some consolation to know that I was not alone in that, however.

"It's too cold to strip," I said. "What I want now is for you to choose leaders and form yourselves into teams. I want each team to be made up half of scrimmagers and half of wing men. Don't worry about goalies. Allow for a few substitutes in case someone gets hurt. Let's see what we have."

Those who expected to play separated themselves from the spectators, and I found there were two castle teams: an older one made up of young knights, and a younger one of squires and a few pages. Townsmen from Caerleon and Caerwent formed a third team, and my squires, with Ayres's sons, a fourth.

Gareth played with us on the farm but chose not to accompany us. "I'm planning with Lady Mal how to come to the notice of the king," he'd told me. "I want to be a knight of the Round Table. I haven't time for games."

"Games." Even my brother saw hurley as nothing but a game! Nevertheless, I thought Gareth could match Pellinore's Geen in strength in the scrimmages, and I was determined to enlist him, one way or another.

Sir Torre and I matched the older castle team against the town team, and the castle squires and pages against our own boys. They played for the better part of the morning, and it became evident our boys, except for three of Ayres's sons, were just too young. The castle squires had several players who were good enough, as had the town team, but the bulk of the players would have to come from the team made up of young knights.

There was no point in delaying. This time I spoke, not Sir Torre. "Sir Torre and I have selected those we think big enough and strong enough to play against the Picts and Scoti at Pentecost. We were impressed by a number of the younger players, as well, and look to them to defend Britain in future matches. For now, you all are needed for scrimmaging, for without opposition this team will not be ready in time."

Sir Torre read out the names of those we had selected, and the others took what satisfaction they could from my words. Perhaps it was not much.

At first the scrimmages were sloppy, for the players were not used to one another; but with practice things improved after that, and I began to feel we might have some chance. King Pellinore often came to watch, and he would leave laughing. "Wait until the Geen comes," he'd say. It made everyone uncomfortable, but I welcomed the challenge. It helped the players to be serious about trying to improve.

Easter was celebrated late in March, which meant Pentecost.

observed fifty days later, came in the middle of May. I would be sixteen. Beltane fell on June first and Gareth would become fourteen then. For the rest, I could see one good thing about it: if practice had been difficult for us, it was even more difficult for our opponents in their colder northern country.

The night before the feast day I spent in the inn with Gareth and Lady Mal. They told me they'd found a way to bring Gareth to the king's notice. "The king delays the feast each year until something out of the ordinary happens. Last year Queen Morgause came. If nothing real happens, Sir Kay's learned to provide an incident to avoid the drunken brawls and ruined food that long waiting occasions." Lady Mal explained.

"Sir Kay told you that?"

"No. Sir Torre did. Everyone knows but the king," Gareth said. "Truly?"

"Bors said the same thing to me," Lady Mal agreed. "He was wondering what it would be this time."

"It'll be us," Gareth confided happily. "Sir Torre talked to Sir Kay about it."

"Gareth is to come to the door of the great hall, overcome by hunger. We're not going to let him eat breakfast; we'll make him walk all the way to Camelot from Caerleon on an empty stomach."

Gareth looked unhappy. "I don't know why I can't just pretend," he complained.

"Because you can't act the part," Lady Mal told him in an exasperated voice. "You know that! We've discussed it a dozen times already! He's always happy unless he's hungry," she confided to me, "but when he's hungry he's pathetic. He won't have to act."

"What happens then?"

"I'll say that I'm a wandering bard," Lady Mal continued, "and, along with my friend, found the boy starving on the road. I'll say he wants to ask a boon of the king."

"Then I say I want to work in the kitchen for a year to regain my strength," Gareth said happily at the thought of being near all that food.

"Back up. You're a bard?" I knew she could impersonate a youth, for she'd done so with me in London, but there were folks that knew her here.

"You've heard me sing at the inn," Lady Mal purred. "When I put on trousers and bundle my hair under a cap, no one will recognize me."

"I would."

"Never," and she stood and strutted across the floor, leering at one of the serving wenches like a demented sailor, pinching her bottom, and causing her to squeal in surprise and nearly spill a pot of ale. Not quite. She'd been pinched before.

"See?" Lady Mal said in triumph. "They'll never know!"

I shook my head, ascertaining only that Sir Kay was in on the imposture before dropping the matter. I didn't want them in serious trouble. "But why?"

"Oh, for a lark. I get bored doing the same old thing all the time," she replied airily.

"And the king will accept this as an unusual happening?"

"Of course!"

"Why?"

"Because Sir Kay says he will," Gareth told me indignantly.

"And you believe him?"

"What's wrong with you? Is there any reason we shouldn't?"

I had no answer. I hadn't warmed to Kay, but I liked few of Arthur's knights. It seemed to me that his eyes never showed any expression, always guarded. What was he hiding?

It fell out as they said. I was invited to dine with the king, along with the rest of the team. Of the five I'd spent at Camelot, it was the first feast of Pentecost I'd ever attended as a guest. There were strange men among us and at the high table, uncouth Picts and

Scoti lords, including the man who must be Lamerok next to his father, King Pellinore. He was big, as I'd feared, and moved with grace for all his size. The queen and her ladies were not present for, among the Picts, men and women eat separately.

There was wine and ale flowing while we waited for the food, though I drank nothing but water. I noticed the strangers were all half drunk already, except for the Geen, who was too big to be much affected. Still, unless he was uncommonly hardheaded, he'd be hung over in the morning. I'd warned our team that anyone who showed the effect of drink would not be allowed to play, and they followed my example, most of them sipping on ale moderately, though they may have privately thought me strange.

A hammering on the door preceded the entry into the king's hall of Gareth and his two companions. Gareth truly looked pitiful, as if he'd been starving for weeks. Lady Mal must have put flour on his face, for he was unnaturally pale; I was afraid she would make a farce of it. With her on one side and one of Ayres's sons on the other, almost hidden by his bulk, Gareth struggled erect, a full foot and a half taller than his companions.

"A supplicant for King Arthur," Lady Mal called in her clear voice. "A starving foundling!"

Foundling? Oh, come now, I thought. How could anyone as big as Gareth get lost in the first place?

"Who are you, boy, and what would you have of the king?" Arthur asked, evidently enjoying himself, by the smile on his face.

"Most noble king," Gareth replied, "I ask three gifts, all within your compass and none that would cause you shame to render."

Lady Mal must have made that up, I decided. Gareth never talked that way.

"Name them and they are yours," the king said with boyish anticipation.

"First, I would have you give me food and drink for a year to recruit my strength. The other two gifts I shall ask for at next Pentecost."

"You appear to be nobly born," the king said. "I can see by your hands you've never had to do common labor." The king looked disappointed. "Tell us your name and ask for something more worthy."

"I have promised I will not do so," Gareth said, flashing a look at Sir Kay, standing behind King Arthur and wearing a spotless apron in honor of the feast day. The king missed the significance of that, but I did not.

Sir Kay flushed in anger. He evidently didn't like to see his little stratagems exposed.

"Very well, I commend you to Sir Kay. Cherish him, Kay, for I can tell he is hiding some noble purpose."

"Not so, Sire," Sir Kay said. "He looks like a slothful fellow to me, interested only in a free meal! But since you'll have it so, I'll put him in the kitchen where he can stuff to his heart's content. Come 'Fair Hands,' " he said sarcastically, referring to King Arthur's remark, and Gareth slouched out, never standing to his true height.

With the special happening concluded, pages scurried about to place steaming joints on the table, with bread and tureens of soup. Sir Torre and I made room for Lady Mal between us.

"We fooled the king," Lady Mal said. "You didn't think we could."

"It's not over yet," I said. "The king has his eye on you. You'll pay for your supper before the day is out."

It was true. The king looked over at her speculatively and when the main gorging was over, called for quiet.

"One of our guests is a bard, I believe," he announced. "Or did you also find that instrument you carry when you found the starving giant?"

There! I thought. He recognized Lady Mal from the inn. She grinned, stood up on the bench she'd been sitting on, and uncovered her harp. Without waiting for further urging, she began a praise song for Arthur, an old one but much embellished, and with new verses I suspected she'd composed herself. It was extraordinary how her voice filled the hall, first high and sweetly, then low and roaring but always musical.

At its conclusion there was a moment of silence, always as sweet to a bard as applause, followed by shouted approval.

"Another! Let's have another!" Unruly knights pounded on the table with the hilts of their knives like pages eating in the kitchen.

The king allowed it to go on for a generous moment, then took a golden bracelet from his arm and tossed it to Lady Mal. "I wouldn't request a praise song in my own hall," the king stated, "yet I thank you for it. Something more sprightly now, in keeping with the feast."

She began a rousing sea chanty from Lyoness, dancing as she played and sang. Dressed in a boy's tunic and with her sailor's rolling gait, her nimble feet and agile leaps enchanted the Picts. They knew the song and kept time to it by renewed rapping on the table and stamping of their feet.

I was happy Lady Mal was not playing hurley for us on the morrow, for she sang and danced half the night. I left before the evening was over, and others of the team followed, coming out in twos and threes. I collected Gareth from the kitchen, and we all slept in Camelot's barracks, for the game was to begin after morning mass. The barracks had fleas, and while we may have slept no more than the Picts, at least we were clearheaded in the morning.

I came to the field barefoot and wearing my seven-colored plaid wrapped tightly about me. I'd roused Gareth and brought him to the barracks to introduce him to the team. "You were worried about Geens," I said. "Geens are not twelve feet tall. They are not monsters likely to eat you; they're merely uncommonly large men. We have a Geen of our own who will face Lamerok and hold him so tightly he'll think he's in love!" Gareth grinned, stood before us, and doffed his thick gray cloak. Naked, he appeared larger and stronger than when clothed, dwarfing all present. He was in a good mood, I was happy to see. I'd let him eat heartily, for he needed the fuel to power his huge frame. He was ready. "Show me this Lamerok," he bragged. "We'll see who's the biggest."

When we walked into the great field and up to the royal box, I saw more people in one place than I'd ever seen in my life. I recognized folks from Lyoness and from London, along with Picts and Scoti and townsmen from Caerleon and Caerwent. Where did they all come from, I wondered? When we were brought before Arthur, he was surprised to see Gareth stand an inch or two taller than Lamerok, even barefooted. Lamerok was shod.

King Pellinore sputtered, "Another Geen? Who's your father, boy?"

"Pelleas," Gareth answered proudly.

"Then you should be playing for us. Pelleas is a Pict!"

"My mother is Queen Morgause," Gareth replied. "I am brother to Gawaine, Gaheris, and Dylan of clan Merrick."

"Why didn't you say so yesterday?" King Arthur asked.

"I promised Sir Kay I wouldn't tell you," Gareth answered. "I didn't promise I wouldn't tell King Pellinore!" He grinned, happy that he had gotten around Sir Kay's stricture.

Sir Kay stood behind the king with a darkened face. He did not share Gareth's joy.

When we assembled on the field in scrimmage, I was matched against a Scoti as tall as Gawaine, but younger. Sir Torre threw the ball down between us and my opponent swiped at it, using a stroke that would have broken my knee had it landed, missing the ball by a foot. I jumped over his stick and jabbed the handle of mine into the soft spot just under the middle of his rib cage. My elbow accidentally caught him sharply under the chin as he leaned over suddenly in pain, and I surprised a look of admiration in his eyes. We understood one another.

It was a brutal game with little of skill about it. I raged up and down the line, rescuing my players from unsportsmanlike assaults, scarcely caring where the ball might be in the early going. I saw Lamerok break his hurley stick across Gareth's head, and the aftermath. Gareth grappled with him, lifted him high in the air, and smashed him against the ground.

After that the two of us, Gareth and I, patrolled the scrimmage line alone for our side. I encountered Lamerok once or twice myself and was relieved to find him measurably slower than I. Otherwise he'd have killed me, as likely as not.

I'd scored no goals, nor had Gareth, but we pulled the ball from the melee time and time again and threw it to one or another teammate. There may have been rest periods, but I was not conscious of them.

Finally, Gareth in a prodigious blow struck the ball high in the air and, unfortunately, in the wrong direction. I saw it soar toward our own goal and stop just in front of it. Running for the ball, I passed Pictish wing men until our goalie could flip it out to me over the heads of the last of them. I caught the ball on the fly and ran back toward the scrimmage line, dropping and striking it to and fro as I ran. For the first time in the match, I was filled with the joy of the game; it was as if I were a boy again. And as I used to, I ran through the entire field and hit the ball past the Picts' goalie, right through the uprights. Ah, I loved hurley.

The game was over. The crowd poured into the field and embraced me, lifting me and carrying me to the king's box. In the crowd I saw Picts and Scoti cheering me along with Arthur's Britons.

"You have won," the Pictish king said to me. "I would go far to see another such hurley game. In fulfillment of my wager, I name you Baron of Caerleon and cede to you and your heirs all my claim to the land between the Usk River and Battle Creek, from their confluence to their sources in the high hills, to hold independently of any liege."

"And I also name you Baron of Caerleon and cede to you and your heirs all my claim to these lands to hold independently of any liege," King Arthur said. Was that pride I heard in his voice? "Well done, Baron Dylan," he added.

He couldn't call me son, even now. Well, at least I had a name of my own that I could bring to Viki. The victory left me as depressed as if we had lost. I realized how much I had been counting on my father acknowledging me before all the folk. I was finally sure he never would, and my resentment deepened. Some day he would regret this!

PART II
The Baron of Caerleon
485 - 487

Clovis, King of the Franks, defeats the Romans in battle and frees Gaul while, in Britain, knights of the Round Table seek the Holy Grail.

CHAPTER VII

hen I awoke the next morning I found the inn full of townsfolk, wishing to congratulate me and pledge themselves to me as Baron of Caerleon. There were hundreds of them, but at Lady Mal's insistence I spent a moment or so with each. Finally she suggested I be given time to eat, or I might have gone hungry in the face of their insistence on a personal audience.

"Will that happen every day?" I muttered when I finally freed myself, planning to flee to the stables.

"It had better not happen here," Lady Mal said darkly to my retreating back. "We only serve regulars and overnight guests in the morning."

"I'll move to the barn," I retorted over my shoulder, carrying a loaf and half a round of cheese with me.

That shocked Sir Torre, who had followed me. "Barons don't live in barns. Besides, it would unsettle the horses."

"What would you suggest, then?"

"Why, you'll have to build a baronial manor, what else?"

I laughed. "I'm but sixteen!"

"I'm serious," he insisted. "Arthur was only sixteen when he

149

started to build Camelot. Now, some of the buildings within the old Roman fort here in Caerleon still stand. We could consolidate what's left into a sizable establishment. Arthur dismantled the fort's rock walls for stone to construct his castle, but he replaced them with oak pilings that serve almost as well for protection against raiders."

"But I don't need such a place!"

"You do! After yesterday there will be more aspirants for sponsorship than you can imagine. They can't all sleep in the barn!"

We found Ayres and his sons waiting for us at the stables. "Has my son talked to you about fixing up the fort?" he asked.

I noticed they all had tools with them. Some of them were shy with me at first, in deference to my new station, but I greeted them, one after another, and they relaxed. They were my brothers as surely as Gareth, for they had treated me as such.

"You look as if you intend to start today," I said.

"No time better." Ayres replied, and led us out toward the road and up to the fort. As we marched through the town we were joined by other men, women, too, once they learned our destination and purpose. Together they swarmed over the fort, first cleaning it of rubble and then tearing down half-demolished buildings to restack the stone for building on the main structure.

It took two weeks to clean up the fort and make a few rooms habitable before spring planting started after Beltane, the first of June. Nothing could delay that if there was to be a harvest. All of June and July, though, and into August there were always men working at the fort until the last piece of slate was laid and cemented on the roof of the main house.

Our last chore was to move Black Nick and the ponies to the new stables we'd set up at the rear of the fort, within the palisade, but as far from the kitchen and living quarters as I could get them. Lady Mal had complained of the flies that plagued her inn and blamed them on the horses when we kept them there. Eventually she arranged for local farmers to take the manure away from the fort daily, a free gift they appreciated, for it was less hot than cow manure, they claimed, and could be laid on the fields fresh. They'd do the same for me.

Lady Mal ran everything. Sir Torre observed, "She knows how to conduct business, trained as she was by her father, and everyone around here likes her. A pity you can't knight her."

"What would be the point?" I asked. "She's able to talk to gentles and commons alike now. You know how snotty knights are to merchants. You've heard Sir Lancelot maunder on about 'trade.'" It was true. It was obvious she didn't spend all her time chasing pigs when she was growing up, despite the stories she told of her childhood, but she'd kept the common touch.

Gareth delayed reporting to Sir Kay to help us build the manor house. "Sir Torre said there are so many lads scurrying about the kitchen, they'll never notice my absence." His prodigious strength was useful in lifting the huge beams we framed it with.

We filled the space between the timbers with stone cemented with quicklime, and smooth-plastered everything but the wood. The roof was made of thin sheets of slate, heavy, but fireproof. The main hall was two stories high, and small rooms attached at ground level served to house the kitchen, storage, and sleeping quarters for guests. There was enough room inside the palisade wall for many other buildings, but we were content to build a roofed walk around the inside perimeter. The roof would shelter folks at need as well as provide standing space for defenders to see over the top of the wall.

When it was finished, Gareth moved back to Camelot and insisted on working in the kitchen to finish out the year he'd pledged at Pentecost. Lady Mal went to her inn and I was more often there myself, staying in the room she'd given me, than at the fort. After some discussion, we decided I should hold a housewarming party and invite everyone in Caerleon. It was harvest and the season for a feast of thanksgiving, anyway.

"I'll don my bard clothes and sing for your guests," she told me. "I've decided on a bard name, 'Dynadan.' Do you like it?"

"From the old nursery rhyme, 'Dynadan, little man, stole a cake and away he ran'? Sure. I like it. Should we invite Camelot?"

"The king, anyway, and Pellinore. It'll serve notice on both of them that you're in residence."

"Will they come?"

"If you don't say it's Lughnasa, the harvest feast in honor of Lud. Pellinore wouldn't care, but the snooty knights from Armorica would deem it a sacrilege."

"Lughnasa's over. It comes August first," I said, "and I don't want Sir Lancelot and his cousins, anyway."

"Doesn't matter. They go where King Arthur goes."

I helped Lady Mal plan the feast, but she was in charge of it. She even selected cooks and serving maids to stay on as permanent servants in the manor house, women who had worked at the inn from time to time. As chief cook she chose one of Ayres's daughters-in-law, with her husband to be house steward.

"If one of them is sick, they can always get a replacement from the farm," Lady Mal explained.

I approved. Indeed, I'd have suggested it had it occurred to me.

"After the party you can eat at home," she continued. "You can't just drop in and eat here like a common farmer anymore. It discourages the other trade." She looked up from the list she was checking. "I'll have a special table set up for you in the corner near the door to your old room. We'll put up a curtain to protect you from the stares of the other diners, and expect you here on Saturday nights. Now, that will help bring a crowd! Even your servants will eat here to mark their night off and to bask in the light of your reflected glory!"

She enjoyed talking like that sometimes.

The party went well, with enough food and drink for all comers and the hall was big enough to hold the crowd. We would have had difficulty in accommodating all the guests at her inn. The squires served the crowd with the dispatch they'd learned from Lady Mal.

"How am I going to pay for all this?" I asked, looking at the great quantities of food being served.

"It's free, part of your tithe." Lady Mal said. "I keep accounts on what's brought in and credit it to the giver."

"I'm uncomfortable about that." I grumbled. "I don't like taxing folks."

"They expect it. They're grateful they aren't required to pay double tithe as before to the king and to Pellinore. These are almost cheerful givers!" I knew her to be both fair and honest and told her to take whatever commission was due her in her transactions. She nodded, but I'm not sure she took anything. I never asked her.

No one from Camelot came, not the king, not Pellinore, not the knights from Armorica, except for my brothers Gawaine and Gaheris, and Morgause, our mother, as a special guest. I was surprised and pleased to see her and gave her the seat next to me. This was the first time I had been able to entertain my family, and I was proud to show off my new palace to them. In its great hall we had set a long table for honored guests on a dais along the wall nearest the kitchen. It would seat thirty comfortably. In the absence of noble folk from Camelot, I seated Ayres, his goodwife, and their sons and daughters-in-law at the high table, though some of the latter spent most of their time in the kitchen preparing food. My family didn't seem to mind. Indeed, Gawaine flirted with the women while Gaheris gorged himself, paying no attention to anything else.

There were four other tables, with benches on either side running the length of the hall for the common folk. Anyone seated there could glance up and see us at the high table.

The low benches were full for hours as townsmen and farmers came in through the kitchen, having first dropped off some contribution to the feast. As they walked by my table I greeted each one, sometimes prompted by Lady Mal, who sat on my other side and knew all their names.

"You remember Giles, Baron," she would say. "He's the shoemaker that gave you the black boots," or something of that order.

"Best boots I ever had," I'd respond. "Glad you and your goodwife and little ones could come!"

Lady Mal told me I must always remember to use their names when I greeted them. "Nothing sounds as sweet to a man's ears as hearing his name in the mouth of one of his betters."

I was half ashamed of enjoying myself so much.

Lady Mal excused herself, ostensibly to check on things in the kitchen, and returned a few moments later in her bard disguise. I wondered how many people she fooled. One she didn't. Morgause looked at her intently and laughed softly. "I knew I'd seen that lady someplace before. She was the bard that brought Gareth to the feast of Pentecost, was she not?"

"Yes, but she'd not have it known," I said. "How could you tell?"

"It's said I'm a witch, is it not?" she asked lightly.

"Not in my hearing," I objected, but I remembered I'd asked Nithe the same question about Morgause. Nithe had said men found her bewitching, but there was no harm in her. She liked Morgause.

My mother smiled fondly at me and squeezed my arm, and I thought Nithe was right. Even if she were a witch, there was nothing malevolent about her.

Lady Mal had composed a praise song for me, a complete surprise. When she'd finished, I left my seat and moved to stand in front of the high table while the folk were cheering. I called her over and said, "Give me your blade, Dynadan."

Lady Mal looked startled, but handed over her belt knife, the one she had from me the day I first met her.

"Kneel," I ordered with a smile.

The hall hushed as everyone craned their necks to see what I was about. Sir Torre had said it was a pity I couldn't knight Lady Mal. Well, I could knight Dynadan if I wished. I was a baron!

I tapped her on either shoulder with the tip of the knife and used the simple words Sir Torre had once spoken to me. "Rise, Sir Dynadan."

She did so to the renewed cheers of the diners. Tears brimmed her eyes, spilling unregarded down her cheeks. Good! I had succeeded in surprising her. It was most satisfactory.

Gareth didn't attend the open house, though Sir Torre had told him about it. I worried about Gareth. His nature was so simple and sweet that he could easily be imposed on. He wasn't so much stupid as trusting, with a childlike faith in the goodness of his fellows.

"He's not like himself at all," Sir Torre told me. "He didn't smile the whole time I was with him yesterday. Something's wrong."

The change in Gareth was on my mind when I awoke the next day, and I went to the inn for breakfast, for my own servants were still cleaning up from the party. They didn't need to be interrupted by me for something so minor as breakfast.

"I want to go to see Gareth this morning," I told Lady Mal. "I feel I've neglected him, and Sir Torre alarmed me about him last night."

"I'll go with you," she said. She said she was bored sitting around the inn, though I thought she had spent much of the last month over at the fort.

We rode across the ford and up the hill to Camelot before the day was an hour old, me on Black Nick and Lady Mal on her palfrey. On arrival, we found Brastius Red-beard watching the sergeants train the new squires. My own were among them, smuggled in by Sir Torre. By rights these should all be King Arthur's men, but a few more were not a cause for objection.

"Where's that giant brother of yours?" Brastius said to me in lieu of a greeting.

"Hiding in the kitchen, probably," I said. "We were on our way to see him."

"Well, tell him to get his ass over here. The king asked about his training the other day and was full pissed to learn he hadn't started yet."

"I'll let him know," I said, and rode past the rows of recruits, listening to a sergeant berating them for being slovenly, slow, and generally stupid. One of my boys winked at me as I passed, and I realized no one took his words seriously.

The appetizing aroma of roast pork was on the breeze as we rode up to Camelot's kitchen door. I was smiling at the thought of how many times I had sent Borre to Samana's back door to beg for food for us when we were growing up. Perhaps there would be something in the kitchen to eat while we were there, like in the old days, though I doubted if Sir Kay was as generous as Samana.

I had food on my mind when we ground-reined our horses and entered the open door, along with a million flies. As soon as my eyes became accustomed to the dim light I was appalled: Gareth was on his knees, stripped to his waist before Sir Kay, who was lashing him across the shoulders with a long thin rod. Gareth was weeping silently.

As Sir Kay swung it back once more, I grasped the rod, jerking it loose. It flew from my hand like a stooping hawk. I have always had an uncertain temper. Like the time I bit Lady Miriam, I heard a throbbing, rushing sound in my ears, like surf beating against a sea cliff. Usually I am careful to avoid situations that might bring my temper to the surface, for I fear I may do someone a serious injury without real intent. Nithe said Pelleas had the same problem. My attempts to keep it under control have earned me a reputation for being aloof, I fear, but that is better than being known as a berserker. Now in some part of my mind I was aware I was in danger of killing this man, and I didn't care.

Sir Kay turned in anger and I caught him moving, clutching his neck in my right hand. I let his momentum carry him to the great pot of soup that simmered on the hob, night and day, and thrust him into it headfirst, up to his shoulders. It was unpleasantly hot to my hand. Sir Kay fought against me, but I held him under until his struggles nearly stopped and I became aware that both Gareth and Lady Mal were tugging on my arms. They both were so weakened by laughter that at first even Gareth's great strength could not prevail against me.

"Oh, give over! Do not kill him," Gareth said choking. "It is not that important! He hurt me very little."

I pulled Sir Kay free from the soup and flung him against one of the timbers that supported the kitchen roof. He sagged to the ground dazed and gasping for breath. To my distress, I had not grown taller, but my strength was twofold over last year. I could have thrown him through the pillar, like as not, had I chosen.

"What's so bloody funny?" I demanded.

"Drowning a knight of the Round Table in hot soup?" Lady Mal stammered. "It's hilarious!"

Gareth nodded, giggling with tears still running down his face. What a changeable oaf! He'd been blubbering but a moment ago. I turned on him, seeing no humor in the situation. "Why do you permit him to treat you so?" I demanded, as angry with him as I was with Sir Kay.

"He caught me stealing food," Gareth said, recovering himself enough to talk coherently.

"Why should you have to steal food?" I asked, amazed. "King

Arthur himself gave you leave to eat your fill. He put you in the kitchen for precisely that reason. I think he wants to see how big you can grow."

"Sir Kay beats all the scullery lads," Gareth explained reasonably. "He likes it."

"That's no reason for you to allow yourself to be treated so! You are no scullery lad!" I couldn't understand Gareth's insistence on what he called playing by the rules.

"I'm supposed to be a serf," he said stubbornly. "No one knows I'm a king's son."

"Fool! Everyone knows!" I raged. "You announced it at the hurley match with the Picts! The kitchen was only King Arthur's joke so you'd be near the food! Well, the joke's over. You're coming with me."

"I'm not, then."

"You're not?" I looked at him. "Very well. But let me warn you, if I come upon such a scene again, I'll show you how serious a thing being beaten can be."

Sir Kay lurched to his feet, his pale face scalded red by the soup and his hand on his belt knife. He glared at me, "Jumped-up bastard!"

Bastard? He knew, then! I watched his hand twitch at the hilt of the knife. "Oh, do it, Kay. Do it!" I urged. "Give me the excuse to end your miserable life!"

His hand left the knife and he wiped his face of soup. "Why did you do that?" he asked in an outraged whine.

"Gareth is my brother. Surely you know! Even more important, he is Gawaine's brother. Can you imagine Gawaine catching you in such an act? You think me hasty? I'm not! Gawaine is hasty. He wouldn't treat you with the kindness and forbearance I've shown you."

"I'll tell Arthur."

"Fine, and I'll tell Gawaine." I retorted. "Be warned."

Before I stamped out. I turned to Gareth and said, "You were supposed to report to the barracks for training. Now! But I'll tell Brastius Red-beard you'd rather scrub pots!"

Lady Mal followed me out, still chuckling, "Oh, what a song this will make."

"Better not," was all I said, but it was accompanied with a look that sobered her up. I was not amused.

Gareth ran after us, pulling on his stained tunic and calling, "Wait!" but we kept riding, leading him up to Brastius himself.

"Don't be mad at me, Dylan!" Gareth was imploring when Brastius saw him, jerked him around, and roared, "How dare you report in such condition! Soldiers are clean! Go take a bath, and get back here within the hour or I'll have you flogged. Run!"

Casting an agonized glance at me, Gareth took off at a lope to obey, and Brastius watched him grimly.

"Take it easy on the boy," I told Brastius. "Sir Kay has been abusing him, and he doesn't understand. He thinks there's something wrong with him instead of with Sir Kay! He'll do anything you want, but don't tell him. Show him. And, he's left-handed. He'll look awkward if you try to teach him to fight any other way." I held Brastius's eye until he nodded.

We rode over to the public bath and found Gareth scrubbing himself and his tunic.

"This will never dry in time," he muttered.

I took it and called a bath boy over. "Clean this and have it back within the hour," I ordered.

He nodded and ran off with it.

"The king told Brastius he wants you to begin training," I told him. "You've lazed around the kitchen long enough."

Gareth started to protest but saw Lady Mal grinning and realized he was being teased.

"Did the king really ask for me?"

"Brastius said so. Go show him what you can already do. I don't think you'll have to spend much time drilling."

"Oh. I want to drill! I want to be a knight."

We waited for Gareth to finish bathing and for the bath boy to return with his tunic. washed. ironed. and dry so we could deliver him to Brastius. "I'll be back to see what progress you've made in a few days." I told him so Brastius could hear. and we set off for home.

"Will he be all right?" Lady Mal asked.

"If the king has taken a personal interest in the boy. he'll be fine." I assured him. I hoped it was true.

Sir Kay organized game drives for winter meat early in the fall. Ayres came to me with the complaint Camelot's knights had trampled the winter wheat he'd sown. The next day I went to the court of justice King Arthur held in his great hall on the first of every month. Riding over to the castle in the usual September rain. I thought I'd rather be sitting in The Pig Girl having a warm drink than out in the weather.

I left Black Nick in the inner bailey and strode into the great hall to bow before the king.

"Greetings. Baron Dylan. Have you come with a grievance?" the king greeted me.

"Yes. Your Majesty. on behalf of farmer Ayres. Sir Lancelot and his men rode over Ayres's field and ruined a growing crop. I want indemnity for Ayres and your understanding it is not to happen again."

Sir Lancelot was standing as honor guard for the king. and the queen was in attendance as well. "We were after a white hart." he said before the king could speak. "I ask no peasant for permission when in hot pursuit!"

"You made the kill in my woods." I told him coldly. "I want the meat. hide. and rack sent to my hall in Caerleon. I also want the value of the ruined wheat."

"You'll get nothing from me," he snarled.

"You're a fine one to be asking for justice here," Queen Guenevere said coldly.

"If you're referring to the theft of your necklace, Your Majesty, I will take oath I never touched it but that one time. Would that I had never seen it!"

"We're in agreement about that, at least. But what would you take oath on that a Christian would respect?"

Was she referring to my incestuous origin before the king? "What would that be in reference to, Your Majesty?" I asked.

"Your celebration of Lughnasa. You even had the effrontery to ask the king to come!"

"You're as wrong about that as about other things," I told her, but she turned away, looking superior.

I turned my attention back to the king. "Am I to have justice?" I demanded.

"That and an apology," he told me. "Lancelot was acting for me and overstepped his bounds. I'll have Kay make amends."

Both Sir Lancelot and the queen looked at Arthur in protest, but he ignored them, though he was aware. His face paled. "I want you to know that I've considered the matter of the necklace and have decided some subtle mind wished to make trouble for you. I do not believe you are a thief. It is not in your nature."

"Thank you, Your Majesty," I said, bowing. I, too, ignored the others. I left without another word being spoken, but my heart soared! If he spoke this way, perhaps he would do more.

What with this and other chores, it was nearly a week before we returned to Camelot. Lady Mal found me happily forking hay and singing, something I do rarely. Usually Ayres's sons managed the stable, but I felt so energetic I could not sit idle. "You should let me give you lessons on the harp," she told me, straight-faced. "We could sing duets."

"I only sing for the horses," I replied, which was true.

"Just as well, probably," she agreed. She didn't have to!

I continued working while she watched until she came out with what was really on her mind. "I think you should go and see how Gareth is faring."

"Something wrong again there?"

"I don't like what I've heard, but best you see for yourself."

So, something was wrong again. I washed my hands and face in the horse trough, pulled on my tunic, and saddled Black Nick. We set off, stopping by the kitchen for apples, bread and cheese, and a meat pasty to take with us, at Lady Mal's suggestion. I gathered she thought Gareth would be hungry, which was likely enough.

We found Gareth standing in line with the squires, listening to a grizzled sergeant exhort, "Basics! Basics! Basics! That's what we're here for, gentlemen. You'll keep at basics until you can do 'em in your sleep!"

"What sleep?" one of the squires muttered.

"Who was that? You there," he yelled at Gareth, "does this bore you? Hand him a sword and shield, someone, and let him demonstrate once more how little he needs this."

One of the other trainers did so, grinning in anticipation, while a few of the other squires snickered.

I saw Gareth bore fresh bruises over old bruises as he took the heavy wooden training sword in his right hand and his shield in his left. "The boy fights left-handed," I said grimly. "Didn't Brastius tell you?"

"Oh, it's you," the sergeant said with some disdain. "This isn't a hurley game. We fight Roman fashion here."

The other sergeants guffawed out loud.

"Then I guess no one ever told you Julius Caesar himself was left-handed," I said, dismounting. "Let me show you something." I took a sword and shield from one of the other trainers and stood beside Gareth. "The boy and I will take on any two of you," I said.

Gareth grinned and took his natural stance, with his sword in his left hand. We placed our shields together in time to catch the sergeant rushing us by himself. I cut at his side and when he shifted his shield in defense, Gareth smashed him on top of his helmet in a crushing overhand blow. He fell at our feet stunned, tripping his friend whom we caught on the shields and flung backward to sprawl helplessly. The others lined up and came against us two by two as they warmed to the challenge, and we defeated them all, leaving them bruised and cursing. The squires were cheering us when Brastius Red-beard rode up with King Arthur.

"What's going on here?" Brastius roared.

"We were giving your sergeants a lesson in tactics," I told him coolly. "They thought being left-handed was a hindrance to a fighting man."

"We train recruits all the same way," he growled. "Your brother has been treated no differently from anyone else. He's just stupid."

"It's your system that's stupid," I retorted. "Do you think the Saxons give a damn if a man fights left-handed or right-handed? All they know is whether he's effective or not. If that wooden toy Gareth holds had been a mace, you'd have a row of dead sergeants lying there."

Before Brastius could answer, King Arthur raised his hand and cut him off. "We may have a chance to test that, Baron Dylan. We have word that a host of Saxons in boats is on the way to our shores. Spies say they plan to land on the south side of the Solway estuary and come upon Camelot by land. Will you fight with us?"

"Against Saxons? Yes. How long do we have?"

"A month. They brag that they will winter in Camelot. They will move with as much speed as they may, helped by the Jutes of Kent in all likelihood. They're cousin to the Saxons."

"We'll be ready," I said, and nodded to my squires to follow. The Jutes of Kent? I thought. Wasn't the king's marriage to Guenevere supposed to keep the Jutes quiet?

I led them back to Caerleon to make preparations, leaving Gareth to make up his own mind about where he belonged. He was torn between his desire to be with Arthur's knights and to be with us.

Sir Torre eased his decision that evening when he brought the boy to the inn. "Sir Lancelot and the other knights from Brittany will remain in Camelot. The Bretons have a treaty with the Saxons and will not fight them unless attacked. If you want to fight Saxons you'd best come with us, for they'll never get past Arthur."

My squires couldn't use the ponies for battle; they were neither big nor fierce. "We'll train to fight on foot," I decided, "all of us that can be spared. Some will have to stay to protect the town if the Saxons break through."

The smaller squires knew this meant them, but I made it sound as important as perhaps it was. "King Arthur has left the pick of his knights to defend Camelot," I said. "He and his men have to know it will be safe, or they will be too worried to risk themselves as they must. Lady Mal will be at the manor house, along with Ayres and his wife and family. They'll be depending on you." They would, too, for the fort was the only defensible stronghold in the valley and had been rebuilt by community labor for that purpose.

We'd assembled with townsfolk at The Pig Girl, drinking and talking, when Sir Torre and his brothers joined us. "Will you lead us?" I asked him.

Sir Torre shook his head. "I must ride at Arthur's side. I'm sworn. You're the baron. It is for you to lead your people."

"Take my stallion then. King Arthur will confiscate it for some other rider if I leave him behind. I don't want his mouth cut up again."

"I'd be proud to ride him," Sir Torre said simply, "but that wouldn't do. A leader must be where he can be seen. Your people will want to see you on Black Nick."

There were growls and nods of agreement, so one of the problems was settled. I would ride, even if everyone else walked.

"I've come for another purpose," Sir Torre said. "The king wants Lady Mal, or rather Dynadan the Bard, to ride with him. He says he wants a chronicle made of the battle so that folks won't forget what we tried to do if we fail."

"He wants me?" Lady Mal said incredulously, with a quick, guilty look at me.

My stomach lurched. What I would have given for such a summons, even now! Each small notice or slight by King Arthur had the power to send my spirits up or down past all reason.

"Yes. He wants you to move to Camelot now, to watch and remember. He knows who you are, by the way. I had to tell him. He said it didn't matter; he knew all the time. He said the Saxons would never harm a bard. Bards belong to the gods, in their reckoning."

"I'll do it. I'll make such a song of Arthur's fight against the Saxons that the folk will remember it a thousand years!" she swore.

Lady Mal was always exaggerating; it went with being a bard. I thought if we failed, it would be lucky if folks didn't spit before mentioning our names.

"You may be safe from the Saxons, but what about our own people?" I asked.

"I'll take a couple of Ayres's sons as gillies. They'll watch out for me. If I have my own tent, I'll have all the privacy I need. And think of the fun!"

I wasn't sure about that last part, but I didn't want to dampen her enthusiasm. It wouldn't have done any good anyway.

Word went out, to townsfolk and local farmers alike, that Caerleon was going to war to fight the Saxons. It took a week to organize a defense for the fort with Ayres in charge and enough supplies to withstand a siege of some months, if necessary.

The women rounded up extra containers to carry and store food, should the word come that we had been defeated and would have to flee to the fort for protection from the oncoming Saxons. Torre told them that the signal would be a column of black smoke from the guard tower at Camelot.

The day before we were to leave to join King Arthur with a hundred men from Caerleon, Ayres sent for me. "I'd come with you, lord," he said, "but my joints are giving me trouble. I want to give you something my father left with me." On the table was a full suit of Roman armor along with a short stabbing sword, a round iron-rimmed shield, a plumed helmet, and finally a long spear.

I inspected the spear, holding it up to test its balance.

"The Romans called that a pilum," he said. On seeing my raised eyebrow, he continued, "I told you my father was a centurion. This is his parade armor. He saved it for the return of the legions to Britain, but he died before that happened. It's gaudy, but it's serviceable. He'd never have owned it otherwise."

"It's the most handsome armor I've ever seen," I told him. That was the truth. I doubted if King Arthur's was as fine. The breastplate was embossed in gold, and the plume was horsehair, dyed a red that was still brilliant after all these years.

I was more interested in the sword, however; good Roman steel, tempered to take a cutting edge you could shave with. The pilum point was sharp enough for boar-killing.

"It's yours, lord."

"It should be Sir Torre's," I objected.

"Nay! He doesn't lead men. Besides, he's no more a son of my body than you are. Besides, he would look foolish in it, tall as he is. This armor was made for a Roman, a man built like you. Take it, lord."

I had never heard Ayres refer to Sir Torre's parentage before, and realized the old man had noticed and been offended by the faint air of condescension that King Arthur's knights bore toward him. I would have been proud if Ayres had been my father.

"I will, then," I said. "Wearing this and riding Black Nick, I'll be the finest sight in Britain. King Arthur will eat his heart out."

Ayres laughed, but I hoped it was true. I wanted the king to notice me. When I embraced the old man before I left, he blessed me. The gesture touched me as much as the gift.

Our point of rendezvous was to be Bath, an old Roman spa that had been deserted for a generation or more. Sir Torre had been there. He said it had never been walled and had escaped the pillage of farmers seeking building stone. He explained that from there we would be able to march quickly enough to meet the Saxons wherever they decided to land on the estuary. If they got between us and Camelot, we'd catch them in a pincers. Sir Torre told us King Arthur hoped to lure them ashore for a direct encounter, however, and to prepare for that.

In the midst of the bustle signaling departure, Lady Mal came by, dressed as a bard, to say farewell. She had a tall slim lad in tow I thought I should recognize. A small dark girl followed the boy like a shadow.

"I have someone who says he knows you, Dylan," she said. "Do you remember Constantine?"

"I do. I also recall how little use we had for each other," I retorted, grasping the youth's hand and grinning. It was hard and callused, not the pampered crybaby's I recalled.

"Losing Samana has brought us together with a common purpose," he said gravely, but he smiled. "This is my friend Eliza," he said, bringing the girl forward to meet me. "You know her father, Colin. It was on his ship, *Hammerhand*, that you sailed from Lyoness with Nithe. Colin thinks we're too young to be betrothed, so we must wait for his blessing, but it will come."

The girl glanced up at him briefly but turned to smile at me. "You have become even more famous since leaving Lyoness, my lord," she told me. "Sir Dynadan sang 'The Battle of the Geens,' for us."

I looked at Lady Mal and she colored. "The hurley match against the Picts. With Lamerok and Gareth in it, the title seemed apt. Hope you don't mind," she said. "Bards have to compose songs about something, and that seemed a good subject for practice."

"I've never heard it," I said.

"Practice was it?" Constantine asked, a trifle maliciously, seeing Lady Mal's evident embarrassment. "You should have heard it, my lord. You are almost as much a hero to Sir Dynadan as to me!"

"Hmmm," I said dryly. "He's been at some pains to keep that knowledge from me."

"Well, King Arthur liked it. That's why he decided to take Sir Dynadan with him as bard," Constantine confided.

Lady Mal turned a brighter red. I had never seen her discountenanced before and decided to take pity on her by changing the subject. I wasn't too comfortable with it myself.

"Will you be going with the king, too?" I asked.

"No, I came to tell him the Saxons have set sail from Kent and the Isle of Wight. They'll be at the estuary in a fortnight. We will harry them with slings from our small fishing boats and eventually with fire pots, hoping to drive them ashore. All of Pelleas's fishermen from Mona will be lying in wait to come down on them at the last moment like biting flies from the north. It should be enough. We'll seal them off."

"How many Saxon longboats are there?" I asked.

"At least thirty," he replied, looking grim.

"Thirty! Why, Horsa took Kent with three a generation ago!"

"The old men say there has never been such a swarming of

Saxons. Over six hundred are coming, they say. It may be the end of the world that's been foretold."

I went to a war council at Camelot that night. Sir Torre and I were late and came to the great hall to find the council in session. Even before we entered we heard loud argument. My brother Gawaine was standing before the king and shouting. "We haven't enough men! The Saxons will eat us!"

"Why so shy?" Brastius replied with heavy sarcasm. He was seated next to King Arthur. "There may be some folk in Camelot who didn't hear that, though I doubt not that every man within earshot is now of your opinion."

Gawaine glared at Brastius but otherwise ignored him. Turning back to King Arthur, he shouted again. "Whatever is on your mind, then?" Did he think the king was deaf, or did he always shout when he was excited? I wondered.

Sir Torre and I sat at the lower table to listen. I had heard Gawaine prided himself on his flawless Latin, learned in Rome as a lad when he was a hostage there, but tonight it was heavily accented with his Gaelic mother tongue. I put it down to emotion and was not surprised to see him lean on the table to stare into the king's face. King Arthur was seated in a wooden chair with parchments spread in front of him. He leaned over backward to avoid being sprayed with saliva, for Gawaine was sputtering in rage.

Gawaine threw his hands into the air, turning to Brastius to say, "Speak to the man! Tell him to stay here in Camelot where he has strong arms and eager hearts ready to defend him. Why does he insist on putting himself at risk?"

"Do you think I have not already told him that?" Brastius answered in rising irritation. "He doesn't listen to me any more than he does to you."

"Enough of this!" King Arthur ordered suddenly. "Am I not king? Will every one of my sworn men question me? I say enough!"

All muttering ceased. The king let the silence drag on while he visibly fought to recover his temper. When he spoke again, it was in a quiet, reasonable voice, and others craned forward to hear him.

"Camelot is good only for defense. In the last instance, if we do not succeed in turning back the Saxons, that will be its fate. If we stay safe behind these walls eventually we will have to sue for shameful peace, such a peace that will leave no man of us whole nor woman undefiled before the Saxons are through with us. I say I will not do it!"

"But a thousand Saxons!" Gawaine said in agonized entreaty.

"I've heard there are scarce six hundred," King Arthur demurred.

"Sire, use reason! If you split your forces, leaving the pick of your men as a defense of Camelot, they will outnumber us, no matter where we meet them," Gawaine continued his argument. "Bring the Round Table along. There are names among the knights from Brittany, like Lancelot, worth a dozen of those you'll have with you."

"Think you so?" King Arthur asked. "Names mean nothing to the Saxons. And they'd have to fight, Gawaine! Have you ever seen any of the knights of Brittany strike a blow in anger? They joust in tourneys with great vigor, but the battlefield is not a tourney ground. There are no rules in battle."

"I was with you against the eleven kings," Gawaine said. "Lancelot and his cousins would fight as bravely!"

"I do not question that," King Arthur said, "but these are not my warriors, just because they are members of the Round Table. Lancelot's father has a treaty with the Saxons. If Lancelot is to honor his father's word, he must wait for the Saxons to breach the peace with Armorica."

"You think he would not even defend Camelot, should the Saxons break through our defenses, as I am assured they will?"

"He will fight to the death to defend Camelot as a private

knight. He is the queen's champion, and she will stay at the castle."
He shrugged, evidently trying to calm himself again, then continued, "Anyway, we don't need them. I have the hundred knights given me in Guenevere's dowry, and others as worthy that I made myself."

"Mercenaries!" Gawaine snorted. "Would that I could find a son-in-law I could give some of my retainers to. The cost of feeding them is ruining me, and they expect presents all the time!"

"The mercenaries, as you call them, are professional soldiers," King Arthur said, "real fighters. Furthermore, my old volunteers, the London Irregulars, have formed and are marching. They will meet us at Bath. You remember how terrible they are in battle with their hooked pikes and their iron flails! And the fisherfolk along the southern and western coasts will follow the Saxons in and join us when they land. We will not be alone, Gawaine."

"At least I will not stay here!" Gawaine declared. "There is no treaty between my people and the Saxons."

"I counted on you to be with me, Gawaine," King Arthur said with a crooked smile.

"Aye, my liege, along with the fishermen!" Gawaine sighed, sitting down. He'd been defeated.

"You have some doubts about fishermen?" Constantine asked quietly, stepping forward. Eliza, the dark girl, followed him, as before. I wondered if she would follow him into battle.

Gawaine looked at him and retorted courteously, "I do not doubt your courage, but that is not the point, is it?"

"The point being that, willing as we may be, we would not be able to stand up against the Saxons?"

"Something like that," Gawaine said carelessly.

"Perhaps you would like a demonstration, Sire," Constantine said to the king. "If you will allow it, I think Eliza and I might change Sir Gawaine's mind if he would pretend to be a Saxon."

Gawaine stared contemptuously, first at Constantine and then at the girl, who dropped her eyes modestly under his stare.

"Demonstration? You mean to fight me, you and this child? Don't be ridiculous!"

King Arthur hid a smile, but Gawaine saw it and jumped to his feet. "You question this? he asked, glaring at the king. Turning to Constantine he demanded, "Where is your gear?" He couldn't stand being laughed at.

"Stacked outside the door," Constantine said. "The guard would not let us bring it into the king's presence."

"Get it. Bring it here. There is room enough between the tables to make good your boast." When Constantine frowned, Gawaine continued, "Wait. I'll go with you. The guard will listen to me."

"He has a net," Gawaine said shaking his head, as he led Constantine back, "a net and a fish spear."

"Are those your weapons?" King Arthur asked, raising his eyebrows.

Constantine smiled, but Gawaine replied for him. "I've seen netmen fight in Rome, though gladiatorial combat in the Coliseum was officially forbidden long before I was there. Net and trident fighters are not to be despised."

Gawaine borrowed a sword from one of the guards and frowned as he swung it back and forth. "The balance is a bit heavy," he remarked.

The man grunted something in reply.

"What was that?" Gawaine demanded, thinking he was being mocked.

"He said it's a fighting sword," King Arthur replied for the guard. "This man is one of the mercenaries who came to me as part of Guenevere's dowry. He's a professional soldier. He and his comrades prefer a heavy sword. They face little armor fighting Saxons, and the shock of blows with a heavy sword like this will break through a wooden Saxon shield even better than Excalibur."

That was too much to be believed, though the bland look on King Arthur's face gave no indication he was teasing Gawaine. However, even I knew the story of Excalibur, the sword that had been given the king by the Lady of the Lake. It lay on the table before him, and he closed his big, battle-scarred hands around the scabbard, a gesture he might make to reassure a child. The sword was precious to him.

Gawaine was not mollified and was in something of a temper even before this. I decided I might have to stop him if he attempted to hurt Constantine or the girl. Unobtrusively I rose and moved over behind the three of them as closely as I could without directly interfering.

"Are you about to join us?" Gawaine snarled, seeing me.

"I hope not," I responded politely, and King Arthur laughed. He shouldn't have. I could cover the distance between Gawaine and me before he could strike, particularly since his sword was so heavy. I would, too, at need. Gawaine might have thought he knew how fast I was from seeing me play hurley. At need, I could move faster. I didn't want Gawaine hurt any more than Constantine or Eliza. Gawaine would have been surprised, though, to learn I was concerned for him, I thought.

Constantine said, "We are ready, my lord," and stepped lightly aside as Gawaine charged. The girl nimbly thrust the handle of her fish spear between Gawaine's legs, and as Gawaine stumbled, Constantine tossed the net over Gawaine's head before he could catch his balance. Gawaine tried to free himself, but the girl jabbed the fish spear toward Gawaine's eyes as Constantine hauled on the net rope. Gawaine fell heavily on his back. To keep him there the girl rapped him smartly on the head, dazing him as he tried to rise, and then poised her spear over Gawaine's chest, ready to skewer him if he moved.

"If we'd been in earnest, my lord, you would be dead now

instead of just knocked about." Constantine said, with a note of regret in his voice.

"He'll be dead yet if he isn't careful," I said, and stepped on the sword Gawaine was attempting to pick up with one hand as he freed himself from the net with the other. "It is over, brother," I added. "You have lost. You won't need this."

We let him recover his wits, stand and peel off the net, shaking his head sheepishly. The king was roaring with laughter, and was joined by most of the others present. I didn't join in, watching this hasty man carefully for fear he'd attempt something stupid.

"I should have known better," Gawaine admitted, and I felt a surge of pride for the man. He was graceful about his defeat when another might have become angry. Immediately I wondered how Sir Lancelot would have reacted under such a defeat.

"I said I had seen much the same thing in Rome," Gawaine continued. "There it was one swordsman against one fighter with net and trident. Often as not that was enough. Two is one too many for any kind of chance at victory."

"There will be hundreds of us following the Saxons to shore," Constantine assured him.

"And as I promised, I will be waiting there to fight beside you. I'm looking forward to it," Gawaine said, and he embraced Constantine.

I turned and left, walked out to my horse where I'd left it standing in the lee of the great wall, and rode back to Caerleon. We were leaving in the morning and I needed rest before the journey started. There was nothing more for me to learn here.

CHAPTER
VIII

e set off from Caerleon for Camelot with five wagons and upward of fifty men. Gawaine and Gaheris rode with us, for Gawaine was still angry with King Arthur for leaving Camelot at all. Gareth was along, talking to his brothers from time to time almost shyly. Morgause had insisted on their recognizing him as a kinsman.

"I can't talk to Arthur," Gawaine complained, still brooding on the king's insistence on leaving the Round Table knights at Camelot. Gawaine seemed to see the king as another younger brother in need of guidance, but stubborn; Gareth was shocked by the frankness of his speech. This was the king!

Gawaine brought his gillies with him, personal servants that his status as a senior knight demanded. Among them were hunters, who never failed to provide meat for the evening meal for all of us; men-at-arms who guarded him as war chief of Clan Merrick; body servants, who seemed mostly to get in the way; and a bard. The bard was to keep his men happy, for Gawaine confessed he was tone-deaf.

"In Rome. when they had boys in to sing at the triclinium feasts, it was all I could do to stay awake." he confided to me.

"I've heard something of those feasts," I said. "I thought they had naked girls to wait on your every whim. How could you fall asleep?"

"Ah. they were slaves." he said. "How can a man practice the art with a slave, knowing the girl has no choice?"

I thought about it. He was right, and it gave me a new perspective on him. I was ashamed I had asked the question.

We stopped at Camelot to load supplies off our wagons into boats for transport to the staging area. Other wagons would take them from there to Bath for distribution. We'd bring with us only what we could carry on our backs, including enough food for six days.

We found the knights of the Round Table in a raking high dudgeon. angry to be left out of the coming battle. Anyone would think they were children who had not been invited to a party.

"I don't see why we have to stay here." loutish Bors said for the tenth time. complaining to any who would listen. He was always the first to complain.

"Where else would you go?" Gawaine asked. lolling against a piling and smirking in the knowledge he would not miss the fun of facing hordes of Saxons intent on cutting off his head.

"Some place where we could share in the action." Bors said, glaring at him. "It's all right for you! You're not made to stay behind!"

"You have a place of honor." I said. finally tired of the talk. "King Arthur is trusting you to defend his queen."

"If you think that is such an honor. I'll trade places with you." Bors grumped. "Just let me have your Roman armor, and no one will know it's not you." He had been admiring my gear openly and. from his remarks. considered me not fit to wear it.

"Why I'd gladly do it if the choice were mine." I said. "It is my firm belief the Saxons will smash King Arthur's defense and then turn on Camelot. You have a chance to survive here."

"Are you afraid?" sneered Blamore. cousin to Bors and another of the contingent that had come with Lancelot from Armorica.

"Of course," I said. "I am not a fellow of the Round Table like you. I can admit to being afraid. Furthermore, I've talked to those who have fought Saxons. The prospect of hundreds of them, maybe thousands, screaming and swinging those foul axes, petrifies me."

"Are you afraid you'll run away?"

"No, I'm more afraid there will be no place to run to," I said. "I may have to stay and fight, despite my inclinations."

Snorting with contempt, they swaggered off, and Gawaine laughed. "Why do you guy them so?"

"They have such an exalted opinion of themselves, it is more than I can resist not to." I said. "I say no more than they already believe. They hold me lightly as a player of boys' games while they engage in men's endeavors. The king was right. They're tourney swaggerers, not warriors. As he said, they've probably never struck a blow in anger."

"Lancelot prides himself on it," Gawaine mused. "He says a cool head is a mark of superiority."

"Well, there's a time for coolness under pressure, perhaps, but I would think the battlefield is no more an appropriate place to exhibit an airy detachment than the hurley field. Perhaps that's what Brastius meant when he said the Picts and Scoti think of hurley as training for war."

Gawaine just shook his head. He didn't want to defend Bors, but he didn't think I was right, either.

Traveling with him was amusing for he told scandalous stories of his past and of Arthur's wars, few of which I believed. Belief wasn't necessary, for his whole effort was directed toward Gareth, whom he felt compelled to tease.

"Lancelot is my hero." Gareth confided in him.

"And mine, too," Gawaine assured him. "Don't let Dylan tell you different."

"Why, he wouldn't do that, would you, Dylan?"

"I know little of the man," I said shortly. I had no intention of gossiping about Sir Lancelot and Queen Guenevere. Let him hear such tales elsewhere. I was happy that Gawaine drew the line at traducing the queen, for I'd have asked him to stop, else. I didn't give a damn about her behavior, whatever it was, but I felt that King Arthur's honor reflected on me, even if he wouldn't see the connection himself.

We went east from Camelot, around the estuary and south behind the hills to Bath. The roads were hard packed after a hot summer and windy autumn, so our men walked dry-shod. Even though we made good time, we found Constantine already waiting there for us.

"Brastius Red-beard ordered the fisherboats to come to the officer with the red plumed helmet," he told me. "I was told to lead you out to the coast as soon as you arrived so they could see you. When the rest of us hide, Brastius wants you to stay visible."

That embarrassed me. I felt like a stallion being exhibited for stud.

"Does Arthur know where the Saxons will come ashore yet?" Gawaine asked.

"He's chosen the place where he hopes they'll land. If they do, they're in for a surprise." He'd say no more except that we could judge for ourselves when we saw the place.

Constantine led me and the men from Caerleon to a small hillock south of the only level land firm enough to beach boats, saying we should hide there until the Saxons had come ashore and passed us by. He pointed out a similar hillock to the north for Gawaine and his followers. Gareth elected to stay with me.

Lady Mal saw us arrive and rode over to meet us. "I'm already working on an epic ballad about this," she said, watching the king ride off with Gawaine, discussing strategy for the coming battle. "I'm calling it 'The Battle of Badon.'"

I but half listened. The king had not spoken to me. "Why Badon?" I muttered.

"It's what the Saxons call Bath. I'll make it sound as if a Saxon composed it so the praise will sound even more honorable, coming from an enemy." It was an interesting idea.

"When the boats come close in, King Arthur will show himself to the Saxons, inviting them ashore. I'll ride beside him," she added proudly.

Seeing me frown, she went on quickly. "If they disembark, we'll retreat to that small hill directly east of the beach," and she pointed to the right. "The Saxons will have to climb it to get at us, and we'll defend the high ground and hold them in combat while the fishermen land and fire their boats under protection from you and Gawaine. You'll form a line between the Saxons and their boats. Then we'll see what happens!"

I thought I could guess: The Saxons would break off the engagement with King Arthur and retreat toward the sea to save their boats. I wondered how the king thought so few of us at the waterline could hold them off. "If I were a Saxon raider, I would leave King Arthur standing on his beach, float on by, capture Camelot, and let the king come to me," I said.

"The king says Saxons do not refuse challenges," Lady Mal said loftily. "He sent word by a captured Saxon sailor to meet us at the mouth of the Severn estuary. The Saxons will come."

I don't know why she found joy in it. For myself, I had a reason of my own to seek out Saxons: Saxon raiders had stolen Samana. I wondered, though, if the fisherfolk who were supposed to follow us would even show up. I had faith there would be some, those with Constantine, the fisherfolk of Lyoness, but I wondered if there would be enough to make any difference.

We slept on our knoll with Gareth's dog beside us, whimpering and growling deep in his throat most of the night. I dozed after the first hour of shushing the animal until I finally fell soundly to sleep. Breakfast was well advanced when I woke up to see Eliza, Constantine's companion, cooking while he talked to Gareth.

"I didn't hear you get up," I said.

Gareth's dog wagged his tail at the sound of my voice but kept his gaze on the cook, hoping for a share of the breakfast.

"If we had been Saxons, you would be dead," Gareth observed, holding out his bowl for more oatmeal porridge.

"The dog would have waked me," I said.

They laughed, and I sat up to look at them more carefully.

"He was talking to you and nudging you all night," Gareth said. "You kept shushing him. Look about you."

I stood and did so. There were dozens of cooking fires all about us, and over on Gawaine's knoll I saw more of the same. "Where are the boats?" I asked.

"This is the first contingent of fisherfolk that came in last night, in advance of the Saxons. Their boats are moored farther up the estuary. They have been walking in for hours." And sure enough, I saw a stream of men coming toward us from the beach.

"The Saxons?" I asked.

"They are still around the point. They will be here before noon."

"Are there more fisherfolk coming?" I asked.

"The water is black with ships. If I were a Saxon, I would consider the possibility of not landing," Constantine said.

"Could that happen?"

Constantine shrugged. "Brastius Red-beard says not. He says the Saxons are bound by fears of what others will think, other Saxons, that is. They have no respect for any other folk."

"Then they will not turn aside," I said. "King Arthur sent them a challenge; they will have accepted it."

Constantine nodded, and turned to talk to Eliza. There seemed to be an understanding between the two of them, young as they were.

After eating, I went to find King Arthur to discover if we could expect any new orders. Lady Mal was with him in high spirits. She smiled and waved as we came close but let the king speak.

"Are you ready?" he asked.

"Am I ready to die?" I replied, rewording his question. "Yes, if necessary, though I find less joy in it than you seem to."

"We will meet victorious in the middle of this field, Lord Dylan," he said smiling. "This is the day we will destroy the Saxon threat to this coast for our lifetimes. It is for that reason I am joyful."

"I will rejoice when that happens," I said without enthusiasm. How could he be so confident?

He laughed and slapped me on the back, as if I were just another comrade in arms, before turning to the next man waiting to speak to him. Lady Mal followed him, her pride in being there evident on her face. It was hard for me not to show my true emotion, but I forbore in order not to cause her pain.

I went back to stand with my people in time to see a line of Saxon boats round the spit of land that marked the mouth of the estuary. They came straight for the beach. I looked carefully around hoping to see that the fires were out and the netmen hidden. Someone hissed at me to take cover.

Instead I put on my plumed helmet and mounted Black Nick, so I was high enough for the fisherfolk to see. I was their rallying point. Looking back up the hill I saw King Arthur on horseback, pacing slowly down to the shore. His mercenaries lined up behind him, on horseback as well, with the London Irregulars lying hidden on the hilltop behind them.

I looked more carefully at the high ground where our main forces were assembled. The trees had been cut all the way up the slope, leaving jagged stumps. The downed timber had been hauled away to either side, with the tops pointing into uncut forest, making an impenetrable barrier every place but straight up the hill where the Irregulars stood. Their line bristled with spears. Suddenly I felt better about everything. Maybe we were ready, after all.

Peering out at the Saxon ships, as their oarsmen brought them to land at a smart pace, I noticed something else. Beyond them, almost close enough to throw stones, was a flotilla of boats, two-man, four-man, and six-man curraghs, all overloaded with extra people, and all headed for the marshy area south of the beach where they could come ashore and make their way up to join us. Gareth was there to receive them. With his height and the morning sun glinting on his hair, he stood like a beacon to guide them in. I saw him point to me, and a line of men trudged forward.

Black Nick was restless. I patted his neck and murmured nonsense to calm him; he could sense battle coming and was as excited as I.

King Arthur rode at the head of his mercenaries, the knights given him as a dowry on his marriage to Guenevere, right down to the water's edge, waiting for the Saxons. Lady Mal rode beside him, carrying her harp. I had hoped the king might try to keep her safe. Neither of them looked safe to me!

When the Saxons came within bow shot, the lead boat pulled up and waited for the others until forty ships were jostling side by side for a quarter of a Roman mile. A score of men or better was rowing each ship, judging from the number of shields hung over the sides. There were more than the six hundred men we'd feared, maybe as many as a thousand!

Arthur held up his hand. "Who leads among you?" he called out in the Saxon tongue.

I could follow it; there was an old Saxon woman who'd worked in Ayres's kitchen, one who gave me extra food when I made the effort to ask in Saxon. I learned fast.

"Who is your leader?" King Arthur called again.

A fat, blond man with a long beard stepped to the bow of his boat and responded, "I am Kesse, chief man of these people."

"I am Arthur, High King of Britain," Arthur said. "I warn you, turn your ships around and leave this island. No one of you who sets foot on this, my land, will live to return to your wives and children."

"I have heard you, Arthur of Britain," Kesse said. "Now hear me. Surrender yourself and your followers before the heat of battle warms the blood of my warriors. I will see you are sold to kind masters."

The men in his boat, and those on either side who heard Kesse's words, roared with laughter and repeated them until they ran the length of the boats and back.

King Arthur waited patiently. Every moment of delay allowed more of the fisherfolk to come. I could see them spreading behind me, all the way to the hill behind the king. From the high ground I occupied, I fancied I could make out netmen on the other side creeping forward from Gawaine's knoll as well.

Kesse raised his hand and the boats surged toward shore, while he stood in the prow of his own vessel to throw a short-handled axe at King Arthur. The king moved his horse disdainfully to one side to avoid the cast, but he also made the beast walk backward toward his line of cavalry.

As the first Saxons gained the beach, King Arthur's cavalry commenced to retreat in what appeared to be fear, but slowly enough so the Saxons came after them in a lumbering run. I thought they would be fair winded by the time they reached the place where the king intended to make a stand, if the retreat were feigned, as I hoped, to draw them onward. I could see the grins on the faces of the mercenaries and realized they thought it was funny, all a farce. It reassured me, but I could hear cries of dismay from our fisherfolk at the sight.

The Saxons passed me, all of them, leaving no boat guard, so greedy for battle were they. I urged Black Nick forward down the hillock toward the line of vessels, out into the center of the open beach, and turned to stand between the Saxons and their escape, should the fight with King Arthur's forces go against them.

I shivered in the cool autumn breeze, but as much from excitement and the anticipation of battle as anything else. Gareth came to stand beside me, wielding a long sword, with Constantine and Eliza behind him. Ayres's sons and the men of Caerleon and Caerwent followed the two of them, along with my squires, looking half frightened to death. I made them bunch up, two or three deep, with spears leveled toward the Saxons' backs. The fisherfolk armed with fish spears and nets ran after them to form a curving line all the way back to the hillock, hemming the Saxons in.

From the other side came Gawaine and Gaheris and their gillies, all on horseback and waving swords, screaming vile Gaelic oaths. They pulled up beside me so a double handful of us were facing the Saxons backed by nearly one hundred foot soldiers and flanked on each side by the fisherfolk. Netmen had followed Gawaine down to the water's edge, completing the trap on that side, a solid barrier to any Saxon retreat.

The Saxons never looked back. They never saw us take our places on the beach. King Arthur and his men kept just out of reach, and the Saxons were so intent on catching him that they had no mind for what might be happening behind them. I turned to see fisherfolk racing boats up to the beach to fling fire pots into the unguarded Saxon vessels; the ships began to burn, one by one, unheeded.

When King Arthur reached the top of his hillock, he turned and the Irregulars rose from their hiding places in the long grass, raising a wooden barrier that separated King Arthur and his knights from the oncoming Saxons. I understood at once. The king had brought the great sectional table from the Knights of the Round Table hall and turned it into a linear fort. Across the length of the table. a hundred paces. writhed the red dragon. its gaping jaws threatening the Saxons. From its nostrils smoke plumed. Could there be someone manning a fire with bellows. blowing that smoke? Whatever it was it gave the dragon the appearance of a real beast. and the Saxon charge halted in sudden fear.

"It not real! It's but painted!" Kesse called out. and threw one of his short-handled axes to stick it into the wood. Moments later there were hundreds of axes quivering in the table shields. and daring warriors running up them like stairs to jump over the barrier. They were caught by spears and pitched backward like hay. I could hear their screams. cut off abruptly as they were hacked to death on the ground.

Some Saxons. faint at heart. perhaps. looked back at the ships and saw the flames break out. "Fire!" one screamed. "The boats are on fire!"

All sailors love their ships above all else. and Saxons are no different. They broke off the engagement and raced back down hill toward the shore. directly at us. King Arthur's dragon wall fell with a crash as the men who had braced it up pushed it over. Across it and after the Saxons came King Arthur and the mercenary horsemen. cutting a swath through the fleeing ranks.

We waited for the Saxons. knowing the longer they ran the less we had to fear from them. You could see the strain of extended exertion twist their red faces. Behind the retreating enemy came the London Irregulars with their ironbound flails and hooked pikes. and farmers from the Mendip hills carrying scythes and pitchforks. as dangerously useful in their hands as any conventional weapon. I could see that the Saxons were nearly out of breath. panicked by the events. Even so. if they had formed a fighting ring. they might still have prevailed. They did not.

I turned to watch the burning ships for an instant: the heat from the fires was becoming uncomfortable. To my surprise. I saw a young man screaming. tied to the mast of Kesse's boat.

Seeing me turn, he called for help, "Dylan!"

Lud, it was Borre! I thrust my pilum into the ground and turned Black Nick toward the boat, leaping from his back over the rail. I slashed the bonds that tied his wrists, and he gave me a fierce embrace before saying, "Give me your sword. I'll free myself. Samana's in the cabin!" I rushed down the slanting deck and looked in. I saw a woman, coughing harshly in the smoke and struggling to free herself from the thongs that bound her to a large chest's handle. Slashing her bonds with my belt knife I freed her, and she looked up in sudden hope. My heart leapt in joy. It was Samana! There were scars on her face that had not been there before, and several of her teeth were broken, but she smiled with her whole face, and that had not changed. Ah, Samana!

"Come" I said urgently and lifted her.

"Dylan!" she cried, hugging me tightly. As Borre joined us, she told him, "Save the chest."

He lifted it and threw it over the side where the flames could not reach it. Together, then, we stumbled up the sloping deck toward the prow where we could lower Samana into the water without fear of drowning and jumped over the rail. My tunic was afire and I felt the bite of flame along my legs.

Black Nick came splashing to reach me, and I caught his mane and pulled myself onto his back. Leaving Samana to Borre's care, I turned him to race toward the shore, for the Saxons were nearly upon us. Grinning idiotically in joy I loosed my pilum, the Roman spear Ayres had given me, from the sand and buried it in the chest of the first Saxon to reach our lines, pulling it free and leading a charge into the van. Samana!

Gawaine's men formed a wedge behind me that shattered the Saxon retreat. Behind them my spear men took a terrible toll of those who escaped Gawaine's men, and the fisherfolk surged around them waiting to pounce on the survivors. For me it was like playing hurley. Black Nick and I danced back and forth, feinting and stabbing at the enemy, wreaking havoc, but untouched. I think I was laughing.

I lost my spear as a man fell, twisting it out of my hand. Borre had the Roman sword, so I dismounted to recover it. Then I saw Kesse. My joy in finding Samana turned to rage! This was the man who had stolen her and evidently beaten her for years! I called his name and he heard me. Glancing back I saw Samana huddled on the ground with Borre, Gareth, Constantine, and Eliza standing guard in front of her, but she was watching me. Good!

Kesse nimbly dodged a thrown net and we met with a crash. He was a huge man close up and surprisingly active. I speared his arm with a jab from my pilum, and he dropped his axe. Ah! I'd hurt him! This was the man who had broken Samana's teeth!

Again the surge of rage, the old rage I feared, came upon me, turning me into the animal Lady Miriam had cursed. I dropped my spear and seized his hand that clutched a sax knife as long as my forearm before he cut me in two. With my free hand I grasped his throat, squeezing to tear out his windpipe if I could. Slowly, as we strained against each other for control of the blade, I twisted his wrist and forced the point into his chest. All the time the thought of his beating Samana was with me. I could not have lost to him.

Though we struggled together in the middle of a great battle, there was nothing in it for me but the face of this one man. He was bearded with sweeping mustaches, and his pale blue eyes bulged from exertion and the effect of my choking him. He had a missing tooth, I noticed, as he panted, slobbering slightly. Sweat plastered his light hair to his head, and he seemed tired, perhaps from the running up and down hill. He was out of condition. Then he was dead. The light went out of his eyes; they glazed over as the blood from his heart ran into his lungs and came out his mouth, covering my hand. He went slack, and I dropped him at my feet.

I was suddenly aware of the noise of battle, the yells of anger and screams of pain. King Arthur's men had trapped the remaining Saxons against our line. Black Nick stood between me and the battle, lashing out with his hooves at anyone who came near, friend or foe alike. I picked up my Roman pilum, mounted and wheeled Black Nick around to see where I was most needed but saw, suddenly, it was over. There was no more resistance. The Irregulars were slashing the throats of the wounded and robbing their bodies. My squires and the townsfolk dashed out from behind us to take the golden arm bands, torques, rings, and brooches from the men we had killed.

I rode back to join Borre and Samana. Some of the townsfolk from Caerleon brought Saxon gold looted from the dead to place at Black Nick's feet. Seeing that, many of the others did the same. Even Constantine's fisherfolk began to bring us gifts from the battlefield. Gareth spread his plaid on the ground in front of us to keep the treasure from getting lost in the sand; the pile grew.

"What will you do with all this?" Constantine asked as one of his fisherfolk deposited several items.

"I don't know. Give it to Lady Mal to hold, perhaps," I said. "She can always turn such toys into useful things. Or you can take it if you want. Your people are bringing much of it."

"Ah, Dylan!" Samana said, coming to me. I dismounted and she hugged me, stroking my face and looking into my eyes. "Gareth tells me Arthur has not claimed you. Has it been very hard?"

"No," I said. How could I tell her after the suffering she had undergone these years past?

We clustered around her, Borre, Constantine, and I, while Gareth and Eliza watched. We stood so when King Arthur came by, looking for wounded men, and saw the growing pile of loot. He was amused. I went to meet him and, taking me by the forearms, he looked into my eyes and laughed.

"I promised you, Dylan, that we would meet after the battle," he said, "but I did not know you would be sitting on all the spoils."

"Certainly not all of them," I said, "though the most precious thing did fall to my hands." And I pointed to where Samana stood. King Arthur walked over to her slowly in disbelief. When Samana saw him, she made a gesture of protest and touched her hair. It had grayed and was cut so short that I might not have known her, except for her magnificent eyes and the warmth of her smile, in which there had been no change. Her broken teeth weren't even noticeable when you looked into her eyes.

I saw the king give a start of recognition. Then he pulled her into his embrace, crying and unable to speak at all. He picked Samana up and wandered slowly over to a sheltering tree before he stopped to gaze in wonder at her once more. I turned away again to meet Borre's eyes. This was none of my affair, but I was happy just the same.

When King Arthur came back to us, Samana introduced him to Borre, his son. I saw the king embrace him and marveled how much alike they looked, both men of middle height, golden-haired, blue-eyed, and strongly made. The king was a little heavier, as befitted his years. Samana spoke quietly to King Arthur and glanced at me. The king shook his head, and I saw his lips form the words, "I cannot!" I knew what he meant, worse luck! It was then that I gave up hoping for some formal declaration from my father. Now I knew it would never come. He knew but would not act.

He came up to me with Samana clinging to his arm. "Will you watch over this lady for me, Dylan?" he asked. "You were right in saying she was the most precious treasure to fall into our hands."

"Of course, Your Majesty," I said formally, no warmth in my voice. "She is precious to me, too."

"Of course," he echoed, but he grinned to see the pile of loot that was heaped on Gareth's plaid. If I could not have his blessing, I didn't want anything that came from his hand. "Do you need this?" I asked, pointing at the sparkling pile. "It is not rightly mine."

"The fisherfolk would take it amiss if you did not accept their gifts," King Arthur said. "And anyway. much of it has come to you through your own folk. Doubtless you will be expected to redistribute it later." As he spoke two of my young squires bustled up with more armloads of trinkets and dumped them, dashing off for more.

King Arthur laughed and moved off to seek out more of his wounded. He would be back. Nithe had told me that the mark of a great leader was success at obtaining loot and generosity in giving it to his followers. There were no great rich leaders, she had said, only great poor ones. That must have been what the king meant. Just as well. If the king didn't want it, neither did I. Gold had no hold on me.

I stood before the Saxons' burned-out hulks with Constantine, who had just brought in more booty. We watched while men waded in the waist-deep water, swarming over the charred wrecks, stripping them of their iron fittings. "Would it not have been wiser to keep the boats?" I asked. "They seem more seaworthy than our frail craft." Indeed a few had survived, and I hoped they might be saved. They were beautiful.

"They are not, though." he responded. "These clinker-built boats are forever parting a seam in rough weather, and the men in them spend more time bailing to keep afloat than rowing. In comparison, the oak bark-tanned ox hides we use for our curraghs are nearly waterproof, after being soaked in sheep wool fat and sewn together with linen thread. We rarely have to bail at all. Those Saxon boats are heavy for the amount of cargo they carry, too, and they need a huge crew to keep moving when the wind dies or against a current. We had ample time to study them these past few weeks and soon learned not to fear them. We can move faster with our small crews in our light boats than they can, and we are ever so much more maneuverable. We considered fighting them at sea, and not letting them land at all, and would have if we'd had any kind of arms."

"It still seems a waste. King Arthur could have used them to carry troops, if nothing else," I grumbled.

"Where to? Would he want to fight in Ireland or Armorica? Maybe take the battle to the Saxon shore on the continent? I assure you as a sailor, he would find many more Saxons there than we have seen here. Would you want Saxon raiders to find a captured Saxon boat in your village? Can you imagine what would happen to the inhabitants?"

"If it could be worse than what usually happens, it would be very bad indeed," I said, but I understood what he meant. "Where are you finding all this stuff?" I asked to stop the harangue.

"Fisherfolk are giving it to us to bring to the pile," he said.

"Why do the Saxons wear so much when they fight?"

"They say a man wears his wealth into battle so the man who defeats him will be rich," Constantine said. "They are used to fighting other Saxons, and they all do that. None of them thinks he will lose, of course, and all dream of coming home laden with treasure."

"They would have had poor pickings from us, had they won," I said.

"They would have taken it from the land instead," he retorted grimly.

"If they come again, they will find Saxon riches in every fishing village," I said. "They can't be bringing everything here. Wouldn't that go hard with the villagers if the Saxons recognize some known piece of jewelry?"

"No, their leaders give away riches in the same manner. The things the warriors wear came to them as gifts. It would add to the value of such a piece to be recaptured, and at its recovery, the person who held it might even be given mercy."

"Good. Then you'll take back half of this with you. There's enough for both of us to gain reputations as openhanded leaders."

Constantine laughed, but he nodded. I guessed he hoped I'd

say that. His father, Duke Cador, would be happy to have his son so recognized, I was sure. I remembered his pride in the boy when we were all young.

King Arthur came up beside us, looking both happy and sad. He hadn't been able to stay away from Samana for long. "Samana insists on going back to Lyoness," he said. "Will you take her for me?"

"Of course," Constantine said. "I will gain much honor from it among my people. And she is my only sister; I would do it for her own sake."

"You might entrust some of that treasure to her to ease her return," the king suggested to me.

"She can have it all if she but asks," I replied.

"Good," the king said smiling. Clapping me on the arm, he went back to his inspection of the battlefield, stopping to speak to wounded men. Samana walked with him, watching him. I could barely look at her, so hungry were her eyes.

I need not have worried about Lady Mal. She was out among the fighters, collecting the names of those who had distinguished themselves, and by what deeds. When she came into our camp on the knoll, where we had moved the loot to protect it from the tide, she said she had enough material for an epic to rival the best lays of the Gaelic bards. She barely glanced at the pile, laughing when Gareth grumbled about the fact that his plaid was in use and he would sleep cold.

"Samana wants to return to Lyoness," I said.

Borre frowned. "I hoped the king would keep her by him," he muttered.

"He is with her now, but he could not well take her to Camelot, with the queen there."

Borre understood but was still unhappy.

"Look at it this way," I said finally, "she will be in her own home, which she must have sadly missed. You will accompany her as escort, won't you?"

The thought brightened him, and there were no more complaints from him on the treatment of his mother. I mentioned King Arthur's request that we give Samana treasure to win the support of the people of Lyoness once more.

"Why doesn't he use his own?" Gareth asked indistinctly. He had found food somewhere.

"He'll give that away to his mercenaries and the men of the Mendip Hills," I said. "I doubt he'll end up with anything himself, past a keepsake or two."

"Then we will do the same," Gareth said. "Lady Mal can take a ring that will glitter when she plays the harp, and I'll take a gold chain, one I can tear a link from when I am broke and hungry in a strange town. Maybe I'll take several, not to run risks," he added.

I laughed. I had already chosen my piece, a golden bracelet set with amber of the same shade as the necklace I had given Viki. I could wear it on my wrist for now, and fit it to hers by squeezing it together a bit. If I ever saw her again, that is.

Samana made plans for herself. She prevailed on King Arthur to save one of the dragon boats from the burning, when those remaining were about to be torched, telling him she had a use for it. He nodded gravely, and she left to go to where the Saxon prisoners had been taken, selecting twenty men from all of those who were willing to go with her. These were young fighting men, commoners for whom no ransom could be expected.

When she sought out King Arthur again, she told him, "I do not choose to wait upon an escort to Lyoness, though it wrenches my heart to part so soon from my boys." She looked at Borre, Constantine, and me with brimming eyes. "It's just that I have been living among strangers for too long, spending half my life on boats. I cannot stand further delay. I want to go home!"

"I can refuse you nothing," the king said sadly.

"Then I ask as a boon that you let me have the boat I have saved and release the prisoners I have chosen to take me back in it."

King Arthur frowned, saying "I do not like the idea of a boatload of Saxons going free, perhaps to raid helpless villages. I would fear for your safety with such as these. Besides, I would have you come with me."

"We've already spoken of that," she said gently. "Our time together is over. You have a new queen, one of whom it is said no fairer woman has ever graced this land. What has she done that you would put her aside? Or would you mean to set me apart in some quiet country house to visit when you can spare the time from your true duties?"

The king merely looked troubled. Sir Torre had told me he could rarely find words when he was distressed.

She sighed. "I will swear the men to my service and take them with me to Lyoness, to answer your first point of objection. They will be a strength to you, not a source of danger."

"Will they serve you faithfully?"

"Why not? I was wife to Kesse, their chief."

The king could not refuse her the boon, and wanted to give her much of the treasure that fell to his lot besides, making her rich enough to afford retainers. She refused, saying that in the chest saved from the fire on Kesse's boat there was enough treasure to keep her, and that it was hers by right. Gareth found it underwater and brought it to shore. She opened the lid and let us gaze upon it. It held the scourings of half of the continent, amber from the Baltic, gold from Ireland, and enameled ware from churches sacked on many lands. For each of us she selected rings that we might remember her, as if we needed that! Mine was an amber thumb ring to match the bracelet I'd taken for Viki and wore on my own wrist.

194

Samana left on the outgoing tide, and her good-bye to each of us was private and touching. I do not know what she said to the others, but later Borre told me she made him promise to visit her in Lyoness. She would not let Borre go back with her, saying Constantine was now Cador's heir, and she wanted no trouble over it.

With me it was something else. "Stay by Arthur," she said. "I fear for him. He will need men who are loyal to him, as I think you are?" This last was posed as a question.

"I love him," I said, smiling. It was true, I thought. He had accepted me as an ally, if not a son, and I still hoped for his blessing. But I also hated him. Which feeling was the strongest, I did not know.

She nodded. It was enough.

As I watched her boat leave, her Saxon rowers in powerful unison, I reflected on how much I hated to say good-bye. Still, I'd found Samana again; maybe Viki would come back into my life.

CHAPTER
IX

t the last moment King Arthur decided to save three unburned Saxon longboats to transport the wounded back to Camelot, rowed by captured Saxons and guarded by Arthur's grim mercenaries. He wintered in Camelot for only the second time since his wedding to Guenevere, for he would not leave his stronghold until the Saxons had sued for peace and ransomed their warriors. The queen fretted but held her tongue; there had been Jutes among the raiders, her kinsmen.

One of the boats was sent to Pelleas, the king's brother, as thanks for help from the Picts at the fight at Badon. Many of the fisherfolk acknowledged Pelleas their king. The other two went off with the ransomed captives in the spring, still in chains and cursing bitterly as they rowed away. I thought it a waste of good iron, but Sir Torre said the ignominy of arriving in Saxony shackled would go far in reducing the possibility of raids in the future. Who would follow leaders who brought back chains instead of gold?

The exchange of prisoners for treasure and promises came the week before Pentecost and gave a new meaning to the celebration of the day. It became a victory feast. It was my sixth feast of Pentecost since coming to Camelot. I was seventeen.

I sat with Gareth, Borre, and Brastius Red-beard at the long trestle table fronting on King Arthur's raised one. I had come to know Brastius on the trip from Bath to Camelot, and found in him a good companion, though old enough to be my grandfather. He'd served Uther Pendragon, King Arthur's father, as a general and compared King Arthur's tactics against the Saxons favorably with those of Julius Caesar's.

"Caesar was a fool," he said, drinking deeply from his beaker of ale. He was continuing an argument we'd started on the road back. "He invaded Britain without proper reconnaissance and had no safe harbor for his boats. At that, he left them without guards, just as the Saxons did. His entire fleet was crippled by channel storms and high tides, and what was left was burned by Britons. Even after that disaster, he did the same thing the following year, with the same result. He should have been court-martialed and executed for incompetence! Imagine! He had hundreds of boats and thousands of trained soldiers but accomplished less than Arthur with his handful of mercenaries and undisciplined crowds of peasant farmers and fishermen."

"Duke Cador always spoke of Caesar as the greatest of military leaders," I said, remembering stories from my boyhood.

"Caesar didn't depend on a bard to tell his story; he told it himself. He lied. Bards don't lie," was his response.

King Arthur held up his arm for silence and we heard Lady Mal's new ballad for the first time. She called it "The Battle of Badon" and sang it while we were waiting for the food. Even the serving wenches quieted in their comings and goings, the better to hear the tale. I recognized tunes from my childhood from time to time: when she sang of the sea black with fisherboats she used a familiar Pictish chanty to carry the words. I guessed she did the same when she sang of King Arthur or the Saxons, making it sound familiar to those who heard themselves praised.

As she'd planned, she composed the ballad as a praise song sung by a Saxon captive, to emphasize the enormity of the occasion: forty longboats defeated by Arthur the King. Even though I had been there, I heard it as if it were new to me, so artfully was it done. I didn't even connect myself to the deeds of Baron Dylan, rescuing Samana, child sweetheart of King Arthur, from the flaming boat, or killing Kesse, the Saxon chief, in single combat, until I saw everyone looking at me. It was embarrassing!

I didn't miss the cold stares bent on me by the queen or by Sir Lancelot, the man Lady Mal claimed gossip held to be her lover. I gathered they would have been better pleased if I'd let Samana burn.

The food and drink were in great bounty, with steam rising in the chill room from the joints of meat that had been set before us. The smell was so delicious it drove everything else from my mind but hunger. Brastius warned Gareth not to touch anything but the ale until permission was granted by the king. King Arthur still insisted upon opening the feast of Pentecost only after something noteworthy had happened, as an omen of approval by the gods. Brastius said something always occurred, nodding sagely as he spoke.

I caught Gareth's eye and he winked at me, remembering the last feast of Pentecost when he'd come in his pitiful disguise, but he shook his head and grumbled, "I'm hungry." He was always hungry.

Sir Kay stood behind King Arthur's chair and glared our way from time to time as we waited. He could not accept the fact that Gareth, his scullery lad, was welcome at the king's feast. Gareth had fought well at Badon, though, and had earned his place.

True to Brastius's prediction, a young woman came into the room and was beckoned by Sir Kay up to King Arthur's seat.

"A boon, Sire," she called. Her sharp voice cut through the buzz of talk and clank of glasses. The knights stopped drinking and boasting to one another long enough to stare at her, nudging one another. She was both young and pretty, and preened herself under their eyes.

"Name it," King Arthur replied expectantly. This should be the unusual event that would allow him to declare the feast underway. He was getting hungry, too, I expected.

"My name is Lady Lynet," she announced. "My sister is held prisoner in her castle by the Red Knight. I beg a champion to rescue her."

"Who are your people?" King Arthur asked.

"We come from a family whose quality is such I cannot name it. If my sister were identified as being under the power of this evil man, its honor would be sullied forever."

"I don't see why," King Arthur said. "How could it be held responsible under the circumstances, if the Red Knight's forces are superior?"

"Nevertheless, it is our wish to remain unknown," the woman insisted.

"Here's your chance," Brastius said to Gareth. "Offer to go with her. Quests like this don't come along every day."

Oh, no, I thought. That damned thing again! I'd hoped Gareth had forgotten his dream of being knighted by Sir Lancelot and made a fellow of the Round Table. Gareth must have confided in Brastius when I was busy elsewhere.

"Before I've eaten?" Gareth asked in disbelief.

"No one will eat until someone takes her quest. It might as well be you, if you are serious about being knighted, that is," Brastius said sharply.

King Arthur looked around the table, then addressed the woman, "I cannot ask anyone to grant this woman's petition for a champion in the absence of a name. Who would risk helping someone against whose family a blood feud might exist? He would suffer kin wreck!"

"I need your mightiest knight," she wailed. "My sister cannot long survive under this foul tyrant!"

"If I promise to go, can I eat first?" Gareth asked Brastius.

"No, but you can stop at the kitchen on your way out," suggested Brastius.

Gareth rose, saying, "Send me, Sire. You promised me a second boon on this day. This may be the quest ordained for me to complete the test for knighthood, my third boon."

"It is yours," King Arthur announced, relieved, and lifted his glass in a toast to Gareth, signaling the beginning of the feast.

Gareth returned the toast, draining his flagon of ale and relieved a waiter of a meat pasty intended to serve six men as he walked out.

"You're sending an unfledged squire to fight the Red Knight?" the woman asked King Arthur in disbelief. "Do you mean to insult me, or is it just that you hate the young man?"

Sir Kay took her arm and led her out, still protesting, with a look of satisfaction on his face. He had started the victory feast on time and perhaps rid himself of a deep embarrassment, the witness who saw him with his head stuffed into a pot of soup. He probably thought Gareth would be overmatched in confronting a real knight. Sir Kay was a happy man. I might have worried about the outcome, myself, had I not known Gareth.

"How long do you think he will be gone?" I asked Brastius.

"It won't be long," Brastius assured me. "Kay arranges for quests from near Camelot to be presented on feast days. It's easier for him to manage. He probably had two or three others lined up, should this one have failed."

I saw the king lean over and speak privately with Sir Lancelot, who nodded and left the table.

"Where is he going?" I asked.

"He'll follow the boy and be his witness. No one would accept

Gareth's unsupported word until he's achieved knighthood," Brastius replied.

I was busy in Caerleon for a few days after King Arthur's victory feast. Lady Mal insisted that we must have one of our own to honor the men of the barony who had distinguished themselves, and to console the families of those who had fallen in battle. Fortunately there were few of those, but six in all. I had brought the families of two fallen men under my care in the manor house. They had no larger kin group to support them, and I could not let them starve.

Lady Mal took over the treasure I'd been given and locked it away. "Some of this can go to Hugh in exchange for iron tools. We need plows, hoes, and scythes. We need iron-rimmed wheels for wagons, too."

"Do you plan on doing that much farming?" I asked in surprise. I didn't think about owning land in that way.

"No, but the folk here need these things. They look to you to provide it. They'll do the farming, and supply your table, but they need tools."

That made sense. "I want to give some of the spoils to those who fought with us," I said. "A Saxon ring or bracelet awarded in front of the whole town will mean more than if I do it privately." Together we selected appropriate items and she set them aside to hand me at the feast when she called out for those who were to be honored to come forward.

At our celebration in Caerleon, Lady Mal sang the ballad again, weaving in the names of my folk, and I gave her a golden bracelet in thanks as I had seen King Arthur do. The feast was a success and left the folk proud and joyous; the Saxon terror was gone for a time, and they had had a hand in it. The one thing I would have wanted to make the occasion perfect was to have Viki sitting by my side. I thought perhaps it was time to seek her out. I did not have my father's blessing, but had made a name for myself that was not despised.

I rode back to Camelot with Borre and Lady Mal in her bard clothing. She'd heard that Gareth had returned, riding a fine horse, big enough to carry his weight, and with two maidens in tow on handsome palfreys, according to Brastius, who had seen them arrive. "Both of the women fawned on him, and he appeared relieved to deliver them to Kay," he'd told her. I had to see that.

Borre knew where to find him, eating in one of the small rooms near the kitchen where food could be found by those who missed regular meals for some good reason. In Gareth's case, however, it was just that he became hungry more often than ordinary men.

"Did you rescue the captive damsel?" Borre asked him. "Lady Mal needs to know all the details so she can write a song about it."

"Talk to Sir Lancelot," Gareth said. "I'm not supposed to brag."

"You can tell me if she was pretty?"

"Yes. She said her name was Lady Lyoness. Does that sound familiar?" Gareth asked.

"Like she made it up," Borre agreed. "Who is she, then?"

"She's a widow," Gareth answered, "Her husband was rich. He owned a number of fishing boats, she said. The Red Knight wanted to marry her and take over her husband's business. After our fight he told me he had no intention of harming her. He claimed the husband had given him the right to marry his widow if anything befell him."

"And it did?" Borre asked.

"The husband got drunk and fell off one of his own fishing boats, according to the widow," Gareth related. "She was tired of being married to an old man, anyway. She likes me," he added smugly, and took us in search of Sir Lancelot to remind him of his promise of knighthood on completion of the quest.

Lady Mal was not satisfied. She always liked extra details,

claiming that's what made her ballads special. "Why didn't his men pull her husband out of the water?" she asked.

"Oh. fisherfolk never try to save anyone from drowning." Borre explained when Gareth could not. "After Lir. the sea god. has claimed a man. it's bad luck to try to go against his wishes."

As we were talking. Sir Lancelot came into the small eating salon and congratulated Gareth again on his defeat of the Red Knight. He spoke to Borre and Lady Mal but ignored me. "You've earned your spurs. and I will tell the king so." Sir Lancelot said. "Usually a man is knighted with a special sword. The one you took from the Red Knight would do."

Gareth was still wearing it and handed it over for inspection.

"Very well." Sir Lancelot said. giving it back. "Come to the Round Table room just after morning mass when you've completed your all-night vigil. I'll dub you in the king's presence and request fellowship in the Round Table for you at the same time. You'll have to be prepared to give your parentage. though." Gareth nodded. troubled.

"What can I say?" he asked us after Sir Lancelot had left.

"Say you're a son of Queen Morgause." Borre told him. "You already claimed that at the hurley game with the Picts. We'll ask Gawaine to come. He'll vouch for you."

Lady Mal followed after Sir Lancelot to hear his account to King Arthur of Gareth's quest. Sir Lancelot had followed Gareth and was his witness as Brastius had predicted. Bards are privileged. Neither the king nor Sir Lancelot would have even considered sending her away.

Later Gareth and I sought out Brastius Red-beard for information about how to do a vigil. for none of us had any experience with Christianity.

"You must sit up all night praying. with your sword laid on the altar so it can be blessed." he said.

203

"I can't do that. I don't know how to pray. Why, I'm not even baptized," Gareth admitted.

"Do you want to be?"

"Is it part of being a knight?"

"There might be some question about it in Sir Lancelot's mind, but I don't think it's a rule. I'm sure King Pellinore is not a Christian, and he's King Arthur's senior knight."

"What should I do, then?"

"It should be enough just to go through the vigil. It's the form that's important. Just stay awake, fast, and think serious thoughts."

Lady Mal and Borre joined Gareth and me at the church to share the vigil. The difficult part for Gareth was the fasting requirement. "How can I think serious thoughts when my stomach is growling?" he asked plaintively, sloshing the wineskin pensively when Bishop Ninian, the queen's priest, came and found us sitting before his church altar. He was scandalized, seizing the drink from Gareth and stomping off.

"What is this?" Lady Mal grumbled. "We can't eat and what's worse, it appears that we can't drink either, just because we have to be here with you."

"I was supposed to ask family to sit with me," Gareth said, looking worried. "You, Borre, and Dylan are the only family I have."

"Ah, I know that. Do you think it would be permitted for me to sing?"

"I permit it," I said, "sing."

Lady Mal sang a ballad she had just composed. It told the story of Gareth's quest, the details of which she had from Sir Lancelot's report to the king. I listened closely, for I had not heard a full account of it. There were several surprising bits, but I did not comment on them for one is not allowed to interrupt a bard, not even when she's your big sister.

I was amused to learn that the sharp-tongued damsel had

scolded Gareth steadily throughout the entire quest. When Lady Mal had finished I laughed, to Gareth's discomfiture. "Why did you ever accept the quest in the first place?" I asked. "It should have been obvious the wench was disagreeable."

"She's not a wench," he objected. "Her name is Lady Lynet. Besides, if I didn't go, no one else would."

"Why do you think that?"

"You saw her at the feast when she came before King Arthur to demand a champion, complaining all the time she craved a boon. Did you want to go with her?" he demanded.

"No, nor would I have stayed with her if she cursed me," I replied. I thought she was handsome enough in her person, but did not seem to have easy ways.

"I was starving," Gareth admitted, "waiting for King Arthur to have the food served. I didn't mind doing something like rescuing a maiden if I could just eat. It worked out, though, as Brastius said it would. I get to be a knight of the Round Table!"

I shook my head. Gareth had been thinking of his belly, not his fame! He had the wrong attitude for a knight. "Why did Lady Lynet vilify you when you were out trying to rescue her sister?" Borre asked, for Lady Mal had sung of all the opprobrious names she had called Gareth on the way.

"At first she was unhappy because I made her wait until after I finished the pasty before I'd start, and later she said she had been shamed by King Arthur because I wasn't even a knight yet," Gareth said. "She said the king held her and her sister in light esteem."

"She must have realized you could fight after you started knocking those bandits about," Borre said. That had been part of the ballad. "Was she just stupid?"

"She said later she was afraid I'd get hurt," Gareth replied.

"What took you so long to return?" Lady Mal asked slyly.

Before he could answer, Brastius Red-beard came into the church, looking for us. He had Sir Lancelot with him. "There you are. thank Lud." he said. "You know that lady you brought back with you, the one with the big-mouthed sister?" he asked Gareth.

"Yes?" Gareth responded, beginning to look alarmed.

"She's with the bishop, saying you took her maidenhead," Brastius said. "You know how that will upset Arthur!"

"I never did! She gave it to me," Gareth blurted. "I would never force any maiden! Would I, Dylan?" he asked, appealing to me.

"No, you wouldn't," I assured Gareth. "Truly," I said to Brastius. "It is not in him to do that kind of violence." At least I knew now what had delayed him, I thought, as I glanced at Borre. Borre's response was a casually lifted eyebrow and a wink.

"I thought not," Brastius said, nodding. "What the bishop will think is something else. I would advise you to find somewhere else to spend some time. Or maybe you'd like being married?"

"I'm too young," Gareth said aghast. "Why I'm not even a knight yet!"

"That, at least, can be remedied," Sir Lancelot said. "Kneel."

Gareth looked to me for reassurance, and I nodded slightly. I thought Sir Lancelot meant him no harm. As Gareth knelt before him, Sir Lancelot took the sword from where it lay on the altar and tapped Gareth on either shoulder, saying, "Rise, Sir Gareth!"

A huge grin lit up the boy's face as he took his sword back. "Sir Gareth!" he cried out, but then asked, "What about the Round Table?"

"Do you really want to see the king just now? Under Roman law, as a dubbed knight, you are allowed to marry," Brastius said, bringing us back to the matter at hand. "What is your wish?"

"What would King Arthur say?" Gareth asked desperately, looking for an excuse to get out of contracting marriage.

"King Arthur was crowned at fifteen," Borre observed. "That is even harder than being married. He won't listen to you."

"Very well," I said to Brastius, thinking the teasing had gone on long enough. "Tell the bishop that Gareth will be free to discuss the prospect of marriage in detail when we return, but he must first ask his father's blessing."

"We're going to Mona to see Pelleas?" Gareth asked breathlessly.

"Well, I was thinking more about seeing Viki," I said, "but I suppose Pelleas will be there. If Brastius will keep the bishop talking for half an hour, we'll be away. And, Brastius, do me a favor. Inform Sir Torre, will you? Otherwise, he'll raise a hue and cry after me."

It took us longer than I'd hoped to saddle our horses and lead them out: we barely made it in time. As the four of us rode over the drawbridge and looked up to the top of the curtain wall, we saw Arthur standing in the dusk with the bishop looking out over the fields toward the river. Someone called, but we pretended not to hear and galloped off down the road that led west toward Caerleon.

"I wonder what the king wanted?" Borre mused as we rode off at a good clip.

I thought I knew. He wanted Gareth to stay and face the bishop. I was riding Black Nick. Gareth bestrode his new charger, and Lady Mal had her palfrey. Borre had one of Sir Torre's horses. By habit we carried swords, spears, and light shields for armament, except for Lady Mal, who was burdened only with her harp and belt knife. We needed nothing more to repel bandits, but we needed food. Lady Mal raided her inn's larders, announcing that she was coming with us.

"You can't do that!" I protested.

"No adventure, no food," she replied coldly.

It wasn't a real choice. She came with us, but may have regretted it once or twice. It was early summer, but even our heavy cloaks were none too warm at night. Thankfully, the weather was superb overall, with the air light and dry, good haying weather if it held.

I thought, with no regret at all, that I'd miss the haying this year at Caerleon. Sweaty work, haying.

It is less than two hundred miles from Caerleon north to Chester, and we did it in a week, pressing along as fast as we could without overtiring our horses. We found hospitality along the road at farms and villages as a matter of course. Respectable travelers are always welcome, particularly armed ones; they discourage thieves. Lady Mal paid for our welcome by singing for our hosts at each stop, a joy to her and an unexpected pleasure for her listeners. There were few bards in King Arthur's Britain.

Few folk live in Chester. The fort walls were dismantled ages ago by the local farmers in search of quarried building stone, but the barracks and storage buildings had been despoiled only of their tile roofs. A market was held on Saturdays in the town plaza, a local farmer told me, but only a few craftsmen still inhabited the town itself. The most notable was a blacksmith. We had him check our horses' shoes and replace a few for a corresponding number of King Arthur's copper pennies. Other coinage was not to be found away from the eastern and southern port cities.

"You want to get to Mona, you say? Best leave your horses here and take a boat," the smith told us.

"No. I'll swim there before I take a boat that far," I said grimly.

He laughed. "I think you'll change your mind when you see how rough the water can be between the mainland and the island, but it's true, you can get a lot closer than this by land. The trouble will be in finding a boat when you want to cross."

I thanked him for the warning, but we continued on another day heading westerly along the coast until we could make out Mona. A second day's travel showed the nature of the difficulty: most of the coastline across from Mona was high cliffs. Reaching the water's edge looked difficult. Fortunately local shepherds offered to watch our horses and took us down secret paths from which they signaled fisher boats. The blacksmith had been wrong. Fisherman were always on the lookout for passengers. It was one of their few sources of coin.

Nothing had changed for me in regard to the sea. I was violently sick immediately, and Gareth had to carry me, almost helpless, to shore an hour later when we made land. We disembarked on a beach where a considerable village of fisherman lived. From there guides took us on a well-trod trail up to the high ground inland, ending at the palisaded manor of Pelleas. The compound's oaken posts were ten feet high and enclosed an area of several acres covered with low, thatched, adjoining buildings. There were swarms of people about, and as soon as we were sighted, we found ourselves surrounded.

"A bard!" one of the children cried on seeing Lady Mal's covered harp hanging on a strap from her shoulder. "A bard has come!"

"I am Dynadan, bard to Arthur the king, and these are my companions, Dylan the Orphan, Borre, son of Arthur, and the big one is Gareth the Geen," she said. The announcement of my name caused a commotion among the young men looking on.

"Dylan, the four-goal player?" one of them asked.

"The only one in Britain," Lady Mal responded for me. I could not have said that.

There was shouting in Pictish, and people boiled from a number of doors. I had eyes only for Viki, who flew to my arms like a stooping hawk.

"I've come for you," I murmured into the mass of curls crushed against my chest.

"Ah, that," she said, pulling away and looking up at me with a troubled gaze. "I'm married, Dylan." She released me and stepped back to turn and hug Lady Mal in greeting.

Too late! The shock I felt must have showed on my face, for I saw the look of dismay on hers as she tore herself away from me. I moved blindly to one side to find myself looking into the eyes of Lamerok; I understood without explanation what had happened. Of course! Lamerok was the son of Pellinore, high king of the northern Picts, as Viki was the daughter of Pelleas, high king of the southern Picts. It was a dynastic marriage. So much for the freedom of Pictish women to choose their mates. Perhaps if I had been the acknowledged son of King Arthur, heir to the throne of Britain, she could have married me! Never had my condition seemed so bitter!

"Lucky in play, unlucky in love," Lamerok said, smirking.

"It wasn't luck, Lamerok. We were better," I snarled, and pushed him from my path. He may have been surprised to find one so small could move him aside so easily, but I could wrestle on equal terms with Gareth, who was at least as big as he.

Before he could remonstrate, I was embraced by Nithe, my first adult friend, not counting Hal, the gardener, though I remembered him with bitterness. "My sons can talk of nothing but the exploits of the famous Dylan," she told me, smiling. "Lancelot is as nothing to them."

"Nor to me, lady." The tension I felt made the words an epithet, but she laughed. "Pelleas will like you; he shares your opinion. But ask him about Gawaine. He played hurley against Gawaine when they were boys. He won, too, if I can believe him."

A huge man came up beside her and rested his hand lightly on her shoulder. "Do I ever lie to you except at need?" he asked mildly.

"Who would know?" she snorted. "This is Baron Dylan."

"I could have guessed. I've heard the name a hundred times in the last few minutes. It is true that I played against Gawaine and his brother Gaheris when we were young. They're your brothers, I believe."

"Yes. Were you friends?"

"No, I don't think we were friends. They were a king's sons and

I was a nameless bastard. And they couldn't understand how lowly Picts could beat them playing hurley. It was very satisfactory."

For some reason I was suddenly heartened. This man had become a high king, starting from much the same position as I. So, I mused, had King Arthur himself. Nithe and Sir Torre as well had overcome adversity to find honor and happiness. Viki was only married, she wasn't dead!

We had come just as the evening meal was being served, so we were ushered inside and seated at the high table. I was between Pelleas and Nithe, with Lady Mal on the other side of Pelleas and Viki next to her. I had the feeling Nithe was determined to keep me from demanding an explanation from Viki or perhaps quarreling with Lamerok. She need not have worried. I didn't want to talk to either of them. For his part, Lamerok sat as far from me as he could get, at the end of the table.

There was one lower table filled with young men, perhaps two score, and Borre and Gareth sat with them. They kept looking up at me, talking and nodding loudly until Pelleas asked Lady Mal if she would sing for them. Lady Mal, who never ate much, tuned her harp saying, "I've been working on a new ballad I call 'The Quest of the Three Brothers.' It isn't finished, but I'd like to try it out, if I may."

Bards do as they wish. The query was merely politeness, and she scarcely waited for permission before beginning. The ballad was unfamiliar to me, but I knew what it would be from the very title. It would be about Borre and Gareth and me in search of our fathers. Whatever possessed her to sing that here? I'd have welcomed something that would have kept my mind off Viki, but I remembered promising to come for her when I'd won King Arthur's blessing. She'd remember, too!

The first part related how Borre and King Arthur found each other; the second, Gareth's quest, broke off in midverse, just after his rescue of Lady Lyoness. She never came to mine. "I don't know what comes next," Lady Mal said.

"I do," Pelleas said, rising, and pulling Gareth to his feet. He put his arm around the boy's shoulders, perhaps the only man in Britain who could do it without looking like a child hugging his father. "Hear me," he announced. "This is my son, Gareth, by Morgause, queen of the clan Merrick of the Scoti. We will have a feast of welcome tomorrow, as may befit a prince of the Picts."

Young men from the lower table surged toward us. "May we have a hurley match, Father? Against Lamerok's men? Dylan can lead us."

"He is a guest here," Pelleas objected.

"Gareth is my brother. If he plays, so will I," I announced.

"Wonderful!" Viki shouted, jumping up on the bench to be heard. "I'll take the winner as a lover!"

Lamerok grabbed her arm angrily, but she shook his hand off, glaring down at him and speaking with quiet intensity, something I didn't catch. He stalked off, and some of the young men who had been arguing at the lower table followed him out of the hall.

I looked at Nithe for an explanation. She took me aside as Viki and the young men all clustered around Gareth, patting him and giving their names while Pelleas watched with a benign smile on his face.

"First," Nithe said, "those young men around Gareth are all sons of Pelleas, much pleased to find a Geen for a brother."

"All of them?" I asked doubtfully.

"They claim it, and he never disputes such a claim," she said. "He remembers what it was like not to have a father. I am not their mother, though I love them all," she added.

I nodded.

"Pellinore asked Pelleas for the marriage between his son and Viki. Viki could have said no, but her father claims Pellinore as his liege lord, and she would never do anything to dishonor him."

"But what she said . . ."

"That she would take the winner as her lover?" Nithe smiled. "Pictish women take lovers when and where they will, though not usually so publicly nor so soon after marriage. However, they are not owned by their husbands. She did it because Lamerok claimed the right to have a traditional marriage ceremony to bring the two royal houses into alliance. It involved public consummation and went on pretty much all day. The practice has almost died out as an institution, as the Picts have become more civilized. Originally it was a symbolic statement on the inferiority of women."

"Viki would hate that," I said with conviction.

"She did. She was almost as furious as her father that Lamerok would subject her to such a demeaning ritual. It was a mistake."

"Viki thinks so?"

"Oh, yes. She won't say anything because she did it for Pelleas. He wanted to combine the two Pictic kingdoms. I said she was furious because I know her so well. Outwardly she showed heroic calm. Just the same, as is her right, she hasn't let Lamerok touch her since the public marriage consummation. She insists she's pregnant. It's too soon to tell for sure, but he must respect her feelings in the matter. If she is truly pregnant, she can insist on sleeping alone under Pictish custom, though it is not required until the seventh month."

"Will she stay here?"

"No, Pellinore has given his son Fort Terrible for a wedding present. They'll move there."

"Fort Terrible?"

"It's what the Picts call the fort Pelleas built about four leagues west of Camelot. Saxons treacherously murdered the women and children sheltered there a generation ago. Pelleas gave the place to Pellinore in exchange for this one, never wanting to see Fort Terrible again."

"I know the place," I exclaimed. "It's on Battle Creek, due west of Caerleon. I've rebuilt the fort at Caerleon. She'll be right next door, almost."

"I know. You're the Baron of Caerleon," Nithe said, reaching up to pat my cheek in approbation. "We heard about it from Pellinore. He said it was the best hurley game he ever saw. Watch over her, will you?"

"Oh, yes," I said. I would, too.

The next morning it continued to clear, the best run of fall weather I could remember. Gareth and I and the sons of Pelleas stripped and took one end of the field while Lamerok and his followers stalked off to the other. The numbers might not have been even, but all who wanted to play lined up behind me or Lamerok. This was to be rough country-rules hurley. People occasionally get killed at this form of the sport.

Pelleas threw the ball high in the air and I leapt for it, catching Lamerok in the throat with my forearm on the way up. I flipped the ball backward to our team, managing to step on Lamerok's foot on the way down before I ran off. Anger welled up in me, anger I'd held in check since hearing Viki had taken Lamerok for her husband. I played in a red rage, running over people I could have dodged. The onlookers loved it. Hurley for the Picts is a form of war, as Brastius Red-beard had said.

Gareth and Lamerok found each other and wrestled for supremacy, Geen against Geen, in a contest that was a continuation of their rivalry and had little to do with hurley. Pelleas's sons played as if they held Lamerok's followers in some way responsible for the humiliation of their sister's ritualized rape during the wedding ceremony. I guessed, as I reflected on the carnage during one of our infrequent rest periods, that there had been some taunting, and that this was the boys' first opportunity to respond.

I do not know what the final score was, but we humiliated Lamerok and his followers. I scored every other goal, passing off to Pelleas's sons on alternate ones. When it was over, the boys lifted me on their shoulders and carried me away, down to the sea to bathe. I made them put me down when we reached the path, but they continued to be jubilant, slapping me on the shoulders and calling me scurrilous names.

Seeing my surprise, Nithe said, "The Picts fear the jealousy of the gods. They call you Lucky Dog and such to fool the gods, who might take an unhealthy interest in you if they heard you praised."

I thought Pictish gods must be unusually stupid. When we came back up the hill, our hair still damp from the sea, but in clean dry clothes that had been brought down for us, we found the feast already begun. Long tables with food and drink had been placed beneath the trees, and villagers joined the folk from the castle in celebration. Pelleas spoke quietly to the boys, and they joined Lamerok's followers in fellowship. Lamerok was not among them. They were inclined to be sullen at first but, under the influence of the ale, seemed to recover their good humor, which might have been what Pelleas intended.

I excused myself to find a convenient tree, because I had drunk more ale than usual, dried out by the exertion of the morning. I needed to find a place to piss. I also needed to be by myself for a bit, to consider what to do next. Once I'd relieved myself, I sat beneath one of the apple trees still in full leaf.

A long, slim hand clutched at my sleeve and I heard a voice whisper, "For a Roman penny, I'll show you what I've got."

"Someone said that to me once before," I said, nearly choking with emotion, "but she didn't mean it."

"How do you know? Did you offer her a penny?" Viki asked, coming to sit beside me and lean against my shoulder.

"No, she was pretty dirty at the time, hanging around the docks." I said. "I finally gave her an amber necklace after she bathed, but I guess it wasn't enough."

"Probably not," Viki agreed, snuggling closer, pulling my arm around her. She had been wearing the necklace all day, glowing against her light blue dress.

"I found the rest of the set it belonged to," I said, and fumbled in my pouch with my free hand to bring out the bracelet, amber set in gold, I had been saving for her.

Viki gasped to see it, for truly it was a magnificent piece. I slipped it over her arm and squeezed it so that it fitted, for it had once been on a warrior's wrist.

"That's worth a Roman penny," she said, her voice a little unsteady. She rose and took my arm, pulled me to my feet, and led me into the woods. She had brought food with her, so there was no need to go back right away. As it was, we saw no one for three days before hunger forced us to return.

I felt shy seeing Nithe and Pelleas, but they beamed at us. "Lamerok has gone on ahead," Nithe told me. "Viki will follow when she pleases, but I imagine it had better be soon if the alliance is to hold."

"Will he try to punish her?" I asked. "If there's any chance of it, I will not let her go to him."

"Nor would I," Nithe agreed quietly. "Her father has told her she must make up her own mind, without concern for whatever political considerations might result. It is her choice to continue the marriage."

"I will try to persuade her not to, you know," I warned. "And if he abuses her, I will kill him. Her power of choice does not run that far."

"I'm relieved to hear it," she told me with a crooked smile. "Will you travel with her escort? She's taking her brothers with her."

"By boat?" I guessed.

"Of course. Arthur gave Pelleas one of the Saxon long ships. They'll use that."

"No. We left our horses on the other side. Anyway, I get sick in boats, and I don't want her to see me that way."

"Still? I thought you'd grow out of it." Nithe was quiet for a moment then said. "I will give you something to take with you that might help." We went inside and she opened a chest. Selecting a great pearl hung from a golden chain. she shut her eyes and held it clasped tightly in her fist against her breast. When she then put the chain around my neck. it was warm. a surprise. for the chain was massy and the house was cool.

"This is a sea gem holding special powers," she told me. "When you find yourself in trouble. do as I did just now and think of me."

"Is this witchcraft. Nithe?" I asked. a bit apprehensively.

"It depends on what you call witchcraft. I would imagine," she replied pensively. "Are you a Christian?"

"No."

"Then it is safe for you. You know I am called the Lady of the Lake. though my mother. Hilda. better fitted the title. Nevertheless, I have her duties now. and among other responsibilities is that of high priestess of the Great Mother. Now. this is not properly earth magic. for the sea is not the Great Mother's domain. but I think it will serve."

I looked into her eyes and saw only truth and wisdom there. With her special capacity for sending emanations of love and comfort. she wrapped me in a soothing cocoon. easing the hurt of Viki's marriage. Oh yes. this was witchcraft! In her hands, however. there was nothing to fear.

When I left her. the sense of loss returned. but I no longer felt hopeless. I would seek Viki out at Fort Terrible. despite Lamerok's sure objections. and continue to do so until she. herself. sent me away.

Next day I stood on the headland and watched the dragon ship carry Viki away from the beach. south towards the estuary of the Severn. until it was out of sight and I could no longer see even the flash of the oars. Another good-bye!

Pelleas and Nithe were waiting to bid me farewell, standing on the beach and talking with Gareth and Borre. "I did not thank you for your service to my daughter when you found her in London," Pelleas said to me. "I will not forget it."

I nodded. What can you say to something like that? I knew how I felt about Viki and how I would grieve if I thought her lost forever in the hands of Saxon raiders. It was bad enough to see her going to another man, who cherished her, for all I knew. It wasn't enough.

As we pulled away from the shore I closed my eyes and clutched the pearl tightly through my tunic. The nausea that had flooded through me ebbed away, and I opened my eyes to see Nithe nodding and smiling at me. It worked. I might survive. If I could do this, in time I might even survive the loss of Viki.

CHAPTER X

We found one of Viki's brothers waiting for our arrival at Caerleon. "She's been worried about you." he told us.

"We were looking for the source of the Usk River." I said. "My domain runs so far under King Arthur's proclamation, and I wanted to know what the territory looked like. Did you know there is a sanctuary for the Great Mother in the upper valley of the Usk?"

The boy said unexpectedly. "That's Avalon. Surely you didn't make claim to it! It's an unchancy place, that. The Great Mother is the goddess held in reverence by women, an older deity than any worshipped by men, except for the Oak King." He made the circle sign of Lud, the sun king, to ward off evil. "Her priestesses are not to be trifled with."

"Actually we were received with every mark of distinction, and gently told not to come back." I said laughing. "They said it was a refuge for women, and men are not generally tolerated. When I told them of the grant of land I'd received after defeating the Picts at hurley, they laughed. They'd never paid taxes to either King Arthur or King Pellinore. When I told them I had no intention of attempting to change that, they smiled, more amused than pleased, I thought." I did not say it, but I also thought at the time that my domain was well guarded from the north. No one would invade my lands through the Great Mother's lands.

"My own mother, Nithe, the Lady of the Lake, is the Mother's priestess," he continued. "She rules there."

"So she told me. Because of it, I offered my free help should ever they need it. I was thanked nicely enough, but received the impression they could take care of themselves."

He grinned in agreement. "You didn't ride down the Usk or you'd have been seen at Camelot," he commented, changing the subject.

"No, we went east toward the source of Battle Creek and down that valley. It is uninhabited until you come to Fort Terrible."

"Then you've already seen Viki," one of the boys said.

"No, I was unsure of my welcome."

"But Lamerok is not living there," the boy protested, knowing what I meant. "Viki is pregnant, and Pictish husbands must live apart from their wives while they're carrying. He's at Camelot, bragging, likely. She wants to see you."

Ah! I went with him the next day, leaving Lady Mal to straighten out any problems that had arisen in Caerleon in our absence. Borre and Gareth went on to Camelot to find out what Arthur's plans were for the coming winter. We'd taken our time returning to Caerleon.

Fort Terrible was a palisaded hill fort, different from mine in that there was no dry moat around it, and the building walls were wood, not stone. It seemed a rabbit warren, much like Pelleas's manor, teeming with women and children. I saw few men.

Viki received me in the midst of her women, who retired to one end of the room to watch and giggle, but would not leave. "I can not be alone with a man, not even Lamerok, until after I deliver," she said. "Sit here beside me," and she patted the bare wooden bench.

"Are you well?" I asked, holding her hand and looking into her eyes. What I wanted to do was take her in my arms and bury my face in her hair.

"I am unwell mornings, but that will pass. Other than that, I feel marvelous."

"You don't look any different," I said, but that was untrue. She looked luminous.

"It's early days yet. I'm glad you'll be gone, for I'll get fat and ugly soon enough." She said it with a certain complacency that led me to think she was looking forward to it and was speaking so without real conviction.

The women brought us food and then let us eat apart from them. I told her of Avalon.

"I've been there with Nithe," she said. "Pictish women do not need priestesses to intercede for them with the Great Mother. I think the women there were shocked to hear it."

"Does the Great Mother have some plan for us?" I asked.

"I do not know her mind," she said. "This child I am carrying fulfills my marriage contract if it is a girl. That would bind the two Pictish kingdoms into one under a single royal line."

"Would Lamerok be content with that?"

"It was the contract he insisted upon. He has no option but to be content."

"And if it's a boy?"

Viki sighed. "I'd have to try again."

I left vowing to Lud that if he permitted the Great Mother to give Viki a girl child, I would never become a Christian. I held no views on the gods, never having seen one or been singled out for their attention. However, I was reluctant to forswear them, as I must if I became a Christian. Why pick a quarrel with the gods or take sides if they quarreled among themselves? I was content not to be noticed.

Another thought came unbidden. What if the baby Viki was carrying was mine and not Lamerok's? We had both been with her, but a few weeks in time apart. I'd count the months as they passed. Perhaps Lamerok would as well, in which case there could be trouble ahead.

At Viki's command I did not return to Fort Terrible. She wanted to keep her mind on the child she was carrying and told me I was a distraction. She was more than that to me. She'd let me kiss her good-bye while her women tittered, but that was all. I'd left frustrated. Damn Lamerok, anyway.

When I returned to Caerleon from Fort Terrible, I found King Arthur had already left Camelot for the winter. Lady Mal had waited for me to return, rather than accompany Ayres's cattle to the London market. I knew I could not honor Viki's request if I stayed in Caerleon, so together Lady Mal and I decided to follow the court to its winter station.

I slept little on the trip to London; the chill night air cut through my warmest cloak. Gareth and Borre came with us and rode together, arguing interminably, mostly about the relative skills and valor of Round Table knights, a subject which had little interest for me. They agreed only on the point that Sir Lancelot was the first in honor, whatever that meant.

Lady Mal rode with me. She talked companionably when I wanted to talk and stayed silent when I wished to think. When I thought, I thought about Viki; but when I talked, I talked about anything else. Among other topics we discussed breeding Lady Mal's palfrey to Black Nick. She wanted another mare, for her mare was getting a little old and would no longer be fit for long journeys in a few years. If the first foal was a filly, she'd keep it, but otherwise it was mine, and like Viki, she'd try again.

When we reached London we found little for us to do there.

Finally, Lady Mal talked with Hugh and arranged to lease a building near his own where she could start an inn. She traded Saxon jewelry for tables, chairs, and supplies, and had it up and running within a fortnight. She named it The Laurel Wreath and made me wear my golden one whenever I was on the premises. At other times it was on display behind the bar.

The city folk of all stations in life, from knights in arms to alley drabs, were served there, and I was offered much more to drink than I could reasonably wish. Lady Mal had a false-bottomed silver tankard made for me that looked generous but in reality held very little, so I could drink with folks and not offend by refusing, and incidentally, she would not lose the sale. Even so, most evenings I returned early to Hugh's and talked with him about the underlying tensions that lay between factions in the city and the court. With that knowledge, I could better judge what I saw at King Arthur's palace in the interactions among the various nobles there.

I came to understand the city people, helped by Hugh's counsel and Gawaine's acid observations. He and his brother Gaheris could be found most nights at the inn. A second brother, Aggravain, had joined them, coming south from Scoti lands. My brother as well, I thought. Aggravain was a slovenly, black-browed fellow with an unkempt beard. How could someone as lovely as Morgause give birth to such a creature?

"Why doesn't he shave?" I asked Gawaine privately. Gawaine sported a flowing red mustache, much like my own, but shaved his jaw.

"He's showing his contempt for fashion," Gawaine said. "He says Lancelot and his kin set it; says they've turned the king's court into a lady's boudoir."

"He drinks too much," I observed.

"How can you drink too much?" Gawaine asked, amazed at the thought.

Gawaine was hasty and made ill-judged moves when he was drunk, and he was little different sober. He thought the same of me, or so he claimed, but I drink less. In his case, at least, his temper could not be blamed on ale. With Aggravain, however, there was a mean streak that came out most obviously in drink. He liked to fight and often hurt people. He liked that, too. Most of the time, though, Gawaine was able to restrain Aggravain, and I could talk with people without fear that I'd have to hit one with a stool within the hour, taking sides in a general brawl. When Gawaine failed, Gareth would deal with him. He kept order for Lady Mal here as he had in Caerleon.

I found the common people of King Arthur's Britain complained about taxes and unequal treatment under the law. Gawaine's argument in such cases was to point out that a generation ago the complainers would be summarily killed and that the freedom to talk was possible only under King Arthur's rule.

I didn't see that being overtaxed while being able to complain was much better than being overtaxed and not being able to complain when the complaining did not lead to redress. I kept my mouth shut on the subject, determined all the same to make sure there was no just cause for complaint in Caerleon.

All in all, King Arthur's London court was unhappy. Quarrels broke out between the knights of Brittany and everyone else. Even the mercenaries the king had as part of Guenevere's dowry took sides, though most of these men had been left in Camelot. Usually the quarrels were based on the rumors that roiled around Queen Guenevere and Sir Lancelot. Aggravain spoke against the queen whenever he could find a listener, even when Gawaine forbade him.

"Why do you gossip like an old woman?" Gawaine demanded.

" 'Tis not gossip, I tell you! They've been seen together. Shameless!" Aggravain insisted, though his face projected a salacious glee rather than moral outrage.

"But why do you care, even if it were true?" I asked.

"Why? Because our cousin the king holds Lancelot in more regard than us, his own relatives, that's why!"

"Sir Lancelot is his relative, too," I said.

"Oh, on his father's side, if Uther Pendragon is really Arthur's father!"

"I've heard different. But who cares who the king's father's relatives are? It's his mother's kin who matter. Anyone knows that!" Gawaine exclaimed.

Spoken like a proper Gael, I thought.

I was glad to get back to Caerleon and away from the trouble I could see coming. I wanted to see Viki so I left early, not waiting for the queen to move the court back to Camelot. At home I found a message was waiting from Viki for me not to come to her. She'd miscarried and didn't want any trouble with Lamerok now that he was living in Fort Terrible again. He had been teased about his wife's lover, a matter that I might have heard about if I'd spent more time around King Arthur's court in London. If I visited her now, he'd wonder if the next child she conceived was his or mine. I still wondered whose the first one had been.

I asked Ayres about it. "Was there all that much talk about Viki and me? Who was doing it?"

"Aggravain, for one, from what Torre said," the old man told me. "He bragged his brother had put horns on Lamerok's head within weeks of his marriage, just as Lancelot had done to King Arthur. Everyone thought it a great jest."

I stayed away from Camelot after hearing that, particularly when the court returned, but not because I was afraid of Lamerok. I wanted to avoid trouble with him for Viki's sake. Sir Torre insisted that I attend the feast of Pentecost, however. It was my seventh at Camelot. I was eighteen. I felt as if I were a hundred.

Gareth declined to come with us. "What if the bishop is there? I'll have to marry that Lady Lyoness," he said.

"You can always say no," I told him, but he was adamant, and we left him behind. When we entered the great hall, Sir Torre and I sat at one end of the low table as far from Lamerok as we could get, at my insistence. We drank for an hour, waiting for King Arthur's miracle so we could eat, and were relieved when four young women came into the hall from the kitchen entrance and walked around the hall. They were all veiled and carried what seemed to be a large, steaming, draped bowl that gave off the most wonderful incense, a combination of cinnamon and clove, perhaps. Rows of servants followed them, placing hot meat and bread on the tables, almost unnoticed by the knights, since the damsels were scantily clad. Some of the knights were already far gone in drink.

"Oh, that's a good one," Sir Torre breathed softly. "Kay's surpassed himself."

Gawaine, at the high table, cried out, "It's a true miracle," and would have followed the girls out the back of the hall except for the fact that Gaheris pulled him back into his seat.

"I swear," he said loudly, "I will find them tomorrow, I swear. The fat one is for me!" He subsided only after Gaheris roughly put a piece of smoking meat on his wooden trencher, nudging him to eat and shut up.

"What is he talking about?" I asked Brastius.

Brastius crossed himself. "It's the Holy Grail," he said simply.

"It looked like a two-handed drinking cup," I said.

"It is. Christ drank from it at the Last Supper and passed it around among his disciples."

So. It was a holy mystery, something known to Christians. It made me uncomfortable.

Sir Kay was furious with Gawaine, muttering to himself all through the meal, standing and directing pages here and there to bring more for the diners. Without a page master, he had to oversee the boys as well as the food, or thought he had to. He probably held me responsible for the fact that the pages refused to choose a new leader after I left. Busy, he waited until the tables were cleared of food and Arthur and Guenevere had retired before speaking his mind to Gawaine, loud enough for all to hear.

"Why did you make such a scene with your coarse comments? You embarrassed the queen!"

"What was I supposed to do?" Gawaine asked, looking puzzled in an unfocused way.

"You were supposed to pray! Don't you know anything? The maidens carried the Holy Grail, whose emanations satisfy all hunger, spiritual and physical."

"I knew that," Gawaine said with drunken dignity.

"Then why did you insist you wanted to find the fat one tomorrow, except to satisfy your lecherous appetite?"

"Not so, not so. Want to satisfy my spiritual appetite! That's it. I'll search for them for a year and a day."

"Them?" Sir Kay asked sarcastically.

"It! It! The Grail thing! I challenge you all," he shouted, "a quest for the Holy Grail. Who will join me?"

"I will," Sir Lancelot said. "I will!"

I judged him to be no more sober than Gawaine, and a chorus of voices echoed, "I will! I will! I will seek the Grail."

Sir Torre tugged me to my feet calling that we would go. His shout fell into a sudden hush and rang uncommonly loud.

"Ah, an angel passed." Sir Lancelot said mockingly, uttering a saying we have to explain a sudden lull in conversation. "You would bring the bastard baron?" That struck him as humorous. "Bastard baron," he repeated. "Bastard baron," and he laughed drunkenly.

Gawaine didn't know who Sir Lancelot was referring to, but looked around owlishly. "Where's a bastard baron?"

"If he goes, I will not," King Pellinore said, pointing me out to

Gawaine. "Should have put his neck under my arm a long time ago. Cheats at hurley!"

I'd heard enough. I left by the nearby side door, followed by Borre and Gareth. A shout of approval came close on Pellinore's announcement, and I could detect Sir Lancelot's clear tenor high above the rest, "Hurley?" followed by laughter.

I would not forget.

Brastius Red-beard and Lady Mal sought me out a few days later at the stables in Caerleon. Gareth, Borre, and I were mending harness. "Most of the Round Table knights have undertaken a bootless quest to seek the Holy Grail," Brastius told us.

I nodded but didn't interrupt him.

"They went out the morning after Pentecost to be gone a year and a day, in spite of the king's entreaties. He fears this will sunder the Round Table, for never have so many been absent questing for so long a time."

Lady Mal was enchanted, however. "Did you ever hear anything so romantic?"

"Brastius just said it's bootless," I objected. "You heard him."

"It is," Brastius said. "The Grail appears as God wills. You can't hunt as if it were a roe deer."

"All the better," she replied lightly. "What a subject for an epic ballad! Why weren't you there?" She asked me.

"I was at the feast. King Pellinore refused to go on the quest if I went."

"And Gawaine refused to go if you didn't," Brastius said. "Didn't you hear the cheer that was raised? He looked for you yesterday."

"I was here," I said. "If I were truly wanted, I could have been found. They all went, truly? I don't believe it! King Arthur would never allow such a thing to pass!"

"Would he not?" Brastius asked bitterly. "After Gawaine slandered the integrity of the Round Table, saying that only he of all the knights had gone to Baden to fight the Saxons while the others had stayed safely in Camelot? How could they refuse? With the exception of a few of the older men, like King Pellinore and me, everyone took the dare."

"After all that, King Pellinore did not go?" I asked.

"No, nor Gaheris either, for he knows how stubborn Gawaine is when drunk, and particularly when he has an aching head from too much wine from the night before. He told Gawaine he was a fool to his face."

"That didn't help much," Borre observed.

"No, it didn't. Except for you two, Arthur, Kay, Gaheris and me, and a few others, everyone who was there set out the next day. They broke into smaller groups once away from Camelot and some drifted on home, but mostly they have not been seen, at least none of them who actually went questing."

"That's terrible," Gareth said. "No one has heard from Sir Lancelot? If I were there, I'd have gone with him."

I glanced at Borre and knew we both had the same thought, one of thanks that Gareth had not been there for, truly, he would have followed his hero.

Into the summer I brooded on the insult I'd suffered at the hands of King Pellinore and Sir Lancelot until it filled my mind, and I was poor company for those round me. It was with some hesitancy then that Gareth and Borre woke me early one morning and told me, "Gawaine is back. He's down at The Pig Girl's stables and wants to see you."

"He can't be," I muttered, sitting up and fumbling for my shoes. "We were told he vowed to quest for the Grail a year and a day and dragged the whole Round Table after him over King Arthur's protests. It has been barely six months. Besides," I grumbled, "no one wants to see anyone this early in the morning."

"He was wounded," Gareth said. "He's thin and ill, Dylan. He's also in a foul mood from not having slept all night. I'd hurry if I were you."

I glared at him. Why should I hurry for Gawaine? But that was churlish. He was my brother.

I was on my feet and adjusting my cloak when Gareth grabbed my arm and tried to rush me. "I'll take you to him," he insisted, tugging.

I don't like being dragged on, particularly when I've just been awakened, so I freed myself as gently as possible, considering who was holding me. "What's he doing in the stables? Why didn't he go to Camelot?" I asked.

"They shaved his head to tend his wound. He looks awful. I don't think he wants to be seen in public," Gareth answered with small pauses between utterances.

Gawaine did look bad, thin and cross, as he lay on a pallet over a hay mattress, and my heart went out to him. His head was covered by a dirty bandage oozing a greenish poultice, most disgusting. Gareth hovered, seemingly distressed. Aggravain watched, seated on a stool, and Gaheris lounged against the inn wall with his arms folded.

"What kept you?" Gawaine growled.

"Whatever happened to you?" I asked, ignoring his question, judging he just wanted to take his spleen out on someone.

Gawaine shifted irritably and grunted in pain.

"Talk to us, Gawaine," Gareth said. "We will listen, won't we?" He looked at the rest of us, nodding his head in anticipation of our agreement.

"I would think so," Gawaine muttered, and settled back on his pallet.

I did not relax. "Why are you back so soon?" I asked.

"Why, indeed? I was informed by a fellow knight that I was giving the quest a bad name, and I had best drop it for the sake of worthier folk. He mentioned himself, for one."

"Who was that?" Aggravain asked softly, his eyes glittering like a rat's in the stable shadows.

"Ector De Marys, a fellow knight of the Round Table," he replied, and spat in the hay.

"Ah, one of Lancelot's kin!" Aggravain sneered. "We told you those Romified bastards looked down on us, but you wouldn't listen."

That was true. Gawaine set high store on acceptance by Sir Lancelot and his kin from Armorica, across the sea. I had not heard Gawaine talk except in the Latin preferred by Sir Lancelot's Bretons since I came to Camelot, and I suddenly realized he was speaking only Gaelic this morning. Perhaps Aggravain, countrified as he was, did not understand Latin.

"Is it just your head or failing in the quest that has put you in such a mood?" I asked, for ordinarily Gawaine, though prickly, is good-humored enough.

"Ah, none of that! I killed our cousin Uwayne in the quest," Gawaine said, "and I must tell Morgan. He was her son."

"I would not wish to tell that witch such a tale," Gaheris said with satisfaction.

"She is not a witch!" Gawaine grated out. He looked at me and continued in a softer tone, "Morgan and I were children together and would have perchance married had we not been so closely related. Our mothers were sisters."

He stopped suddenly, perhaps realizing how closely his words touched on my own condition, but I merely stared back at him a moment before saying, "You haven't said what happened."

"The kind of thing you might expect," he answered, irritably now. "I was in company with De Marys and he saw three knights posting toward us. The fool ran off ahead to challenge them. When I got there he had engaged all three, like the buffoon he is, and I had to come to his rescue. I knocked one off his horse to even the odds, and when I got back to him and pulled his helmet off, I found it was Uwayne."

"You'd killed him?"

"He died the next day in my arms. I've never felt so bad about anything in my life."

"What about De Marys?"

"Oh, he wandered off. Said I was acting like an old woman."

A silence ensued, Gawaine brooding and the others intimidated by his sullen, uncommunicative mood.

"But how did you get hurt?" Gareth blurted.

Gawaine glared at him, sighed deeply, and said, "Lancelot's get, that damned Galahad, blindsided me." He shut his mouth, and I could see he'd work himself into a rage if he continued talking about it. He looked feverish.

"Another one of the damned De Marys clan," Aggravain snarled.

"I'm sorry," Gareth said, apologizing, perhaps, for Sir Lancelot, his hero.

"What do you mean, 'sorry'?" Gawaine growled. "Do you think I brought you here for sympathy?"

"What, then?" I asked.

"It's as I'll tell Morgan, I'm sick of Camelot and Gaels like us pretending to be Romans. I'm sick of trying to be civil to Pellinore, the man who killed my father, just because he's a member of the Round Table. I'm sick of the whole damned charade!"

"What do you plan to do?" Gareth asked.

"First, I have to see Morgan and try to explain what happened to her son. We don't need her for an enemy. I don't look forward to it. Then I may have some other plans." He looked up at Gareth and me and spoke to us directly. "Come with me," he urged. "If you stay here, you'll be the target of more challenges than you can handle because of me. Besides, I need you all with me. Will you come?"

"Why do you need us?" I asked, ignoring the implied threat.

"Because I do," Gawaine roared. "Are you kinsmen or not? I want to reestablish our claim to Lothian in the north, once our father's land. If you are with me, you can share. If you stay here, you'll bear the brunt of the resentment the Britons will show as they lose fat holdings. Well?"

"Lot was your father, not mine or Gareth's," I said. "Besides, Arthur will never let you do it. Pelleas is his brother. And you're forgetting Pelleas. He'll have Picts around your head like hornets."

"By the time Arthur or Pelleas know about it, it will be too late," Gawaine said in a low growl.

"Brastius Red-beard, the Warden of the North, will tell Arthur," Aggravain said slowly, shaking his head. "He has gone back to Hadrian's Wall since Arthur no longer fears the Saxons. He must send regular reports, and he'll hear about our activities. Arthur won't be able to ignore them, as he does some other things."

Gawaine frowned at this veiled reference to Guenevere and Lancelot, and I didn't want to listen to another discussion about the rumors of their adultery, so I said, "Brastius Red-beard? Don't tell me he is really up there someplace."

"He decided he didn't want to go questing for the Grail," Gawaine said, "having more sense than the rest of us. He took a group of people north with him to have an excuse to avoid it."

"What was the excuse?" I asked.

"To watch the Picts."

I hooted. "The Picts are not raiding! Brastius himself told me that King Arthur sees no danger from that quarter."

"No more is there, but that's the excuse he gave," Gawaine said sourly. "The point I left out is that Brastius is tired and wants to sit around a hermitage for a while. Arthur knows this. We're going to ask Arthur to appoint me as the new Warden of the North. Then Arthur will hear only what I tell him."

"That makes some kind of sense," I admitted. "It is said that the king is very fond of you and can refuse you nothing. However, he'll object to your running away where he may never see you again. I've heard him complain about missing Brastius."

"Will you come?"

"No. Lothian means nothing to me."

"It's claimed by King Pellinore. Have you forgotten his insult?"

"Pellinore's insult? That's my business, not yours. I'll handle it man-to-man one of these days."

"He'll eat you," Aggravain snorted.

"If he does, I absolve you from any responsibility to seek blood debt," I said coldly.

Gawaine sent Borre to find King Arthur, and Borre insisted I go with him. I was not surprised when we found him in the mews with his hawks.

"Have you heard that Gawaine has returned, Sire?" Borre asked him after greeting his father.

"Wonderful! Where is he?" The king had nodded pleasantly enough to me, but no more than that.

"At The Pig Girl's stables in Caerleon, Sire," Borre replied, explaining further when the king raised his eyebrows in surprise. "He was wounded, and they cut his hair. His vanity prevents him from coming to court, but he wants to see you."

"Was he badly hurt?" King Arthur asked in a worried voice.

"I think it may have been a closer danger than he now admits, and he still looks bad enough, in all truth. He has sent me to prepare you for a boon he would beg of you, Sire," Borre continued.

"I would grant Gawaine almost anything," King Arthur said. "Let us go to him, and you will tell me about it as we ride."

Borre and I had left our horses at the gate, and a page brought one around for the king.

"Have you seen him, Dylan? How is he, truly?" King Arthur asked me as we approached Caerleon.

"Recovering, I think, but he needs diversion," I said. "He feels keenly his failure in the quest for the Grail and has no stomach for waiting to hear stories of those more successful."

"He was always proud," King Arthur agreed.

"He is no less so in his present humiliation," I said.

"Surely. it is not so bad as that," King Arthur said.

"It's worse. Our cousin Uwayne died at his hands by accident. He grieves for it."

Pain passed across King Arthur's face. "Do you have any idea how many people have been killed on this ridiculous quest?" he asked bitterly.

"Gawaine said there were many."

"And so there have been: more. I am sure. than he knows. Among them there are some I could spare more easily than Uwayne. He's son of my own sister Morgan. I've always been fond of the boy."

I bit my tongue. The king valued kinsmen. just not me.

"Just what is it that Gawaine wants of me?" he asked.

"Gawaine wants you to fulfill Brastius's request to retire by appointing him Warden of the North in Brastius's stead." Borre said. "It is a thing within his compass. as the quest was not."

"The border is quiet. though. What does he expect to find there?"

"In Gawaine's mood it may not remain quiet." I said. "I fear part of his desire to go there is to change the policy these many years of ignoring Pictish encroachments on the holdings of the Gael: many Gaels were driven out of the north by Pelleas. I know Pelleas is your brother. but he does not keep order among his people."

"Pelleas denies that it is his responsibility," King Arthur said. "He does not accept himself as high king of the Picts. though in truth. he knows better. We both have let matters go untended there: perhaps it is time to change somewhat."

We reached the inn and found Gawaine in better appearance. having covered his wound with a clean bandage. changed his clothing. and trimmed his beard. Nevertheless. King Arthur was concerned by Gawaine's appearance. as well he might have been.

"You have been more ill than I had believed, Cousin," he said. "I doubt you weigh more than my old dog, Cavell, did."

"Hardly," Gawaine replied, "but I was always thin, Sire. It is the pallor of too many days out of the sun that alarms you, though."

"It may be," King Arthur said, "We must bring you to Camelot and feed you huge meals to alter that."

"I cannot be seen, Sire. You, of all men, know how it is with me. I have come to beg leave to be absent for a pace and to request a mission from you that will take me hence."

"My son Borre told me," King Arthur said. "Gladly would I grant your request, although the court will miss your presence, none more than I. Are you sure you are fit to undertake this?"

"Yes," Gawaine stated emphatically. "I will mend the quicker now that I don't have dirty hermits telling me how sinful I am and how God has granted me grace in allowing me to be wounded so severely. I listened to lectures and prayers to the point I could renounce my faith if they were continued."

"So be it." King Arthur sighed.

"I am not wholehearted about this," I heard the king grumble as Borre and he left to return to Camelot. I was not invited to accompany them.

"You have the king's blessing, Gawaine," I said, gazing after the pair walking together. King Arthur with his arm around Borre's shoulders and talking earnestly to him.

"Will you come then?" Gawaine asked hopefully.

"I'll have no part of it." I answered flatly.

"And if you don't come, neither will Gareth." It was a statement, not a question, and needed no answer.

I took my leave without ceremony and went into the inn's kitchen to beg breakfast. Gareth divined my destination and came along, always ready for a little something early in the morning. "You could go if you wanted," I told him.

"No, I wouldn't want to leave just now."

There was a dreamy quality to his voice, and I looked at him sharply.

"Another girl?"

"The same one, actually," he replied, almost apologetically, "the one I rescued on my quest. She waited for me, Dylan." He said it simply, as if amazed at her constancy, though he'd been away only a few months.

"I didn't know you'd been seeing her," I said suspiciously.

"I hadn't. I ran into her accidentally last night. She was as surprised as I was."

I'll bet, I thought. "I gather from Lady Mal there's been no one else much around. You might have been better off on the Grail quest after all."

"No, I truly like her," Gareth disagreed mildly. "I've been considering talking to the bishop. You know he said I ought to marry her after I took her maidenhead."

"But she wasn't even pregnant," I objected. "Did she try to trap you into marriage with such a claim?"

"She's so innocent, she thought pregnancy was inevitable," Gareth explained.

"But, what maidenhead? She was a widow!" I shouted in exasperation.

"Her husband was impotent," Gareth said, blushing.

"She said that?" I couldn't believe how simple Gareth was.

"Yes," he replied, turning pale. Now he was angry! That was so rare an event that I held my peace; it truly was none of my business if Gareth wanted it that way. Maybe it was for the best if he was right about her; though properly he needed a keeper, not another child to play with.

Once Gareth decided he would take the girl, the matter was handled with great dispatch, but it still took ten days to arrange. The king sponsored the wedding and surprised everyone by giving the bride's sister, Lady Lynet, to Gaheris to wive in the same ceremony. Lady Lynet had no other protector, so her hand was the king's to dispose.

Dowries for the two women had to be verified, and the Bishop Ninian took it upon himself to counsel all parties on the responsibilities of the married state in the interim. Both Gareth and Gaheris had to be baptized before the bishop would consent to marry them to the sisters. Baptism was necessary before Gareth would be eligible for induction into the fellowship of the Round Table anyway, so he made no demur, but Gaheris was more obstinate. He liked neither the idea of marriage nor the necessity of becoming Christian. Eventually only Lady Lynet's rich dowry won his reluctant consent to the union.

A Gaelic knight owns only his horses and weapons until he takes possession of his wife's dowry. At that, ownership of the land remains with the bride's family. Still the income from rents of the lands belonged to the husband. Poor Gaheris, I thought, to be so torn between greed and revulsion.

Gawaine insisted that the wedding be held in The Pig Girl inn so he could watch from the shadows unobserved. He was so amused at Gaheris's evident distress that he quite forgot his own problems and mended apace. When I caught King Arthur looking with silent satisfaction at Gawaine as he teased Gaheris, I realized the king had intended that outcome and had created the delay to give Gawaine more time to heal.

I had not been to a Christian wedding before and barely knew how to behave, so I stood in the back where no one could watch me make mistakes. From there I could see striking differences in the behavior toward their brides displayed by Gareth and Gaheris. Gareth, though years younger, was much the more practiced lover; Gaheris seemed to be embarrassed that he was dealing with a lady and not a serving wench.

Immediately after the breakfast next morning, Gaheris insisted on leaving for the north to help Gawaine set his plans in motion. "The bloody woman talks in her sleep, even," he complained. His bride did not rise to bid him farewell and secluded herself in her room at The Pig Girl the rest of the day. Gareth and his lady came to demand food about noon, the first time since I knew him that Gareth had missed eating when food was available.

I envied him, thinking of the three days Viki and I had spent together. I wondered if such a time would ever come again.

CHAPTER
XI

I stayed away from Camelot during the fall and winter months, working with Ayres, Borre, and Gareth to establish a herd and fields to feed my manor house at Caerleon. We cut timber and dug stumps to prepare ground for planting next spring and took Ayres's surplus cattle as a nucleus for our own dairy and meat supplies. Since King Arthur would not leave Camelot while his Round Table knights were out on the Grail quest, Ayres would not have the protection of the king's large party to bring his cattle to the London market. Ayres was happy to make the cattle available to us in exchange for Saxon jewelry.

Gareth's wife, Lady Lyoness, became one of the queen's ladies-in-waiting, and she chattered artlessly about the castle folk when Gareth brought her to visit us in Caerleon. She thought the king and queen became closer in their common worry about absent friends. Whether the queen did not care to be in London without Sir Lancelot at her side was a question I could not answer. Indeed, I little cared, though it was a matter of endless speculation for others.

Lamerok stayed on at Camelot, not being Christian and under

no obligation to search for the Holy Grail. Lady Mal told me she'd heard Viki was pregnant again. From hints dropped by Gareth's wife, I gathered he was paying court to my mother, Morgause. Gossip . . .

I wondered if Lamerok sought to dishonor Morgause in exchange for my three-day affair with Viki. His interest might be an honest one, but I worried about it. If he'd gone questing, I'd have visited Viki despite her wishes, but he'd hear gossip at Camelot and might retaliate against either Viki or my mother.

I didn't accompany Gareth when he went to Camelot to help celebrate the feast of Pentecost, the eighth held since I had come to Camelot. I was nineteen. The knights that had set out on the quest were due to return, and Sir Lancelot should be among them; I didn't want to see him.

Lady Mal had sung at the feast in her guise as Sir Dynadan and returned to The Pig Girl inn with a new ballad based on Sir Lancelot's account of the quest. She sang of Sir Lancelot's son Galahad and Pellinore's son Percival as the only knights to have successfully completed the quest for the Holy Grail. Sir Lancelot said he and Bors had seen them sail away in a boat with the Grail, but had been refused passage themselves, as being too sinful and not worthy of the vision of the Grail.

Lady Mal told us later that Sir Lancelot was much changed, so dark of mood as to be dangerous. His friend Lavayne and the queen were in despair over the man. I little cared.

In early summer Gareth brought news that Gawaine had returned to Camelot amidst rumors that Pellinore had been murdered by him and his brothers.

"Remember he told us Pellinore had murdered his father. Well, they say Gawaine has made Pellinore pay blood debt for that."

"If that's true, the king will never forgive him," Borre exclaimed. "Pellinore was the Round Table's senior knight. The king loved him."

Borre and I joined Gareth to attend the welcome-home feast for Gawaine. We saw that King Arthur's greeting to Gawaine was restrained. "What have you done with your stewardship?" he asked Gawaine after he had embraced him and Gaheris. Aggravain was not with them.

"We have taken steps to secure the frontier," Gawaine said.

"Steps?" King Arthur said, with raised eyebrows.

"Yes, Sire. We found the mountain land empty north of Hadrian's Wall but feared it would not remain so. The Romans settled Gaels there generations ago as a buffer between their lands and the wild Picts. When Pelleas drove the Gaels out of Caledonia, they did not stop running until they were south of the wall. We mean to bring them back where they belong, to serve you as they did the Romans."

"If they ran once, why will they not run again?"

"Because I will be there to stop them," Gawaine said. "Brastius was content to squat behind the wall and watch. I am not. He tried to tell me the wall would keep the Picts out if they attempted to invade, but the wall is seventy-four Roman miles long. We walked it from end to end. There are forts or sentry stations every mile, and it would take six thousand men to hold it properly. We will not have six hundred."

"Can you stop any force with so few?"

"If I have adequate intelligence, I can," Gawaine said. "The Picts do not form armies or fight under generals. Only Geen giants can lead the men of several villages at the same time, and there are few of those."

"There are fewer than there were," King Arthur said sadly. "Word has come that Pellinore is dead. The Picts say his body was found hidden in the mountains to the north with dead fighting men, Gaels and Picts, buried not far away. It looked like an ambush."

"I fear it is true," Gawaine said. "It grieves me."

"Do you know aught of it?"

"Yes, but I will keep my counsel at this time," Gawaine said. "No good would come from a discussion of it. As Warden of the North, I will deal with it appropriately in due time."

I was surprised that King Arthur dropped the topic. It was possible he knew already what occurred and did not wish to challenge Gawaine with an accusation of murder. He would have understood if Gawaine had admitted the deed and claimed vengeance for his father's death, but he could not forgive him for an injury to a fellow of the Round Table. The oath of brotherhood was supposed to override blood feud.

The company at dinner was thin. Few of the knights had yet returned from the quest, though it was to have lasted but a year and a day, and it was well past time for them to come home. The news of casualties on the quest dampened the spirits of those who had. The queen greeted Gawaine and Gaheris with the charm she reserved for those closest to King Arthur, and for once I was in the right company. She did not call me by name, though. Morgause looked me over with an indolent but searching glance, for I had not come to see her over the winter. She had not invited me, either.

"I am happy to see you among us again," Guenevere said graciously to all of us. "You will be happy to see Arthur's sister Morgan is visiting," indicating the woman sitting between her and Morgause.

Gawaine paid scant attention to the queen, his interest all on Morgan. To my taste, Morgan was the more striking of the two in appearance, and evidently Gawaine agreed with me. I bowed and raised my head to find Morgan watching me with amused interest. Looking from her to Morgause to Guenevere, I remembered one of Lady Mal's ballads and realized that I was in the presence of the three most beautiful women in Britain. I recited, ". . . the three graces of Britain, like the birds of the goddess, the goldfinch, the raven, and the dove . . ."

Where Morgause was fire red and Morgan raven black, the queen was gold and white. Which was the most beautiful I was happy not to be required to say. None of them looked as if she would be willing to take even second place in such a judgment.

"Oh, hear, sisters," Morgan said, "our cousin is a poet!" and smiled on me, ignoring Gawaine.

I glanced at Lady Mal dressed as Dynadan the Bard, who grinned wickedly, strumming the tune to the ballad quietly on her lyre from her seat behind the king. She had not been invited to play yet, and I could guess what she would offer the gathering after the meal was over.

"Sit beside me and tell me what is happening to the north," Morgause said to Gawaine, patting the empty seat beside her as Gareth claimed the seat on her other side.

I sat by Morgan at her smiled invitation. Samana trained me how to behave in company, even under eyes as bright as these. "I am honored, my lady," I said.

Morgause's clear voice dominated the table talk. I had not seen her in company before and realized she captured the center of attention as naturally as if she'd had it all her life. I could believe it to be true but wondered how the queen felt about such a presence at her table. The rest of us ate, most of us content to listen. Indeed, Morgan's interest was such that she ignored me, but not spitefully.

"Arthur says you've claimed the land between Hadrian's Wall and the Antonine Wall," Morgause stated.

The king glanced at Gawaine out of the corner of his eye but said nothing to challenge that.

"Reclaimed it, Mother," Gawaine replied. He made no pretext of eating, but drained his wine cup, clicking his fingers to a page for a refill. "It was always the property of us Gaels, as you know," he added.

"Do you believe Gaels will come to settle so close to the Picts?" Morgan asked.

"Yes, my lady. There is free land. Parties of men have already built palisaded villages. Some have sent for their women and children."

"Is there not danger?"

"These lands were never Pictish," he said, "at least not after Roman times. There is no reason to suppose the Picts will object to our presence there, so long as we do not stray north of the boundary of the Antonine Wall. Our settlements may be close enough to Pictish raiders for them to come after our cattle, but we can take care of our own."

Guenevere had been listening to this and said, "Gossip has it that the Picts have a cause Arthur will listen to."

"What might that be, Your Majesty?" I asked, for the question had been addressed to me.

"Why, it is said that Gawaine knows more than he should about the death of Pellinore," she replied casually. Her voice had a natural quality that carried it more widely than ordinary voices. The sudden silence that filled the room was proof that others had heard and understood her statement. We were in the queen's hall rather than the great hall. With so few people at table, the queen's hall was more than adequate.

How could I respond to that? I did not.

"I know what all know, Your Majesty," Gawaine said in the silence that lingered. From his tone, he could no more understand than I why she had voiced the statement. "I know Pellinore was a gallant knight. His death, if he has truly died, is a loss to match any of these last sad months. More than that, I cannot say."

"Cannot or will not?" Guenevere asked, continuing the conversation with honey dripping in her tone.

"Cannot, will not, choose not," Gawaine said, irritated by her continuing the discussion. "What is it to you, my lady?"

His tone of voice and insolent question brought a frown from the king, but Guenevere placed her hand on his arm to quiet him while she continued her examination of Gawaine. "If you could shed light on the manner of his death, it would be of interest to all."

"I trust he died like a gentleman," Gawaine replied.

At a signal from King Arthur, Lady Mal began a song, and courtesy demanded that conversation cease. The ballad was about the three graces of Britain, as I had anticipated. Morgan smiled at the stratagem, but Guenevere merely looked bored. She chose not to reopen the quarrel when the applause died away. I would not have done so either, in the face of Gawaine's barely contained fury, but I believe she had merely become disinterested in the subject. Fury from a male would have been no hindrance to her.

After the meal I encountered Morgause in the hall and inquired, "What information does the queen have about Pellinore's death that she has not shared with others?"

"I rarely gossip with the queen," she replied, shrugging. "I do hear tales, though, and might guess at the truth when I do not know it and knowing it would be useful. Which do you wish me to tell you about, the tales or the guesses?"

"Neither. It is not my affair. I fear the queen has made trouble for Gawaine, though."

"The queen is tormented by Lancelot's coldness since his return. She is bored. Perhaps it is no more than that, but I agree that it is still dangerous to speak openly of such a subject. Arthur may not be able to ignore it."

With that friendly warning, if it was that, I sought out Gawaine. I found him with Gaheris, as usual.

When I related my conversation with Morgause, Gawaine sighed, considering. "I am concerned about our mother," he said, finally. "She is more credible than other gossips, such as Kay, although I do not really know why. But if she believes this and says as much to others as she did to you, she could do us more damage than the queen. I must find out." He looked shamefaced and added in a low voice, "I dread going alone. I was ever fearful of displeasing her. Will you come with me?" He spoke as if Gaheris were not there.

The three of us found her in quarters that much resembled a draper's stall with rich fabrics strewn around, rugs, and tapestries. When I'd been here before, most of the space had been taken up by her loom. It was nowhere in sight, and I gathered she'd found a new interest.

Gawaine blurted out his concern. "Why does the queen attack me, Mother?" he asked.

Morgause looked at me and shook her head. "It is nothing so organized as an attack. The queen is merely unhappy. She is indifferent to what the effect of her words might be."

"She didn't appear to be unhappy to me," Gawaine objected.

"Oh, she hides it well, but she's quarreled with Lancelot and driven him from her side again. It's not the first time that has happened. She'll send for him eventually, when she thinks he's been punished enough, and he'll come back. He always does. In the meantime, she takes her spleen out on other males."

"You could counter such remarks," Gawaine suggested.

"Me? I am dependent upon Arthur's charity! Why should I quarrel with his queen?"

"We're your kin!" Gaheris exclaimed.

"So is the king! He's the son of my own sister Igraine! I'd rather he remembered that than that my sons conspired to kill Pellinore!"

"No one who knows you would believe you mourned our father, Lot, enough to seek revenge for his death," Gaheris said bitterly.

"No?" she asked, looking with surprise at Gaheris. I gathered he did not often speak so to her. "Nor did I," she responded, shaking her head after a moment's reflection. "Your father was not a loving man. We had quarreled and separated years before Pellinore killed him, if he did. I have heard it was Balin, anyway, not Pellinore at all. Even Pellinore said so."

"Lot was our father!"

"He was disowned! Dishonored!" she retorted in anger, "exiled by the clan! You were there the night he raped Morgan, were you not, Gawaine?" she asked appealing to her oldest son.

When Gawaine nodded grimly, Morgause continued in a more subdued tone. "Anyway, had he lived, there would have been no rapprochement." She turned back to Gaheris and asked with some asperity, "And tell me, what business is it of yours, anyway?"

"If you bring shame on his sons, it is our business," Gaheris said.

What shame? I wondered. What was he referring to?

"I relieve you of any responsibility for my conduct," Morgause said, white with anger now. "Do you also wish to censure me?" she continued, turning my way with a sharp look.

"I would not dare." I spoke lightly, but it was true. Morgause was one of the few persons in this world I would have think well of me. And I wanted to love her, if only for the ideal that was in my mind of what a mother should be.

"You fear me, Mordred? That is unkind, but you are the only wise one of my sons. You may all leave me now. I'm expecting a visitor who would not be happy to see you here."

We left, by chance to meet Lamerok, Pellinore's son, in the hall leading to Morgause's rooms. He glared at us, but did not speak.

"I think he suspects us of killing his father, Pellinore," Gaheris said.

"Why would that lead him to Morgause?" I asked.

"Who knows? But all Camelot is buzzing about Pellinore's death, and his son would hear of it from a dozen mouths," Gaheris said.

"Small matter," Gawaine said carelessly. "We must seem unconcerned. I like not his calling on Morgause, however," Gawaine said. The corridor was too narrow for the three of us to walk abreast, so I dropped behind and missed the gist of what they were saying to one another. My mind was on Morgause. I was concerned about more than talk. Gareth's wife had said that according to court gossip, Morgause had had numerous lovers since coming to live in Camelot. Could this be another? Was this what concerned Gaheris, that Morgause would have an affair with the son of the man he believed had killed his father, Lot?

I was angry for Viki's sake. Lamerok should respect her more than this! Still, Lamerok might have some other thing in mind besides pure lust, and I did not wish to see Morgause hurt.

Full summer came, and gossip about an affair between Morgause and Lamerok heated up along with the weather. I had stayed away from Camelot for I had little desire to participate in the life of the court and was unaware of the tensions building around the affair between Morgause and Lamerok. However, Gareth enlightened me. "I'm worried about Morgause and Lamerok. I'm afraid I won't get into the Round Table." He sometimes spoke elliptically that way. He made sense if you took the time to sort it out.

"You mean because of the gossip? Stay away from Morgause," I said. "She would not be pleased to find you concerned with her affairs. It isn't as if she ever showed any special interest in you, or me, for that matter."

"It's not that. I just don't want any trouble to rise between Lamerok and Gawaine," Gareth said. "They are both knights of the Round Table, and now that I've been knighted myself I must be sponsored for Round Table membership without anyone's dissenting."

"You really wish to join the Round Table?" I asked in surprise. "I would wager even Arthur thinks it's in the process of dissolution. So many knights were lost in the quest for the Grail, or just went home during it, that only the mercenaries are left. They don't even seem to care about the Round Table."

"It's all I've ever wanted," he said simply.

"All right," I sighed. "Why do you think Lamerok will object? Your father is Pelleas, acclaimed high king of the Picts, even though he acknowledges Pellinore, Lamerok's father, as his liege lord. I'm surprised Lamerok doesn't offer to sponsor you himself."

"That's not needed," Gareth said. "Sir Lancelot will sponsor me if Gawaine doesn't spoil it all by entering into a quarrel with Lamerok. He promised."

I started listening seriously, guessing this was what he had come to tell me. "So, what is likely to happen?" I asked.

"Lamerok keeps hinting that Gawaine has guilty knowledge of Pellinore's death. He doesn't come right out and say it, or Gawaine would be able to challenge him, but people are beginning to take his hints seriously," Gareth said. "Do you think something happened out there?"

"I don't know," I grunted. I wasn't about to talk to him about it. The quarrel between Gawaine and Lamerok was obviously not over Gawaine's being irritated by a scandal about an old woman taking a young man for a lover. I wondered if Lamerok was just using Morgause. I had thought he sought to seduce my mother in return for my seduction of his wife, but this sounded like something more.

"If Lamerok challenges Gawaine, he may find he has to fight not only him, but some others as well," I said, "but King Arthur would never permit dueling between fellows of the Round Table. You know that."

"It could happen," Gareth said stubbornly, "but that's not the worst of it. Lamerok talks about Morgause when none of us is around, and the serfs who serve them in Morgause's rooms talk in the kitchen about what they say." Even though as a knight Gareth was free of kitchen duty, he often visited there to see friends and to beg food. "The scullery boys are wondering how available she is, thinking they might be able to scratch her itch if Lamerok tires." There were tears in his eyes, and his hands were clenched into fists.

I understood his confusion. In the absence of action from Gawaine or his brothers, he didn't know what was expected of him. I had always loved the thought of Morgause, even when she ignored me except when I was in her presence. Then she charmed me as she did all men, effortlessly. I had chosen not to judge her conduct and deeply resented anyone who did so. Morgause was Morgause. And now my throat tightened as it did on those rare times I lost my temper. A pulse began to throb in my temple.

I rode back with Gareth to Camelot to go looking for Lamerok. I thought it well that we talk. Inside the castle, I pulled off my boots, fouled by the mud of late spring. Since it was already evening, I thought I knew where Lamerok might be found, and intended to head for Morgause's room at the near end of the women's quarters. A white-faced page ran up to me before I could don the light shoes I'd taken from my saddlebag. I knew the boy; he'd promised to pledge himself to me as soon as he was free to do so. Now he clutched my arm, out of breath and in great agitation.

"Oh, my lord, you do not know what has happened!" he said desperately.

"Then tell me," I said, finding a smile for the boy.

"Gaheris has killed Morgause," he blurted, "killed her in her bed! Come before Gawaine goes mad!"

Morgause! Killed, he said? I pushed him gently to one side and set out at a dead run for Morgause's door, filled with an overwhelming sense of loss. I had not given up hope of finding a closeness with my mother, but now it was forever too late!

It was as the boy said: by the dim light through the narrow window in her room, I could make out Morgause sprawled in the bed with her head cut from her body. I seemed rooted to the floor, just looking. There was an astonishingly great amount of blood. Gawaine had Gaheris backed into a corner, leaning toward him as if he would impale himself on the dripping sword Gaheris held ready.

"Dog! Ass! Snake! What are you? Monster!" Gawaine screamed. He was so angry he could not speak coherently.

As for me, I stumbled over to Gawaine, vaguely aware my feet were in something warm and sticky. I grabbed Gawaine by the tunic and thrust him tumbling into a corner to get at Gaheris.

Gaheris was in shock. "I struck at Lamerok," he gasped in a flat voice, gazing out of unfocused eyes, "not Morgause. Never Morgause." He reversed his sword, held the blade in his bare hands, and drove it toward his chest. I grabbed one of his wrists and twisted it until something snapped. The sword dropped. I stooped to pick it up, but as I rose I sensed Gawaine behind me. I turned just in time to see him strike me with a stool. I was conscious of a blinding light and the single thought, Oh, he will pay! then nothing.

I woke in a small room, with Gareth sitting near me, looking worried. He was washing my feet.

"Are you all right?" he asked when he saw me awake.

"No, I am not," I said. "What happened?" I felt it was something bad, but I couldn't summon my thoughts. Gingerly I felt the back of my head. Hmmm . . . a large lump. As I probed it, a lancing pain caused me to hiss. With it came such a sense of loss that I closed my eyes to contemplate it.

I remembered: Morgause. Ah, Morgause!

"Gawaine did not want to hurt you, just stop you from killing Gaheris," Gareth said.

His words were an intrusion. "Why would he want to do that?" I muttered. I hadn't meant to kill him. I'd intended to beat him with the flat of his sword, the traditional punishment for a coward.

"Maybe to kill him himself," Gareth said. "He was angry with me when I took Gaheris to the leech to set and splint his arm. You broke it," he added accusingly.

I didn't remember that. "Where's Gawaine?"

"He's getting men together to go after Lamerok. If Lamerok

passes the guards on Hadrian's Wall before Gawaine can warn them to hold him, he'll be unreachable. Once in Caledonia he can rally the Picts against us to keep Gawaine away from him."

"Why Lamerok?" I asked, thinking slowly. I seemed to be able to deal only with small bits of information. What was wrong with my head?

"Don't you know?" Gareth sounded surprised. I glared at him until he said. "Gaheris found him in bed with Morgause."

"And Gaheris killed Morgause for that?" I asked, outraged. "Everyone knew they were lovers!"

"I know. Gaheris tried to kill Lamerok, anyway," Gareth said. "Finding them together was too much for him. Maybe Lamerok taunted him. When Lamerok ran away, Gaheris was so mad he killed Morgause instead."

I didn't believe it. Maybe Morgause had been killed accidentally in a struggle between Gaheris and Lamerok, or even perhaps Lamerok himself had killed her. Gaheris would never harm his mother purposely.

On my trying to rise, nausea much like seasickness gripped me. I clutched Nithe's pearl on the chain around my neck and thought of her until my head cleared. "What are you doing?" I asked finally as Gareth began to towel my feet.

"I thought to relax you," he said in a confused voice.

I rose on one elbow, but had to close my eyes against a sick new wave of vertigo, and desperately clung to my amulet. Ah, Nithe! When it passed I looked at him searchingly. The water in the basin he had used to wash my feet was tinted red. I suddenly realized what I had waded through in Morgause's room while reaching for Gaheris.

I thrust Gareth violently away and toweled my feet myself, cursing savagely. There was little room for grief in the strength of my distress as I lay back, shuddering. "Go away!" I ordered. I closed my eyes, still cursing. I wanted no ministrations. Why was Gareth not in pursuit of Gaheris, anyway? Lud, I had to get up! Ah, Morgause!

"I thought you would not recover consciousness for hours," a voice said.

I opened my eyes to see Morgan regarding me, a half smile on her face. Behind her stood Gareth looking apprehensive.

"Don't attempt to rise," she said as I made the effort. "You'll do yourself an injury. You have been badly hurt and any exertion just now will make it worse."

"Where is Gawaine?" I demanded.

"You wish to call him to account for striking you?"

"Something like that," I muttered as I attempted to rise, only to be overcome again by giddiness. Morgan had little trouble in pressing me down again.

"Gawaine has gone after Gaheris, or Lamerok, one or the other," she told me. "He didn't say which. What he intends to do if he catches one or the other, I have no idea; I've never understood Gawaine. What is sure is that you were not fit to go with him, and he would not wait. Would that he had." She turned to Gareth. "If you love Dylan, don't leave him, or he'll take off as soon as he can stand alone. I am convinced you are ready for the Fellowship of the Round Table. Treat this as that sort of responsibility. Fulfill it, and I'll speak to the king in your behalf."

"Oh, lady!" Gareth said, overwhelmed. "But Sir Lancelot was to sponsor me and he's not here. They say the queen quarreled with him and sent him away."

"He will return," she said confidently and, looking at Gareth a moment, smiled kindly.

I guessed then that Morgan knew Gareth was Pelleas's son and probably knew about me, as well. I smiled ruefully myself, despite my throbbing head. There were no secrets in Camelot, it seemed.

"The more Dylan rests now," Morgan told Gareth, "the sooner he will be able to follow after Lamerok, if that is his wish. See to it." In leaving she looked back at me. "It is good to find a new young cousin. Lud knows the clan needs new blood."

At that word I saw in my mind the crimson pool surrounding the body of Morgause, and a weakness came upon me. I shut my eyes. When I opened them some time later, Morgan was gone and Gareth was polishing the sword he'd won from the Red Knight.

Despite what Morgan had said, I could not stay in bed. I rose, brushing off Gareth's remonstrations. I vomited when nausea washed over me, but I grasped my pearl and my head cleared. I was afraid I would not catch up with my brothers in time. If they teamed together to murder Lamerok, Viki's husband, it would start a blood feud between our two families, and I'd never see her again.

I couldn't dress and hold Nithe's pearl at the same time, particularly hindered as I was by Gareth, and fainted before I could finish. I wakened back in bed with Gawaine standing over me, shaking me.

"They got away," Gawaine said, "both Lamerok and Gaheris. I couldn't find either of them. We bury Morgause today, or I would still be in pursuit. If you can rise, we need you to mourn our mother."

Part III

The

Prince Regent

487 - 489

Justinian, the greatest of the Byzantine emperors, is a village boy playing near the Adriatic while, in Britain, Mordred and Arthur meet at the battle of Cammlan.

CHAPTER
XII

I do not recall much of Morgause's funeral except that it was raining. There were puddles in the open grave. I remember objecting when Gawaine or someone cut long shallow grooves into the backs of my arms until blood welled up and dripped freely. The same person ignored my protests and smeared my blood across my face so it appeared I had cut my face as well. Someone else then tore my shirt and threw ashes in my hair, so I must have presented a most villainous appearance standing between Gawaine and Gareth at the funeral rites. Gareth was holding me upright with Gawaine growling when I muttered I wanted to lie down.

Gareth was weeping. Why wasn't I? I could not concentrate on thinking about Morgause, though I tried. The light and noise kept narrowing down, fading at the edges and turning white. If it had not been for Gareth, I would have been disgraced for falling asleep more than once as the druids intoned the burying rituals and the women keened. It took forever and my light-headedness did not diminish.

"What is wrong with me?" I muttered.

259

"Gawaine hit you with a stool. He bruised your brain," Gareth told me under cover of the noise of the mourners.

"Why would you do that?" I asked, casting a puzzled look at Gawaine, wondering why I was not more angry. He ignored me.

"You were about to stab Gaheris," Gareth whispered. "He killed Morgause. Don't you remember?"

I shook my head, to be rewarded with a sudden nauseating pain that flooded my awareness, sending me into near oblivion. Fumbling to touch the pearl Nithe had given me, I held on to it like a lifeline and, though I still could not see, I faintly heard Gareth say, "Help me, Gawaine. He's going limp."

I was grasped in an iron grip on the other side and hauled back to my feet. "Hang on, laddie. It's but a short time," Gawaine muttered in my ear.

"You hit him too hard," Gareth told him bitterly.

"If I had hit him more gently, he would have succeeded in killing Gaheris. Not that it would have been a loss, but later he would have resented my not stopping him," Gawaine explained quietly. "It's bad enough to have a son killing his mother not to compound it by having a brother kill a brother! The clan would never live it down. It would be thrown in our faces at every feast! He'll thank me for it when he stops hurting."

I heard the words and wondered, had I been trying to kill Gaheris? I remembered: no. In any case, I could not believe I would thank anyone for making me feel as bad as I did. I must have fainted again, for when I awoke, I was in my bed in the military barracks. I recognized the ceiling, the same dirty boards. I was beginning to hate that, too.

I am uncommonly hardheaded, a legacy from my Scoti ancestors, I am sometimes given to understand. That did not protect me from having a headache that was almost too much to bear.

Borre was asleep on a pallet, and Gareth was polishing his great sword again and glancing at me from time to time. "Ah, you have awakened! I thought you would sleep forever!" His tone was light, but did not entirely conceal his anxiety.

"Where is Gawaine?" I asked.

My voice awakened Borre and he answered, "He has gone after Gaheris."

"And where might that be?" I asked, attempting to sit up.

"Gawaine says Gaheris went after Lamerok," Borre continued. "Gawaine says Gaheris means to kill Lamerok to erase the shame of killing Morgause."

I concentrated on his words and found I could think again. Ah, Lamerok! I knew why Gawaine had gone after him, and it wasn't to stop Gaheris. It was to help him hunt down Lamerok! I swung my legs over the side of the bed, fighting off the nausea that accompanied the movement.

"You're not supposed to get up," Gareth informed me.

"I don't have much choice," I said. "I have to ride after Gawaine. Lamerok is Viki's husband."

"You want to protect Viki's husband?" Gareth asked in disbelief.

"I want to keep a blood feud from developing between our two families," I said.

"Oh. Well, you can't ride out in your condition," Gareth protested.

"Were you considering trying to stop me, little brother?" I asked.

He did consider it briefly and gave up, looking to Borre to reason with me, instead.

"Morgan says you are to stay here until she comes back," Borre stated.

"Morgan? What has she to do with me?" I grunted as I tugged on my boots.

"Can't you remember anything? She's been taking care of you!" Borre exclaimed, a tone of concern in his voice.

"Well, I'll relieve her of that burden," I said. "I must try to reach Gawaine in time."

"Well, King Arthur told you to stay in bed, then," Gareth insisted, trying a new approach.

"No, he did not. He pays no attention to me," I corrected him crossly.

"Well, he would have!" Gareth said, nodding emphatically. "After the funeral he told me to stay with you. You were unconscious. He couldn't tell you to stay in bed, but he would have. I'll get him, and you'll see."

I could always tell when Gareth was lying. He assumed a spuriously innocent look. "I'm not unconscious now," I said, "not quite. Close, maybe, but not quite. Besides, I don't want to talk to King Arthur."

"Why not?" Borre asked.

I thought about it as I was folding my plaid to throw across my shoulder. "If the king wants to see me, he'll have to come to me," I said bitterly. "I'd die before I sent for him!"

"Why do you care what happens to Lamerok?" Borre asked. He liked him no better than I did.

"I told you! If Gawaine kills him, he'll set up a blood feud and we'll be drawn in. I'll never get to be with Viki!"

Gareth nodded once in agreement, and said, "Wait but a moment. I'm coming with you. I must bid farewell to my wife." He said it self-consciously, but with pride.

"Meet me at the stables, then," I said. "I'll have your horse saddled for you." Borre left with Gareth, and I struggled by myself to get to the stables, reaching them in time to see Borre ride out toward Caerleon. I wondered if he thought Lady Mal could stop me when he couldn't.

Gareth loved the charger he had won from the Red Knight for, in truth, it proved to be up to his weight and had enough spirit to serve as a war-horse. Holding the pearl tightly, I ordered the grooms to bring Gareth's steed out along with Black Nick. I inspected the feet of both beasts as I waited for Gareth, telling the grooms to lead out a pack pony as well, knowing part of the delay was because Gareth was after food for the trip. He would no more leave on a journey without an adequate supply of food than he would leave without the great sword he'd won.

I dipped my head into the watering trough, trying to cut down on the ache, and while it refreshed me, I was still slightly dizzy from the pain when Gareth came. As I had foreseen, he lugged a bulging leathern sack with him, which he proceeded to tie on the packhorse with no hint of embarrassment. I mounted and moved out, letting him scramble after me, muttering under his breath. I paid no attention, trying to concentrate on staying in the saddle. The continuing rain had made the going slippery all the way to Caerleon. I didn't dare risk a trot, well aware that my head would come completely off and roll into the ditch if I tried.

"We must swing by Fort Terrible," I said. "Lamerok would have stopped there, and we may pick up his trail." I knew it was just an excuse to see Viki, but not actually untrue.

Borre and Lady Mal were waiting in front of The Pig Girl as we rode into Caerleon. They and my squires were mounted and carrying weapons. My war band! I nodded at them, at the cost of another wave of nausea, but did not speak. Lady Mal looked sharply at me, and I could hear her speaking urgently to Gareth behind me.

The gate to Fort Terrible was closed when we reached it. A lookout posted on the catwalk behind the palisaded wall saw us, turned, and called out, "Dylan has come!" The gate swung open to admit us. Several of Viki's brothers took our horses' reins as soon as we entered. "Lamerok has come and gone," one said in a bitter tone. "Viki said we must wait for you but would not let us send after you."

"Take me to her," I demanded, and lost my balance and fell heavily to the ground as I attempted to dismount. The jar nearly caused me to loose consciousness again, but my vision cleared when I grasped the pearl.

"What's wrong with him?" The question was sharp and anxious.

"Gawaine knocked him out to save Gaheris; Dylan was going to kill him. Morgan says his brain is bruised."

The man hissed in concern as he helped me regain my feet. "He's in no better shape than Viki was."

"What's wrong with Viki?" I insisted. But this time others were crowding around, mostly women.

"She lost her baby again!" one of the women burst out.

"Lamerok beat her," another said angrily.

Beat Viki? My own anger welled up; my hands started clenching and unclenching. "Why?" I asked. I vaguely intended the question in a broader sense, but the answer I received was specific.

"Lamerok wanted to move her to Camelot, where he could watch her better, but she said it was too near her delivery time. He said then that it wasn't his baby. That's when he beat her."

It was my fault! He was suspicious. "I want to see her," I said in a voice I did not recognize, so thick with anger was it.

"Our brothers took her back to Mona as soon as she could travel," one of the men said.

She hadn't sent for me. Still I knew what I must do. The hate that had built up in me over the years flowed over and centered on Lamerok. I owed him payment both for Morgause and Viki. Why hadn't Viki sent for me?

They helped me mount, for I could not have done it myself, and we set out, joined by half a dozen of Viki's brothers. We retraced our steps to Caerleon to take the northern stone-faced Roman road. The rains had turned the British dirt tracks into impassible quagmires, so we stayed on the old Roman stone roads going ever northerly.

My vision faded, and only my grasp on the pearl was real to me. I seemed to hear Nithe's voice, giving me courage to go on.

Perhaps others spoke to me, and perhaps I responded. I do not know. There were periods of rest, and occasionally attempts were made to feed me, but I could retain nothing.

I was not even conscious of time passing until Borre thrust his face close to mine and said with vehemence, "Wake up! We have found him; he's ambushed Gawaine and our brothers. You must tell us what to do!"

I seemed to be looking out from the back of a long dark cave. I grasped the pearl and saw Borre's face form out of the mist. As I turned my head, I observed Gawaine, Gaheris, and Aggravain in the valley below with their gillies, fighting desperately against a score of men who surrounded them. Of these, I recognized only Lamerok.

Borre thrust my Roman sword into my hand, and I wheeled Black Nick around, urging him into a running gallop straight downhill for Lamerok. Black Nick crashed into Lamerok's horse as he turned it to face us, knocking it back on its haunches. Lamerok was jolted from the saddle, and before he could fully regain his feet, I'd dismounted and attacked. I hit him and hit him until Gareth wrapped his arms around me, and I could see Lamerok writhing on the ground, screaming in pain.

"Enough!" he shouted in his huge voice.

The fighting ceased.

"It is over!" I whispeted harshly, looking down at Lamerok.

Two of Lamerok's gillies came to carry their master away, but I commanded them to stop. "Let him lie!"

They backed off and I said, "He will die, in time. Perhaps while he lies there he will remember that I promised I would kill him if any harm came to Morgause through him. Perhaps he will even think of the unborn child who never lived to see its mother's face. What he will not do is move from this place. Leave him!"

I stood glaring until my vision narrowed and disappeared completely. For a time after that, I drifted in and out of consciousness, barely aware of riding or of stopping. Dimly I felt someone lift me and carry me to a bed. Then there were dreams of being fed warm broth and having my head bathed, but it must have been days before I was conscious enough to open my eyes and look around me. When I did I found myself lying on a low banquette against the wall of a house that appeared to be dug into the earth. The linen cloth I lay on was damp. I had been sweating; my fever must have broken. A woman with a plump, pretty face mostly in shadow was watching me anxiously. Behind her I saw an older woman spinning flax by the central fire pit. She was tattooed around the eyes. Pictish, she was, then.

"How do you feel?" my watcher said.

"Hungry," I said, "thirsty." My grasp of Pictish is limited, but she spoke simply. "Sick at heart," I added honestly, too weak to lie.

She smiled and left, coming back with a bowl of savory soup which she fed me out of a big spoon. She also saw me glance at her face. She was tattooed like the older woman, but not as heavily.

Touching her face she said, "Pictish women are allowed to be tattooed only if their male relatives kill enemies in battle. My son is a great warrior."

"Where is Gareth?" I asked, embarrassed to be caught staring.

"Out hunting with my son Galahad," she said.

"Galahad?" I asked. "Lancelot's son? I thought he had been lost in the Grail quest."

"No, he just no longer wants to be a knight. He says he has become a Pict."

"Did you say 'not be a knight'? I do not understand Pictish all that well," I admitted.

The woman repeated it in passable Latin and conversed with me in that language thereafter. "He has taken a new name, a Pictish one."

"Hmmm?" I asked. I really didn't care, but she wanted to talk.

"He calls himself Paynur, after my uncle, Pellinore, who is dead."

"Pellinore?" I lay back and moaned, thinking the rumors of an ambush were true then. "I cannot stay here, lady," I said. "I fear my kinsmen may have killed Pellinore. And I killed Lamerok," I added as I remembered the battle.

"Be easy," she said, smiling, urging more soup on me. "Call me Elaine: we are related now. We know about Pellinore's death. And Lamerok's. Galahad wished to be freed of the responsibility of seeking your life in vengeance, so we adopted you to replace Lamerok, as one lost to us. Look!" she insisted, and showed me the backs of my own hands. I saw blue lines there. My hands had been tattooed!

"What is this?" I asked, lifting a hand for her inspection.

"This is the mark of the Moon Goddess, the Great Mother," she said, pointing at the back of my left hand. "You can see the broken spear cast at her by the hunter god." And, indeed, the tattoo was a circle with an angled line drawn through it. One half of the circle was blue.

"On the other hand is the mark of the southern Picts," she said. "The kingdom is divided into north and south, and here only the southern division is shown as occupied."

On the back of my right hand I could see another blue circle, this time with a zigzag line slashing across it. It took some imagination to see in it all she said was there.

"I'm a Pict now?" I asked, astonished.

She laughed. "Yes, a Pict. You will have to earn further tattooing, if you wish it."

"This is why the Picts are called the painted people," I mused. "I know very little about them."

"You know some of our leaders, like King Pellinore and Pelleas," she said.

"They don't have tattoos."

"No, tattoos are considered old-fashioned," she admitted.

"Some of our people are changing, now that Bishop Ninian has been bringing Christianity among us. Even before that, some Picts like Pellinore and Pelleas followed Roman ways; the Romans do not tattoo. My father, Pelles, is not one of those who have dropped the old ways."

I asked about Gareth again.

"Oh, we didn't adopt Gareth. He has always been a Pict, by our reckoning," she said. "His father, Pelleas, is my brother. Pelleas is the son of my mother, Brusen," and she nodded to the woman who was spinning by the fire. The spinner turned and smiled at me. I could see that once she must have been as good-looking as her daughter.

"How could I take Lamerok's place?" I asked. She had said that!

"When a young person dies, we sometimes give a captive his name and treat him as we would have treated the one who has left us, had he lived. Lamerok was married, and you are expected to look after his wife. Her brothers said you would be willing," and she laughed again.

This was too much to understand. "A captive?" I asked.

"You came to us helpless," she said. "You were in our power. Any revenge we might have wished to take, as blood debt for the death of Pellinore, was available to us. We chose to adopt you instead, in Lamerok's place, as I already told you. No, you are not a captive."

"I will be called Lamerok?" I asked.

"Among us, at least," she said seriously.

"But I killed Lamerok," I said again.

"We know," she assured me. "We found the place where he died and burned his body. If you had not killed Lamerok, we could not have let you take his place," Elaine added grimly.

I was quiet for a spell while her eyes were focused on something in the middle distance, her mind busy elsewhere. When she turned her attention to me again, I asked, "Do I need to undergo some sort of trial to prove myself worthy?"

"No more than a newborn baby would," she said. "What needs to be done has already been done while you lay ill. Our shamans decided that you would die of your head injury, for they saw your lifeline shortened; there was a shadow on you. They gave you the rest of Lamerok's life so you could have more years on earth."

I didn't feel any different as a Pict than I had as a Gael, though my headache was gone. I had no new memories that might have been Lamerok's. I still spoke Pictish with difficulty and decided there was nothing in it but the symbolism of taking Lamerok's place. Still, I did think about being Lamerok and about my brother Aggravain's killing Pellinore. Pellinore was Lamerok's father. The one man kin to them all was King Arthur. Now that I had a new identity, was I expected to avenge Pellinore's death? If I were to kill the king, would I be doing it as Lamerok to avenge Pellinore's murder by King Arthur's kin, or as Dylan to avenge Morgan's father who was killed by Uther Pendragon, King Arthur's father? It was too much. I wouldn't do it. I had no desire to kill King Arthur. I wouldn't accept responsibility for a blood debt.

"What is this about learning to hunt?" I asked. "Gareth has been hunting since he could hold a spear."

Elaine laughed, a joyous sound. I could see how she might have captivated Sir Lancelot. "He didn't learn how Picts hunt, however. Pictish boys learn to hunt after they take their grown-up name following their eighth birthday," she said. "They live with the hunters and learn secret lore, particularly how to propitiate the god of the woods when they take life."

"Gareth is learning what he would have learned as an eight-year-old boy, had he been raised among Picts?" I asked.

"Yes."

"And Galahad?"

"He already knows. He was raised amongst us," she answered,

"and you must call him Paynur, not Galahad. That is his Pictish name. He will call you Lamerok."

I fell asleep thinking over what she had told me, and slept through the night. Next morning when I awoke I was much better, and Gareth came to see me, spending some time telling me what was in store for me when I underwent training. "You have to talk to the animals," he said earnestly, "asking permission to kill them and thank them afterwards for giving you their lives."

"Do they respond?" I asked with heavy irony. I wondered if Lamerok was happy to have me given his life.

"No, but the hunters say the god of the woods hears you," he replied seriously, as if my question had also been. "If you do not go through the ritual, you will get no profit from the hunt. Even if you make a kill, you will find the taste of the meat is sour, and it will spoil before you can eat it."

"That is always true if the game is not cleaned properly or taken out of season when the bucks are rutting," I said.

"True, but this is something different, something more." He shook his head at the wonder of it all.

I did not argue with him, for it was clear he believed it. I did not.

I was still bedridden when Morgan found me, accompanied by Cornu, her shield bearer. She was a warrior-queen as well as a healer.

"You here, my lady?" I asked in surprise.

"Did you expect I would let my patient just walk away and do nothing?" she asked lightly and sat beside me, placing the back of her hand on my forehead. She was smiling.

"Gareth told me of your care, my lady, and I thank you for it. I'm afraid, however, I have no memory of you beside my bed like this," I said apologetically.

"Small wonder," she commented. "Blows on the head are apt

to knock out more than memory of things happening around the incident. What do you recall of recent events?"

"I remember Gareth waking me and telling me Gaheris had killed Morgause. I remember being told that Lamerok had beaten Viki so that she lost her baby. From that time to this I have hazy impressions of wandering with Borre and Gareth. I can remember killing Lamerok, but I'm sorry, I cannot tell you more."

"At least your fever's gone, and you seem rational enough to me now," she said.

"I gather I was babbling when last you saw me," I said.

"No more than most young men," she said, smiling again. "You'll soon be active again, thanks to the excellent care you have had here and your own stout constitution." And she nodded to Elaine, who smiled.

She means my head is as hard as a stone, I thought, and looked at Elaine to see if she agreed. Elaine sat so that the firelight shone upon her tattoos. As I drifted back to sleep, I wondered if that had been so when she and Sir Lancelot were lovers. I wondered if that was before Sir Lancelot met the queen. When I awoke I found Morgan had gone back to Camelot. Lady Mal had gone with her, along with Viki's brothers. Gareth, Borre, and my squires waited for me to be well enough to ride.

My strength returned quickly, and within a week I had recovered enough to set out for Caerleon. Maybe Viki had returned from Mona. Gareth didn't want to leave. Borre said that both Gareth and Galahad were considered special because of their great size. Galahad was a Geen, like Gareth. Between them, they could carry a gutted beast weighing two or three hundred Roman pounds by thrusting a long pole between its lashed legs and placing the pole ends on their shoulders. Usually several men may take their turns in bearing this burden, as much to lay claim to a part of the meat as to spell off a tired porter, but the Geens could even manage a slain boar by themselves.

Gareth had a new hero, which explained his reluctance to depart for home. "Paynur is the perfect knight!" he exalted. "Only he was pure enough to take the 'siege perelous' at the Round Table."

"Galahad," I corrected him, "Galahad did that."

"And did you know he defeated Sir Lancelot in jousting?"

"Galahad? You mean the same way he defeated Gawaine, by hitting him on the back of the head?"

"Oh, no, there was something wrong with Gawaine's account. He would never do a thing like that!" Gareth said, scandalized. "And his name is Paynur now."

"Not to me," I said flatly.

"It's truth," he insisted, starting to become angry.

I found I didn't much care. It took too much strength to quarrel, particularly about someone like Galahad. Let Gareth believe what he wanted. "Then Gawaine lied," I remarked. Gareth made no response to this, perhaps not wanting to think a Round Table knight might deliberately lie.

However, I didn't try to make it easy for Gareth. The truth was, I didn't like Galahad and made a point of forgetting to call him by his new name to the point of irritating him. When I'd said I wanted to leave, I was told it was too early, and I thought perhaps I was a captive after all. I blamed Galahad for the delay. Galahad spoke about my choice of address in front of the hunters, saying insolently, "What will it take to impress on you my proper name?"

"Perhaps if I were as impressed with you as you, yourself, seem to be, I would not be so forgetful," I replied. "Maybe it is only that."

"Do you mean to quarrel with me?" he asked, blushing like a maiden. Galahad was very fair and showed every emotion in his face.

"It is nothing I would humiliate myself to avoid," I replied coldly.

The hunters did not seek to intervene until Galahad reached

for the knife at his belt. "No!" the head warrior yelled. Galahad was not used to being checked so rudely and glared at him, but the man explained, "Among us when there is a disagreement, it is settled hand to hand. No weapons may be used unless both men agree."

"I need no weapon," Galahad said, untying his knife belt and tossing it to one side.

"Well, I do," I said. "What do you say to hurley sticks?"

He flushed again, not sure whether I wasn't suggesting that this was the type of quarrel boys might have, but he accepted a stick thrust at him, and I did the same, though looking it over first to assure myself that it was sound.

We stripped down, and the hunters formed a ring around us, bright of eye, to see their newest warriors fight. I wasn't much larger than the average Pict, and they were curious why I had pushed the challenge. I wondered myself.

I began warm-up exercises, and Gareth joined me, rubbing my back to loosen it. "You may be in trouble," he warned me quietly. "I have wrestled him and not defeated him. He is almost as strong as I, and faster. Are you well enough to risk this?"

"Do you know how I could get out of it?" I asked.

Galahad was watching me curiously, waiting for me to come to the mark. I noticed he looked bigger stripped than clothed while, from what I have been told, I looked smaller, more compact. When I stood up against him, he was over a head taller than I, within two inches of Gareth's height.

Galahad struck at me, using the hurley stick as if it were a sword. I dodged to one side, allowing it to miss me by a shadow's thickness, and jammed the blade of my stick into his ribs to teach him respect. He looked startled as well as pained, and I guessed he had expected an easy victory. Perhaps it was mere petulance that caused him to kick at my groin. It would have been a crippling blow, and one not permitted in any sort of duel unless the match was to the death.

My temper flared, surprising me, for there had been no precursor, no drumming in my head. I chopped at his collarbone, breaking it so that he dropped his stick. I grasped the stick with my toes and flicked it into the crowd. It was the end of the match. Gálahad was too shaken to continue and, by the looks given me by the hunters, it was well for me I had not seriously injured him. Gareth walked with me back to the village.

"I have never seen that hit before," he ventured.

"You're not likely to see it again," I said. "I would not repeat it, now that I am no longer so angry." Galahad wasn't the only one shaken. My temper had risen so fast I could not soften the blow. Had I struck elsewhere, his temple, for instance, I would have killed him. Was my temper growing within me, a something that would come and go of its own will?

When we reached Elaine's house, I told her Gareth and I would be returning to Camelot before winter set in, a transparent excuse since it was yet early fall. I explained what I had done to Galahad and told her I feared that the hunters would no longer see me in a comfortable light.

"It will do the young man no real hurt to lose some of his arrogance, even though he is my son," she said. "I don't expect he will see it that way, but I assure you the hunters will, even if they don't say so. He was becoming difficult to live with."

"You do agree it would be best for me to go," I said, looking for approval.

"Oh, yes. The good that has been done could easily be lost if he sought to recover his status," she said.

"I am by no means sure I could defeat him again, at least not unless I became angry again," I said. "I fear I am a berserker!"

"Do you hear the surging of the sea when that happens?" she asked.

"Usually something very like that," I admitted, surprised.

"I thought so. The shamans said you had been touched by Lir, the god of the sea. He is notoriously quick to anger and very dangerous then, becoming much stronger than he is ordinarily. Those who are his creatures share much of his temperament."

"That is why they looked at me as they did?" I asked.

"Yes. The shamans do not know how to propitiate Lir, and those who are ruled by Lir are difficult for them to control. That is why Picts do not sail out of sight of land when they fish," she added.

"I was found as a baby adrift in a ship's boat. The boat was lost in a storm and only I survived. The fisherfolk said Lir had marked me for his own."

"That would explain it then," she nodded sagely. "When Lir has set his mark on someone, it never leaves."

We left the next morning. I was surprised to see Galahad among those who wished us farewell. He came up to me and extended his hand. "I was wrong to attempt to kick you as I did," he said. "Sometime I would like you to teach me how to properly conduct myself in a match."

"I would be happy to," I said, taking his hand firmly. I am sure he had no idea how hard his hand was and how paralyzing his grip. He was not trying to cripple me; he was trying to show sincerity. I thought about saying "ouch" but immediately discarded the notion. He would be embarrassed, and this time might not come forward in friendship again. As it was, I released my hand as soon as I could without being abrupt. I thanked Lud for the time I had spent at hurley, which made it possible to smile as my bones nearly crunched. Hurley is a rough sport.

On the way south, Gareth asked me about his new hero. "Did you really come to see what a splendid fellow he is Dylan?"

He wanted my approval, so I spoke cautiously, "I will never come to love him," I said, shaking my head, "but I can see how others would." I am afraid it was not enough, for Gareth did not bring the matter up again.

I dismissed it from my mind, wondering what we would find when we reached home. Mostly I wondered if Viki would be there.

CHAPTER
XIII

Gareth wished to practice his new hunting skills on the trip south to Caerleon. I was in a hurry to get back to be near Viki. She'd be at Fort Terrible, but a few hours' ride west of Caerleon. So, Gareth, Borre, and the squires hunted, but only at dusk and in the light of false dawn, when it was still too dark to travel safely. I fished; I like that better than hunting. I caught a salmon or a trout for each deer or rabbit they brought in, and we ate fish for our evening meal and meat for breakfast. Fish has to be eaten fresh, and meat is better if it hangs awhile.

We praised one another for our separate contributions, but in truth, we all liked eating rabbit or venison better than fish, even me; no one said so. Gareth and I treated each other with special consideration, having been somewhat estranged over Gareth's friendship for Galahad. Gareth loved heroes.

Gareth and I dropped Borre and the squires off at the manor house and rode straight to The Pig Girl, ever a center for fresh gossip of doings in the countryside.

Lady Mal was delighted to see us, hugging first Gareth and then me. In truth, I was more than happy to see her as well. She never changed but was as steadfast a friend now as when I'd first known her. "Where have you been?" she exclaimed. "We've watched for your coming for weeks!"

"It took a little time for me to recover," I said.

"But you're all right now?" she said a shade anxiously, looking sharply at my face.

"Gawaine hit me with a stool, a little harder than he'd intended, perhaps," I shrugged. "You know how brothers are. If I'd rested a few days, as my cousin Morgan told me to do, I'd have come to no harm, but I thought I had to go after Lamerok."

"I know that story," she interrupted. "Sit! Sit! We hear most things here sooner or later."

"Is there anything to eat?" Gareth asked, impatient with the small talk.

I, too, was impatient. I waved my hand to put an end to the polite conversation and asked the question that was most on my mind. "Where is Viki?"

"She was at Camelot. She came in with Nithe and Pelleas in their Saxon longboat, but went on with the queen as one of her ladies-in-waiting when Guenevere moved the court to London."

"Gone?" I asked with a sinking heart. "But it's early in the year for that. Why so soon?" And why isn't Viki here, waiting? I asked myself silently.

"It's hard to be sure what occurred in truth," Lady Mal said slowly. "From the different stories I've heard, the queen was accused of witchcraft and had to undergo trial by combat. Her champion won, but she was so incensed at the need to be defended from such an infamous charge that she moved the court to London a month early. She swears she'll never return to Camelot. Without the court, trade at the inn has been terrible!"

"Who would be such a fool as to traduce the queen?"

"Gawaine," she said grimly. "The queen gave a party for him to spite Lancelot, whom she has not forgiven for whatever slight

278

it was he put upon her. She served apples, knowing Gawaine's partiality for them, and an Irish knight died of eating one. They tried the queen for witchcraft."

"But Gawaine could not believe the queen capable of that," I said in disgust.

"Aggravain could. He worked on Gawaine while the rash fool was drunk. When he sobered up, the damage was done."

"But why witchcraft?"

"Poison is a witch's weapon."

"Or a Pict's," I said. "So what happened?"

"Oh, there was a trial by combat. Lancelot appeared at the last minute, riding up from wherever he'd been in seclusion, and defeated the queen's accuser."

"Not Gawaine!"

"No, a knight named Madore. He was cousin to the dead man."

"He must be a man of courage, to ride against Sir Lancelot. No one ever stands up against him!"

"A trial by arms, invoking God's judgment, is different," Lady Mal said. "I could ride against Sir Lancelot if God were on my side, and fear no defeat."

I took a long drink. I'd not ride against Sir Lancelot unless I no longer cared if I lived or died. "There's nothing among the Picts to compare with British ale," I said idly but thinking furiously. What I said then was, "Viki did not wait for me to return. Did she fear Lamerok might be the one to return?

Lady Mal ignored my question. "I may as well shut up shop if Camelot closes down. Maybe the king will hold court here without her, though. Do you think that's possible?"

I shook my head. If Lady Mal didn't want to answer my question, it meant that she had no word of comfort for me. "I don't know what's possible," I replied.

As we sat together, with Gareth's stomach rumbling, a number of boys, perhaps a year or two younger than my own squires, brought us ale, bread and cheese, and then hot meat. Some I knew: King Arthur's pages. They eyed me expectantly. I wondered what they were doing here.

"These lads?" I prompted, nodding at the boys hovering around.

"Well, they're runaways. The queen vowed to give a dozen pages to the church in thanks for her delivery. They ran away to escape that fate. She left without knowing they were gone, but the boys expect she'll send for them. They say they won't go. We could ask your cousin about the king's plans," she suggested. "If he decides to abandon Camelot to please the queen, I have to know."

"Which cousin? Morgan? She's still here?"

"Yes. She bought that manor house next to the river north of Ayres's place, she and Cornu. You know the man, that short, hairy body servant of hers. They needed a place for their horses. There's been sickness among her grandchildren, and she wasn't able to go when the court left."

"The sickness didn't reach Camelot?"

"Oh, no. Camelot lies far enough above the river so that the clouds of smoke from the smelter downstream didn't poison their air," she said bitterly. "Children here in Caerleon died of it, and more would have done so if Myrddin and Cornu hadn't come with medicines to help."

"I'm sorry to hear of it," I said.

"We did all that could be done."

"Lud! I shouldn't have stayed so long!"

"Don't swear! From the look of you I'd guess you came on before it was wise."

"Hmmm. I'll stop at my fort tonight, but tomorrow I'll seek out Morgan. I'll ask your questions of her. These boys can come with me if they like. I'll put them with the others. The queen's mandate does not run in Caerleon."

"Take them," she agreed. "It's what they hoped for. As for Morgan, I'll ask her myself. Stop by for me."

The pages scrambled after us so closely that I feared one of them would get stepped on by our horses before we got home. None of them had spoken to me yet, but every time I looked at one, I found his eyes on me. I recognized several of them.

Gareth came home with me. "There will be no one to cook if my wife is in London," was the reason Gareth gave for avoiding his wife's house. It might even have been true.

My people welcomed all of us with food ready, having been warned of our arrival by Borre. They stuffed Gareth until he finally stopped eating, though it panged him. I marveled at him. I'd eaten my fill at The Pig Girl, and he'd matched me bite for bite. Even now, Gareth looked wistfully at the uneaten food.

Before I excused myself for bed, one of my squires said, "The new boys want to pledge themselves to you, Sire," nodding at them as they stood looking at me with anticipation.

One by one they knelt before me, giving me their names and kissing my hand as they promised fealty. There were princes among them, sons of foreign kings.

Next morning Gareth, Borre, and I picked up Lady Mal at The Pig Girl and rode companionably side by side to Morgan's place, a smallish manor in good condition. "It belonged to a widow who wanted to go back to her people. Her husband had been killed at the Battle of Badon," Lady Mal told us. She knew most of what went on near Caerleon.

We found Morgan telling stories to a number of children. She looked as pale as they did. "Greetings, cousins," she said. "Welcome to my house, you and your friends. It's good to see you again."

"You look about as shaky as I feel," I said. "Have you been ill?"

"No, just tired from nursing little ones who were. And yourself? You look as if you'd been overdoing again."

"He had a fight with Galahad, and we had to leave before he was fully recovered," Gareth said unexpectedly.

"Who won?" Lady Mal asked, looking for another ballad theme, like as not.

"Why, Dylan. Did he ever lose?" Gareth asked.

"It was more a misunderstanding," I hastened to say, to cut off further explanation. "Cousin Morgan, this is one of my best friends, Lady Mal of Caerleon. She keeps The Pig Girl Inn there."

"Cornu speaks highly of it, which is a great compliment," Morgan said, smiling. "His standards are very strict."

"He particularly likes my ale," Lady Mal said. "We brew it ourselves." She gave me a look that promised there would be more questions of me later on.

"Ah, he would favor it, then!" Morgan exclaimed. "Children, these men are your cousins, Gareth, Borre, and Dylan, and the lady is their friend, as you heard them say."

The children who had been watching with bright eyes suddenly tensed, looked at one another until one ventured, "Our cousins? Are you that Dylan? The four-goal hurley player?"

"He is that," Lady Mal replied. "The only four-goal player in Britain!" She liked teasing me about it, knowing it embarrassed me. Her behavior was frequently someplace between naughty and wicked.

One of the children, a young girl, stepped forward to speak to me as Morgan mounted her palfrey. "Can we come and be squires for you?" was the question she asked. "King Arthur won't take girls."

"With Morgan's permission, you will all be welcome," I said, looking from face to expectant face. What I would do if they held me to that vow I had no idea.

The trip to London was blessed with fine weather. Soft summer rains kept the air clear of dust, and Cornu played his flute for us at night, accompanying Lady Mal and her harp, bringing sleep and sweet dreams. Cornu seemed not to need sleep himself, mounting guard each night.

My dreams were all of Viki: it was over a year since I'd seen her. When we reached London we found Hugh was happy to see us.

Morgan took pity on me, knowing I wanted to go to Viki, and we left Cornu with Hugh while the rest of us rode to King Arthur's London palace, the refurbished Roman public baths. We borrowed respectable cobs from Hugh to give our own horses a rest: London is too muddy to walk in for it rains every day in the late summer and early fall, sometimes all the damned day.

Morgan conducted us to the women's quarters, and I found Viki waiting for me. Gareth sought Lady Lyoness, his new wife, and Morgan and Borre disappeared on some business of their own, but I barely noticed. Viki's welcome was all I could wish it to be in such a public place. She had changed but little from how she had looked on Mona. Perhaps there was a shadowed grief that gave her a new gravity, but she didn't speak of the miscarriage.

In turn, I didn't speak of Lamerok. I wanted to, though. "When will we have a chance to be alone?" I asked her as privately as I could manage.

"I'll leave with you," she whispered back, pushing me gently away.

Sir Lancelot came by and greeted Gareth, his protégé. "I've spoken to the king," I heard him say. "We will be able to induct you into the Fellowship of the Round Table this winter." He frowned when he saw me with Viki. "You're rather free with another man's wife, Baron," he said. Lamerok had been a fellow of the Round Table, and Sir Lancelot evidently felt I'd overreached myself.

"Widow, not wife," I shot back, stung into anger. "Would you take up his quarrel?"

Before he could respond, Morgan appeared from nowhere, took his arm, saying, "The king is looking for you, Lancelot," and dragged him away. He glared at me over his shoulder, but he left.

"Have you no respect?" Gareth demanded.

"For Sir Lancelot? None," I stated, looking him in the eye.

"But he's the foremost knight in the world!" Gareth was near tears, a dangerous sign, for he cries when he's angry.

"I pity the world," I said flatly, balancing on the balls of my feet to move quickly if I had to.

Viki and Lady Lyoness moved between us and, though I don't know what his wife said to Gareth, Viki scolded me. "You must not tease Gareth so!"

"I wasn't teasing."

"What's the matter with you?"

"It's nothing a dustup wouldn't settle. Gareth has been my little brother too long. He won't see himself as a man until he's able to put his foot on my chest."

"Well, let him then!"

"Not a chance," I told her coldly. She didn't understand. Gareth didn't really want to, he just had to try. One of these days he would.

"Why is there bad blood between you and Lancelot?" Viki asked, studying me.

"Lancelot is the queen's champion, appointed by King Arthur," Borre answered her. He'd returned with Morgan. "The queen doesn't want the king to acknowledge Dylan as his son. If the queen had produced a legitimate heir, it wouldn't be such a problem."

"That's only part of it," I said, still irritated. "I'm not just a king's bastard, in her Christian view I'm a child of incest, a monster. She'd loathe me in any case, and Sir Lancelot would support her."

"Does King Arthur feel that way?"

"I don't know how he feels," I told her. "He has been generous to me as Dylan, the hurley player. I don't know how he feels about me as Mordred, his son; I no longer much care." That wasn't

284

true, but what kind of man would refuse to recognize a son to have peace with an unfaithful wife?

The old baths had been added to, incorporating some of the old Roman-built private houses, to construct King Arthur's residence in the city. The original Roman palace had been demolished for its building stone, and the basilica and forum had become the city market. The only public buildings left had been the baths and the royal warehouse. Both had fallen into disuse after the Romans left and before King Arthur claimed them. There were no taxes gathered in kind to be stored and sent to Rome to need a warehouse, for one; and for the other, Britons don't bathe much, not like Romans, anyhow. I understand that. Bathing weakens a man; that's probably why Rome fell, I thought. Its people bathed all the time.

The quarters assigned to Morgan were on a quiet street, away from the public rooms. Viki and I had privacy there. I told her about Lamerok, and she told me about the miscarriage, crying as I held her. Viki examined my tattoos and listened quietly to my claim to be Lamerok by adoption and, consequently, her husband.

"We'll deal with this later," she said. "I cannot think of myself now."

"Then think of me," I said. "How long must we wait until we're together?"

"But we are together! And you must know I have vowed to serve the queen as a lady-in-waiting. I can't leave her now; I'm concerned for her. Borre tells me that Aggravain and his friends are speaking ill of the queen, saying her friendship with Sir Lancelot is adulterous."

"Do you claim it's not?" I asked. Why did she hold the queen in higher regard than me?

"I know it's not. When the king comes to stay the night with her, all her ladies are obliged to leave her quarters. She's very fastidious about such things."

"So you'd know if she were to see Sir Lancelot?"

285

"Of course! There are no secrets here."

"Does she know about us?"

"Well, no."

"Hmmmm."

"Don't hmmm me!" and she punched me on the shoulder. "Anyway, Borre says Aggravain is plotting to take Sir Lancelot and the queen by surprise and expose their guilt for all the world to see. Why does Aggravain hate the queen so?"

"It's not the queen, it's Sir Lancelot," I said. "Aggravain thinks the king slights his Gaelic kin and favors Sir Lancelot and his cousins." To myself I admitted I agreed with him.

"He's wrong about the queen and Lancelot, though," Viki said. "I'd know if they were lovers. I would! How can Aggravain expose something that doesn't exist?"

"I don't know! It just worries me. Aggravain is clever and devious. He's not even thinking of himself. He's jealous of Sir Lancelot for Gawaine's sake," I said. "If Aggravain can discredit Sir Lancelot, he thinks Gawaine will take his rightful place."

"And it's the queen who keeps Lancelot at the king's side," Viki added, understanding at last. She went to sleep before I did, but eventually I joined her. When I woke up later that night with Viki's head pillowed on my arm, I thought about it. Brothers are a problem, I admitted to myself; but in this instance, Aggravain was right.

CHAPTER
XIV

Borre burst in on us, awakening us from sleep.

"Aggravain has trapped the queen!" he shouted. "Come!"

"Good for him," I said.

Viki hit me sharply in the ribs. "No!" she cried. "It's terrible! You must help her!"

I shrugged and rose, pulling my tunic over my head, pausing to wait for Viki, who searched frantically in the dark room for her dress. I was in no hurry, myself. I'd tossed her clothes in a corner last night without thought of the morning. Borre grinned as he watched her in the light of his lantern while she untangled them, muttering to herself. Though Pictish women have little modesty about nakedness, she glared at him as she yanked down her dress. Borre was no Pict, and she knew what he was thinking.

We proceeded directly to the queen's quarters to see what had been done. I had some vague notion of trying to talk to Aggravain, shaming him if I could. If I couldn't, I'd threaten him with exposing his part in the murders of Pellinore and Lamerok, though that was pure bluff. I knew nothing.

I went unarmed. It was a mistake, like everything else that

happened that night. I should have known better, for I knew Aggravain.

We found Aggravain with a dozen men, all armed and drunk. They were beating on the wooden door to the queen's rooms, and shouting, "Come out, bitch!" "Bring your stud and we'll castrate him for you!" and such sentiments. I pushed my way through them until I found Aggravain.

"What madness is this, brother?" I demanded.

"You've come to join us, have you?" he asked. "You want first crack at the golden lady? You'll have to wait your turn!" And he laughed drunkenly, to be joined by the others.

"You're speaking of the queen?" I asked, amazed. "Arthur will have your head on a pike! Even Gawaine won't be able to save you this time!"

"Tell him, if you must," Aggravain snarled. As I turned to do so, he thrust at my back with his naked sword, slicing through muscle to the bone. My ribs saved me from being pierced through.

"Here, now!" one of the others admonished him. Borre and Viki lifted me from my knees and half dragged me clear. Viki was crying in frustration and anger, and Borre was cursing bitterly.

I seemed not to have the breath for either; the pain of the wound nearly paralyzed me. I staggered along between them until we reached the courtyard before my legs collapsed and I pulled both Viki and Borre to the floor with me. Viki was crying in panicked horror. I realized I'd never seen her cry like that before, not when she was cold and hungry on London's docks, or when she told me about losing her baby.

"What is this?" I heard Cornu demand.

I struggled to my knees, and Borre and Viki tugged me upright again. "Aggravain and his friends are trying to break into the queen's quarters," Borre said, gasping for breath from the exertion. "They have Lancelot trapped there. We must get help to them!"

"Fetch some then, but I think I'll carry Dylan to Morgan. We'll

288

see what she says," and Cornu picked me up as if I were a child. The man was a head shorter than me but was so strong, he made little of the task of bearing me, though I was no lightweight.

Morgan had not retired to Hugh's room this evening. She had been sitting up with a sick page in a makeshift infirmary she'd commandeered for his care. She was a notable animal doctor, preferring to treat them, but would on occasion serve people as well. Cornu laid me on a bed in response to a gesture from her.

"What is this?" she asked me.

"It's Aggravain," I said faintly.

I grunted in pain as she and Viki rolled me over on my belly, cutting away my tunic the better to see my wound.

"He's trapped Lancelot in Guenevere's rooms and brought a dozen men to seize him there," Viki explained urgently. "Dylan told me Aggravain has been plotting with his friends to bring proof of his accusations against the two of them."

"Damn him!" she muttered. "This is too much. He will pay for this in dear coin! But, how came this wound?"

"I tried to go for help," I said, gasping as she put pressure on the wound to stanch its flow.

When I could speak again, I said, "He stabbed me."

"Aggravain? Your brother? Arthur will have his head for sure . . ." Her voice faded out of my consciousness.

I came to enough to realize Morgan was sewing up the wound with a series of stitches as though I were a canvas sack of grain ready to be stored. I wished I hadn't. Sometime during her ministrations, wondering if the animals she tended were as little grateful as I felt . . .

I woke to find Gareth sitting beside me. He was asleep on a stool, leaning up against the wall. In the deep window seat I saw Borre, strumming his lute quietly and humming.

"Is the queen all right?" I asked.

Gareth sat upright with a snort, "Ah, you're awake! Good! I

thought you might have died, but I was afraid to say so. Viki would kill me for holding the thought."

"The queen?" I persisted.

"She was not harmed. Viki is with her."

That was enough for now. I slept again. Next time when I awoke, Viki was there, looking tired and worried.

"My love," I said in greeting, and she bent quickly to hug me. I grunted in pain as she pressed against me.

"Oh, sorry! I didn't mean to hurt you," she exclaimed, releasing me but hovering, her eyes huge with concern.

"And I'm sorry, too," I said, smiling. "I'll miss a lot of hugs that way."

"How do you feel?" she asked.

"Very light-headed," I told her. "As if I'd taken a fall from a wrestler twice my size." Actually, I didn't feel that good.

She put a hand to my brow and rose, saying over her shoulder, "Morgan asked me to fetch her if you awakened." She all but fled from the room.

Before she returned I must have dozed off again, for I awoke to hear her say to Morgan, "I hurried as fast as I could. He's burning up, isn't he?"

"Yes, I am," I answered for Morgan and attempted to sit up. Cornu materialized from somewhere and pressed me back down.

"Rest," he insisted.

Just before I went back to sleep, Viki asked in despair, "Oh, what can we do with him?" It was the kind of question Samana used to ask in jest. I chuckled at the recollection, marking Viki's quickly indrawn breath as she realized I had overheard. Those were the clear recollections.

Gareth came and went, came once more dressed soberly in black, and then came no more. And I missed Viki's presence. Where was she? Finally there was a time when I awoke with a clear head and posed the question, "Where is Viki?" Her dogs were beside the bed, so she must be about.

"She is with the queen, as one of her handmaidens, you know," Morgan said calmly.

I looked for Borre. "Where is Borre, then?" I asked.

"Borre's worn out. He's been at your side for days. I gave him something to make him sleep."

"Gareth?"

"You ask too many questions. Am I not good enough company for you?" She touched my forehead and nodded in a satisfied way at whatever it was she had learned. Smiling to take the sting from her words, she said, "Sleep!" as if she were ordering a dog to sit.

Such was her power over me that I did sleep, to awake this time with a thirst that would not let me be. "Water," I whispered. Borre was there with the king, watching over me. My father! King Arthur himself held a cup to my lips with his own hand.

"What has happened?" I asked, for I could see how worn King Arthur looked, and how concerned Borre was, not only for me but for the king.

"We are waiting for you to get your strength back enough so we can tell you," the king said. "Morgan made us promise not to talk about anything until she gives permission. When she does, there are many things you must know." And he shook his head sadly.

"Will she let you find me something to eat?" I asked. "I'll never get well if I'm allowed to starve to death."

Borre grinned hugely, saying, "I have more trouble getting food out of Kay's kitchen than I ever did on Cador's Island, but I still have some of the old skill." And he left whistling. I wondered why he was so pale.

King Arthur looked after him with his brows raised.

"When we were young . . ." I began, testing out my voice which was hoarse from disuse. "When we were young it was Borre's chore to beg food from Cador's kitchen when we hungered between meals, which was on most days. He was good at it, but he resented the need. He welcomed Gareth as a younger brother to rid himself of the responsibility."

I noticed that the king's face suddenly went blank when I mentioned Gareth's name. He'd been looking concerned. "It's something about Gareth, isn't it?" I asked him. Nithe once told me King Arthur never lied, not even as a child. He didn't this time, but he didn't respond, either. He just patted my arm, looked bleakly away, and called for Morgan. What was he doing here?

That Gareth! Like as not someone's teasing had gone too far, and he had responded for once. He was so good-natured he treated the grossest insults as jokes. That was fortunate for wits like Aggravain, who thought it amusing to see how far they could go with him. If Gareth had ever become angry, he would have been dangerous to taunt. Something came to my mind. Aggravain?

"Aggravain did this to me!" I declared indignantly.

As I said this, attempting to rise against the pressure of King Arthur's hand, Morgan came in, followed by Cornu.

"What he did will pale in comparison to what I'll do if you don't behave yourself," Morgan admonished me sternly. "I'll turn you over to Cornu, who will show you some things about wrestling you've never learned until now."

Cornu grinned.

I remembered how he had picked me up with little effort. I didn't want to wrestle with him. "I told the king that Morgan is keeping me weak for some purpose," I complained. "Maybe that's it."

Cornu glanced at Morgan and they both laughed, happy to see me on the mend.

"I've sent Borre for some of Kay's famous soup," she said, without breaking a smile. "If Borre says it is for you, doubtless it'll have something extra in it."

"It needs to be Gareth who asks, or the something extra will be spit," I said.

She nodded, smiling now. She evidently knew the story about my ducking Sir Kay in the soup cauldron.

Borre entered with a steaming pail. "I watched carefully while this was filled," he said, having overheard our conversation. "It is so clean I could eat it myself. I won't, mind you, for I am not partial to soup. But I could, if I had to."

He looked so doubtful I laughed, and the wound in my back hurt suddenly. I gasped. "How bad is it?" I asked.

"Aggravain's stab cut muscle, but the gash ran along the strands of fiber, not through them. A lung was pierced and collapsed, though, and I had to follow the wound in to sew it up. His blade was not clean, or there would have been no problem at all. Even so, if you were a horse, you'd be out in the pasture by now."

"Nothing about Aggravain was ever clean," I said.

"He probably never wiped his blade after cutting Pellinore down," King Arthur said.

"Do you know for certain he did that?" I asked, dismayed.

"Gawaine was there," the king said sadly. "He confessed to me. He said Aggravain put an arrow in Pellinore's horse and brought it down and then stabbed the man as he lay with his leg caught under his mount, just as he struck you from behind."

I remembered how it had felt. "I'll break him of that habit when I get my strength back again."

"There will be no need," King Arthur said quietly, ignoring Morgan's frown. "Lancelot was there before you. Put your mind at rest on that matter."

Morgan dipped a cup into the pail of soup and thrust it at me to cut off conversation. I drank it, found it savory, and smacked my lips to decide what it was made of. "Some kind of fowl?" I asked.

"Yes, chicken, among other things," she said, after tasting it herself. She made me drink it all, and then another cup, before she drove everyone out of the room so that I could go back to sleep again.

"I am not at all sleepy," I protested.

"Do you want Dynadan to play you a lullaby?" she asked ironically.

I supposed I did sound like a child. If I needed to sleep in order to regain my strength, that's what I would do. I willed myself to doze off while Morgan was still chiding me gently.

No one told me anything until I had been free of fever for a week. By this time I realized that both Viki and Gareth were somewhere else, for they never came to see me, and Borre spent most of his time in my room.

I waited patiently until I was by myself, feigning sleep, before I tried to rise. After a slight giddiness, I found I could balance on my two feet. It felt good to be up again.

Morgan found me thus. She entered carrying another bowl of steaming soup in both hands and, after setting it down carefully on a small table, turned to me, hands on hips.

"What is the meaning of this, pray?" she asked sternly.

"Since no one will answer my questions, I am about to seek answers for myself," I responded mildly. I wondered if I could walk.

"Sit down and eat this," Morgan said in a peremptory voice. She seemed cross that I had risen without her permission.

"Do not be offended, lady," I said. "I feel a need to be about."

She smiled and nodded, gesturing again toward the bowl of soup. "That's why I like doctoring animals better than people. They never talk back."

"What's in it?" I asked suspiciously. I had wondered if she had put sleeping draughts in my food to keep me on my belly while I healed.

"Soup," she replied, evasively, I thought.

"Well," I said. "I have had all the soup I am ever going to eat. I want bread and meat and wine."

"Do you think you know more about what's good for you than I do?" she asked in mock astonishment. "Remember what happened last time?"

"I'm hungry," I complained.

"That's a good sign. Eat the soup and I'll find you something more nourishing."

I complied, but with a bad grace.

"How much do you remember?" she asked when I'd finished.

I recalled she'd asked me a question much like that before. "I remember being awakened by Borre and going to Guenevere's quarters to stop Aggravain from embarrassing the queen," I said slowly. "I remember Aggravain struck me from behind when I would have gone for help. That's all," I concluded, looking at her.

"Well, help didn't come in time," she said. "Sir Lancelot broke the trap and killed those he found at her door. There were thirteen in all, including Aggravain."

"Thirteen?" I asked in disbelief. "One man killed thirteen?"

"They had to come at him one by one in that narrow corridor. They were all drunk," she said.

It was possible. "Aggravain is dead, then? Lancelot saved me from killing a kinsman," I added grimly.

"Florence and Lovel, Gawaine's sons, also fell," Morgan continued.

"Both boys?" I asked. I was shocked! "He had but the two."

"Both of them," Morgan replied.

Florence and Lovel. I had not known them well and liked them even less, but I grieved for Gawaine. "How is Gawaine taking it?" I asked.

"Gawaine is wrapped in deepest sorrow, but not because of them. He had warned them not to harass Lancelot, and they had laughed at him."

I nodded. I'd also spoken to the boys about Aggravain and, while they hadn't laughed, exactly, they had let me know they would make up their own minds on things. But she had said Gawaine was in deepest grief. "There is something more, isn't there?" I asked.

"Arthur condemned Guenevere to the stake for treason," Morgan said.

"There could no longer be any question of her innocence," I said.

"Catching Lancelot in her rooms at night doesn't prove anything," Morgan protested. "Lancelot is the queen's champion. He would come to her call, night or day. And," she added, "Lancelot does not love her in that way. His true love is Lavayne."

"Lavayne?" I said in disbelief. "But Lavayne's a knight! How could Lancelot love another man?"

"Many in the Round Table have taken comrades as lovers," she said, evidently astounded at my ignorance. "It's an old custom from Roman times. Look, I'm just showing you how sure I am there was no treason."

"Sir Lancelot? Lavayne? I can't believe it. I don't think anyone would believe such a story."

"You are not much around Camelot, or it would not be such a mystery. I gather it is not talked of in the taverns?"

"No," I said. "I would have heard of it from Borre or Gareth if it were even a rumor. Are you sure it is true?"

"Arthur says so," she responded.

"Then why did he condemn his queen?"

"He had to. Things had gone too far, with thirteen men dead at the queen's door. You could hardly hush it up. Adultery is merely a sin for ordinary persons, but for royal lines it's treason. It sheds doubt on the legitimacy of heirs.

"But he has no heir," I said obstinately.

"It doesn't matter, does it?"

"Was there a trial?"

"To what purpose? If Lancelot had not fled the king's justice, perhaps the truth could have come out. By fleeing, Lancelot himself condemned the queen. All that was left for Arthur to do was to pronounce judgment."

"Judgement, but not justice. She did not deserve to burn," I said.

"Oh, the king agreed with you. He expected Lancelot to rescue the queen as he had before. He even disarmed the guards so there would be no resistance."

"And Sir Lancelot came," I prompted her, trying to bring her to whatever point she wanted to make. Obviously there was something dire to tell.

"Oh, he did," she said bleakly, urging more soup on me.

I ate without tasting it, waiting for her to continue. Morgan was not one that could be bullied. Her hands were folded in her lap, and she looked into the middle distance. I sensed she had been there. She was seeing it in her mind. "Lancelot came riding out of the forest," she said, not looking at me, "and cut them down before riding off with the queen."

"Cut down the queen's guards? Cut down unarmed men?" Shock thickened my speech. "Why? He had only to free the queen. No one would hinder him!"

"It is a question much asked. Gawaine asks me a dozen times a day."

"Gaheris was there? Sir Lancelot killed Gaheris?" I guessed, at last understanding what she was hinting at.

"Yes. Gaheris was one." She sighed again and looked at me with compassion. "Torre was another," she said.

Lud! Sir Torre! Was there to be no end to this?

"And Gareth?" I asked, fumbling my way back to the bed and lying down.

She nodded sadly.

"How could he? Sir Lancelot was his hero. He knighted Gareth," I said. "He'd never kill Gareth." I turned my face to the wall in rejection. It wasn't so. The idea of family meant more to me than to most people, I thought, perhaps because I had grown up not really knowing if I had any or not. Gareth had depended on me! I'd never have let him stand by the stake as honor guard for Guenevere! Never! What could King Arthur have been thinking of? I must have slept again, though in my restless state, I couldn't be sure.

I was aware of suddenly knowing that it was true. I knew for sure when Lady Mal came in with Borre and started playing the songs Samana had sung to us when we were children. Borre knew them all, singing along with Lady Mal in his untuneful voice. Evidently he thought I'd take comfort from hearing the old songs again.

"Tell me about it," I said.

"I wasn't there. I was here," he said.

"I was there," Lady Mal stated. "I was standing at King Arthur's side." I could see a song had been forming in her mind on the topic.

"Lancelot must have thought he had to rescue Guenevere by force," Borre said, "as if he didn't know King Arthur expected him to come."

"But why Gareth? And Sir Torre?"

"Why, indeed? After Lancelot struck him, Gareth fell beneath the hooves of Lancelot's horse. He was trampled, Dylan," Lady Mal's voice broke.

I tried to visualize it. It was monstrous!

When she recovered herself, she struck dissonant chords on her harp and said harshly, "Brastius Red-beard had to hold Arthur back to prevent him from attacking Lancelot with his bare hands. Dozens of men were killed and wounded when Lancelot's cousins followed him, slashing at everyone who stood in the way. It was Lancelot's sword that took Sir Torre, though."

"No one struck back?" I asked, to help myself understand.

"With what?" Borre asked wearily. "Don't you understand? They were unarmed, a guard of honor. Honor!" he said and spat.

I didn't want to hear any more. "Why is Viki not here?" I asked, for I knew her absence from my bedside had some dire meaning, and I could no longer put off the question.

"After Arthur condemned Guenevere, Viki rode off to fetch Lancelot. She followed him back. When Lancelot carried the queen away, she followed the queen. No one has seen her since."

"She left me?" The bitterness I tried to hide embarrassed Lady Mal, and she continued to strum without responding, so I asked, "Where did they go?"

"To Joyouse Garde, Lancelot's castle in Armorica."

Lud, that was across the sea! I closed my eyes and thought about what they'd just told me. I guessed Viki held herself in some measure responsible for what happened to Gareth, since she had brought Sir Lancelot word of Guenevere's plight. The queen she'd hold blameless. She might choose exile with the queen rather than face me.

"What is Gawaine doing about it?" I asked, looking up again.

"Gawaine insists his honor requires that he take blood revenge on Lancelot for killing Gaheris and Gareth, not to mention Aggravain, Florence, and Lovel."

"Gawaine's honor?" I asked, incredulous, thinking of Pellinore. He'd been there! Why hadn't he stopped Aggravain then?

"So he says. He says he wants to see you. You're the closest relative he has left."

"Well, I don't feel related to him," I said. He should have stopped Aggravain! "Is King Arthur listening to Gawaine?"

"Yes. King Arthur has only been waiting for you to recover. It's been three weeks, Dylan!" Lady Mal said grimly. "He will appoint you regent in his absence. Then he is going after Lancelot."

I shook my head. Regent? "To what end?" I asked.

"To what end, indeed! Vengeance! Blood debt! All of the old tribal hatred is alive again," she exclaimed in disgust. "Lancelot's kin have gone back to Armorica with him. The Round Table is dead along with all the knights Lancelot killed at Guenevere's door and before the stake."

"Still, Sir Lancelot cannot refuse the king battle, were he to stand before Joyouse Garde with but a single squire," I declared. "I'll go with him!"

"No, I told you, you'll be regent."

"I don't wish to be regent. Let Borre be regent." I turned from Lady Mal to Borre. "You're King Arthur's acknowledged son. I will go to Armorica. Viki's there."

"She's with the queen. She won't be able to see you," Borre said sadly.

I hesitated. What he said was true. I would never be allowed inside Sir Lancelot's castle. No matter. If she loved me truly, she'd find a way out.

"We'll see," I said, as Samana used to when she had no intention of granting a request but wished to avoid an argument over the matter.

I swung my feet over the side of the bed, rising unsteadily as Borre sprang to help me. Wincing as my healing wound pulled slightly, I shook my head at Borre's unvoiced question. "The sooner I start to move about, the sooner I will mend," I said. "If the king is waiting for me, I'll make that wait as short as I possibly can. I'll talk to him about the regency then." I intended to refuse it.

Walking up and down carefully, I turned on reaching the wall and marched back across the room. Sweat stood out on my forehead at the effort, though the day was not warm. I was not up for long, but I rose again that afternoon and again that evening.

By the end of three days' passage, I demanded clothes and shoes from the page Morgan and Borre had left with me, and walked from my room to call upon King Arthur.

"Mordred!" King Arthur exclaimed as I entered the great hall. He came over to me, almost running. "You should not be up yet. Morgan would have told me else."

He'd called me by my name! He meant nothing by it, however; for as he stood, ready to come to my aid should I need it, his look was one of concern and courtesy, not love.

Morgan entered behind me and came to my side. "Indeed, I would have told you, had I known what was afoot," she said, looking at the king curiously. She must have heard him call me by name. I wondered what she made of that.

"I may not be at full strength, madame," I said lightly enough, but with full conviction. "However, I need no one's permission to walk about."

"You have no color in your face at all," the king said peering at me. I saw that I stood nearly as tall as he; he was beginning to stoop from the burden he carried.

"I can't get anything but sops from Cousin Morgan," I responded, grinning at her. "If I may have meat and wine, food and drink meant for a warrior, I will begin to look like one soon enough." Morgan had been augmenting my soup diet with eggs, milk, and bread for days, but had ignored my request for stronger fare.

Morgan smiled back at me as I voiced my complaint, but did not protest at my exaggerated characterization of her treatment of me. I thought she understood how indebted I felt toward her.

The king escorted me to the table and sat me at his side. There had indeed been changes! It was early for the evening meal, but a page brought cheese, apples, still-warm bread, red meat, and wine at King Arthur's request. Morgan watched me eat, standing on the other side of the table with her arms folded. Lady Mal was on her stool behind the king, playing and singing quietly to herself. When I caught her eye, she winked.

"Do you know about Gareth?" King Arthur asked me bravely, but with obvious reluctance.

"Yes, Sire," I said with my mouth half full. I swallowed convulsively and put down the bone I had been chewing on. I'd called him Sire! This was a day for firsts!

The king sighed. He had not noticed. Most men called him Sire, but the word had a special significance for me. It meant "father." "I can't tell you how much I regret what has happened here," he began.

I stopped him from going further by putting my hand on his arm. I didn't want to listen to apologies. This was too great a matter for apologies. "Gareth died believing the best of you, and of Sir Lancelot, for that matter." I didn't tell him that Gareth and I had quarreled over that part of it. I went back to eating. The sooner I was at full strength, the sooner I could go after Sir Lancelot. I didn't believe that the king truly wanted me to be his regent, and even if he did, what did I owe him?

The king was quiet as he thought about what I had said. "I hope it was so," he replied finally.

I looked up to see Morgan did not agree with me, but she held her peace. Just as well.

Next evening when I came to the great hall there were others present, Gawaine for one, talking forcefully to the king, who looked troubled. Pelleas and Nithe were also there sitting quietly, close to one another. Morgan was by herself, studying a glass of wine, swirling it, and watching the surface as if to divine some mystery. I was surprised to see Sir Kay as well. Usually at mealtime he was in the kitchen overseeing preparations.

"Brother," Gawaine called, rising and coming to meet me. "Add your voice to mine. We must avenge Gareth on the false traitor, Lancelot."

"We?" I asked coldly. "What have you to do with Gareth?"

"Why, he's our brother," Gawaine said in amazement.

"He was my brother, Gawaine! I'll avenge him! Aggravain was your brother. He answered to no one but you. Why did you not stop him?"

Gawaine staggered back as if I had struck him, his hand to his mouth. Before he could respond, Lady Mal struck a cord on her harp and began to sing. From the half smile on the king's face, I thought perhaps he saw that she was trying to protect me from Gawaine's importuning. In that she was successful, for Gawaine walked away to sit at the far end of the table, with his face averted.

I took the seat the king indicated across from him. He waited patiently until the song was over and then spoke to me in a low voice. "Baron Dylan, we have taken council and think it best to set our plans in motion. Are you recovered enough to take on the responsibilities of regent in my absence?"

"Never," I said. I was no longer Mordred to the king. I would respond as Baron Dylan, not as his son, then! "You can find a fitter person. Cousin Morgan is royal and experienced in ruling; let her serve you in this. I'm going to Joyouse Garde to challenge Sir Lancelot to single combat. It is my right."

"Morgan's healing skill will be needed in Armorica to physic warriors," King Arthur replied grimly. "Besides, she tells me you shouldn't undertake any violent action for some months or you'll be crippled permanently. You must stay in London." He raised his voice and all other talk ceased. "Those here will take witness that I name Baron Dylan, prince of Britain. He will act as regent in my name while I am absent on business of state. He is to consult with Kay, but final decision on any matter concerning the kingdom will be his."

I glanced at Sir Kay. No expression crossed his sour face, least of all approval.

The king rose, and I stumbled to my feet as well, trapped into a responsibility I didn't want. No one else moved, but everyone watched us intently. The king reached up and pulled the great golden dragon torque from his neck. He held it outstretched in his two hands, so I had to bend over the table for him to place it around my neck as a symbol of my new authority. I thought briefly it must be difficult to sleep with it on. I wondered if he took it off at night.

"Hail, Prince Dylan, the Regent!" the king toasted me with an uplifted flagon.

Gawaine, Nithe, Pelleas, Morgan, and Borre rose to stand with Arthur and joined the toast. Gawaine's face was impassive, showing neither pride nor anger.

"Hail, the Regent!"

"Hail, Arthur of Britain!" I responded. I noticed Sir Kay's flagon did not touch his lips when he joined the others in the pledge I made. I wondered why.

As the others settled down to an evening of quarreling and drinking, the king took Morgan and me aside. "We will set out as soon as we can load the ships."

"How many men go with you?" I asked, wondering about defenses against raids by Saxons, Picts, and Scoti that would occur when his enemies learned the king was no longer in Britain.

"Every able-bodied man within reach," he answered briefly.

I was stunned. "This is a personal quarrel. Sir Lancelot will meet you on the field of honor. You need no more than an escort! Surely you would not leave this land defenseless?"

"Lancelot has all of Armorica at his back. He will outnumber us vastly, no matter how many we can bring to the fray," the king said patiently.

"Your father, Uther Pendragon, went to war over a woman and brought his kingdom down," Morgan said bluntly. "Who knows that better than you, who had the task of putting it back together again? Are you as much a fool as he?"

"Speak to Gawaine," the king said, his face grimacing in pain in recognition of the truth of her words.

"Gawaine is headstrong and hasty," she protested. "You are the king. You cannot indulge yourself so."

"It was I who demanded that Gawaine persuade his brothers, Gaheris and Gareth, to stand beside the queen in the path of Lancelot's sword," the king explained, though loath to do so, perhaps. He seemed not used to being questioned. "Gawaine holds me responsible for their deaths: he who forgave me the deaths of his brother Aggravain and even his sons, Lovel and Florence. Dylan is the only one of his kindred left alive."

"Is it because Gawaine is my brother that I am to be regent, sheltered here in Britain?" I asked, not daring to add "not because I am your son?" I cursed myself that I could not make him face the matter for once!

"I honor you as Gawaine's brother, my blood cousin, and for yourself, Baron Dylan," he said smiling, nodding his head.

"I see," I replied. He would not say it, could not in all likelihood. Probably the church would never allow him to acknowledge me. He dared not lose the blessing of the church if he were to hold his kingdom together. He'd lost everything else. I thought bitterly that Christianity had come in the train of the Roman legions but had strengthened as the military power of Rome waned. Even non-Christians like myself were constrained by its power.

The king looked perplexed, waiting for my answer. "You honor me for the wrong reasons, Your Majesty," I muttered softly. A moment later I added in a firm voice, "But honor demands I say to you, 'Think well on this, Arthur of Britain! As regent, I will take care of Britain as if it were my own.'" I thought the king was betraying Britain, taking all of the able-bodied men out of the country and leaving it defenseless.

"I can ask no more of any man," the king said in surprise.

"You ask too much of this one," I said in bitterness. "You strip it of every fighting man. Who will protect it?"

"It will be your task to answer that question," he said sadly.

"Then I will," I grated. "I swear, I will guard it with what dogs I can whistle up against the wolves who will be circling our flocks. But those I raise I will call my own!" I left in fury, finally at terms with my father's intention to leave me nameless. So be it . . . I had made something of a name for myself already. Now I would do more!

CHAPTER
XV

King Arthur asked Sir Kay to issue me three purple surcoats to wear over my brown linen tunic. A surcoat is sleeveless and hangs open all the way to the knee and serves more as a symbol than as a useful garment. Sir Kay did so grudgingly, giving me ones that were royal purple but faded and mended, with the gold thread that once lined the borders thriftily removed. The first time King Arthur saw me in one, he lost his temper and had Sir Kay brought before him.

"Are these my stores or yours?" the king asked him, with eyes as cold as sea ice.

"In truth, Sire, they are the kingdom's," Sir Kay said sulkily.

"They are not, then," King Arthur roared in a voice more suited to a troop muster than a royal audience. "They're mine!"

"You hold them in trust for the kingdom," Sir Kay maintained stubbornly.

"I do not!" the king corrected him harshly. "The kingdom owns nothing her king does not give it. Think well. When I acceded to your father's request and made you seneschal over all my lands, I was speaking of my lands, not the kingdom's lands, which is fortunate for you, for you'd have naught to oversee, else. But I will not have this discussion with you. I told you to issue garb for Prince Dylan so that people will know he is regent in my absence. What will they think if they see him in these rags?"

"They'll probably think what I think: that he's not much of a king," Sir Kay retorted snidely.

"Let me speak to Sir Kay," I requested. "It is I who will have to deal with him in your absence."

King Arthur nodded.

I grasped Sir Kay by the slack of his tunic and jerked him up against me. Sir Kay was taller than I, but not as strong for all that, slack-muscled from his easy life.

"Hear me," I said quietly. "For myself, I care naught whether I wear king's purple or peasant's brown. I'd sooner go to Armorica to challenge Sir Lancelot than skulk in Britain, out of harm's way here with you. However, I've been told by the king to act as regent in his absence. You have been told to assist me. If I discover again, as I have this day, that you seek to diminish my effectiveness, I will hold you personally responsible. I did that once before, for your mistreatment of Gareth. I trust you remember?"

He squirmed in my grip.

"Now," I continued, "I've sworn no oath to your father to hold you as seneschal as King Arthur once did. So, if any act of yours materially damages my authority here, I will kill you. Do I have your attention?"

Sir Kay attempted to break free, kneeing me in the process. He missed hurting me, but it would have been a crippling blow had it landed squarely. In response I shook him until his teeth rattled, throwing him against the wall hard enough to stun him. The old black anger gave me strength enough to snap him in two, but I desisted. King Arthur made no move to interfere. As Sir Kay attempted to rise unsteadily to his feet, hatred in his glance, I stepped up to him again, grasped his tunic as before, and hauled him upright. "Shall we start again?" I asked.

"Loose me," he rasped. "I will do my part."

"Good, then," I said, stepping back, stripping off the surcoat and flinging it against his chest. "Take this rag and exchange it for something that befits the regent of the king. In future it is your place to make me as acceptable as you can in the eyes of King Arthur's people. I will tolerate nothing less than your best, and I will soon enough know what that is. I will ask others when I have doubts!"

"You will have no cause for complaint," he said in a surly tone, wiping at his face. He had bitten his tongue and was bleeding slightly from the mouth.

"I will not complain again," I said with outward calm. "I will act." What I wanted to do was smash him flat again. Knee me, indeed!

While King Arthur gave me detailed instructions about the responsibility he had laid upon me, Sir Kay left to return with three new surcoats. He gave them to me without comment. I selected one and handed the others back. "Send these to the guardroom. As regent, I will live in the captain's quarters there."

"Where will the captain live?" Sir Kay queried.

"I will answer you this once, but do not ever question an order of mine again," I said. "The captain will go with King Arthur, along with the rest of his men. I will find my own guards."

Sir Kay turned, seeking a page to carry out my instructions. He was too proud to carry them out himself, though it would take longer to do it his way.

"You need not sleep in the guardroom," King Arthur said. "You can have my quarters, or Guenevere's for that matter, if you wish."

"Guenevere's women would be furious if I moved in on them," I said, "and I do not wish to take your place in any way. I will make a place for myself."

"I see," the king said, nodding, and together we went out to inspect the men he had ordered to assemble. The king's old London

Irregulars, fathers and sons, turned out for the muster. King Arthur accepted all but the oldest for service abroad. He left me these two dozen veterans, explaining to them the need for experienced fighters to train the men I would raise and send to London. They seemed disappointed but took it in good part, promising to drill daily while waiting for the recruits to arrive.

As we left the muster I said to King Arthur, "One more thing, if you permit. I would interview the women Guenevere left behind. Those who wish to join the queen, I will dispatch by the first available transport. I do not want them here making scandal and plotting intrigue to bring me down out of jealousy or worse."

"What will you do if they refuse to go to the queen?" he asked.

"I'll send them back to their families," I said. "I would put London on a war footing, an assembly post for recruiting and training men to defend Britain. Since you will take everyone you can rely on to defeat Sir Lancelot, I will do what I can to bring in replacements in readiness against the Picts and Saxons."

"It is well," the king agreed. "Do it. I will worry no more; Britain will be in good hands." I'd become resigned to staying in England while the others sailed off. I didn't like it, though.

It took another week for King Arthur and his army to embark for Armorica. Even the weeks he had for preparation, while he waited for me to recover enough to take the responsibilities of regent, had not been enough. Small wonder; there was much to do. To add to his worries, it was late in the season to begin a war. Winter was less than a month away.

The king had found ships to carry his London Irregulars, the heart of his forces, and Sir Kay had gathered enough supplies to last for the journey and the first few weeks of fighting. If it took longer, King Arthur and his men would have to live off the country.

When, finally, he was ready to sail, I wished him Lud's speed and watched him sail off with something like tears in my eyes.

Borre turned once and waved, and I waved back. I envied him his place at our father's side.

Good as my word, I dismissed all persons in the king's service who would not aid in the task I had been set. The few women who would not risk the journey to Armorica, but had no families to claim them, I sent back to Camelot.

No one left in London was trained in war, with the exception of the few London Irregulars, too old and battered for active service, and my squires. I had not let my squires go with King Arthur, though he had requested the use of them. I would not send them across the sea to die in such a bootless cause.

I had hoped Morgan and Cornu would remain behind, along with Nithe and Pelleas, but they did not. Both Morgan and Cornu went with the king, as he had wanted. Morgan's man, Cornu, spoke to me on parting, "I would leave something with you, something I have long carried." He unwrapped a sword cased in a jeweled scabbard and handed it to me.

I drew the blade and swung it back and forth; it had a curious lightness in motion. The blade itself was cloudy, an effect of many almost invisible lines that coursed its length.

"It is layered steel," he told me. "The edge is hard enough to keep its sharpness, but the whole blade is so flexible it is virtually unbreakable."

"How came you by it?"

"It once belonged to Morgan's father. I was his shield bearer while he lived. His death is unavenged."

"Who killed him?"

"Morgan holds Uther Pendragon responsible."

"King Arthur's father," I said.

"Exactly."

I understood. His ghost would walk until King Arthur's death. I felt a chill as I examined the blade. "Ah, well, what will be will be," I sighed, though I still refused to accept responsibility for blood debt.

Nithe and Pelleas decided to sail back to Mona in their dragon ship, rowed by their sons. Nithe was torn between her love for King Arthur and her feeling, whatever it was, for Sir Lancelot. She would not take part in any quarrel between them.

Nithe might have conflicting loyalties, but Pelleas promised me help. He said, "The Picts will not raid Britain in Arthur's absence. I must go north and tell my people how Pictish knights fell before Lancelot's sword. I most miss Torre."

Another debt to be paid, I thought. I would not forget Sir Torre, either.

"You can count on me to hold the northern marches for you," he added.

"Will you send me men?" I asked.

"I will permit those who will to join you. Viki's brothers will likely lead them." And Pelleas smiled.

"He only regrets he cannot stay himself," Nithe told me wryly after Pelleas had patted my shoulder and stalked off to ready his boat for the trip home. "He would, too, except that I've convinced him he can do more good holding the north."

Nithe and I walked together and climbed the stairs to look out over the Thames. Pelleas's dragon ship was tied to the dock and nearly ready to depart.

"Have you heard any word from Viki?" I asked her, without turning my gaze from the scene before me.

"None since she left," Nithe replied. "We had a long talk before she joined the queen, and she told me how wrong she thought it of Arthur, when he knew Guenevere to be innocent, to allow her alone to pay the cost of Aggravain's plotting. Lancelot should have been adjudged as guilty as the queen by any fair-minded person."

"Or as innocent," I said. "I do not believe there was any treason from what Morgan told me."

"She said you didn't believe Sir Lancelot loved Lavayne instead of Guenevere."

"You know that, also?" I asked.

"Everyone in court knew it, dummy!"

"Not us peasants," I muttered.

"Poor Guenevere," Nithe said, shaking her head. "Torn between two men, one who didn't love her and one who couldn't."

"The king never loved her either, then?"

"Arthur is a loving person and was very fond of Guenevere, but Samana held his heart," Nithe said, laying her hand on my arm as we leaned against the wall. "It was Samana who insisted on holding true to her bargain with her father, to end the marriage when she got pregnant. Arthur could not dissuade her."

"And Viki has sworn to serve Guenevere? Is that what you're saying?"

"Yes. Women honor vows the same as knights. Viki's one regret in staying loyal to Guenevere was that you might think her disloyal to you."

"Not disloyal," I murmured.

"What would you call it? You were dangerously wounded and sick with fever when she left. She wanted to stay by your side, and I'm sure she intended to do so, once Guenevere had been rescued. When Gareth was killed at the stake, she must have feared you would hold her accountable, since it was she who summoned Lancelot and she is the queen's handmaiden. I know I would have felt that way in her place."

"Well, I would not have done so," I said, "but I would not have left her, either, to follow some other responsibility."

"You see it as desertion, then?"

"Something like that, perhaps," I muttered. I didn't want to characterize it more clearly, for then I would have to face the fact: Viki held me in light esteem.

"She will grieve for Gareth, as we do," Nithe said, pressing my arm.

"She will that. Perhaps Gareth was not fated to grow up," I said slowly, turning to look at her. "He was a child in many ways, for all his size and strength, and could not have survived long away from Borre and me to think for him. At the end we left him too much on his own. He probably married because he was lonesome, but his wife is no more worldly than he, hardly someone he could lean on for advice."

Nithe nodded. "He seemed unhappy the last time I saw him, though I didn't quite know why. I think I do now. You probably don't know I view Lancelot in much the same way you do Gareth," Nithe added thoughtfully. "Lancelot has never grown up, either, and I have always felt responsible for him in a way."

I shook my head. "I do not understand Sir Lancelot," I said. "I cannot see how he could kill unarmed men, men who were his old comrades."

"I admit I do not understand that either," Nithe said. This time it was her gaze that locked on the view of the river. "The only thing I can guess is that Lancelot panicked. He had never been in a situation before where there were no rules to follow. He is a tournament fighter, not a warrior, you know."

"That's why King Arthur did not take Sir Lancelot or his cousins to the battle of Badon," I said.

"Lancelot was hurt by that," Nithe said. "He thought Arthur held him in light regard."

"I know. The king said Sir Lancelot was sent to him in trust by Lancelot's father, King Ban. King Arthur insisted that he could not let Sir Lancelot be risked. Gawaine was furious, though, when the king left Sir Lancelot and his cousins behind."

"Well, Arthur has little enough regard for the Round Table

knights now. I fear." Nithe said. "Lancelot and the queen destroyed it between them, with no more wish to do so than children would a sand castle. I'm not sure either of them are aware yet of the enormity of what has happened."

"I do not grieve for it." I said honestly. "I grieve for Britain."

I accompanied Nithe to the boat and stood there while they debarked, rowing downstream with the tide. Before they left, most of Viki's brothers came to me, one by one, saying that, unless their father forbid them to come, they would return to help me as soon as they could get away from home.

I could not allow Britain to be guarded by Picts and children alone, however. I sought out Colin, Constantine's old fisherman friend, whom King Arthur had left behind, deeming him too old for war. "Will you take me to Constantine in Lyoness?" I asked him.

"Aye. I have been planning a visit, anyway, to see my grandson," he said.

With Colin in charge, our plans were put into action by the next day. I called Sir Kay in and gave him orders to cover my absence. "I will be sending back men and stores collected as I travel," I said. "Receive them and care for them so that I will find them here when I return. I do not wish to hear of your refusing to provision men because they have not been entered on a formal roster. It will be enough for them to say that they come from me. Do you understand?"

"It will make record-keeping easy," he sneered.

"No, it will not. I will have a good idea of what stores should be here when I return. I'll keep a record of what I send. I already have a good idea of what we have now; your present records have checked against actual holdings. I will expect to see the same meticulous accounts kept for me as for King Arthur. Again, so there be no mistake, what I do not want to see is your refusal to issue needed goods to my recruits. If I find they have turned around and gone home again because you would not feed them, it will go hard with you."

Threats mean little unless there is a history of experience to back them up. The difference between King Arthur and me was that the king allowed Sir Kay to have entirely too much freedom in his management of supplies. Sir Kay had come to feel a proprietary interest in everything under his control. I had no intention of allowing him to exercise independent authority. I was sure he understood how I meant it to be but realized he would test me.

Trusting to Nithe's pearl to keep me from being seasick, I ordered Colin to sail me to Lyoness. His boat was still called *Hammerhand* but had a riper smell than when Nithe, Gareth, and I sailed in it from Lyoness.

We stopped at fishing villages along the coast where Colin was known. Everywhere we were hailed and honored, Colin as kinsmen and friend, and me both as Dylan the hurley player and as regent for the king. I was asked to judge hurley matches rather than to play. Seemingly, my new status was too exalted for me to roll in the dirt, a privilege of rank for which I was not grateful.

I told the young men who crowded around that they should go to London if they wished to fight for King Arthur. They would find people there who would train them to be warriors, and I promised to lead them when I returned. Many promised they would go, and Colin told me they could be relied on to keep their word.

We stayed in sight of land until we left the western tip of Cornwall and made straight west for Lyoness across open sea. Nithe's pearl was never out of my grasp, and I could feel the threat of seasickness at the edge of my consciousness waiting to overwhelm me. When we made landfall on Cador's Island, we found word of our coming had preceded us. I was relieved to be ashore once more.

"Father!" a young woman called, running down to meet us, when we rowed in to the beach. She jumped up and down, splashing in the shallow water and waving in greeting like an eager child. When Colin could free himself from being hugged fiercely, I recognized her from the battle of Badon, when she had been Constantine's companion. Colin introduced her as his daughter Eliza.

"I know Eliza," I said, and kissed her in greeting. "Has your father resigned himself to the attachment between you and Constantine?" I asked.

"Hardly that, but we are married now, anyway," and she hugged her father again.

Constantine followed her down to the beach and clasped arms with us. I inquired as to how they knew we were coming.

"We have been waiting for days!" Eliza said accusingly, while clinging to Colin's arm and gazing up at him fondly, "What kept you, Father?"

"I go when my Lord Dylan orders it," Colin said, grinning.

"If we had known we were expected, we might have hurried more," I added, "but we would have missed meeting some interesting folks."

"Oh sure, 'we.'" she said mockingly. "Don't tell me. I know that women are fighting each other in the most appalling way to be the one who warms your bed, my grand Lord Dylan, in village after village."

"That might have happened to one of my brothers but not to me," I responded. Fisherwomen were pert!

"Ah, I was so saddened to hear of Gareth!" Constantine exclaimed. "Everyone loved him."

"And he tried his best to love everyone in return," I said, "at least all the young women in Britain. There was a great wailing when he married."

"He never tried anything with me!" Eliza said indignantly.

"I told him I'd knife him in his sleep if he even looked at you out of those puppy-dog eyes of his," Constantine said teasingly.

He immediately turned to me and added, "I shall miss him, Dylan."

"Yes," was all I could manage. As yet I couldn't handle direct statements of sympathy over Gareth's death. "You haven't told me how you knew we were coming," I said to put the conversation on a safer topic.

"Fishermen have been sailing into the harbor for a month announcing your imminent arrival," Eliza said. "Constantine has had his things packed to join you for almost that long."

"You are not coming?" I asked her.

"Of course not! Someone has to look after Lyoness!" But for all her bravado, she seemed anxious. She didn't like the idea of being separated from Constantine.

We spent a few days on Cador's Island, and I instructed Constantine to take fishermen north along the coast of Cornwall as far as Camelot to spread the word that we needed men in London.

"I will call on Samana on Ector's Isle," I said. I had expected to see her on Cador's Island, but Colin said Lady Miriam had not welcomed her back, so she settled in the manor house on Ector's Isle. Sir Ector's goodwife had died, and he was happy to have Samana take over his household.

Samana had also heard we were coming and had set out watchmen for us. "Samana said to bring you to her as soon as you arrived," I was told on landing.

"Has something happened to her?" I asked, slightly alarmed.

"Oh, no. She just wants to see you," he confided. "She's eager for news of King Arthur."

I found Samana was concerned over King Arthur.

"We cannot tell truth from rumor at this remove," she said. "What really happened?"

I explained the tragic events and spoke of the trap set for Sir Lancelot that had caught the thirteen conspirators. I then told her about Gareth being butchered by Sir Lancelot.

"And the queen?" Samana asked.

"She was last seen clinging to Sir Lancelot, covered with the blood of men who had been her friends," I said bitterly.

"Oh, how terrible for Guenevere! And is Arthur very sad, then?" she asked, knowing the answer.

"More than that, I think; resigned, perhaps," I answered. "The Round Table is broken. Though I had no part in it, I cannot regret its passing."

She sighed, "You never found the father you were looking for in very truth, did you?"

"No," I admitted. "He has made me regent, but not as his son. He has never told me what he feels for me, if anything." I had always been able to say things to Samana I could say to no one else. Certainly King Arthur did not know how I felt, either. I was not sure myself; some mixture of hate and love, perhaps.

"I'm sailing for Mona in the morning," I told her. "I have promises for help from the sons of Pelleas."

"Take me with you," Samana asked.

"You would be safer here, perhaps," I replied.

"When everything is at risk, there are no safe havens," she retorted. "At least take me as far as Mona. I must convince Pelleas and Nithe to send men. I know Arthur is going to need all the help he can get."

"Pelleas said he would not hold back any who wished to come," I said.

"Then I will tell him now is the time," she said, smiling.

Samana had already inspired every young man on Ector's Island to make his way to London, having heard I was seeking recruits. And it fair looked as if I would be the last person to reach London, such was their eagerness.

Even so, Samana found further reason for delay. "Have you asked King Mark of Cornwall for his knights?" she wondered.

"Cornish knights? They have little reputation for valor," I protested.

"That's because their king is such a buffoon. The men of Cornwall are valiant enough. We can stop off at Tintagel on the way to Mona," she coaxed.

I had little hope of aid from King Mark, but I was willing to ask Constantine to approach him, for Britain needed every fighting man available.

"Bring whatever men you can raise to Mona, and we will sail back to London together," I told him.

Constantine pledged to join us, and we sailed directly to Mona, almost up to the dock before Colin decided it would be necessary to row the rest of the way. We found hundreds of boats tied along the shore, and hundreds of tents dotted the great commons in front of Pelleas's castle. On meeting Pelleas, I learned the reason.

"We have found men for you," Pelleas told me. "Some of my chiefs came to me for advice, and I told them to fight under your banner. They have been recruiting, as you see." I felt immensely better. At the feast of welcome I even found some dozen of the sons of Pelleas who had pledged to serve with me. For the first time I felt that we might prevail against any threat posed against Britain.

GHAPTER

XVI

hen Viki's brothers came to me one by one and
pledged themselves to me by name, I understood
it was a matter of some seriousness for a Pict. In
accepting their service, I called them that one time
by name. Except for kings and heroes, who showed their courage
by allowing their names to be publicly known, names were used
only within the family. The boys had everyday call names for one
another, scurrilous ones based on their baby names, which they
varied from time to time. I never mastered them, for I do not
understand Pictish that well. Fortunately, it was not needful. I
called them all cousin, for that's what they called me. Their father,
Pelleas, and mine, King Arthur, were half-brothers, sons of Uther
Pendragon. The young men all seemed to be about five years
younger than I, tall for Picts, stoutly built, active, and dark of hair
and eye. They determined among themselves to become my personal guard, and I was rarely out of the sight of one or more of
them.

Personal service among the Picts is not honorable unless it is
voluntary, so it is the Pictish way to serve without appearing servile.
Therefore, I found meals cooked and placed before me, a tent

raised at night, a horse saddled in the morning, and no one to thank for it.

I missed the feeling of having a brother at my back, as I had in the company of Borre and Gareth. I missed holding Viki in my arms. I had never been so lonely, even as a child. Most of my life I'd had someone to take care of, someone who looked after me as well. Now, my responsibilities for kingdom and servants were so numerous I could not tell one from another. Since Borre was with King Arthur, Viki with Guenevere, and Gareth was dead at Sir Lancelot's hand, it seemed I had no one I loved near me.

I mentioned this to Samana when she asked why I was so somber, and that evening Constantine came to me. "Would you let me be your shield bearer?" he asked. "We are foster brothers and no one has a better right than I."

"You want to do this? You have your own boat to look after."

"I'll leave it for Samana. She wants to remain on Mona to see that Pelleas sends these men off to you in time. I meant to beg you for a ride in your boat, but this will give me unquestioned passage."

I gave him the great round shield that belonged to the Roman centurion's armor Ayres had given to me, along with the pilum and Gorlais's sword I had from Cornu. I was relieved to pass on the burden and found in Constantine a wise confidant as well.

Pelleas gave us his dragon ship and his boys rowed it for me, so we reached London in a matter of days, not weeks. Lud, I hated boats! I no longer vomited when I felt the slow rising and falling of the sea, but I never felt at ease on the water.

We met other crafts going in our direction. When we hailed them and asked their business, they were all bound for service with the regent, Dylan the hurley player, or sometimes four-goal Dylan. Constantine advised me to don the Roman armor with the red-plumed helmet so the fisherboats would see we weren't Saxons and, though feeling something of a fool, I followed his advice.

It proved to be particularly useful when we came ashore at night, landing at one fisher village or another, and ate fish caught by hand line on spits over fires even before our tents were pitched. Picts have a healthy notion of the importance of eating regularly. I wished I liked eating fish better. The village folks offered us what hospitality they could, seeing we were not raiders, but I liked dried fish even less than fresh ones.

It was a relief to get to London. I was clutching Nithe's pearl reflexively whenever the breeze kicked up. If Lud loved me, I'd never have to do this again!

We disembarked in midafternoon. I wore my Roman gear ashore and, with Constantine at my side and Viki's brothers behind me, made a royal entrance into the city. At first we attracted no notice, for London had not given up the Roman habit of long midday rest periods, but gradually a crowd formed and followed us, calling, "Dylan! Dylan is back!"

I thought if we had been Saxons, we could have put London to the torch before an effective defense could be mounted. I resolved to have adequate guards out by nightfall.

We walked down the street that passed Lady Mal's new inn, The Laurel Wreath and, alerted by the crowd, she met me in the street with the golden circle in her hands. Bending it slightly with her strong harper's fingers, she reached up and placed it on my helmet.

The crowd cheered her action, and she took advantage of the noise to say in a low voice, "Come on inside, all of you. Things have happened that you should know."

Pelleas's sons stopped the crowd from following us by shutting and barring the door. The inn usually didn't open until evening and had no customers.

"What is wrong?" I asked as soon as we were free from the crowd's pressure.

"Nothing, maybe," she replied evasively. "It's just that much has changed. I fear I am to blame," she added.

We sat at her own table in the rear corner, joined only by Constantine. Viki's brothers busied themselves in rummaging around to find ale, bread, and cheese, bringing some to our table before feeding themselves.

"Words should not be hard for a bard to find," I said over a foaming beaker.

"I meant well," she said with a sigh. "I made up songs about King Arthur's son, how he was hidden away at birth, how he became the greatest hurley player in the islands, how he stood with his father against the Saxons at Badon when Arthur's knights hid at Camelot . . ."

"They didn't, you know; they wanted to come."

"Oh, I know, but let me finish. It gets worse."

I nodded, thinking how good it was to see her and hear her telling a story again. She continued, "I sang of how Dylan's wife was attacked by a knight and lost her child, how his mother was killed by another knight, how Dylan was stabbed in the back by a knight when he tried to protect his father's queen, and how Sir Lancelot's knights killed Dylan's unarmed brother when Dylan lay near death from that terrible wound. I sang of how Sir Lancelot's knights abducted the queen, forcing King Arthur to strip Britain of all its warriors to rescue her, and how the king appointed his son, Dylan, as the island's sole defense against her enemies."

"That's quite a song," Constantine said. "I'd like to hear it sung."

"The queen was not abducted," I said in protest, though there were other things that bothered me more, such as the implication that King Arthur had acknowledged me.

"It's not just one song, but a dozen or more, all tied together," she said, answering Constantine, then turned back to me to add,

"I know it's not strictly accurate, but we bards call that embellishment. Sometimes the truth is just too dull!"

"I call it lying," I grumped.

"Whatever you call it, the point is that most of London knows them all by heart now, and your recruits learn them as part of their indoctrination."

"Is that what you're afraid to tell me?" I asked, though I thought it was more than enough.

"I'm afraid of what the consequence may be. I fear the way people feel now, they won't let King Arthur come back. They believe he deserted them by seeking his vengeance overseas, leaving Britain unprotected. Now they think that his knights betrayed him just as he betrayed his people."

"I feel much the same," I said after I considered her tale.

"Do you also feel you should be king of Britain?"

"I don't even think I should be regent!" I said bitterly.

"Well, no one agrees with you. If you don't take charge of London this very day, it will be destroyed by its own people. Hugh tells me there are plans afoot to loot the palace as a first step."

"Will that crowd outside let me go there?" I asked.

"There's a tunnel in the back that leads under the street to Hugh's stables. This place used to be a house of assignation and needed secret access."

We used her tunnel and found Hugh out in the stable yards. He was boarding King Arthur's horses, and I bespoke them in the king's business, signing a written order to that effect to relieve Hugh of any blame for letting me take them. Pelleas's sons were thrilled to be given war-horses, although these had been left behind as too old for active service. Black Nick was glad to see me, as I him. I'd missed him.

When we rode up to King Arthur's London palace, we found the doors barred. Recruits in tents occupied much of the great public square before the palace, and as we rode through them, they came out and followed us, cheering.

Constantine hammered on the closed door until it opened. I turned and greeted the crowd, quieting them by raising my hand. "Constantine of Lyoness is my shield bearer," I told them. "These men with him are my wife's brothers from Mona, come to join us. Tell them your needs, and I will be out to see they are taken care of as soon as I have taken whatever messages are awaiting me." Claiming Viki as my wife sounded strange to my ears. Would that it were true!

I dismounted and found Sir Kay waiting for me. "Guenevere has returned," he said without preamble when I walked in.

"Where is she?" I asked.

"In Kent with her Jutish relatives," he replied with some satisfaction. "The church at Canterbury is sheltering her."

"Why doesn't she come here?" I asked. "I am King Arthur's regent."

"She is under sentence of death," he reminded me. "She may be a traitor, but she is not a fool. Kent is loyal to her, not Arthur. When Lancelot rescued her, they fled together into Kent, using friendly Jute sailors to bring them across the Channel to Armorica."

"Jutish fisherboats are small. Sir Lancelot must have left his horses behind," I said.

Sir Kay did not respond. He evidently thought his only responsibility in holding conversation with me was in saying things that might distress me. Well, I had need of more horses, ones that could be used in battle, not just for show. Perhaps I should pay a visit to the queen.

"How many recruits have come in?" I asked.

"Six hundred and twenty-seven at roster call this morning," he replied. "It sometimes takes a day or two for new ones to find where they belong."

I thought that in Julius Caesar's time a Roman legion had six thousand men. With three legions Rome could not prevent the Picts and Scoti from raiding Britain. What could I do with six hundred untrained men?

I went out to talk to the recruits, finding they had been issued spears, tents, and blankets along with daily rations. There was no one to drill them though, so I made all of Viki's brothers sergeants and told them to organize the recruits into squads. I assigned one of my squires to each squad. They'd all been trained in weaponry and could at least teach the rudiments. More I could not do. There wasn't time.

I formed six squads of twenty men each, all horsemen, to take into Kent as a training exercise and also possibly to requisition the horses Sir Lancelot must have left behind. Before we departed I made Hugh quartermaster for the army we were forming. He had contacts with all the merchants of London. "When you need anything, requisition it from Sir Kay," I told him. "If he gives you trouble, warn him I will hear of it when I return."

"I am accustomed to dealing with Sir Kay," he said dryly. "Have no fear."

One of Viki's brothers assured me before we left, "The men will be ready when you get back."

I doubted it, but I thanked him, saying, "There will be others coming in. See that they're welcomed. I do not trust Sir Kay for that. Be particularly welcoming to King Mark's knights from Cornwall. They're trained and will expect special treatment."

"Cornish knights? They don't have much of a reputation for valor."

I could not disagree . . . I had said as much, myself. "They'll look good on horseback, and more important, bring their own horses. Appearance may be all we have," I replied gloomily.

As we left for Kent, I rode Black Nick as usual and Constantine was mounted as well, but the others, including two of Viki's brothers, walked, grumbling like all soldiers. They meant nothing by it.

We would all ride back from Kent on Sir Lancelot's horses, Lud willing.

I thought of what we might find at Canterbury as we marched into Kent. Canterbury was Kent's principal town and rated a cathedral ruled by a bishop. It was he who had given the queen refuge; Viki would be there. How would she greet me? The men marched in two long lines so they could talk to one another, but I rode with Constantine at the head of the double column. Constantine was occupied with his own thoughts. It turned out his young wife, Eliza, was pregnant and much on his mind. I'd had little leisure time myself recently for thinking private thoughts and welcomed the chance. It took little self-probing to learn that the raw hurt of Viki's choosing Guenevere over me had not healed.

I had worried about food, but each man carried oat flour and dried fish that could be made into a fish porridge with the addition of hot water. It was good marching food, for all that it was nearly tasteless. Little space was required to carry it, and it was filling. Since nothing else was available, I came to look forward to eating it, hungry as each day's exertion made me.

We saw no people on the trip, just deserted fields and houses; peasants are wary when an army is on the march. The wise ones hide their food and women. Only fools will put themselves in reach. Our foragers found eggs and chickens to piece out our breakfasts, and sometimes we could hear shouts of anger from the bordering woods at our thievery. We would have paid for the food if anyone had claimed payment.

It took us three days to go from London to Canterbury, a distance of about sixty Roman miles. The wall that ran around the town was three meters thick and twice as high, something that would keep out any but the most serious raiding party. Canterbury was close to the coast, and the townsfolk understood about raiders.

I was surprised to see how small Canterbury's town gate was, a single open door set into a tower. I could stretch out my arms and touch both sides of the jamb as I rode through; if I had not bowed my head, I would have bumped the top.

In the tunnel under the thick wall, I looked up and saw men were watching me through slits in the ceiling. "We have come to see the queen," I announced.

The door porter came to meet us, looking us over carefully before responding in broken Latin, "All strangers must come before the Captain of the Guard before they are free to move about the town."

I was surprised he could speak Latin at all for he was tall, red-haired, and could have been the brother of Kesse, the man I had killed in combat at Badon. I dismounted and left Black Nick with Constantine and allowed the porter to conduct me to the guard-house, after he carefully shut and barred the gate. Before I could question his intentions, the guardhouse door was thrust open, and Viki came flying out to hug me fiercely.

"Ah, Dylan, love," she said. "I knew you'd come!"

Like hell! I thought. A moment only I hugged her back, then pulled free and caught her by her shoulders, looking at her without expression. I said formally, "I am here as regent to the king, on his official business."

Her welcoming smile died, and she bit her lip, stepping back. "The queen sent me to greet you," she said, imitating my tone of voice. "She is waiting to give you audience."

"Do you vouch for this man, then?" the captain asked dryly.

"Oh, yes, I do that!" she exclaimed, glancing up at me and then away.

"And your brothers, who are waiting outside," I added.

Looking at me with a startled glance, she tugged at the gate bar to hurry the porter in opening it. I waited with the captain until Viki led Constantine and her two brothers back through. The captain was not happy to see armed men in his town and required that we surrender our spears and swords before leaving the guard area. They allowed us to keep our helmets and belt knives.

Viki assured us it was all right, and I left my Roman sword to show an example, though it made me uneasy. The squires and other followers stayed outside to wait. If we did not return in a reasonable time, they would come after us.

"You must talk to the town's council first," Viki told us, "though the local bishop is as important as the magistrate."

The town was laid out like all Roman-built towns. A wide street split the town into halves, and I could see another even smaller gate at the other end of the main road. Another dividing street ran at right angles, creating four separate areas.

"On the left is the Jutish quarter," Viki told us as we walked through the town. "Jutish mercenaries were once housed there, and their descendants still live in the same houses." I paid scant attention to what she said, registering without conscious thought that the Jutish area had been portioned into small squares served by other smaller streets swarming with people, mostly blond. The sound of her voice and cadence of her speech filled my mind. Ah, Viki!

"The quarter on the right is where the shops and storage areas are, handy to the gate," she went on, pointing. "The theatre is over there." She seemed determined not to show she was hurt by my rejection. It was just as well she couldn't see into my heart. It was in such turmoil that even I was frightened.

I could see the large building against the wall. It appeared to be D-shaped, like the one in London. The stage was set up along the diameter of the half circle with tiers of seats around the curve. After the Romans left, the cut stones facing the structure were removed for use in building houses, leaving rough rubble exposed. It had started to decay and appeared to be little used for its original purpose.

When we came to the wide cross street, I saw there were small gates, only big enough for a man to walk through at either end. The only gate that could admit a wagon was the main one to the south. If those we left outside had to come after us, the only feasible way would be through the main gate or over the walls. We should have brought felling axes to make scaling ladders on speculation, I realized.

"The queen lives in the commandant's suite in the forum," Viki said. "The council will be waiting there." She led us to the principal crossroads of the center of town. On opposite corners were the church and an imposing forum. I could see what Viki meant about the equal importance of the bishop and administrative council here. It was not so in London. There were guards at the forum's doors, but they let us by without hindrance.

"I would not have let strange men pass without question," I said as we entered.

"You're with me," Viki said matter-of-factly.

"Even so," I muttered, and she grinned sardonically. Perhaps she understood I had placed myself in her hands without means to defend myself.

Inside the great hall we found the walls lined with grim Jutish warriors in full battle gear. It was I who was foolish. If this was the trap it appeared to be, we had no chance. I gave Viki a bitter look, and she paled at the unspoken accusation. Regardless of how she might feel about me, her brothers were with me! On the dais at the end of the hall stood the queen in full royal regalia, crown and all, flanked by a mitred bishop and a dozen older men in robes and chains of office.

I strode to the foot of the dais, and the queen extended her hand to me. I bowed over it, but stared down the bishop who would have had me kiss his ring.

"I am told you are the king's regent," the queen said coldly.

"Regent, son, and heir."

331

"Regent only," I corrected her, just as coldly, "as close cousin to the king." Damn her! She had known all these years!

"Close, indeed," she retorted with a look very like a sneer. "What venture do you seek in Kent with so warlike a following?"

"In King Arthur's behalf, I am honored to welcome you back to Britain, Your Majesty," I said. A shadow passed over the queen's face at the implication that she was to surrender herself into my custody.

Viki frowned, but I persevered. "I am fortunate that my duty lies with my desire," I added. My amendment did little to ease her mind.

"Your loyalty humbles me, Prince Dylan," she said with but little evident conviction. "I wish Arthur felt the same." She put the best interpretation on my words that she could.

"I am sure he does in his heart, Your Majesty," I said. "I do not understand the responsibilities of kingship that hold him from your side, though part of it must stem from the bitterness of my brother, Gawaine, over Gareth's death."

"Lancelot mourns for Gareth as if he were his son," Guenevere said earnestly.

"He came to it late," I said bitterly.

"Lancelot? He knighted Gareth; he was proud of him!"

"Not enough, Your Majesty," I retorted. I remembered that Sir Lancelot had never sponsored Gareth for fellowship in the Round Table as he promised. He'd done little for him living, but even if he had, nothing would have made up for Gareth's death at Sir Lancelot's hands.

After this unsatisfactory formal meeting, the queen and her bishop withdrew. Viki gave me a troubled glance as she followed the queen out, but I did not acknowledge it. What could she expect of me? I might have died of Aggravain's wound while she followed the queen. I saw no reason for me to become the queen's friend.

Members of the town council came up to me informally after

the queen left. They dismissed the guards, and I asked the boys to go back outside to await me there. If an ambush was being planned, I didn't want to have them cooped up here with me. I had feared I would have difficulty in securing Sir Lancelot's horses, but this did not prove to be the case.

"We did not know what to do with the horses," one confessed when I broached the reason for my visit. "They are all stallions and of no use to anyone but a warrior or a mare in heat, it would appear."

"I would have thought they could be gelded," I said.

"We were expressly forbidden to do so by Prince Lancelot," the magistrate sighed. "Jutes don't ride horses in war, so even our guards don't want them. They spoke of eating them," he added, shuddering.

I could understand his worry. If Sir Lancelot heard that his war-horses had been eaten, he would likely return to punish whoever was responsible, even if he had to cut his way through King Arthur's men, who held his castle under siege.

"I will give you a written order requiring the horses to be turned over to me," I said. "You can show it to Sir Lancelot if he comes back to claim them. Tell him I arrived with armed men, if you like, for it is the truth."

"There is still the matter of the queen," one of the older men murmured.

"A special problem?" I asked cautiously.

"She rules in Kent, not King Arthur. If anything were to happen to her, Kent would rise against the king."

"I will leave that to the king," I said firmly.

"That is what you cannot do. You must swear to protect her as her champion, against the king if necessary, or you will be treated as her enemy."

It was a trap, then. Ah, false Viki! "I promised the king only that I would do what is best for his realm," I said. "If Kent rises, the Saxons will overrun Britain. I will protect the queen even against King Arthur, if that is what is needed to hold Kent."

"She must remain queen."

"I would not depose her."

"More than that, you must espouse her! The bishop has agreed to a betrothal, conditional upon King Arthur's death."

"You're mad! Do you not know that the king is my father? Everyone else seems to, though it isn't openly spoken of."

"He has not acknowledged you, and in the eyes of the church your father was King Lot, the husband of Morgause. It was so recorded at your baptism."

Another man, dressed in a cleric's robe, brought a bound parchment record for me to see. The entry had been made, as stated. I had not known I was baptized.

"Queen Morgause ordered it done," the cleric said smugly.

No wonder Morgause said to me that Christianity had its uses, I thought. Though if she had me baptized, at least she had acknowledged me right from the first. The upshot was that Guenevere was not barred to me. I was little grateful.

And Viki! Viki had led me to the queen. She had known what would be asked of me. If I wanted proof that her loyalty to the queen was greater than her feelings toward me I had it. "I will, then," I said.

"Perhaps you can raise us up an heir where King Arthur could not," one said slyly.

I glared at him, "You ask too much! There are limits to what I am willing to do for king and country. Bedding my father's wife is not therein."

Viki was waiting for me outside. She took my hand and looked into my eyes. "I became the queen's handmaiden before I was pledged to you," she said. "I cannot break that vow just because I would rather be with you. To me a vow isn't something to disregard. How would you feel if I did? Maybe I'd see some handsome man like young Galahad and just go off with him because for the moment I liked him better than you."

"And yet, no vow could have kept me from your side," I said.

"You took long enough to seek me out while I waited for you in Mona," Viki retorted hotly. "You have doubts about my feeling for you. Do you think I have never wondered about your commitment? Even now?"

"And yet you're with her, not me."

"It's not like that," Viki protested, with tears in her eyes. "It's just that I can't leave her when she has no other friends. Don't you see? The queen has letters from Lancelot saying Gawaine has been badly injured in a fight before the walls of Joyouse Garde. Only Gawaine has kept the quarrel alive. Now the siege may be lifted, and King Arthur will come for the queen. He's condemned her to the stake! We can protect her if we have enough men. Stay here with us. You can be regent here as well as in London, and here the Jutes will fight for you."

"On the other hand," I said, "if things go badly, the king may need more men to settle the quarrel with Sir Lancelot. Sir Kay will send them if I'm not there to stop him. The men I have recruited are for the defense of Britain, not for fighting in Armorica. So, I am needed back in London and I must go." I thought, in London I would be away from the queen and from Viki as well. I wondered if Viki knew how tormented I was about what she had done. I couldn't speak more clearly without losing control of myself.

Guenevere would have none of it. "I must be where my new champion can take care of me," she said. The local worthies provided Guenevere and her ladies with wagons for the trip to London and ponies to draw them. I promised to send them back after we arrived. They also delivered Sir Lancelot's horses, enough to mount all my squires. I wondered if some had been held back to provide meat for the Jutes, but did not ask for an accounting. I had no way to audit it.

We were also given flour ground at the numerous donkey-powered mills around the town, a gift that earned Canterbury remission of taxes for two years by my order. Viki quietly suggested that to me, though I thought it was possible the idea came from Guenevere. Guenevere knew what ruling a country was all about, after twenty years of it. Much of the sovereign's responsibility had been hers while King Arthur was off fighting Saxons.

Sir Kay was surprised to see us when we arrived in London, particularly with Guenevere in tow. "She is an attainted traitor," he told me.

"She is none of your concern," I told him in turn. Why did I have to defend her? Damn the man! "I am her champion now, appointed by the people of Kent, and betrothed to her should aught befall the king, by dispensation of the Bishop of Canterbury. Beware how you use her name."

"I will write Arthur," he said, setting his jaw.

I looked at him. Sir Kay was a coward but was also stubborn. "Do so," I said. "Be sure to tell him the queen is under my protection. Let him make of it what he will."

I walked away, not happy with Sir Kay but not seeing how he could do anything to hurt me directly. I settled the queen in the royal suite, much to Sir Kay's consternation. Viki stayed with her to help her unpack. The rest of the queen's ladies had long since dispersed.

"I cannot countenance this!" Sir Kay cried the next morning. "She must be confined to await Arthur's justice!"

"Where would you suggest we find a suitable place to confine a person of quality?" I asked with seeming meekness.

"We have a prison!"

"Ah, yes. We have a prison. Correct me, but isn't it used to hold thieves and rapists and murderers until such time as a sufficient number have been collected to justify the expense of a public execution?" I asked, quoting the regulation I had recently read as part of my new duties.

"Yes, that's the prison," Sir Kay said. At my look of disgust, he added, "There is no one there now. All of the condemned prisoners were given a choice of serving with Arthur or being summarily hanged. Most went with him."

"Yes, I would have, I think," I said. "For the queen, however, I have something else in mind. She had made decisions for the management of King Arthur's affairs for years while he was out fighting Saxons and the like. Why should she not do so now?"

"But Arthur named you regent!" he exclaimed, red of face and shouting. "It was bad enough to pass me over, but at least he left me as seneschal. I cannot longer serve the queen, knowing what she is."

"And what is she, then?" I asked in exasperation.

"She's a whore!" he screamed.

Without thinking twice, I struck him with the back of my hand, knocking him up against the corridor wall. "That is from the queen's champion," I said. "You have just been challenged, Sir Kay."

He stepped away from me, wiping the blood from his cut lip, and said, "Me? Fight you? A jumped-up bastard like you? I'll have you beaten from the throne like the nameless beggar you are! Arthur was insane to leave you in his place!"

As I watched him, he turned and ran out into the great hall, calling "Guards! Guards!" The racket brought out Viki and Guenevere from the queen's second-floor quarters, and they leaned over the balcony railing to watch what transpired.

From the guardroom near the hall entrance door stepped two of the sons of Pelleas. One said to Sir Kay, "We sent your people down to the muster grounds for training, though they seem too young to be of much use."

"Anything we can do for you, Dylan?" the other asked. The sons of Pelleas are not overgiven to awe of rank.

"Why, yes," I said on consideration. "You might escort Sir Kay down to the prison."

"You can't do that! Arthur said you were to consult me!"

"I am doing so. I am putting you in the way of making an inspection of the prison to determine if it is a fitting place to confine a queen. I doubt it, but it was your suggestion, you know. I just want more information from you on the subject."

Sir Kay turned as if to flee, but another of Pelleas's sons strolled down the hall behind him, eating a chicken leg he had stolen from the kitchen. The boys took him away, put him in a cell, and took charge of all the keys to the prison.

"I am afraid Sir Kay will never forgive you for confining him," Constantine sighed. He had followed Pelleas's son from the kitchen and was also eating a chicken leg. "Are you sure it is wise?"

I looked at him. "It is done, for better or for worse. Sir Kay is disloyal to me and, I think, to King Arthur. It would be truly unwise to let him be free to stir up further discord. I am more comfortable to have him where he can be watched."

"But who will coordinate all the movement of requisitioning and dispensing supplies? Sir Kay has always done that."

"Sir Kay has followed the queen's orders these many years, has he not? All she needs is someone energetic and intelligent to carry out her orders, and no one will miss him."

"How do you know so much?" Constantine asked, a smile lifting one corner of his mouth. He was, perhaps, a bit startled at my frankness.

"Gareth worked in the kitchen. He saw how things were and told me," I said simply. "Do you think he was wrong?"

"Perhaps not, but Kay is right when he describes the queen's status. Would anyone obey her now?"

"You will," I said. "Any of my people will. I might suggest that an experienced person like Lady Mal should act as a go-between. Relying on my authority, you could do as well as Sir Kay. Talk to Lady Mal about it."

Thereafter, Constantine and Lady Mal took orders from the queen, not from me; and the affairs of King Arthur's Britain soon appeared unchanged from what it had once been. Viki's brothers told me Viki was happy to be busy again, for entertaining a fretting queen gave her less pleasure than being an aide to a busy one. For me, I saw little of any of them, working with the sons of Pelleas to train the recruits. It was just as well. I had no stomach for further discussion with Viki. One thing all of us did together: we all waited for tidings from Armorica.

"Do one more thing for me," the queen requested, summoning me after we had reestablished her position. It had taken but a few days, so skilled was she and so highly regarded by the people of London, many of them originally from Kent.

"Name it, Your Majesty," I said. Anything to be away from her presence, particularly with Viki peering at me from behind the queen's shoulder. What did Viki want of me?

"Let Kay out of prison," Guenevere said. "I can coax him to work with me, and Constantine will see that he does. You know Arthur won't be pleased to hear you have ignored his advice to consult Kay. Arthur has a blind spot where his foster brother is concerned, I fear. He truly believes Kay is his loyal retainer."

"But not his friend?" I asked.

"Arthur is not a fool! No, he does not consider Kay a friend, but long ago he gave his word to Sir Ector, Kay's father, to allow Kay to be his seneschal. Arthur would not break his word just because he dislikes someone."

I nodded. I would not have kept Sir Kay beside me, promise or no promise, but I was not King Arthur. "I will do so, telling him it is your recommendation," I said. "Perhaps he will then treat you in a civil manner."

"Oh, trust me for that!" she said.

I wished I could trust Sir Kay for as much.

iki's brothers had delivered the horses to Hugh's stable yard to hold for me. With Constantine at my side, I rode down to the public square where I found Hugh himself handing out weapons to the newest band of recruits.

"My lord, we have need of you," he said in greeting.

" 'My lord' to me?" I said with a grimace.

He laughed. "You are King Arthur's regent. What else would I call you?"

"Dylan," I responded as he came forward to grasp my hand.

"They say you brought the queen with you," he said looking at me expectantly.

I shook my head. "It is more correct to say that the queen brought me," I said. "She had me named queen's champion and said I must take care of her. I promised the folk of Kent I would do so to keep them loyal. Consequently, she traveled with us to keep me in range of a call for assistance."

"Ah," Hugh said with understanding, "an honor to be coveted."

He was sincere. "I wish it had been yours," I told him glumly.

Hugh was eager to show me what had been accomplished in

my absence, now that I had time to see it properly. As before, I found that most of the entire central square of London town was covered with tents, the pegs hammered into cracks between paving stones. The rest was devoted to men training in various exercises under the direction of veteran soldiers, King Arthur's old Irregulars. They had turned out in numbers, glad to still be of service. We dismounted for a closer inspection and found squads were learning to work with sword, spear, and flail, listening to instruction, and practicing strokes under the watchful eyes of these teachers. Viki's brothers and my squires kept order in the ranks.

"Men who know each other will be fighting as units," Hugh said. "Each village has its own squad under its own leader. The instructors are from elsewhere, partly to assure equal treatment, and partly because the villages have no trained men."

It was well done. I watched a limping veteran instruct teams of men in pair fighting. Two men, thrusting at the same time behind overlapped shields are a match for any single fighter, no matter how experienced. I nodded. It would be useful to help the villages defend themselves against raiders later if their men trained as a fighting unit now, learning to depend on one another.

I was less pleased when I saw the pages I had left behind in Caerleon working out together. I rode over to speak to them. "Ayres sent us," one of them blurted before I could form a question. Indeed, there were several of Ayres's sons with them, looking at me anxiously.

"He did well," I responded. "We need every fighting man we can get." What else could I say? Yet, I would rather have them safe in Caerleon, I thought.

Sir Kay found me there. I had not seen him since his release, and seeing him walking towards us in his disdainful way now reminded me of something. "One of the sons of Pelleas said that Sir Kay's guards had been sent to you after I imprisoned him," I said to Hugh. "How did he get control of guards?"

"Guards? They were the pages King Arthur deemed too young to take to Armorica," he answered. "They have taken to training, however, with eagerness. I gather they had not liked being left with Sir Kay as kitchen drudges and worse."

Barring the knights from Cornwall, who had come in and made themselves obnoxious by strutting around London, I had an army of children, I reflected. First my young squires, then the runaways from Camelot, and now these. They might be useful for bluffing, perhaps, but they could never stand up to trained fighters in combat. Indeed, I would not risk them.

Bustling up to us, fairly panting, Sir Kay blurted, "Arthur is dead!" bringing practice to a halt, not only immediately around us but everywhere within earshot. Sir Kay had a singularly piercing voice. He should have been a herald. But the man was either a fool or a traitor to make so public a declaration.

Constantine struck Sir Kay to the ground, so angry was he at the man's lack of discretion, but I stayed his hand when he drew his sword to give Sir Kay quittance. Sir Kay might well have deserved death, but not for so minor a thing. Still, too many men had heard him.

"Next time show a little more grief when you give tongue to lies about King Arthur," I said. "Sir Lancelot's spies send word of the king's demise with every new moon, hoping to shake our resolve." I watched Sir Kay gather his legs under him to stand. "Only a child would believe such a thing," I added scornfully, and loudly enough to be heard by all.

I hoped Sir Kay had enough sense to follow my lead, but he took a rolled parchment from where he had thrust it into his belt and waved it at me. He was clearly too angry to consider his words carefully, but he might have spoken as he did out of some malicious intent.

"Read it for yourself, if you can read," Sir Kay sneered, struggling to his feet.

343

In response, Constantine snatched the parchment from his hand and unrolled it, perusing it quickly. Samana had seen to his education, I observed. He handed the parchment roll to me, flushing in irritation. I gathered Sir Kay's statement was born out by the missive.

It started, "The Honorable Kay of Lyoness, Royal Seneschal . . ." I skipped down to see it was signed, "Morgan of Gore." I didn't know her hand.

The message was blunt. "Arthur, my brother, is dead at Lancelot's hand. Lancelot is preparing to march on Britain to claim Arthur's crown and will be upon you almost as soon as this reaches you. You must resist him. It was Arthur's last wish that you should take the crown, being the only man left capable of ruling. Honor his request, and find me your grateful liegeman. Morgan of Gore."

No word for me? I thought. Could this really be from Morgan? I shook my head and read the message aloud so all could hear. There was doubt on many faces when I finished. Sir Kay was not loved, and few could accept King Arthur's holding him so high. Certainly Constantine didn't, and his doubt influenced the crowd.

"Kay is to take the crown?" he asked scornfully. "We are to believe that King Arthur would give his crown to such a one as this?" Constantine slapped Sir Kay's chest with the back of his hand.

"I do not believe it," I said, holding up the scroll. "We must be prepared for anything, though. Where would Sir Lancelot land, if there were any truth in this?"

There were many suggestions: Dover, London, even Exeter, where he had landed once before, were most prominently mentioned. I ended the discussion by sending mounted men to each of the port cities with instructions to light beacon fires on the hilltops if ships were sighted. One messenger was dispatched by boat to Ector's Isle requesting Samana to order her dragon ship with its Saxon warriors to Exeter. Without professional help, the

344

merchants of Exeter would be so fearful of raiders they would open their gates abjectly to any armed force, in cowardly hope for the best.

Once the news from Armorica became common knowledge, the training took on a new intensity. I told the queen myself and made Sir Kay come with me to show the letter, should the queen wish to read it.

"Words of woe travel faster than those of good cheer." She had been crying. "We have already heard," she explained, but took the letter to confirm her fears.

"Do you believe the tale?" I asked, as she finished.

"I scarcely know," she said, with a troubled look. "She signed herself 'Morgan of Gore.' I cannot believe she would style herself so. She left Urien of Gore and founded her own kingdom of Galloway."

I felt a sense of relief. The letter had seemed false to me, too. "I will believe it only if a fleet comes against us," I said. "I cannot think the king would pass me over for Sir Kay, though there are doubtless others more worthy of the crown." I looked at Sir Kay for some response but could not read his face.

"Will you now keep your promise to the Jutes to wed the queen?" He asked the question I had carefully avoided. Damn the man! I glanced at Viki, but she stared through me.

"Whatever prevails, you will still be queen, Your Majesty," I said, "but it is early days for any vows. I believe King Arthur is still alive."

"I hardly know what to believe," she said, "or what to pray for. Who will accept me as queen when Arthur rejected my claim of innocence?" she asked bitterly.

"I will, for one. As Sir Kay reminds me, I am bound by oath to do so." I answered her. "I can keep a vow as well as any man, or woman, for that matter." I had hoped Viki would look distressed, but she nodded gravely in approval.

"Very well. I have already named you the queen's champion. I also accept you in the king's place as my protector, should the need arise, as my Jutish people have insisted. The need may become manifest if Arthur demands that you give me into his hands."

Sir Kay drew his breath in sharply. "What will folk make of this, Your Majesty?" he asked. "As Arthur's foster brother, I should take his place here. It was his wish, as Morgan writes," and he thrust the parchment roll at her. He insisted the letter was from Morgan despite the queen's doubts.

"But, it is not my wish, Kay," Guenevere said, and dismissed him with a wave of her hand. He left, pale of face and biting his lip. An angry man and a hurt one. I wondered if he were secretly in love with the queen?

"He will do you ill if he can," Viki said darkly.

"Kay would do everyone ill if he could," Guenevere responded carelessly. "Fortunately, everyone knows it."

That evening, signal fires were seen burning to the west, and we knew Sir Lancelot had landed. We mustered the men for an early morning march.

"How ready are they?" I asked Constantine privately.

"They will never stand up to men on horseback, but I hope Sir Lancelot will not have any. He probably expected to find his chargers waiting for him in Kent. Where would he get others?"

In addition to our trainees, King Arthur's old London Irregulars had brought out their grandsons. Their sons were with Arthur, and these boys looked over-young to me. Lud, more children! They swaggered like veterans, however, speaking of how they planned to deal with Sir Lancelot personally. Even the Cornish knights, braggarts though they were themselves, were amused. I was merely appalled.

Everyone gathered to listen as I gave instructions to the townsfolk. "It will be your responsibility to guard the city in our absence."

I told their self-appointed leader, a grizzled man with a determined air. Hugh stood beside him as my deputy.

"Watch for ships from Armorica, and close the city's gates against them," I counseled. "They will hold against any force Sir Lancelot can bring. Be aware, they will use their ship masts to make scaling ladders. Man the walls against them with every able-bodied citizen in London, including your women. Use rocks and boiling water for your weapons if you have nothing else.

"Sir Lancelot will need food to feed his army; deny it to him. Bring all the stock grazing on the commons outside the city under the protection of its walls. Harvest any ripening crops to prevent them from falling into the hands of the invaders. If you have archers among you, fire their ships with blazing arrows to destroy the supplies they brought with them. If all this is done, the invaders will have to forage in the countryside in small parties. Ambush them! Take them by surprise! Always remember, we will be back with help. Do not surrender!"

"Dylan! Dylan, Four-goal Dylan!" they shouted; the youngest were the loudest. I wondered what acceptance I would have had I been a two-goal player.

We looked better on the march than we were, for we had two hundred men mounted on good horses, including the fifty knights from Cornwall. Sir Lancelot's chargers that we'd taken in Kent looked even bigger than usual because some of their riders were so small. Most of our grown men were fisherfolk, slight of stature and small-boned. I was thankful again for the men from Cornwall. They at least looked as if they might be fighters.

Messengers met us a day west of London, Jutes speaking their halting Latin, who told us we were too late. "They've landed. We sent boats out to set theirs afire, but they kept us off and sank us. They were met at the beach by our best warriors, but cut through almost as if we hadn't been there at all. Those of us who lived set off for Canterbury."

I remembered how big the Jute guards had been. If they could not stand up to Sir Lancelot's forces, how could we?

"Lancelot is seeking the queen," Constantine said. "When he doesn't find her at Canterbury, he'll search for her in London. We must return to meet them."

I could only agree. As we turned our column back to London, I wondered what the men of Canterbury would think of us. We had promised them aid. Then I realized bitterly most of them would be dead. How could we hope to fight Sir Lancelot's experienced warriors with these fishermen, new-fledged squires, and dock boys? Even the oldest of Pelleas's sons was but sixteen. I was little older!

It took less time to reach London than it had to leave it. I dismissed the locals, pledging them to return when summoned by the battle trumpets. It would be easier to have them fed at home than from our stores. I sent out scouts, men serving under Constantine, with instructions to locate Sir Lancelot's column, mark its numbers, and report how it traveled. If we had a few hours' notice, we could be ready, I hoped.

We waited. Two days went by, then three, before Constantine returned. We met in council with Hugh and Lady Mal. I trusted no one else but Constantine. "They landed south of us, dismissing their ships and marching to pass London by," Constantine reported. "Lancelot may plan to surprise us by crossing the Thames over the old Roman bridge, a day's march west of here. If he comes east down the Roman road against us, we should be waiting for him."

"How many men does he have?" I asked.

"No more than four hundred in all, I would say. Only a dozen are mounted."

Only a dozen mounted! He had counted on finding his horses waiting for him in Kent. Even though Sir Lancelot had brought a mere honor guard, they would be trained warriors. Ours were not. "We'll make a stand at the Roman bridge in the morning," I ordered. "Have scouts find us on the road if Sir Lancelot appears to change his mind about London. He may be going to Exeter to meet his fleet. In that case we would be outnumbered past all hope."

"Perhaps we should force a fight," Constantine said. "We may catch Lancelot before he adds to his numbers."

"What I can't understand is how he was free to come at all," Lady Mal said. "If King Arthur lives, surely he would have tried to stop him. And what of Gawaine and Arthur's other knights?"

"The queen said Gawaine was already badly wounded," I answered. "What I fear is that this means the king has met with some massive defeat in Armorica."

From the troubled look on Constantine's face, I saw he held the same thought. "These things may become clear in the passing of time," he said. "For now, we have an enemy marching on us. Let us meet him at the bridge."

We mustered our men before the sun was fully risen next morning. I was surprised to find a number of the original London Irregulars standing side by side in line with their grandsons. We had fewer than two thousand men in all, a pitifully small number to stand up against Sir Lancelot's seasoned troops. I welcomed every graybeard I saw.

We reached the bridge before Sir Lancelot did. Constantine and I took stations on its middle to deny its use. Lady Mal in her bard costume accompanied us on her palfrey. Some of the sons of Pelleas stayed on the riverbank with the foot soldiers, who were fanned out behind us. The rest of the sons of Pelleas were stationed on a low hill flanking the bridge. All of them were well-mounted. We may have looked more formidable than we were, in actuality.

A herald rode up to meet us. "The king bids the false regent to surrender himself along with the traitor queen and receive judgment."

I did not recognize the herald. "What king? Tell the oath-breaker I am a true man and will hold the true king's authority until he asks for it back in person," I replied.

The herald carried my words to the small knot of mounted men, who waited safely out of bow shot. They had no worries, for we had no archers. One of them, on a black, blaze-faced horse, broke away and rode toward us on receiving my challenge, but two others caught him and brought him back, protesting.

"That man on the black horse rides like King Arthur," Constantine said in wonder. "Can it be he?"

"Sir Lancelot would not call Queen Guenevere traitor," Lady Mal offered.

"We do not know the circumstances under which she left Joyouse Garde and returned to Britain, though," Constantine responded. "Perhaps they were such that he would deem her so."

Joyouse Garde! What an misnamed place that was, I thought bitterly. I strained to make out the features of the man but could not at this distance. They were dressed in blue surcoats over chain mail and looked much alike. It was a clever way to hide the identity of a leader, if that was their intent.

"If he is the king, why is he fighting?" I asked.

"The men of Kent would deny him entry, no matter who he was," Constantine told me. "They are subjects of the queen, not of his."

"We are not men of Kent."

"Believe me when I say that the people of London would not welcome Arthur with mounted knights at his back, either," Lady Mal said. "I know the temper of the people better than either of you. It makes no difference who it is if he comes armed against us."

I didn't know. I gathered that the argument we witnessed was over whether to fight or ride away. Seemingly, the decision was made to pass on by. The man on the black horse with the white blaze, who had tried to accept my challenge at the bridge, rose in his stirrups and shook his fist at us in defiance before leaving. I had never seen King Arthur show so much passion. Why would he be angry now? I thought of the endless hours I'd been in the saddle or on boat deck, clinging to Nithe's pearl with desperate intensity. All this in his service, and he was angry at me? Suddenly, I didn't care who it was, King Arthur or Sir Lancelot! Damn them both! "Shall we follow and give battle?" I asked. I wanted to.

"Every day we have to drill is another day we have to live," Constantine responded. "Men are joining our lines even as we ride. Our numbers will grow. Theirs will not."

"Lancelot's men will provision themselves from the countryside," Lady Mal agreed, nodding. "Every field despoiled, every cow stolen means another angry farmer to fight on our side."

"We cannot allow Sir Lancelot to meet his fleet at Exeter, if that is his plan," I decided. "We must hit him before he gets there." I thought, but if it is the king, how can I surrender Guenevere to suffer a traitor's fate when I gave my word to guard her? Surely, Kent would rise, and Britain would be lost, and all for nothing. If this was King Arthur, he had forfeited any right to rule.

"Our watchers are still out along the coast," Constantine said. "If ships come, there will be signal fires. There have been none. If Sir Lancelot is waiting for ships, he may wait long."

"Very well, we will follow the raiders from this side of the river," I said, planning aloud. "Let them use the Roman road. They will have to come through water to get at us. We may want to flank them and beat them to Silchester. There the road forks, one route going to Exeter the other to Camelot. We can deny them the town itself if we reach it first, for it's walled. From its watchtower we can see which fork they take, the north or the south."

The London Irregulars were too old for quick marching, so we left them at the bridge to light a signal fire should the enemy turn back and attempt to cross the river to attack London after all. A pillar of smoke from their signal fire would bring us to their aid. I led the fishermen we had raised on the islands, the sons of Pelleas and their friends, the Cornish knights, the dock apprentices, and my squires. We kept Sir Lancelot's column in sight from the north shore of the Thames River.

"Do you think they might go to Camelot after all?" Constantine asked.

"Perhaps. Sir Lancelot knows as well as we that Camelot lies at the other end of the northern road," Constantine replied.

"Then let us flank him and place a force between him and Silchester, in case he turns north. Do you think the townsmen will help us?" I asked.

"We will encourage them to," he said dryly.

"How does he think to take Britain with so few men?" Lady Mal asked in wonder. She had too much imagination and chattered when things became tense. I knew she would show courage though, if it came to actual fighting. She had done so at Badon.

Constantine answered her when I did not, "Two generations back, the Saxons, Horsa and Hengist, came with three boatloads of warriors, not over threescore in all. They were enough to cause Britain's high king, Vortigern, to cede all of Kent to them. Lancelot has enough men for his purposes."

We cut north and quick-marched to reach Silchester before Sir Lancelot, sending the bulk of our forces, including all of our horsemen, on half a league toward Camelot. Constantine, Lady Mal, and I entered the town to convince the town's elders to bar the gates against invaders. They seemed to think we were as big a danger until they saw the size of Lancelot's forces from the city's walls.

The ruling council came to confront Constantine and me in

the gate's guardroom, which we had taken over, while Lady Mal wandered on into the town. "We want no trouble here," their spokesman said nervously.

"None of us wants trouble in life," I said, "and yet it comes. Arthur, the king, sent word throughout his lands that he was leaving for a time and that his cousin Dylan would become regent in his absence. Surely word has reached you."

"That is known," the man said.

"Well, I am Dylan. This is the king's dragon torque around my neck, placed there by his own hand. Do you recognize it?"

"Oh yes. It is his! The very one!" the man said, and fell awkwardly to his knees.

"Don't be foolish, man," I said, raising him. "I am not the king, merely his regent! I ask your help now, in his name."

"What would you have?" he asked, a note of caution back in his voice.

"Those coming upon us now are from Armorica. You'll have heard that Sir Lancelot stole Queen Guenevere and fled with her to that land. King Arthur followed to recover the queen and to punish Sir Lancelot for his disobedience. This is Sir Lancelot who is coming now. We know no more than you do how he slipped away from King Arthur's certain justice, but we mean to keep him at bay until the king returns to save us. Will you help?"

"Yes, yes. Only tell us what to do."

"Keep Sir Lancelot from entering your town. I will stand by your side with the king's authority. Send him on his way with no food or men to swell his ranks. It is what Arthur, the high king, would wish."

"We will do it then," he said, and the council agreed as they filed out, setting in motion the actions that would accomplish our wishes.

We were on the parapet when the enemy's herald rode up.

"Open this gate and allow the king to enter as is his right," he called.

"We have the king's regent here among us, and he has told us not to listen to you, bold man," the town magistrate replied. He had armed himself, as had the council and dozens of the townsmen, some in antique Roman armor. Where it had come from, I had no idea. It was bronze, not iron.

"The king's regent has had his power stripped from him by my master," the herald replied.

"That can only be done face-to-face by one who speaks for himself," I said, stepping up beside the magistrate. If these were King Arthur's men and not Sir Lancelot's, surely the king would step forward for recognition at this invitation.

The herald rode back and spoke to the mounted men. They, in turn, stared long at the town and finally rode around it, passing behind it to camp a league up the road to Camelot. From there they could guard themselves should an attack come out of Silchester.

"We will follow them," I said. "We will tell the advance forces to retreat to Camelot ahead of them. Those of us here can cross around them in the dark and join forces again. If they think to occupy Camelot, they will find they have to fight for it."

"What will happen if they turn and come back against us?" the magistrate asked.

"Then we will return also. We will have to fight them somewhere. Catching them between the city walls and our army is not the worst thing. Just don't let them in if they come. Know that we will be coming to your aid." I remembered I'd said much the same thing to the men of Kent.

We left a worried magistrate behind us when full dark fell, and men from the city guided us around Sir Lancelot's camp. They knew where the rest of our forces were. When we were all together once more. I ordered the men to march toward Camelot along the Roman road.

"I want to be a day ahead of Sir Lancelot," I said. "If he sends out scouts, he will know we are here and may attack in the dark."

"Sir Lancelot has no scouts," one of the men from Silchester told us. He seemed the spokesman for a few of the younger men from town who had elected to join us, looking for glory.

"Can you be sure?" I asked.

The spokesman was considered a wit by his friends, I would judge, by the snickers that followed his utterance when he said, "As sure as anyone can be without owls' eyes."

"These clods from Silchester don't know," one of Pelleas's sons observed.

"Tell them," I said.

"Look you," he told the wit, "like all Picts, we have owls' eyes. We see in the dark. We will keep Prince Dylan informed about Lancelot's movements." And he melted away into the fringes of the forest along the road.

I was gratified to see that the men from Silchester looked embarrassed. They had just received a lesson in the art of talking to kings. They'd been too familiar for peasants.

That evening Lady Mal was looking unaccountably amused. "What is it?" I asked. "I could use a laugh."

"I stopped by several inns in Silchester," she said. "I nearly didn't leave in time to come with you. Everyone here knows my songs, and I had to sing them several times. They say King Arthur's time is gone in Britain."

"They think this is King Arthur who has come against us?"

"Yes, don't you?"

"I truly don't know," I responded. "Perhaps I don't care."

For whatever reason, the invaders did not send out scouts the next day and marched slowly, making no more than twelve miles before camping again. Some of the time was lost in foraging, of course, but this group did not act concerned about fighting. We went on ahead, convinced that they were truly making for Camelot.

I slept poorly. Old anger burned in my belly and washed up into my throat when I lay on my pallet, anger at King Arthur, at Sir Lancelot, and at Viki. I ached to be free of the torment.

When we arrived at Camelot we found only old servants in occupation, along with a few of Guenevere's attendants I had sent there from London. We settled our troops, closed the gates, and sent out word to Caerleon that the people should come to Camelot for protection, bringing their families, their cows, and their stores. All morning, from first light on, the road from Caerleon to Camelot was black with folk, moving as fast as they could to save themselves. My army was augmented with the men from the local villages, men from my own barony, led by Ayres. We had over three thousand men now against Sir Lancelot's four hundred. We were still overmatched. With luck, though, sheltered by Camelot's walls, we would not have to meet in direct combat. For the first time I thought we had a chance.

We expected to see the enemy that night, but only Pelleas's sons came in, laughing and singing. "They are still a day behind us," they reported.

I decided to send the sons of Pelleas to Fort Terrible to ready that place for a siege, and gave them my squires and the runaway pages to help. We could not save Caerleon should it be attacked, but Fort Terrible was more defensible and manned by Picts, allies of King Arthur. I doubted if Sir Lancelot would attack there and wanted the boys somewhere relatively safe. Though no one was happy to leave, they understood the need for it. Their absence did not measurably weaken my forces, which, in any case, I did not intend to engage in open combat.

By midday only a few straggling families from the outskirts of the barony were still arriving. King Arthur had built Camelot for just such a purpose as this. The cattle were penned in the larger of the two stone-enclosed circles, downwind from the castle itself. In the four-acre enclosure of the smaller circle there was space enough to shield all the folk, including those from Caerleon. Great cisterns held enough water to save us from thirst, and runoff from the roofed areas kept the cisterns filled. There were granaries, with slate roofs to protect against fire, where enough grain was stored to feed everyone for a year. We were impregnable.

On the evening of the next day, Sir Lancelot's men straggled up to the river and made camp. The herald came to the gate.

"Open to receive your ruler!" he demanded.

"We will know our ruler when he comes," Lady Mal replied for me. Bards often are used as heralds. The man left, having delivered the message entrusted to him.

Next morning he returned. "I am bid to request a meeting with you to discuss terms," he said.

"Terms? What terms could we expect to hear from traitors?" Lady Mal called.

"You do not know," the herald countered. "You will not know that until you and my master have talked."

I looked at Constantine and he shrugged.

"We will meet at the stake where the queen was to be burned when she was falsely accused of murder and witchcraft," Lady Mal's clear voice announced. "Make it at dawn, the hour of her trial. Let no man draw a sword at our meeting, least there be treachery. If we see one sword flash, we will not wait to be cut down as the queen's guards were in London."

The herald turned and left without reply.

"A little long-winded, and not too accurate," Constantine observed, looking at Lady Mal sardonically. "The queen was tied to the stake in London."

"That was the second time. She was tried here for poisoning an apple. Besides," Lady Mal laughed, "I have to think how it will sound in the ballad I intend to write about this."

On the morrow I set out with Constantine and walked to the stake, arriving with the first dim rays of the sun. He carried my sword, and I wore my red-plumed helmet so that I would be recognized. Otherwise, we were unarmed as befitted a truce talk. The day was mostly overcast and a fitful breeze was blowing, smelling of rain. A tent had been set up, and Sir Kay was standing before it, barring my way.

"Have you turned your coat, Sir Kay?" I asked.

"I am not the one who seized the queen," Kay sneered.

"Nor am I, as you know. The queen named me her champion when there was no other person left near her to fill the role. I am her protector, pledged to her by oath to the men of Kent, in the advent of the king's death."

Sir Kay laughed. "Her protector?"

"That is all," I said, my gorge rising to where I could taste it, burning my throat and hindering my speech. "I warn you, do not traduce the queen, or these proceedings will wait until you have met my challenge."

"You are not fit to act for the queen," a voice growled from the tent.

"It was not I who hacked unarmed knights to death," I shouted, hoarsely. "If I do not raise that issue here, I will not allow questions of worthiness to be raised by anyone else. I speak particularly of the queen. She will be dealt with by her true lord in his own time."

"That time is now!" The tent flap was thrust back with a violence that made the canvas crack like a thunderbolt, and King Arthur strode into the clear air of dawn.

"You?" I cried in surprise and dismay.

Sir Kay laughed. He knew! He'd known all along that the king lived! The anger that I had kept under tight control for many weeks rose and threatened to overwhelm me.

"How dare you call me unworthy!" I shouted. "How have I been untrue to my pledge?"

"You've usurped the crown and think to bed my queen!" King Arthur retorted, as angry as I. We were standing close enough to touch, or to strike, more likely.

"Bed your queen? I'd sooner bed a serpent!" and I tore off the dragon torque he had placed around my neck and dashed it on the ground at his feet. "There's your regency!"

As the king glared in doubt at Sir Kay I saw, from the corner of my eye, a flash of steel glinting in the early light and heard the cries of "Treachery!" raised by the sons of Pelleas.

I turned at the sound and saw one of the king's men striking at the ground to dispatch a viper that had been disturbed in the dewy grass at his feet. Sir Kay's sword was out and swinging, nearly catching me as I stumbled, moving backward.

"No! Wait!" I cried, but it was too late. Constantine fell at Kay's feet, taking the blow meant for me; bright blood sprayed over my legs as he fell. If the boy died, I'd follow Sir Kay to hell for vengeance!

I'd come to the parley unarmed, but as my shield bearer, Constantine carried Gorlais's sword. As I freed it from it's scabbard and snatched up the round Roman shield, men rushed from the meadow behind me and from the invaders' camp by the river. I tried to reach Sir Kay, to pay him back for his foul blow, but he slipped away, and I faced one of King Arthur's mercenaries instead.

We fought toe to toe, exchanging blows until I beat him down. His place was taken by the king himself, fighting in battle fury equal to my own. Before we could do more than exchange blows, the men of the two armies converged upon us and swept us apart.

The storm that had been threatening broke, and pelting rain

wet my tunic so that it clung to my arms, hindering my movement. I ripped it from my body, fighting naked except for my leather boots and red-plumed helmet.

I had seen a real battle unfold at Badon, but this was more like a tavern brawl, with knots of men coming together and beating on one another. The footing became so slippery in the deepening mud, it was a wonder that anyone could strike an effective blow.

The dawning sun disappeared behind black clouds, leaving us in near darkness, a fitting omen, indeed. The one thing that was the same as Badon was the sound of men screaming as they died. The uselessness of it infuriated me, and anger thickened my own voice as I shouted, cutting into the men I faced. Gorlais's sword seemed to have no weight, almost swinging itself back and forth, hewing a red swath through King Arthur's ranks. I wondered why it didn't jar to strike though a man's steel-rimmed helmet into his brain.

My Roman helmet acted as a beacon for my followers, who rushed to aid me. King Arthur's knights dismounted, horses being of no use in the mud, and joined the foot soldiers meeting my spearmen with drawn swords. With our greater numbers we pushed the king's men back toward the river, though many of them slipped away into the trees that bordered the bank.

Men melted from before me, avoiding the terrible weapon I held, as if it were accursed. Perhaps it was. Eventually, I found myself alone in a clearing and turned to a challenge. It was Arthur the king. He attacked me without waiting, and I had never met a man of such strength, at least my match. One of his spearmen appeared behind him, but didn't interfere.

King Arthur had never once given me a chance to love him. He'd thrown me away at birth and rebuffed every attempt I'd made to win his acceptance. The bitterness of a lifetime strengthened me as I met him shield to shield. He raised his famed sword

Excalibur for an overhand blow, but I countered with a mighty backhanded stroke with the sword Cornu had given me that tore it from his hand.

He snatched his lackey's spear, and he thrust at me from under his shield. Ah! It cut shrewdly into my left shoulder, drawing at the flesh as it passed.

The shock of it brought me to my knees and, before the pain could unman me, berserker rage seized me. Arthur! My vision dimmed except for what was just before my eyes. I dropped the shield, grasped the spear with my left hand, and pulled it farther through my shoulder until he was in reach of my sword. Rising, still grasping the spear with my left hand, I struck with all my strength at his unprotected side, following it with a slash at his helm. Oh, to kill this man who had so wronged me!

His helm came off, leaving his head bleeding freely. It was King Arthur's turn to fall to his knees, still clutching the spear which had drawn us close together. I raised my sword to strike again when he raised his face to look at me. his color had drained away, but he smiled. He smiled! Had he sought death at my hands?

Was this my enemy, smiling? "Father!" I cried, lowering my sword. choking as I felt the rage leave me in a shuddering flood. My lifelong fear of injuring in rage someone I loved had come to pass. "Truly, Sir Kay said you were dead!" I gasped. I didn't understand, and I saw he didn't either. Then the pain from the gaping wound in my shoulder claimed me, and I swooned.

When I woke I could see King Arthur, leaning against a tree a dozen paces away. A knight knelt at his feet. I saw the king kiss the sword Excalibur and give it to his man. "This river flows from the lake where the Lady abides," he said. "Take it and throw it into the water. Return to tell me what you saw."

Another wave of pain washed over me and I lost consciousness again, awakened by the sound of King Arthur's voice. "Why will you not do as I command, Bedivere?"

The knight seemed in dire distress. "But it is a wondrous thing, lord," he said. "I could not do it! Excalibur should be held before men's eyes to reunite the kingdom!"

"That is not its purpose. I have but little strength left," he sighed. "I must know before I die whether the service I have put it to was acceptable." He pointed at his miserable follower. "For the third time I tell you, do as I bid!" Such a note of power came into his voice that Bedivere fled.

He returned before I had taken a dozen breaths, each showering a mist of blood over the ground where I lay. I, too, was dying.

"It is done, lord." I heard Bedivere say, and turned my head to see him kneeling again before the king, weeping into his two hands. "A hand rose from the water, caught the sword in midair, shook it three times, and drew it silently down! A miracle!"

"It is well. Keep watch there for me," the king ordered, dismissing his retainer.

As soon as he left, another figure strode up to stand before the king. "Do you believe such a tale as Bedivere just told, or have you finally realized how simple you have been?" It was Sir Kay. I recognized his high voice and sneering manner.

King Arthur replied in a voice that sounded as if he might be seated before his own board about to take his supper. "Yes, I believe Bedivere. It was the way the sword came to me, given in trust by the Lady of the Lake."

Sir Kay spat at King Arthur's feet in wordless contempt.

"So, Kay, you appear to have survived the battle when better men did not," King Arthur said slightingly. "I might have known."

"And you, Arthur, appear not to have done so," Sir Kay observed coldly.

"My son has done for me in truth," King Arthur agreed. "He seemed to think I should be someone else when I came out of the tent. Who did he think I should be?" I turned my head and saw that the sun shone on his face; it was waxy pale. He winced in pain. A rough bandage had been wound around his head to stop the bleeding, but not by Sir Kay, I'd warrant.

"Surely it is apparent at last, is it not?" Sir Kay sneered. "He thought you were Lancelot come for Guenevere after killing his father, Arthur the king."

"And you told him that? Why would you do so vile a thing?"

"When my father begged you to make me seneschal, I promised only that I would not steal from you. You might remember I made no other pledge of loyalty."

"And that excuses you for bringing about the deaths of so many men?" King Arthur asked in amazement. His voice was still strong.

"I should have been made King of the Britons," Kay said in answer. "I was better born, legitimate, and Christian. I will be king now."

King Arthur laughed grimly. "I have named Constantine my heir and successor. He and his child-wife, Eliza, will rule after me, though one might well ask, 'What is there left to be king of?'"

"You grieve for the Round Table? I am glad it is shattered!" Sir Kay snarled. "It was I who brought that down, for it would not serve me. And it was I who sent a kitchen page whispering to Lancelot that the queen had desperate need of him that night, and I who told Aggravain the trap was set for springing. I even sent word to Lancelot that he'd have to cut through a knot of defenders to rescue Guenevere! It may have been Lancelot's hand that wielded the sword, but it was my strategy!"

Arthur struggled to rise but could not. I thought if I could get my hands around Sir Kay's throat, I would shut off his lying tongue for good. I strained to reach him, clawing at the forest soil to pull myself to where I could grasp his foot. As Sir Kay stepped back to deliver a vicious kick into Arthur's wounded side I caught him.

"Stop it!" I shouted. A wave of pain left me retching. "Traitor!" I roared in frustration, inching myself ahead as I held him fast.

Sir Kay tore loose and turned to me, leaning down to inspect me for a moment. "I have a present for you," he said, and taking a chain from his neck, dropped it near my face against the ground. A gem blazed in purple fire.

"It's the amethyst bead! It was you who stole the necklace," I gasped.

"And saw you damned for it," he agreed. He grasped the spear and, putting his foot against my chest, pulled it out of my shoulder.

I screamed, "Oh, Lud!" and pressed the wound with my right hand. My left seemed not to be working.

"I trust he will bleed to death comfortably now," Sir Kay said in a conversational voice to King Arthur. "As dead as he thought you were. It may comfort you to know he was as loyal to you as any knight of your famous Round Table. More than most, actually, but perhaps you will not like to hear that. You did strike the killing blow, didn't you?"

"No," King Arthur said. "You did, Kay. And you do comfort me. The most bitter thing of all was thinking that the son I had longed for . . . though I could not tell him so . . . that son was untrue to me. You will pay for this, Kay. I name you oath-breaker and leave you for the gods."

He had loved me! He had! Surely, he had!

"Gods," Sir Kay sneered. "You forget, I am a Christian, Arthur. I will do penance and be absolved. But now it seems fitting that the spear that killed the bastard should serve as well for his be-getter," and he bent over King Arthur, holding the spear to thrust it home.

Before he could ram it into King Arthur's chest, he was picked up from behind and thrown violently to one side. Pelleas had appeared, followed by Myrddin, Cornu, and three women draped in dark robes. One threw back her head covering and knelt beside King Arthur.

"Oh, my dear Bear!" she sobbed. It was Nithe. She touched his brow; he caught her hand in his and smiled.

On his other side knelt another woman, who also uncovered her head. It was Samana.

Arthur cried out "Sam!"

Samana hugged him as Nithe clutched his hand. I lay back down from where I had raised on my elbow. The movement brought the third woman to my side. It was Morgan.

"What have we here?" she asked, stooping over me. "Mordred! This makes the third time I have found you bleeding and in need of care." She pulled away my hand to inspect the wound in my shoulder.

"Third time pays for all," I said, remembering a story Samana used to tell us.

"The way I heard it, the story ends with the words, 'If I win it three times, I get to keep it,'" Morgan said absently. There was more, but nothing I remember clearly, other than the fact that Cornu turned me over so she could inspect my back. Then together they removed my mail shirt, an undertaking that dimmed my vision as waves of pain coursed through me. Their voices became indistinct as the pain increased. It was worse than when Aggravain had stabbed me, I thought. With my last conscious thought, I clutched Nithe's pearl and hoped the pain would go away, and it did.

I awoke in my old room in The Pig Girl. In the next bed lay Constantine, a bandage swathing his head, and a sudden joy came to me. I'd thought him dead! Sitting beside him were Eliza and Borre, talking to him earnestly. He was frowning, obviously in disagreement with what he was hearing.

"Even if it were King Arthur's wish, I cannot take his place. No one could, not even Dylan, though if he lives, his claim supersedes mine!" Constantine exclaimed.

"Granted," Borre agreed. "No one can take King Arthur's place.

He and his handful of knights united Britain and kept it from Saxons while two generations of children grew up in peace, but his time is past. As for Dylan, he slew King Arthur. He would never be accepted as Britain's king."

"Then you do it." Constantine pleaded. "You're King Arthur's acknowledged son."

"No, I will go back to Lyoness and take my place as Cador's heir. It is what I was meant to be," Borre said firmly.

"It just doesn't seem right." Constantine fretted. "Besides, I don't believe King Arthur is truly dead. He'll be back!"

I found someone had placed the dragon torque around my neck once more, so I unclasped it and held it out to Constantine. "Until he comes this is yours." I said. "I heard the king say it with my own ears."

All three turned to me in surprise. When I grinned, Borre's face lightened in relief, and Constantine beamed. I'd solved their problem. Whoever would have thought that Crybaby Constantine, as Borre used to call him, would grow up to become high king of the Britons? And that Borre would approve? Still, Constantine had saved my life at some cost to himself, and I would not forget it.

Eliza rose and patted me in passing. "Dylan's awake!" she called at the doorway. The summons brought Lady Mal and Viki.

Ah, Viki, my love!

"You win the bet." Lady Mal said in mock sorrow. "I was sure Dylan would die."

"No, you won, Baroness." Viki said sitting beside me and taking my hand. "He did die at King Arthur's hand, like everyone believes."

I raised my head. "Baroness?" I asked, though a thousand other questions needed answers.

"The people chose her following the death of Prince Dylan, Baron of Caerleon, on the field of battle," Viki said primly, but there were tears brimming in her eyes, and she was smiling tremulously. "His great horse, Black Nick, came home without him."

"Then, who am I?"

"My own true husband, Lamerok, given me back by the mercy of the Great Mother," Viki said, and her smile steadied and widened.

I nodded, squeezed her hand, and thought, Lamerok? Ah, well, if that's what she wanted of me, I'll do it, though I hated the bastard, before drifting back into sleep, conscious that Viki was holding my hand as if she'd never let go.

COURTWAY JONES is a cultural anthropologist and ethnohistorian who earned his Ph.D. at Columbia University. He has taught at Indiana University and Pennsylvania State University. His bestselling first novel, IN THE SHADOW OF THE OAK KING, began this uniquely lively and original trilogy on the world of King Arthur, DRAGON'S HEIRS.